A WARTIME FRIEND

Leah escapes from a train bound for a death camp – along with a surprising friend, a kind-natured German Shepherd dog. Discovered in France by an RAF pilot, the traumatised Leah wakes to find she's forgotten everything. Leah is renamed Lily and is fostered by the kind RAF pilot and his wife, Meg. Before long their lives are disrupted once again by the war and, with their home in ruins, they are forced to flee to the country. In Somerset, Lily is reunited with Rudy, the heroic dog. However it soon becomes clear that Rudy is not just her companion, he is protecting her too, and someone wants him out of the way...

A WARTIME FRIEND

by

Lizzie Lane

Magna Large Print Books
Long Preston, North Yorkshire,
BD23 4ND, England.

British Library Cataloguing in Publication Data.

A catalogue record of this book is
available from the British Library

ISBN 978-0-7505-4604-1

First published in Great Britain in 2017 by Ebury Press,
an imprint of Ebury Publishing

Published in Large Print 2018 by arrangement with
Ebury Publishing

Magna Large Print is an imprint of Library Magna Books Ltd.

Printed and bound in Great Britain by
T.J. (International) Ltd., Cornwall, PL28 8RW

CHAPTER ONE

In her dream she was back in Austria, the country where she'd been born, dancing around a picnic table spread with food of every description: creamy slices of confectionery, pies and succulent pieces of chicken; puddings, plums, pears and freshly baked bread spread with bright yellow butter.

Her father's English friends were visiting and she had the chance to practise her English on them. Her father smiled with pride on hearing her.

'Perfect! Just perfect.'

The sun was shining across the great expanse of lawn and the air was full of the smell of flowers. The breeze whispered through the leaves of the oak tree beneath which the sumptuous picnic had been set. White linen tablecloths flapped on square iron-framed tables.

Walking across the lawn, his head and shoulders dappled with sunlight, she saw her father looking handsome and strong in his dark grey suit, smiling through the thickness of his beard. Her mother drifted through the assembled guests, nodding and smiling at each one, her chiffon tea dress floating behind her like the open wings of a butterfly, pale lilac streaked with purple. The laughter and animated conversation mingled with the sound of bees buzzing from one summer rose bush to another. Their buzzing became louder and, as it did so, petals fell from the roses, the laughter and conversation diminishing.

Her attention was suddenly drawn to the edge of the pond where what looked like bees rose in a gigantic pillar, spiralling upwards in a noisy black swarm. Mesmerised, she watched as the buzzing changed to something else, a terrifying sound like the clattering of many feet pounding on a wooden bandstand. Her father back by her side, she tugged at his sleeve but he did not answer. His expression was grave and her mother's face had turned white, her pale skin tightening over her high cheekbones. Her mouth opened unnaturally wide, her dulcet voice suddenly a blood-curdling scream. The dream vanished. Reluctant to leave the dream and the past behind, Leah squeezed her eyes tightly shut, willing herself to go back to sleep, to return to how things used to be: full of colour, happiness and light. Not like now. Not the horror of what was now. In the feeble light of a candle she saw an elongated shadow stretch across the wall, its legs and arms as thin as sticks, half its body trailing over the ceiling. Elements of her dream resurfaced as she sucked in her breath. Who was this creature? What was he doing in her bedroom, a lovely place of lilac and mauve with pretty white furniture?

'Get out of my room!' she wanted to shout, but no sound came out, the words stilled in her throat like a lump of food she'd failed to chew and swallow properly. Not that it could be food. Food was precious and eaten quickly.

Her pretty bedroom of pastel colours was replaced by mud-like tones and lumpy walls, dark green window frames and dingy curtains

8

bearing more than a passing resemblance to old potato sacks – which they might once have been More awake now, she recognised the smell of the room they all shared: the damp mouldiness of crumbling plaster, the accumulation of cooking smells from both this room and others nearby; rooms lived in by refugees like them, people with little choice of where they could go and what they could expect from those who begrudgingly gave them shelter. She knew now that the scrawny shadow twice the height of a normal man was that of her father leaping from his bed.

Reality crowded in on her. This place was not Austria. This place was not her bedroom. Back in Austria she'd had her own bedroom with a violet-coloured counterpane and wallpaper sprinkled with tiny lilac flowers. They'd lived in a beautiful house with many rooms. The garden had been idyllic. It was always summer in the garden, or had seemed that way to her. Her father, a professor of economics at the university, had his own study and their kitchen had been large. There had also been servants. But everything had changed when Hitler came to power.

At first her parents had done their best to protect her from the truth, teaching her at home when she was no longer allowed to go to school. 'The school is being renovated and reorganised,' they had said, but something inside told her otherwise. Her school had gone. Her friends had gone. Her world had turned upside down and fear had made her nervous and disbelieving of anything her parents told her. She didn't need to be told they were living on the edge of a precipice.

She could feel it.

'Your father is on a sabbatical,' her mother had told her when her father no longer went to the university. Then their house had been taken and her father, Professor Rudolph Westerman, had taken the decision to leave Austria and head for France.

'The French motto is "liberty, equality, fraternity"; we will be safe in such a country,' he'd confidently declared. So with the minimum of money and a few belongings stuffed into three shoddy suitcases – expensive ones might look as if they contained valuable items and were likely to be searched – they had fled to France.

For a while there had been safety but no beautiful house with a study and a garden. At first they'd had two rooms, but so many people were now fleeing Austria and Germany in hope of a safety that seemed increasingly precarious as jackboots marched and subjugated one country after another. Then there was only one room and, although the roof leaked and the shutters didn't quite fit, they'd felt safe – until now. War was declared and France was invaded.

For a while, before Dunkirk, they had held on to a faint hope. Her father had been full of confidence: 'The allies will hold them back.' But Rudy Westerman's hopes had been in vain. Germany stormed through the Ardennes and into a country still fighting in the manner of the Great War: a static defence from behind the Maginot Line. The Germans had merely driven round it. Paris had fallen and, like a plague, the invaders had spread swiftly across the country. Now here they were.

The tall apartment block echoed with noise,

thuds, screams and shouted orders. Leah cowered at the side of her bed. If it wasn't for the suitcases stuffed beneath it, she would have hidden there. A draught of cold air filtered into the room; Leah shivered. Her father had opened the door a fraction. He peered through the gap before shutting it firmly with both hands, palms flat as though that would keep out the threat to his family.

'We have to go.'

'No–' Her mother's voice was a long wail.

'Rachel! We have to go. We cannot stay here. They are ordering us out. We must obey or...'

His wife broke down into tears, shoulders trembling, her face hidden in her hands. Rudy Westerman turned to his daughter.

'Dress, Leah. Quickly.'

'But I thought we could stay here,' Leah whined, hoping her plaintive pleas would have some effect. 'Anyway, it's still night-time.' She glanced tellingly at the mantle clock. Two o'clock in the morning. It was still dark and she was sleepy. Hungry too. At least hunger wasn't so pressing when she was asleep, even though her dreams were full of food.

Seeing her reluctance, her father dragged her from the bed and pushed her towards the chair where she'd placed her clothes the night before.

'Dress. And pack. We cannot refuse them. We dare not refuse them!'

His heart was heavy. His original plan had been to escape to England but he had felt for his tired family. Persuaded by his wife, he had fallen in with her wishes to settle in France. Her reasoning was not unsound.

There was a sound like thunder as the German

11

soldiers used their fists, then their rifle butts on the doors of their neighbours living on the lower floors, finally kicking them in with their boots, splintered wood flying into the room. *'Schnell! Schnell!* Get out! Get out! All Jews get out!'

Once he'd checked their suitcases were packed and they were dressed in warm clothes, Leah's father opened the door to their apartment. Screams and shouts of protest rose from the lower floors as people were turned out of their rooms, told to bring only what they could carry. Children cried and babies wailed. Her father closed the door swiftly as the sound of thudding boots came closer.

Leah shivered as she pulled on her clothes. She badly wanted to go to the lavatory, but her legs were shaking so much she didn't think she'd make it that far.

Her mother made a pitiful noise, her long white fingers curled against her mouth, her eyes wide with fear. 'You said we'd be safe here, Rudy. You said they wouldn't dare do in France what they did in Germany...'

Rudy grabbed his wife's shoulders. 'I am sorry, my love. It is now happening in France. Dress and pack only what you can carry. Now! And remember to wear those clothes into which we sewed some money. Your fur coat, yes? Leah, help your mother. Quickly. Both of you.'

Going to the lavatory was forgotten as she helped her mother throw a few things into a suitcase, including half a loaf of bread and a sausage. It was her father who'd insisted on the food. Up until then her mother had been piling underwear

12

into the case along with family photographs in silver picture frames. Her father told her to hide anything that was silver or gold. 'Just take the smaller frames. The bigger ones will take up too much room.'

Rachel Westerman's face crumpled with despair. 'This can't be happening to us. We came to escape this.'

Rudy had no time to explain or ruminate on what they had hoped for, and what was now actually happening; he only wished he'd acted sooner and travelled on to England. *Complacency. You are guilty of complacency. If only...*

But there was no time for regret. He had to ensure his family's survival.

'Pull yourself together, Rachel! We have our daughter to think of.'

His wife wailed hysterically. 'But when we left Germany, you said...' She wouldn't let go; she was on the verge of hysteria.

'Rachel!' He slapped her face. Her look of despair was replaced with one of total shock.

Feeling instant regret, Rudy folded his fingers into the palm of his hand. Never before had he raised his hand to either his wife or their child, but the tactic worked. The threat of her sliding into outright hysteria receded and a blank, un-comprehending expression came to her face. As though in a dream, she put on her fur coat and wound her favourite pink scarf around her neck. It didn't match the coat. One was for winter, the other a thin silky thing fit only for summer.

Rudy turned his attention to his daughter. Smiling weakly, he told her they must all be brave.

13

So far she appeared calm. He wished most sincerely she would stay that way. The sound of tramping boots was getting closer.

'Listen to me.'

Leah smelled the pipe tobacco on her father's breath as his face came close to hers. She felt his hands trembling on her shoulders and she trembled too. Although she needed the lavatory, she didn't say so. Despite this room of shadows, the intense look in her father's eyes demanded her full attention.

'We have to go. We have no choice, but if we get separated head west. Get to England. Here is my friend Daniel Loper's address. I will put it in here.' He took his wife's pink scarf from around her neck, sliding a piece of paper into a gap in the hem. 'Keep it safe.' His voice broke as he tied the scarf around his daughter's neck, tucking it beneath her coat collar.

There was a resounding crash as the door slammed open. Huge dark figures blanked out the meagre light from the landing.

'*Schnell!* Out! All of you out!'

Like upright parcels, they were pushed outside, Rudy doing his best to protect his daughter from the thudding rifle butts, the violent pushing. The noise of furniture being overturned and glass smashed sounded behind them from within the shabby room that had been their refuge.

Along with their neighbours, Leah and her parents were bundled down the stairs, most of which they took two at a time because the soldiers were pushing them, slamming their rifles across their backs, all the while urging them to be quick.

Once out in the street Leah fixed her gaze on the familiar buildings opposite, almost as though she had never seen them quite so vividly before now. A searchlight mounted on the back of an army truck lit up the street. Canvas-covered trucks had their headlights on. Leah had never seen Rue de St Auguste so well lit.

Rue de St Auguste.

Some deeply buried instinct convinced her she was seeing these buildings for the very last time. The light softened their dirty grey stone. There were details she'd never really noticed before that she now felt obliged to save to memory: stone cherubs holding up a balcony, the weed thrusting up at roof level above the guttering, the bright brass door knocker and matching brass plaque outside the doctor's house.

'Schnell!'

Intently studying the buildings of the mediocre street, she failed to hear the shouted order. The soldier's rifle butt threatened just inches from her head, serious injury only prevented by her father stepping between her and its impact. She heard him cry out, a cracking sound as his back arched like a bow about to be fired. She gasped with fear and the urine, which she'd so far held in check, trickled down her legs and into her socks.

The yawning mouth of the tarpaulin-covered truck awaited. The pushing and shouting was unrelenting. 'Get going! Up! Up!'

Assisted by her father and those already inside the truck, her mother climbed in first. There was little room. Everyone had to stand. Nobody could sit down.

'Leah! Take my hand.'

Leah felt her mother's long fingers reaching for hers. She did as asked, surprised at her mother's new-found strength dragging her up on to the tailboard. When had her fingers become so thin? She couldn't remember her ever having so little flesh. Her father assisted, his movements urgent and jerky as he lifted her up into the truck, groaning in pain from the injury done to his back.

The interior of the truck was stuffy and stank of stale sweat and other, more disgusting, smells. She wasn't the only one who had wet herself – but there was worse.

Body was packed against body. Leah felt she was almost suffocating. There were so many people and so little room. Not enough to breathe properly. Some people were crying softly. Others were slumping against their companions, dependent on the next tired person to keep them upright.

Her father did his best to reassure her, his breath warm on her face. 'Don't cry, Leah. Everything will be all right. We're merely being relocated because of the war. It is only because of the war.'

Leah wasn't crying and she already hated the war. It was the war that had caused her family to flee from Austria to France. Now the war had caught up with them. It seemed nowhere was safe.

Her mother added her own reassuring words. 'Listen to your father, Leah. See? I am not crying.'

But you are, she wanted to say, though her comment was smothered against the silky fluffiness of her fur collar.

Her mother was almost choking with the effort of trying to hold back her tears. They came out anyway. As more and more people were loaded on board, Leah was crushed more tightly against her mother's chest. Her mother's body pulsated with sobs.

It was hard to see anything in the truck, but Leah was reassured by the smell of the soap her mother used, the sweetness of her father's tobacco. She could feel the softness of her mother's fur coat, a wedding anniversary present if she remembered rightly.

What if other people smell like my father and another woman has a fur coat? It wouldn't hurt to check. Reaching up with both hands, she felt her mother's face, the little piece of net hanging from her hat over her wet eyes. She felt her father's closed eyes and with her fingers followed the line of sweat down his face into his pointed beard.

Fumes from the truck's engine blew in beneath the canvas surround as it burst into life and surged forward, its wheels bumping over the cobbled street. People coughed and spluttered as they jolted into each other. Others prayed. Some froze as though they were already dead. Others tried to lend some logic to their situation.

'Where are they taking us?'

'They're taking us to the railway station,' someone said. 'We're being shipped east. That's what I heard.'

There were mutterings of disbelief.

Leah felt her father's body stiffen against hers and heard a barely suppressed wail from her mother. Her fingers followed the movement of her mother's head as she hid her face in her husband's shoulder. 'They're going to kill us,' said her mother, her alarm muffled.

Rudy Westerman tried to sound brave. 'Shush, Rachel. Don't be so foolish. You're frightening the child,' he whispered. 'We're just going to be resettled to do war work in factories in the east. Normandy will be a battleground if an attack comes from England. They will move everyone they can.'

He'd picked up on hearsay, rumours and reassurances from the small Jewish community that had congregated in the town; some were of French descent and many had fled west from the devilish hound that was the Third Reich. Everyone believed what they had been told: they were being taken to labour camps in Eastern Europe. But being a logical man, there was no disguising the disbelief in his voice, a result of the leaden sickness he felt inside. Why had nobody come back from these labour camps? Why no letters, no postcards, nothing?

The answer chilled him, though for now at least he would keep it to himself. His voice failed to boom with the familiar confidence of a man used to lecturing and throwing his voice to the back of a room. He only hoped his simple words were enough to calm his wife and daughter. It was all he had to give them.

CHAPTER TWO

The smell of coal dust and the sound of escaping steam heralded their arrival at yet another railway station. The tarpaulin that shielded their existence from the sleeping world they'd passed through was pulled aside. There was little light except for the cold white globes above the signs revealing that this was Rennes. Somebody remarked at the lights being on.

'As though they've nothing to fear from British bombers,' someone else added.

'They will. In time.'

Every statement was murmured in hushed tones. The yell of rougher men barked out into the night.

'*Schnell! Schnell!*'

More shouts, more wielding of rifle butts.

Rudy Westerman cupped his hand around his daughter's eyes so she wouldn't see the blood spurting from the head of a man close by. She saw it all the same, her footsteps faltering as she took in the sight of blood running down his face and dripping from his chin.

This time they were dragged rather than pushed.

The sloping roofs of railway goods warehouses pitched a black visage directly in front of them. Tumbling like dead flies from the back of the truck, they were hustled to a waiting area where their belongings were searched for 'contraband'.

19

Only a few people cried. Even the children were silent, eyes big and round, wondering at this horror world they had entered.

'What do they mean by contraband?' whispered Leah's mother.

Her husband answered, 'They mean anything of value.'

Everything of value was taken, the soldiers ripping at outer clothes, snapping open suitcases, bundles and valises. Only the small things people had slid into clothes about their person escaped the search. Leah retained her coat and the pink scarf that had belonged to her mother.

Her father attempted to inject some humour into the sombre scene, though purposely kept his voice low. 'Rachel, I am really glad you never mended that hole in my pocket.'

'I forgot,' she replied, totally oblivious to his attempt to lighten their circumstances. 'Oh dear. Oh dear, I am so sorry...' Her sobbing returned anew.

'Never mind. A few coins and your favourite silver earrings have fallen all the way down into the lining of my coat,' he whispered back, more concerned that the guards had taken the small suitcase containing their food. 'Now isn't that lucky!'

'And I have money,' whispered Leah, referring to the small sum sewn into the hem of her dress.

All day they waited, sitting on their luggage, now emptied of their food and valuables. It was cold. Soon there would be frost. The sky was overcast, the clouds as grey as their moods.

A few enterprising souls smelling of sweat and fear wove among the forlorn crowd trying to sell what remained of their pathetic belongings. Not many people were interested. What was the use of a handsome ring or tiepin when you'd eaten nothing since the day before and were unsure of when you would eat again? Only those who had had time to grab and hide a little food had any success, though unsure of when they might eat again, people clung on to what they had.

Leah's mother protested when her husband handed over a gold watch filched up from the lining of his coat in exchange for half a loaf of bread. His response was blunt: 'Our suitcase is gone. You can't eat a gold watch.'

Rumours continued to be rife. Leah overheard somebody ask her father whether he believed they were really going east to work. Her father was non-committal. 'I am not privy to Nazi war plans,' he replied.

'I heard that nobody comes back. Those that go are never heard from again. It's not a work camp. It's a death camp. They're going to kill us all.'

This last comment resulted in her father springing to his feet, grabbing the man by his collar and threatening him with a beating if he didn't keep his filthy comments to himself.

It was six o'clock in the evening when they were finally herded towards a goods train. Leah was tired and it had been some time since she'd eaten the bread her father had given her. The station was a bare, dismal-looking place smelling of manure and urine, as though animals were usually boarded there.

Leah's mother remarked that she could see no carriages, only cattle wagons. 'Surely they don't

21

expect us to travel in those? Especially if we are going on a very long journey – I think we should protest.'

Her hurrying footsteps came to an abrupt standstill.

'You must move,' urged her husband.

'No!'

The crowd, herded onwards by the bellowing guards, parted to either side of her. Frightened by her behaviour, Leah grabbed her mother's arm, tugging at it, pleading with her to move.

Her father hissed a warning. 'Rachel. You must move forward. If you don't, they will punish you.'

Guards with fierce dogs on chain leashes shouted and pushed those who dared loiter, beating them with staves if they didn't move forward fast enough. The sharp teeth of the snarling guard dogs bit a few unfortunate men, women and children.

So many people were being loaded into each cattle wagon, though not fast enough for those driving them forward. The wagons were quite high and not easy to climb into, especially for the old and those with children. When a bottleneck occurred, Leah found herself pushed to the edge of those waiting to board.

With the queue at a standstill, the guards seemed to relish the opportunity to beat anew, the dog handlers goading their overexcited dogs to leap forward and take a chunk out of those at the edge of the crowd. In the ensuing panic, Leah's parents got sucked into the centre of the throng, leaving Leah isolated from them on the edge. Her father tried to pull her back but the crush of people severed their contact. The touch of his fingertips melted away.

'Leah. Come here! Come here!'

People surged into the gap between her and her father.

'*Schnell! Schnell!*'

Always that word. Always the flailing arms, the snarling dogs.

The wooden staves beat down all around her, hitting shoulders, arms and backs, cracking heads. A guard with a dog saw her wavering on the edge of the crowd. 'Get going. Now! Now!'

The dog he held wasn't crazed like the others, barking and snarling, but was wagging its tail, looking up at the guard before eyeing the little girl within its reach. Instead of biting her, it looked at Leah as though she were a friend. There was no malice in its eyes, no snarling or bared fangs threatening to rip her flesh from her bones.

The guard's face was electric with blood lust, urging the dog to attack. 'Go on! Go on! Attack! Take your first taste of a Jew!'

The dog did nothing. Its gaze fixed on Leah, its tail wagging in greeting; it was almost as though it recognised her, welcoming her as a long-lost friend.

The guard swore at the dog, wrenching the chain leash cruelly so that it tightened like a noose around the animal's neck.

'Damned hound!'

The dog yelped. The guard, deciding that if this child were going to be injured he'd have to do it himself, raised his stave. It was only inches away when her father's arm clapped on to her shoulder, dragging her back into the centre of the crowd. The last she saw was the guard kicking the dog and shouting that he would shoot it at their next stop if its attitude didn't improve.

'It should be acting like a wolf, not a mouse!'

In the meantime, it was due a good beating. The other dog handlers laughed at him.

'You got the one that's soft as boiled cabbage,' shouted one of them. More laughter, raucous comments and jibes.

The crowd closed around Leah, too dense for her to see any more.

They were packed even more tightly together than they'd been in the truck, everyone standing up, fear simmering like a warm stew in the bitter cold, her face muffled in the thick fur of her mother's coat. Some people prayed in French, some in German and many in Hebrew.

The Old Testament mantra of the chosen peoples' exile into slavery in Egypt was an apt comparison. 'By the Rivers of Babylon ... let the words of our mouths and the meditation of our hearts...' It was happening again, though this time they feared never returning to the Promised Land. Many Jews had fled Germany for safety in France. Many other tongues would be spoken before the horror finally came to an end.

There was no light inside the cattle wagon. Only by feeling and information passed mouth to mouth did they learn that the only facilities was a bucket in one corner for women, and one in another for men. Leah told her mother that she'd wet her knickers, but her mother didn't appear to hear, or perhaps she didn't want to because she could

24

not supply her daughter with clean underwear.

'Tonight will be cold,' somebody said. Everyone knew what this person meant: at night they would be spared the stench of the buckets, but by day they would soon stink.

As was her disposition, Leah's mother did her best to keep apart from those she considered inferior to herself: a professor's wife and daughter of a rich mill owner. 'Herded like sheep,' she said.

Leah bit her bottom lip and squeezed her eyes shut. Perhaps it was all just a dream; no, not a dream – a terrible nightmare. If she opened her eyes she would see that, but when she did nothing had changed.

Her mother had always been of a whiny disposition, something Leah and her father had often shared looks over. But it was too dark to exchange those familiar and predominantly humorous looks. Fear permeated each of them, seeping through their soiled clothes; a cloying sweat enveloping all, sticking them one to the other as fast as glue.

The shriek of a whistle announced their departure. Miles and miles they travelled, through the night and all the next day, though daylight was barely discernible in their cramped quarters. There might have been gaps in the sides of the wagons, but the sheer number of bodies blocked out most of the daylight. On and on they went like this. Nights should have been colder but they were so squashed together, a series of bodies staying warm, that it provided the only comfort on a journey of pitiful souls.

Not all the bodies remained warm. Blessed with

the release that only death can bring, the dead remained upright, wedged in among the living. Already starving, already weary from travelling in trucks to meet the train, the elderly and the very young were the first to weaken. They were given no food and only one cup of water a day. Small children, smothered by the close proximity of adults, suffocated. Old people gave themselves up to the inevitable, closing their eyes and falling asleep, never to wake again.

Leah rested her head against her father, his arm wrapped around her to hold her upright. Her legs were aching. She dreamed of her bed, even the narrow one in France. The pretty violet and white one back in Austria was only a fantasy; something from what seemed a very long time ago.

The train rattled slowly onwards, stopping for a few hours overnight at small towns. At one there was a lot of shouting. Her father managed to look out and saw people with baskets of bread trying to get close to the train. The guards were holding them back, shouting at them that approach was *verboten*. Forbidden. When they didn't immediately retreat, they were pushed back with rifle butts, their fallen loaves picked up by the soldiers, their empty baskets kicked after them.

After a few days six in their wagon were dead. *Multiply that by twenty*, thought Leah's father, taking a guess as to how many wagonloads of people the train was towing, *that makes 120 people in total*. His analysis was sickening and he didn't want to believe it. Sadly, he knew that although it was only a guess, even three in each truck would bring the total to sixty. Sixty people dead. How many more would die before they reached their destination?

The dead continued to remain where they had died, some still upright. Leah's father suggested they lay them on the floor in layers, two on top of two. Those closest did just that. The dead were piled up. There was a little more room, though still not enough to enable sitting down. Heads rested on the shoulders of neighbours.

A woman next to her mother began to scream. 'My baby is being born! Please! Please help me!'

Leah's mother panicked. 'There's no room for her to lie down! She should be lying down!'

Rudy exchanged looks with other men. There was only one place where the woman could lie down.

'On top of the dead?'

'Where else?'

In normal times they would never have committed such sacrilege, but these were not normal times. They were the most abnormal times they'd ever known.

Room was made for her on top of the piled bodies. A midwife pushed her way forward.

'I will do what I can. You men should not be here. This is a woman's time. Give her privacy.'

A circle of women formed around her.

Not wishing her daughter to witness what was about to happen, Rachel Westerman held her daughter's head tightly against her, but Leah struggled and, as the train lurched, her head became dislodged from her mother's grip. The acrid smell of unwashed bodies mixed with one she did not recognise, except that it was female and somehow feline.

Her heart thudding, she watched as the woman's clothes were hitched up above her thighs, her underwear removed. The woman gave no sign that her dignity was being invaded, her private parts on view to the world. The old woman who had professed to be a midwife commented on every little thing she was doing, as though somehow her skill and knowledge might keep their minds off where they were and what the future held.

There was blood, a bulging of something between the woman's legs. The feline, raw, blood smell intensified.

'Now I will turn the head so the shoulders come out sideways. How far gone are you, my dear?'

The woman whimpered but did not reply. From somewhere among the banished men her husband answered for her. 'Seven months.'

The midwife pulled the baby from the woman's body. 'I need to cut the cord, but I can't see... It's too dark...'

Meagre as it was, a cigarette lighter was passed from hand to hand, throwing some light for the old woman to see by. Silence hung in the air, the only sound the rattling of the cattle wagon and the squealing of iron wheels against iron rails.

Somebody passed her a sack. The old woman sighed. 'There's nothing I can do. Open it please.'

The sack was opened, the baby slid inside, and the neck of the sack was folded over.

'Lydia? Lydia?'

The father of the child shook his wife's shoulders. Finally convinced there was nothing he could do, her clothes were put in order, one more body added to the pile. The sack containing her dead baby was placed beside her. There was no ceremony. No prayers. Only blank acceptance that she was gone where others would doubtless follow.

A man, unknown to Leah and her family, suggested they should inform the guards about the dead the very next time they stopped for food and water. 'It is not healthy to leave the dead with the living. If they do that there will be no workers arriving at the end of this journey. What good will that do?'

Up until that moment Leah's father had not engaged with any of his fellow passengers. As if their cramped closeness was not enough, he'd travelled with one arm around his wife, one around his daughter. Tired and suffering from the blow dealt him at the beginning of their journey, Leah realised from the sounds he was making that her father was in pain. When she felt his face she found that his mouth was firmly clenched. Sometimes he wheezed, his breath seeming to whistle down his nose and from his throat. When that happened, blood trickled from the corner of his mouth and she felt it sticky on her fingers.

'I think that is a very good idea,' he voiced somewhat thoughtfully in reply. 'It will give us more room.'

A few other voices rose in support.

Rudy Westerman had made his mind up. He didn't really believe they were to be used as labour in the east. He'd heard those dreadful rumours that had turned his stomach. War made monsters of men. If he died then so be it, but Leah? She was only ten years old. She deserved

29

to live. His brain worked feverishly. He had to save her. He *must* save her.

Leah felt her father's arm tighten around her.

'Listen,' he hissed, his blood-caked mouth close to her ear. 'The moment we stop we will suggest en masse that the dead bodies be taken off the train. If enough of us protest, they might just listen. After all, the journey has barely begun and if they truly want labour in the east, they won't want any more to die than is necessary. You will be one of those bodies, Leah, my darling.'

Presuming that he meant she was shortly to die, Leah was about to protest when she heard her mother sucking in her breath; she too had interpreted that this was what he meant.

'Listen carefully,' he whispered. 'You will not really be dead. You must pretend to be dead. The guards will offload you. It is the only way you will escape this madness. Do not worry about your mother and me. We are strong. We will come looking for you when the war is over. In the meantime you will be flung among the poor souls who are dead. Let us pray they will leave the bodies lying there for a while, just long enough to give you time to get away. You must run as fast as your legs can carry you. Do you understand?'

Leah started to protest; she would not leave unless they were coming too. 'Mamma will cry if I leave.'

Her father's voice was dull with sadness. 'We will all cry if you don't. Now listen. You will make your way west. You must try to get to England. My friend Daniel Loper lectures at Cambridge University. You will go there to him. Now remember that, my darling daughter. Remember. Daniel Loper. Cambridge University. His address is in the hem of the pink scarf.' He went on, warning her about not trusting anyone, that even some French people collaborated with the invaders.

Leah did her best to take it all in. The thought of leaving her parents alarmed her, but dutifully she memorised what her father had told her. Daniel Loper. Cambridge University. Somewhere in England and the address was secreted in the pink scarf.

It was almost midnight when the train came to a hissing, clanking standstill, billowing steam rising from the belly of the beast and up into the cattle wagons.

'Now – we must do it now,' Rudy Westerman hissed.

A cacophony of voices rose like a storm, pleading from within the cattle wagons for the dead to be offloaded.

'Please. There are so many dead. Many more will become sick if you do not offload them.'

'There will be no workers left for your factories.'

'No workers for your factories.'

'None. All dead,' shouted Rudy, raising his voice along with all the rest. Through a narrow gap he saw the insignia of an officer within range of his booming voice. 'We are only at the beginning of our journey. Nobody will be left by the time we get to our destination, and then the Reich will have no workers for the war effort.'

Nobody came back from the 'work camps', and nor were any letters received from family or friends there. Even so, many people believed what the guards told them, because the alternative was horror on an unimaginable scale.

The man who had mentioned the factories was, like Rudy, one of those sceptical about resettlement. They exchanged a worried frown. 'We must hope they really are sending us to labour camps,' he murmured. 'If so, they won't want any trouble.'

Rudy was inclined to agree with him. Despite the great lie, he knew that fear could cause panic and panic could send the crowded people into hysterical rebellion. He was counting on the commander of this little outfit not wishing to have a riot on his hands. He had to remind himself of how many women, children and babies were on board. Removing the bodies would give some comfort and a few more moments of life – their animal-like submission being a small price to pay.

There was some hesitation in answering their demands, but Rudy perceived some running backwards and forwards, boots thudding along the hard ground, plus intense discussion followed by snapped orders. He breathed a sigh of relief. 'They can't risk a mutiny. They have to keep us believing we are really going where they say we are. Let us hope they see reason.'

Before Leah knew what was happening, her father ripped the yellow Star of David from her coat, leaving only ragged stitching. Shouted orders were followed by a loud clunking and rattling as the sliding doors of the cattle wagons were wrenched open. Rudy closed his eyes and thanked the Almighty before whispering in his daughter's ear, his voice trembling over each word.

'Close your eyes, Leah. Make yourself go loose

32

like a rag doll. Let your head sag on to your chest. Lean into me.'

'No. I don't want to leave you.'

'You must! Now, be a good daughter. Do as I say.'

Leah trembled. Her father was giving her an order and she'd never ever disobeyed him.

'Loose,' he whispered. 'Fall against me. Let me lift you up. Close your eyes.'

Her mother took hold of the pink scarf that was around Leah's neck and wound it around her face. 'In case they look at you too closely.' Her fingers lightly brushed Leah's forehead. 'Don't cry. They must not see tears.'

'Good girl. Goodbye, my love. Be brave. Go limp,' her father added.

Even after he'd removed his hand from her shoulder, it felt as though it were still there, its warmth flowing into her flesh.

Her mother's voice sounded as though she were breaking into pieces. 'My child. My child.' She heard her mother's despair but did not open her eyes.

She remembered that her rag doll had been stuffed with sawdust, imagined how that must feel and did her best to replicate a rag doll's arms, a rag doll's legs. Something of her father's desperation flowed through her in an icy stream. It frightened her.

Closing her eyes was a welcome necessity. She had no wish to see the horror around her, the dead bodies, the angry-faced men and snarling dogs.

Those still living were ordered to unload those who would never see the night sky again. Leah did not see the tears streaming down the faces of fathers as they offloaded their children, of mothers as they wailed and hid their faces as babes in arms were taken and added to the pile of dead. Old folk were flung on top of the heap without any respect.

The guards gave them no quarter, some wielding riot sticks, some jabbing with the butts of their guns or kicking with their shiny leather boots, just as they had at the beginning of the journey.

Goaded by their handlers, three out of the four guard dogs lunged, snapping and barking, their sharp teeth white with starlight. The fourth dog, the one that had regarded Leah as though they'd been reunited from another place, looked confused; the more its handler urged it to be vicious, the more the dog resisted, at one point baring its teeth threateningly at the guard.

Its inability to act like the other dogs angered the man who held it. Instead of kicking at the people offloading the dead, he aimed a kick at the dog, which yelped.

'Gutless! You're gutless.'

He aimed another kick. Seeing it coming, the dog bounced on to its back legs, the guard's boot missing.

Another guard ridiculed his handling and laughed. 'Perhaps he has no taste for this kind of meat!'

The guard resented being made to look the fool. 'He's a coward and stupid!'

'Not that stupid. He moved fast when he realised your boot was on its way again.'

The guard had been a bully even before he'd donned a uniform. Preying on the weak was something he'd always enjoyed. Face red with anger, he tugged backwards on the dog's chain with his meaty fist, then forwards so that the dog was swung in among the living and the dead. In the hope of igniting some viciousness in the animal, he grabbed those offloading the dead, pushing and punching them, anything to get the dog to lay its formidable fangs into their flesh. He was adamant that this breed of dog was endowed with the same bloodlust he felt himself.

It didn't happen. Although buffeted and pushed, the dog resisted any attempt to get it to bite.

If the handler had understood anything about dogs, he would have seen intelligence shining in this dog's eyes. This was no unthinking bully but a clever animal willing to defend those it loved. It was a magnificent animal, but its past was not the same as the others. It had once known a loving home.

The dog the handler had named Wolf had only been with this man for a short time, but from the start he had not warmed to the guard's disposition. His instinct, much stronger than in humans, sensed this was not a good man. The other dogs responded instantly to their masters' brutality, but Wolf was stubborn. He would not be bullied, by humans or other dogs.

The German army usually depended on specialist breeders for their guard dogs, but in view of the current demand for purebred German shepherds, they'd begun requisitioning household pets. 'The more vicious the better,' Heinrich Himmler, proud and merciless director of the 're-settlement' scheme, had declared. 'I want killers.'

Wolf looked the part, but as a puppy he had belonged to a little girl. They'd done everything together. He'd loved her dearly and instinctively knew she'd loved him. All that was gone now. The little girl had become ill and died. Her parents, racked with despair, couldn't bear to look at the dog that had been their daughter's constant companion. They'd donated him to the war effort.

His handler couldn't comprehend that he was in charge of a dog that could think for itself. Livid at what he perceived to be cowardice, the handler pushed and shoved everyone he came into contact with, dragging them to within his dog's range even if they were moving fast enough to get the job done.

'Go on! Bite him! Bite him! Taste his tainted blood, you stupid dog!'

The dog refused.

As the bodies piled up, Rudy Westerman held his wife. 'Have we done the right thing, Rudy?' she whispered. 'I believe so.' It was all he could say.

Finally, the last of the dead was carried from the train. The bodies were piled four high in a rough square on the cold ground. The living who had assembled the corpses were reloaded and the doors closed.

The bodies were counted and entered in a ledger. The officer in charge grunted his approval. 'Now we wait here a while. There is a troop train en route for the coast. We will receive the signal to leave once it has passed. They have priority and it should be some hours yet.' He glanced con-temptuously at the pile of bodies. 'The sooner the better,' he muttered. Then, pointing at the pile with the riding crop he always carried with him, 'The trucks will fetch these in the morning.'

This wasn't quite the job he'd had in mind when war had broken out. But he was a Prussian and considered himself naturally superior to the men under his command.

The guards relaxed. Cigarettes were smoked, hot coffee brewed and food distributed. The handlers fed their dogs before feeding themselves – all except the man paired with Wolf. His face was red with anger.

'You chose him,' one of the other handlers said, as the rest of them grinned from ear to ear. The accusation was well founded. He had gone for the biggest and most handsome of the four new canine recruits, a choice he now regretted.

His surly look passed from them to the dog. 'He has to go,' he said grimly.

The others shook their heads and looked at him as though he were the biggest fool they had ever seen. 'You're going to shoot him?'

They'd seen cruelty in all its forms but a dog was as close to them as their gun, even their greatcoat. The prisoners – the Jews they herded on to packed cattle trucks – were a different matter. The dog handlers and other guards chosen for this gruesome task had become immune to human suffering. The thing that set a dog apart was that it was a working companion. They ordered and it obeyed. But Wolf was an exception. It was obvious to all of them that he lacked aggression but, despite what his handler might say, he was brave. All German Shepherd dogs were brave. Even the Allied powers in the Great War had recognised the fact, though the English had chosen to call them Alsatians, inferring that they originated from Alsace in France rather than Germany.

Swearing under his breath, his temper more foul than usual, the handler dragged Wolf away. 'I'll teach you a lesson you'll never forget,' he muttered, spittle spotting the corners of his mouth, his eyes slits of anger. By now he was holding the dog's chain so tight that the animal was choking and being forced off its front paws, running along on its back legs to keep up.

The handler chose a spot away from his colleagues' mocking laughter. The dog was whining and yelping, music to his ears. The dog's behaviour had embarrassed him: it was a weak, ineffectual animal that wouldn't hurt a fly. Well, he'd see about that! He'd make this dog vicious by beating it into him – even if it meant he got bitten himself.

Wolf heard a swishing sound as the guard whipped a birch stick through the air and feared what would happen next. He must escape this man. His life with Helga, his first owner, had been a cosy world of running through meadows and playing with sticks and balls, swimming in the river, going on long walks. But this life was different. These people were different. He didn't understand them. He didn't like them. He had to find the life he'd had before and the little girl who had loved him.

The stick whipped through the air again and he knew what was in store. Up until now he'd been an obedient dog and not shown any sign of temper, but if roused he would respond. The man holding his chain so tightly did not perceive that. He was ignorant, a bully, and the fact that his colleagues were laughing at him doubled his need to lash out, to pick on someone weaker. That someone was his dog.

He dragged Wolf away from the main line to where two railway tracks forked around an open drainage ditch where water mixed with coal dust before finally toppling into a deep tank. It was darker here than by the train.

'Now,' he grunted, his anger at boiling point.

That swishing sound again as the stick came down. It connected with Wolf's back. He yelped, at the same time spinning round on his back legs so quickly that the chain tightened around the man's hand. Now it was the handler's turn to cry out in pain.

Bursting with fury, the man raised the stick again. 'I'll teach you...'

Wolf spun even more quickly, again tightening the chain around the man's hand, who cried out in pain as his skin was caught in the links. The birch stick fell to the floor. He swore even worse punishments for his dog as he sought to free his trapped flesh.

Concentrating on his hand rather than his feet, he loosened the chain. As he did so, the dog leapt to one side yanking the chain from his hand, then bounded back over the gaping mouth of the drainage tank.

Fuelled by temper and his determination to catch and punish the dog, the man spun too quickly, toppling over and twisting his ankle in the process. Immediately behind him was a three-inch lip running all around the drainage tank. This would usually enclose a series of railway sleepers as a cover for the tank. Somebody had neglected to replace them: the deep pit was wide open. A few loose pebbles fell into the oily water. The handler followed.

He yelled only once, the sound unheard by his colleagues who were laughing and drinking on the other side of the track. His helmet came off and fell in first. His head snagged on a jagged piece of metal. The last sound the dog heard was a loud splash. Then there was silence.

The dog, unsure what to do next, stood for a while before going to the side of the pit. He could neither hear nor smell any sign of life. The only scent was a mixture of oil, coal and rancid water.

The rest of the men were inside the watchman's hut, eating and drinking, clinging on to every last minute before they would yet again have to sit on the outside of the train and guard the prisoners on the last journey they would ever make in their lives. Wolf had no wish to go there. He'd had enough of these men and their unbelievable cruelty, which for some reason they seemed to regard as courage. There was no courage in attacking helpless people. He could not do it.

Remembering the little girl he'd been urged to bite, he turned to where the train waited. His chain-link lead clinked across the ground as he headed that way.

The sound of crying and sobbing from the cattle wagons, even that of softly spoken prayers, disturbed him. He did not understand why these people were locked away, or why others could treat them so cruelly. Humans were difficult to understand.

Wolf's nostrils twitched. The pile of bodies left beside the train smelled of death.

The muffled sound of sobbing from inside the long line of cattle wagons desisted, except for a few coughs and the low murmur of prayers for help that would never come. He pricked up his ears. He'd heard something, but it was not from within the cattle trucks. Turning, he headed for the bodies. His sensitive nose twitched as it caught a certain scent, that of something living among the dead.

CHAPTER THREE

As the bodies had been piled on top of her, thudding one after the other, Leah had been terrified. She'd wanted to scream that she was still alive. Even though her father had told her to be like a rag doll and play dead, the urge to burrow out of her prison and run free was hard to resist.

The smell of decaying, sweaty, dirty and malignant bodies was suffocating, and despite having promised her father not to move, she felt crushed under the load and could barely breathe. She had to escape. Although only ten years old, she was sensible enough to know that if she didn't escape from beneath this stifling mound, she would die.

Torsos, legs, arms, heads and clothes weighed

41

heavy. Bit by bit she heaved them off her, pushing away arms, burrowing beneath legs, closing her eyes each time a lifeless head lolled close to her face. *Be as quiet as a mouse,* she said to herself. *Like a mouse!*

Her breathing laboured, she stopped every so often and listened. Were the soldiers coming back? Or the dogs? The dogs were frightening, their teeth white and sharp beneath furled back flews.

The top half of her body was free of the weight of dead bodies. Sharp stones and pieces of grit grazed her palms but she was determined not to cry out. A little more effort was needed before she was entirely free.

The night air was fresh after the cloying stink of dead bodies. She took great gulps of air. Her body trembled. Her parents in mind, she took a moment to look towards the long trail of cattle wagons. Which one had she been in? Her gaze swept those nearest to her and the pile of bodies. One wagon looked like another. There was no way of telling.

The desire to run back and implore her parents to come with her was very strong. At the back of her mind was her father's face and his strong words urging her to go on, to get away from here no matter what she saw or what she heard. Gritting her teeth, she dragged the lower half of her body out from under the pile, struggling as a leaden weight pressed down into the small of her back. One shoe caught on something but she pressed on. Not until she was lying crumpled and free did she realise a shoe and sock had been left behind. Exhausted, she lay there. She was so tired. Her eyelids fluttered then closed. She was back in Vienna.

The scene behind her closed eyes was preferable to where she was now and, for a moment, she considered lying there, getting colder and colder, until she froze to death. What was the point of being alive if she was alone, with no parents, no friends, nobody?

I might as well die, she thought. *I might as well die!*

Sobs threatened, but she held them back. *Be as quiet as a mouse!*

Suddenly, hot sticky breath covered her face. Then a warm tongue licked her. Startled, her eyes flashed open. The unmistakeable muzzle of one of the guard dogs was only inches from her face. Panic tightened her chest. She'd seen how fiercely these dogs could bite, how excitable they became when blood oozed from a deep gash left by their sharp teeth.

Except for one. The one the guard had encouraged to bite her. She'd seen the dog's handler kick the animal in the ribs because it had refused. But that didn't mean to say he wouldn't bite her now.

Leah shivered. Slowly, very slowly, she raised herself up on to her hands, her fear-filled gaze fixed on the dog. There was little light from the station, but enough to see it reflected in his eyes. He had kind eyes. That's what she thought.

The dog's ears pricked. His tail began to wag. His muzzle came forward. When he licked her again, she shivered thinking it might be a prelude to tearing her to pieces. The other dogs would have done. Fear paling her face, she looked

43

around. If the dog was here staring at her, then surely his handler was not far behind.

The sound of men's raucous laughter came from a short distance away. Hearing it jolted her into action. She had to get away before they found her. She could not let her father down. *Daniel Loper, Cambridge University. Not London. Cambridge University.* She'd memorised the address just in case she lost the scarf and the fragment of paper hidden in the hem.

When she looked back the dog was still there, staring at her, a melting look in his eyes. As he wagged his tail he whimpered, almost as though he knew her and was waiting for her to take charge.

She noticed the chain hanging down, the blood around his neck. 'You're hurt,' she whispered, her voice trembling. 'You're hurt. Are you going to bite me now?'

The dog whimpered. Blood flecked her face as he shook his head.

'You're hurt,' she said again and thought of her father. He would know what to do. He would know how to stop the bleeding.

Eyes wide with fear, she reached to touch the choke chain, thinking that if she grabbed it she could tie him up so he wouldn't attack her. After all, that was what he was for; this dog was bred to give service to men, to do whatever he was ordered to do.

'Nice dog,' she said softly. 'Nice dog.'

The dog whimpered and wagged his tail, his gaze fixed on her face.

Tentatively she reached for the chain. The dog

looked at her expectantly. Swallowing her fear, she forced herself to keep going until her fingertips touched the chain, her fingers hooking into it.

The dog whimpered at the increased pain but stopped as her fingers loosened it. She felt stickiness. Without needing to see it, she knew there was blood on her fingers. The guard had tightened the chain so much it had bitten into the dog's neck.

'There. Is that better?'

She didn't know much about dogs, but thought he looked happier. 'You poor thing,' she murmured.

Her plan to tie him up somewhere and leave him behind melted away. Let him go wherever he wanted. She had to travel west. She had to get to England.

With this in mind, she attempted to get to her feet. Once upright, she staggered a little. The dog nuzzled closer, preventing her from falling over. Wearied by hunger and despair, she sank to her knees and threw her arms around his neck. A wet nose nudged at her face, then nudged again as if telling her it was time to move on. They had to save themselves. But where to go?

Head west. That was what her father had told her. Head west to the sea and somehow get to England.

The sound of men's laughter came from behind her as they and their dogs moved towards the train. If the train was going east then she must go in the opposite direction, just as her father had ordered. Darting from shadow to shadow, the dog loping behind her, she headed in what she thought was the right direction. Her only clue was that she knew the sun set in the west, and that way was England.

Her common sense told her it would be safer to keep to the shadows and away from army trucks and train lines. The dog also moved instinctively into the shadows.

The goods yard was quite large, with various sidings hosting both goods and passenger trains, though mostly they had been taken over by the invading army. There were French people working at the station, but she knew they were best avoided. 'Be careful who you trust,' her father had said to her. 'There are traitors everywhere, people who would betray you in order to gain favour with the Nazi regime.' She understood that. He had meant for her to do this alone.

Something brushed, then pressed against her side. The dog was still with her and, though she appreciated his company, she felt it was best to escape alone.

'Go away,' she hissed. 'Go on. I'm going to England. You can't come.'

Despite this, she and the dog moved quickly onwards. One more shadow to hide in, then another and another, keeping low, running silently despite only having one shoe. Her father had told her to trust no one, but he'd meant people. He hadn't foreseen a dog wanting to accompany her.

Leah sighed. 'You can't come with me. I've already told you that. Now go. Go on home.'

Home. The dog didn't have a home, just a kennel in an army barracks, and it seemed he wasn't going back. So now there were two of them running away to freedom.

The night was dark. No moon or stars. Although her heart throbbed with a feeling of loss and fear, and stones cut into her shoeless foot, Leah made not a sound. The dog padded beside her, the warmth of his body close to her side, his breath turning to steam in the cold night air as they hurried away from a situation neither of them could understand.

Beyond the pool of light and the rough surface of the goods yard, the frost crisping the grass cooled her bleeding foot. Although she was not consciously aware of it, the dog had led her away from the road leading to the yard, to the edge of an open field.

The dog came to a halt in the lee of a hedge and dropped down as though on a given command. In the absence of anyone telling her otherwise, Leah did the same. Only seconds after she'd done so, the cold white beam of a searchlight swept over them. Her eyes opened wide as she watched it arc across the indigo sky. She wondered what the beam of light was looking for. Was it her? Had they counted the bodies and found one missing?

The moment it had gone the dog got up. Leah did the same, clutching his ruff and keeping low as she moved alongside him. Twice more he repeated his action, and Leah followed suit, noticing that the light was diminishing in strength the further they travelled. It struck her suddenly that the dog had known the searchlight was about to arc over the sky.

Her knees weakened and she stumbled. The dog stood silently beside her and licked her cheek, his breath hot on her face, waiting patiently until she was firmly on her feet again. She looked over her shoulder. Nothing disturbed the darkness. The dog licked her face once more, at the same time attempting to lead her forward. She felt a draught of air and heard a swishing sound. The dog was wagging his tail. He'd been agitated back at the goods yard, keen to get away as quickly as possible. She felt no fear of him now. He was all she had in the world.

All through the night they plodded onwards, Leah impeded by having one bare foot, the dog sometimes stopping to lick the blood running down his chest, then turning and doing the same to her foot. She found it soothing and for a moment fell asleep.

The fierce sound of steam escaping from a train funnel sounded some way in the distance. She couldn't know for sure, but wondered if the train she had been on – that her parents were still on – had left the station and was finally heading east. Soon there would be no sound, nothing but silence and a great void in her life where her parents had been. She hoped she would see them again – one day.

She blinked once, twice, three times, not to hold back the tears but in an effort to retain the memory, the vision of her parents: her father's black beard streaked with white, like a zebra, his gold-rimmed spectacles; her mother's glossy hair and total dependence on her husband.

The dog nudged her. She just about refrained from shouting at him. 'I have to remember them. It may be a long time before I see them again.'

The dog gave a whining yelp, his eyes bright with interest as though he understood.

They moved off, but even though her stomach was empty she didn't care to eat. Even if she'd had food, she couldn't eat. She had to go on. She had to find England, Daniel Loper and Cambridge.

They travelled until just before dawn when the black night sky turned to pewter and the grass was damp with dew. Leah curled up under a hedge, a field of long grass sheltering her from any passing observer. The dog lay alongside her, the warmth of his body giving her enough comfort by which to fall asleep. Her more pleasant dreams were of food. Her nightmares were of being buried beneath a mountain of dead bodies.

Although weary, sleep was intermittent. When she awoke, the dog awoke too. Her eyes flickered as she studied the animal that had been meant to follow orders, to attack people unable to protect themselves, without regard for how old or feeble they were. He looked back at her steadily, his ears erect. The blood the chain had drawn was dry now. The dog did not make a sound as she removed the wicked-looking choke chain.

'There,' she said. 'That's better.'

He gave her his paw.

'Oh. We're shaking hands,' she said and laughed. Her laughter was short-lived. She shuddered. It was wrong to laugh after such a horrible day.

'I wonder where you came from,' she murmured, desperate to think of something else, any distraction while she adapted to the present situation – and its horrors. 'Never mind. I'm glad you ran away with me.'

He stretched his neck and held his head to one side, his eyes inquisitive.

Suddenly she felt a great urge to tell him about herself. If they were going to spend any time together he should know what he was getting himself into.

'My name's Leah,' she said to him hesitantly. 'My parents have told me to head west across the sea and find an old friend in England. It won't be easy, but if you want to come you're quite welcome.'

The dog's jaw dropped and a pink tongue flopped out. He looked as though he were laughing, or at least smiling. She couldn't know for sure but she told herself he'd understood every word she'd said.

Sighing, she nestled back down in her place under the hedge, comforted by the smell of the dog. She stroked his neck as he rested his head on his paws.

Just as she was beginning to doze off, something important came to her. 'You know my name, but I don't know yours.'

The dog sighed, as though the same thing had occurred to him and he wasn't sure what to do about it.

'I don't know what you were called before, so we'll have to think up a new name. Shall we do that?'

The dog's ears perked up as he tilted his head to one side, totally attentive.

'You tell me which name you would like. How

50

about Hans?'

The dog growled, recognising the name was linked to his handler.

'You don't like that?'

He growled again. Leah soldiered on.

'Wolf?'

The dog shook his head so heartily that his ears flapped.

Leah thought deeply. She recalled the names of some of her father's friends. In England, he'd told her to contact Daniel Loper. 'He will look after you,' he'd said. 'Remember his name.'

Leah thought carefully. One of her father's friends would look after her because her father was not around to fulfil his responsibility. But the dog was. This dog had looked after her.

He was all she had and would take her father's place – at least for now. Her father's name was Rudolph – Rudy.

She looked into the dog's keen eyes, the dark tan colour between his ears, the blackness around his muzzle reminding her of her father's black beard. 'How about we call you Rudy?'

Responding to her tone of voice, the dog yelped, his mouth wide open and his tongue lolling to one side. Despite everything, Leah beamed at him. 'Rudy. Rudy the dog.'

That night she wound her mother's silky pink scarf around the dog's neck. It was light and pretty but did nothing to keep out the cold. In the morning she found a piece of charcoal in the dirt and wrote his name on the pale pink fabric.

'Rudy!'

Burying her fears for the night, she wrapped

51

her arms around him and fell asleep with her nose buried in his ruff.

For the first two nights, they slept in the fields. By day, Leah foraged for apples and nuts that had survived the winter. Her best find was two or three potatoes left behind when the field had been harvested. After rinsing the mud from them, she considered how she might light a fire. Racking her brains brought no result. There was nothing to do but eat them raw. Tentatively she sunk her teeth through the skin and into the interior. One bite and all she wanted to do was throw up.

Rudy found a vole. It wasn't much but he seemed contented as he chomped it to pieces after ripping its fur from the flesh.

In the morning, Leah decided she needed to plan her journey more carefully. There had to be an easier way of heading west than trudging through fields.

A steam train sounded in the distance. Roused to investigate, Leah stood up on a gate and searched for its source. Her heart beat with hope when she spied a cloud of white steam furling upwards like a triumphant banner. She wasn't to know it but the railway line was the main connection from east to west – from Berlin to northern France – and was being used to help fortify the Normandy coast.

Sunlight bounced off the hard metal of the rails behind the train. From that she worked out that it was heading west, the early morning sun bright behind it in the east. So, if she could follow the railway line... Her mind was made up. That was exactly what they would do. Stopping en route in small wayside stations that trains rarely used, they might also find food, perhaps in a railwayman's hut or left behind in the solitary railway station.

'We will only search for food at night,' she whispered to the dog once she'd climbed down from the gate.

Alert to her father's warnings, she kept to the hedgerows, avoiding the narrow lanes that were numerous in this part of the French countryside. She felt safer once she was close to the gleaming rails that were hedged in by shrubs growing freely around the drainage ditches. They drank water from a stream.

By nightfall, the sun ahead of her, she could pick out a series of stone buildings forming a small railway halt where the rails split into sidings. She feared somebody might be there, but had to take the risk of being seen. Her stomach was so empty and she hadn't managed to keep down much of the raw potato. Hopefully she might find food here.

Kneeling down beside Rudy, she whispered into his ear that they were going to explore the railway huts and stations but that he had to be quiet. 'No barking. We need to find food.'

Quietly and carefully she edged her way down through the long grass to a small stone building sat beside a wooden platform bordering the railway line. The dog padded silently along at her side, his ears alert to the slightest sound.

A man came out of the station house when they were only a short distance from the door. He was holding a coffee cup in one hand and a hunk of bread and cheese in the other.

Leah froze.

The man stopped dead when he saw them.

He was an old man with white hair and keen eyes. In his youth he'd been a crack shot on the Western Front. Like many, he'd been told it was the war to end all wars but here they were, fighting again. Dying again. He'd seen starvation before and saw the hollow-eyed gleam in Leah's eyes, the licking of her bottom lip on spotting the bread. He was only vaguely aware of the dog skulking at her side. All that registered was the look in the child's eyes, the sunken cheeks and the overall air of neglect. He held out the food.

Leah regarded him as silently as he did her. Could she trust him? The imagined taste of the food encouraged her forward. The urge to snatch it and run was overwhelming, but her mother had always insisted on being polite to others. She took the bread and cheese and would have thanked him but the words seemed to stick in her throat. Hunger had rendered her speechless but so too had his kindness.

The stationmaster watched as the girl and the dog hurried off, disappearing into the long grass and straggling shrubs at the side of the track. He stood there motionless until the silence of the late morning was broken by the sound of motor vehicles winding along the road from the village, no doubt on their way to Rennes where the Resistance had blown up a section of railway line.

His eyes narrowed thoughtfully as he drained the last of his coffee. Once that was done, he prepared to face their questions, the answers to which he'd already rehearsed.

The cars pulled up, and several officers got out.

'We saw someone leave here,' one of them said, in German-accented French. 'Who was it?'

'Just a child. My granddaughter,' said the stationmaster. 'She brought me coffee and food as she does every morning.'

They seemed satisfied enough with his answer. He had not heard the enemy was looking for an escaped Jew and they'd not mentioned it. It was possible. He'd heard a train was going east, loaded with poor souls destined to never see their homes again.

As for the girl, he hoped she was long gone by now.

CHAPTER FOUR

Leah welcomed the night. Although it was cold she was glad of the darkness cloaking their steady progress westwards. Nobody could see them at night and she could afford to sleep snuggled against the warmth of Rudy's thick fur.

Sometimes in response to sounds she did not hear, he would jerk awake, ears erect. Sometimes they would see dark shadows moving through the night, keeping low as though they too preferred not to be seen.

Nobody saw them. They remained undiscovered.

Weighed down by recent events, Leah had forgotten about the coins her mother had sewn into her threadbare dress. She smiled at the thought of her father, a keen reader of Sherlock Holmes and other English detective novels. 'Always prepare for the unexpected.' A tear slid from the corner of her eye.

Perhaps she could buy a loaf of bread in a village. She closed her eyes and imagined the taste of warm bread on her tongue. Back in Vienna she had relished warm bread spread with bright yellow butter, the butter melting so quickly she used to add even more. Butter was now a luxury. The bread and cheese given her by the stationmaster was all gone.

The next village she came to was very small, just one street bordered by a jumble of small houses with square windows set into sloping roofs. She was frightened but so hungry she had to do something – even if it meant being discovered. Sheltering against a tumbledown wall, she ran her fingers along the hem of her skirt but found only one coin. Only one! There should have been more. Without noticing, she'd torn her dress on a thorny bush and not seen the coins dropping out.

Sighing, she began to make plans. She decided it would help if she didn't have the dog with her. Wrapping her arm around his neck, she explained to him as best she could. 'I have to go by myself. You must stay here.'

Struggling to her feet, her knees weak and her heart thudding, she began to walk away. After a few faltering steps, she turned round. Rudy was sticking with her.

'No,' she snapped, shaking a finger. 'You must

stay here. Sit!' So firmly did she speak that the dog did exactly that. Again, she pointed her finger. 'Stay! Lie down.' The dog whimpered but much to her relief he obeyed, his head resting on his paws.

It was just before sunset. The street was deserted and the houses threw solid shadows across the road. An old woman in black, her hair a concoction of wispy grey sitting like a nest on top of her head, was bent over the doorstep of a small shop, seemingly the only one in the village.

Leah's steps slowed as she approached. Her nervousness rising like a rock in her throat. The woman, sensing somebody was close by, looked up. On seeing Leah, her eyes widened in surprise. Having lived in Fougères all her life, she knew every man, woman and child by name. This skinny urchin was unknown to her so she was immediately on her guard. There were so many vagabonds nowadays, likely to steal anything that came to hand. The child approached stealthily, which only increased the woman's suspicion.

'Go away. I have nothing for you. Go on! Shoo!' She waved her hand as though flicking away a particularly pesky fly.

Leah's stomach lurched with hunger and the vision of bread, perhaps even some cheese, made her mouth water. It also gave her courage.

'Please. I want a loaf of bread. I have money.'

She fetched out the coin that had been hidden in the hem of her dress. The old woman's fierce look tempered at the sight of the coin, far too much for a pre-war loaf of bread, but just about right for a wartime village shop.

The old woman squinted. 'You are alone?' she said at last.

Leah nodded nervously. Desperation had brought her to this course of action even though she knew that there were people who would hand her over to the Germans because of what she was. It seemed odd to her: she could see no difference between herself and any of the other non-Jewish girls she'd known back home in Austria.

The old woman seemed to consider her next course of action very carefully before holding up a handful of work-worn fingers, the joints misshapen and gnarled, beckoning her into the village shop. Inside it was dark and full of a mixture of familiar and not so familiar smells. Oil for kerosene lamps mingled with the spicy aroma of a smoked ham hanging from the ceiling, the warm smell of freshly baked bread, autumn fruits and the earthier smells of freshly dug potatoes, celeriac and coffee.

Half a loaf of bread was produced from somewhere. The woman shoved it into a sack, the sort used for storing garlic.

'Give me the coin.'

Leah handed it over, thinking it was far too much to pay for half a loaf. The old woman brought the coin up close to her eyes. After satisfying herself that it was genuine, she grunted something that sounded like approval, slapped the sack on to the counter and opened its yawning neck.

To Leah's astonishment, out came the remains of a meaty bone, the only remaining flesh the dark brown skin clinging on with a fatty sinew.

Next came the end of a cooked sausage, the thick rind of a piece of cheese and three apples. Leah's eyes opened wide and her stomach rumbled. Her family had not been strictly observant in the eating of kosher food, and, anyway, Rudy was hungry too. The sausage was his.

The old woman heard the noise and raised her eyebrows. Leah murmured an apology. The woman jerked her chin and did not smile as she pushed the sack across the counter. Her brow was furrowed with wrinkles as though she thought too much. Her thin lips, creased with age, stretched into a straight line.

'Go. And don't come back here. Ever.'

Although the woman had given her more for her money than a loaf of bread, her sour face made Leah want to run. Grabbing the sack, she bolted for the door thinking that the old woman might have been playing a game, and would tell the authorities she'd not paid her for the food. Perhaps somebody would follow her. They might have a gun. She ran from the village without looking back, fearing that if she did she would see the old woman watching her from the doorway of her dingy shop.

Madame Serena Bertrand was indeed watching from her shop doorway. Where was the child going? She answered her own question. The child was running away from something that had hurt her badly and that she could not understand. And neither do I, thought Serena. What I do know is that tonight I will be going to bed with no supper. The child was in need. It was all she could do. And, anyway, there was always coffee

59

and a cognac, perhaps an apple and the last piece of cheese. The country was starving. Everyone was starving.

CHAPTER FIVE

The bread lasted for two days, the piece of fatty smoked skin peeled from the bone she held on to, sharing the fat between herself and Rudy who had already devoured the end of sausage. He had also crunched the bone to nothing on the first night.

There were no more coins. Although Rudy could fend for himself, he feared going off and leaving her. Leah was getting weaker. She slept fitfully now, her stomach convulsed with hunger pangs, and because she was growing weaker, their progress across the countryside was slow.

Rudy hunted for food, but Leah had no way of cooking it and she couldn't bring herself to eat anything raw. Once he brought her a loaf of bread. She had no idea where he'd got it from, only that it was a bit stale. Not that it mattered. She ate it regardless, washing it down with cold water scooped in her hands from a swiftly running brook.

The mud at the side of the brook was slippery and the night was dark. Making her way back up the bank, her feet slipped from under her. She went down, slamming her head on a rock as she did so. She lay there getting colder and colder, her legs immersed in the icy water, a trickle of blood flowing over the rock and into the mud. Eyes closed, she didn't hear Rudy's small cries of concern. Neither was she aware of his teeth snagging on her coat as he dragged her away from the water into the tall reeds.

The next morning, she came to with him lying at her side licking the crusted blood away from her eyes. She saw the name written on the silky scarf hanging from his neck. Rudy. Instinctively she held on to the dog's neck and struggled to her feet. She still feared moving by day but the nights were cold and it was very appealing to fall asleep against the warmth of her dog's body.

She couldn't quite recall when she had decided to call him her dog, as though he'd never been anything else. But he was all she had to cling to, to tell her troubles to and cry against his thick fur. Her energy was draining fast, all the springiness gone from her step, dragging her legs as though they were made of lead.

In her dreams, bodies pressed around her, their weight crushing her into the ground, their eyes staring and lifeless. In her dreams she smelled dirty clothes, blood and death, the rank smells of bodies that no longer lived. All she knew was that it was better to be alive and sometimes she awoke screaming, not stopping until Rudy licked her face and nuzzled his cold nose into her cheek.

Tonight the moon was bright, a silver disc hanging in an indigo sky. There were no clouds and the land was bathed in a gossamer light. Leah was staggering now, her strength almost gone, her mind weary and wandering between

61

what was now and what had been, between dreams, nightmares and reality.

She thought she was on a train with plush seats and brightly dressed people all on their way to a concert in Salzburg where they would stay in a smart hotel, eat lovely things and talk about their families, their lives, their hopes for the future. Then halfway through, the dream would change into a nightmare, the train from one of luxury to a cattle wagon where people were squashed into a small space like sides of meat packed in a cold store, en route for the butchers' shops in up-market Vienna. Then the people became carcases and the butchers chopped them into tiny pieces...

Her head aching with remembrance and fear, girl and dog snuggled down in the long grass, all that remained of a field of lavender, the smell lingering on the air. The field was flat and very large, enclosed by a thick hedge, thick enough to shield them from the worst of the frost.

Leah shivered. Her muddy, worn coat did little to keep out the cold. She barely noticed her runny nose and couldn't stop her eyes from closing. Neither could she prevent her knees from giving way, so she fell on to the spiky remains of the lavender. Finding herself on the ground came as a surprise, but all she could do was snuggle down between the hedge and the dog.

Cold, hungry and weary, she fell into a deep sleep and, without knowing it, grew colder and colder. She didn't hear Rudy's concerned whining or feel his hot breath as he licked her face. Instinctively he knew that he had to keep her awake if she was to live, had to move, make

62

noises, do anything to stop her freezing to death.

He'd had to do this before. She'd awoken then, her eyes flickering as she came to, seemingly surprised to find herself in a strange place with a dog and without her parents. But on this occasion, her face lit ghostly white by the full moon, her eyelids remained closed. Rudy snuggled closer to her, trying to warm her with his own fur-covered body. He barked sharply, nudging her with his nose and licking her face.

Leah remained motionless. She was yet again on the train to Salzburg, seeing her mother enjoying the glittering company, the smell of her perfume, her happy face and avid conversation. The train rattled onwards. The plush upholstered seating and amber light from pretty glass shades went out. The light and the happy atmosphere were replaced by darkness and the smell of fear, of people travelling to the butchers.

Leah felt helpless. This was the last stage of the journey. The butchers were waiting to cut them up. If she didn't leap from the train she too would be cut into little pieces. But what would it mean to leap from the train? Something better than being slaughtered like cattle, came the answer. Cattle travel in cattle wagons. Cattle get slaughtered.

Somehow the door of the cattle wagon was jerked open. The train was racing through the night. In the distance she could just about make out the spires and towers of her native Vienna. If she jumped, is that where she would end up?

Encompassed in her nightmare, Leah was not aware of the brightness of moonlight or of the low drone of an aircraft getting closer. She was not

63

aware of Rudy's protective instinct kicking in as his nose twitched in response to smells and sounds he perceived close by. No matter who they were, he would be here for her. Nobody would approach unless he sensed they were trustworthy.

His gaze turned upwards to watch a dark shape cutting through the sky. He heard a rumbling, thudding sound as it came down, its wheels flattening the shorn stubble of the field, its propellers slicing through the air before slowing and coming to a stop.

Crouching figures, the ones he'd smelled and heard, emerged from the hedge to either side. Rudy got to his feet and growled, disturbing the hedge at his back.

'Who's there?'

There was a clicking sound the dog recognised. A gun. The guards had carried guns. He knew the sound of them, knew what they could do. His first instinct was to run away. His second was to stand firm beside his new friend. He would not – could not – leave her. In compromise he merely growled, a deep throaty growl, ears erect and every sense alert.

'*Un chien.*'

Language meant nothing to him. Tone of voice was everything. The crouched figures were speaking to each other. He growled another warning as one of the figures leaned closer and saw Leah.

'*Une fille!*'

'Are you lot ready?' Another voice. Another tongue.

The droning of the aeroplane engine had stilled. The pilot had climbed out. Ray Malin, a broad figure made more bulky by his sheepskin-lined flying jacket, loomed out of the darkness.

'Come on. I haven't got all night.'

'We have interlopers,' said the softer voice that had spoken first. 'Shoot them.'

'It's a child. And a dog.'

Ray, a confirmed dog lover, was instantly diverted from the tough job he'd been sent to do – picking up a British spy. He held out his hand palm down so the dog could sniff it and ascertain that he was no threat. 'Hey, boy. It's all right. Nobody's going to hurt you. What are you doing here anyway? And who's your friend?' His voice was gentle, his manner mild and not at all threatening.

It had been many days since Leah had bought the supplies from the old woman in the village shop. Eyes closed, oblivious to the situation, she lay cold and still. The dog growled a warning. He'd grown wary of men, especially those in uniform.

Ray kept his movements slow, his voice even. 'It's all right, old chap. I'm not going to hurt you.'

Serge, codenamed Blue Dove and the man he'd been sent to pick up, spoke again. 'It's a child. A little girl. What the hell is she doing here?'

'Hold the dog a moment.' The speaker was Alphonse Revere. Besides being a member of the Resistance, he also happened to be the local doctor. Fearing the worst, he checked the cold little face already wondering what he was going to do with her, noticing the ragged yellow stitching still left on her coat. 'This child is very sick. She won't last long if she doesn't get help shortly.'

'Is she local?' asked Serge.

The doctor shook his head. 'I don't recognise her. I've treated every child around here. I don't know her.'

Serge grunted, 'A train full of Jews went through here a few days ago, heading across the border into Germany. I wonder if she could have escaped. As for the dog...'

He went to grab hold of the dog's ear. The dog growled, leaving Serge in no doubt that he was treading on dangerous ground. He snatched his hand away.

'Here. Take my flashlight. Look into his ear ... if you dare.' Ray looked at him in consternation before doing so. 'Easy boy,' he said gently. 'Nobody's going to hurt you.'

The uniform of the RAF pilot was partially obscured by his flying jacket. His manner was reassuring. Rudy allowed him to look into his ear.

'Hello,' said Ray. 'There's a number tattooed into his ear.'

'Let me see.' A slim hip nudged against that of the pilot, easing him gently but firmly aside. Ray fancied he smelled something flowery and knew he'd been nudged aside by a woman. He saw her face in profile, her nose rising pertly from a sleek face, strands of dark hair fluttering from beneath her oversized beret.

'He is right. It is a serial number.' There was something tenacious in the look she gave him, as though she was weighing him up with a single glance.

Serge nodded. 'An army number. The Wehrmacht tattoo all their dogs. I bet you, my dear friend, that this dog was also with that train. A guard dog.' He frowned, curious as to how and why the dog was with the child. Part of him wanted to kill this animal. It was a German Shepherd, a dog bred by and beloved of the enemy.

The woman, Nicole, suggested they shoot it.

Ray stiffened. 'Why?'

'There is precious little food for people, let alone dogs.'

'He's a useful animal, aren't you?' said Ray, ruffling the dog's ears. The dog's initial growling had ceased. Ray had the feeling he'd been weighed up and found to be acceptable.

'What's he doing with the little girl – if he was with the train, that is?'

Ray wished her perfume wasn't so enticing. Concentrating on the dog helped him ignore it. He addressed the dog rather than actually answering her question.

'I bet you've gone absent without leave, old boy.'

Nicole smiled at him. 'You RAF boys always say that – old boy – even when someone is young.'

Ray grinned. 'A term of endearment, my dear. Merely a term of endearment. Still,' he shone the flashlight on the face of his watch, 'I can't stand around here chatting.' He turned to the small group of French Resistance fighters and the agent he'd been ordered to pick up. 'What will you do with these two?'

There was a great shrugging of shoulders and shaking of heads.

'We can't keep her here. We can't take her back to the village. The risk is too great.' Although Serge was the leader of the group, the speaker was

Nicole. 'And before anyone calls me hard-hearted, may I remind you that we have orders not to jeopardise our circumstances for anyone or anything. The girl has to be disposed of. The dog too.'

An angry silence descended.

Ray clenched his jaw. He had come to fly the agent to safety. He would obey the order. However, there was no way he was going to leave an innocent child behind to be slaughtered. She at least had to be taken to safety.

Before anybody could stop him, he scooped the child up into his arms and strode off across the field to his waiting plane. Her eyes flickered open. 'Rudy. Rudy.'

'If Rudy's the name of your dog, I can tell you he's right behind us. See?'

He held her so she could see that the dog was bounding along behind them. A smile of satisfaction came to her face before her eyes closed and she lost consciousness.

Serge, the doctor and leader of the group, prepared to shoot the dog. The agent stopped him, his intention uttered in a low voice. 'I have a knife. I will deal with it quietly. It will not be getting on that plane.' Hand resting on his knife, he raced off across the bumpy ground. By the time he got to the plane both the child and the dog were already on board.

'You're taking the dog too?' Disbelief frayed his voice. 'I am sorry. I cannot allow that. Let me...' He half pulled the knife from where it was concealed beneath his jacket.

Ray was adamant and the fingers that gripped the man's wrist were strong. 'Can't allow it, old chap. Haven't you ever heard that the British are a nation of dog lovers?'

The man codenamed Blue Dove winced but gritted his teeth. He would have his own way. 'I am giving you an order. It is bad enough that you took that child on board...'

'Sorry, mate. You're not my superior officer. I'm in charge of this plane. The little girl looks as though she needs urgent hospital treatment and somebody to care for her, and the dog seems to be the only friend she's got. So get in or stay put. The choice is yours, but I warn you: touch that dog and I'll throw you out without the benefit of a parachute. Do I make myself clear?'

'I must protest! Taking passengers is strictly against orders...'

'Damn orders. The kid's sick.'

'I'll concede that, but the dog...'

'Is a military decision. It suits me to take him. Now settle down and we can all be away from here.'

The agent's eyes flashed with anger in the dim light. He was used to giving orders and having them obeyed. His mission, his presence and his decisions were what counted.

The navigator, Chris, turned round and grinned as Ray settled himself in front of the controls. 'Extra passengers, sir? How do we list them on our manifesto?'

'Children of the storm. Well, one child and one dog. Handsome fellah, don't you think? By the looks of it I think dog and kid are devoted to each other.' He frowned. Would the kid survive? She was in a pretty bad way. There'd been mention of

69

a train going east. Had she been on that train?

His face crumpled with sympathy. 'Poor kid. I can only guess what she's been through.'

There was something about the look on the agent's face that made him pause before starting the engines for the flight home. If there was one thing he was good at, it was reading peoples' minds.

'Hey, buddy. Let's get this straight. I like dogs a lot and I'm in charge of this plane. Anything happens to him and I'll keep my promise about throwing you out over the Channel.'

Chris chortled into his charts. Not that he needed them yet. Head due west and they would swoop across the English Channel; the charts would come into their own when flying low over the dark landscape that was wartime England.

The propellers whirled into action. Ray set the aircraft up for take-off, choosing the portion of the field that would give him the longest run. The field was bumpy and far from ideal, but Ray was experienced enough to know to get the wheels up as quickly as possible. Tufts of dead grass and brown earth passed like waves before them, and the smell of lavender retained in the soil wafted upwards.

This was the time during the mission when gut-wrenching nervousness erupted in full strength. The secret was to get in and out of this war blasted country as quickly as possible. He'd been a little slow tonight but considered it worthwhile. There would have been no help for the little girl, and as for the dog...

He understood the agent's concern and that of

the Resistance. They lived on a knife's edge. Emotion was a commodity they could not afford and it would have been expedient for them both to be killed. Ray couldn't allow that. If it were his child he'd want someone to help. If only he had a child. Although he'd been married for four years there had been no patter of tiny feet. He only wished there had, then perhaps he might have persuaded his wife Meg to let him buy a puppy as a companion for the child. But there had been no child and likewise no dog.

As they swept over the Channel he marvelled at the sight of it glowing like tinfoil beneath the light of the moon. His navigator asked him what plans he had for their extra passengers.

'Well, hospital first. The girl needs medical treatment, then we can find out who she is and if she has any family in England. I'll look after the dog while she's in hospital. He'll come in handy around the base. The chaps will love him.'

Chris agreed. 'He can be our mascot. That's if the little girl doesn't object. She might consider the dog belongs to her.'

Ray had to admit he could be right, but seeing as he was in the habit of jumping in with both feet, he chose not to dwell on the prospect. Anyway, he'd noticed the dog wore a military tattoo in its ear. A German tattoo. He was, in effect, a prisoner of war, part of the booty that war always brought to those who grabbed their chance.

'I think him becoming our mascot is a great idea; a great welcome coming back from an op, don't you think?'

The navigator nodded. 'Whatever you say, boss.

71

Whatever you say.'

'Or I might take him home. If I can.'

Keeping the dog with him at the base was the only option he had. His wife Meg wouldn't have a dog in the house. But first he had to sort out the little girl.

Leah could feel the train vibrating as it hurtled down the rails, the cattle wagons rattling and rolling from side to side. If she didn't jump off soon she would be dead! Suddenly she was screaming. 'Stop the train! It's not going to Salzburg. It's going to the butchers!'

The man they'd been sent to pick up, who Ray disliked on sight, translated what she had said.

The spy also pointed out that she spoke French with a German accent. 'I would hazard the guess that she was born a German Jew but escaped to France.'

'With her family, I suppose.'

'Presumably.'

Ray exchanged a quick look with his navigator. They'd both heard rumours of trains going east, to so-called labour camps, but certainly not to Salzburg!

Blue Dove, the son of a French woman and a Scottish father, had sold sports cars in his former life, besides getting involved with the shadier side of London nightlife. Being an agent was far more exciting and set him apart from those who pursued 'ordinary' lives. He was that indoctrinated, all he cared about was the mission. He had every intention of reporting this incident. Given the chance he'd throw both the kid and the dog into the Channel.

Not a chance! The dog lay between him and the child. The dog growled a warning.

Ray settled into his seat; the girl's words had rattled him. She was just a young kid who'd got caught up in the war and it wasn't right. It just wasn't right. He radioed ahead for an ambulance.

Ray held the girl's hand while she was being loaded on to the ambulance. Her eyes flickered open as they had on the plane, wide with fear, darting all over the place.

'My name's Ray Malin,' he said to her. 'Just you remember that if you need a friend. Got it?' He repeated his words in French, though it wasn't too good. She looked terrified of her new surroundings and gave no sign that she'd understood what he'd said to her.

'Can't blame her for that,' he said to Chris.

Chris agreed.

Whose child was she? Someone had once loved and cared for her. Where were they now? He could make a shrewd guess. Did she have anyone to care for her at all? Shaking his head, he voiced his thoughts out loud. 'Wish I had a kid like that.'

'It'll happen one day when you least expect it. Mark my words.' Chris was his usual pragmatic self, but then he could afford to be. He had four children and another on the way. Like shelling peas, thought Ray. And all he wanted was just one child for him and Meg to call their own, then perhaps she'd have something more to do than clean the house from top to bottom every day. Sometimes it seemed she lavished more attention on that house than she did on him. Perhaps... The thought came to him that here was a child needing a home, and he and Meg were in need of a child.

Ray stood watching the ambulance drive away, the dog sitting beside him, Ray's hand on his head, the pink scarf entwined around his fingers. He looked down at the dog. The dog's gaze was fixed on the disappearing ambulance.

'No need to worry, old chap. She'll be well taken care of. In the meantime, we'd better get you fed. Better get you a collar and lead too,' he added.

It was when he was removing the pink scarf before placing the new collar around the dog's neck that Ray saw the scribbled name in faded black charcoal. Rudy.

'Rudy? Is that your name?'

Recognising the sound, the dog's ears pricked up, his tail slowly brushing the floor. He was beginning to trust this man, though he also missed the little girl with whom he'd gone through so much.

'Rudy,' said Ray, the name rolling off his tongue. 'Your name's Rudy. I take it that's the name the little girl gave you.'

Rudy whined, lifted his paw and raked it down Ray's leg a few times.

Somehow Ray understood what he was about. 'Don't worry,' he said, gently massaging the dog's velvety ears. 'I promise you she'll be fine and if I can arrange for you to see her again, I will. So how do you fancy being a squadron mascot?'

The dog gazed up at him, his eyes full of trust.

'Yeah. Seems a good idea to me too. Come on. Let's check in.'

CHAPTER SIX

The dog settled in well, seemingly liking everybody except for Warrant Officer Dodgeson, who had a bright red face and the voice of a foghorn. An assistant in an ironmongers' before joining up, Dodgeson in a uniform was an overbearing and arrogant bully. He couldn't bully the officers of course, but he could bully those of lesser ranks – which he did quite often. A dog also fitted into the lower ranks.

'Acquired yourself a dog, sir?' He drew his chin in as he said it, as though he were swallowing his tongue.

'Yes. This is Rudy. He's a handsome fellow, don't you think? Ideal to be the base mascot.'

Dodgeson didn't look convinced.

The dog growled his dislike, which was instant.

Rudy accompanied Ray wherever he went, though on occasion, usually when Ray was in a briefing, he wandered the base. The men took to him, fed him titbits and threw an old tennis ball for him to fetch time and time again until their arms were worn out.

Only Dodgeson refused to warm to him, his top lip curling so high that his pencil-thin moustache looked in danger of disappearing up his nose. Man and dog glared whenever they came into close contact. Dodgeson decided to complain.

'I don't trust that dog,' he said to Ray when the

animal had bared his teeth at him. 'I reckon he should be muzzled – just in case he takes a bite out of somebody.'

That somebody being you, thought Ray. He'd had dogs all his life, knew them well and swiftly made his own judgement. He looked sidelong at Dodgeson. He'd disliked the man from the start and his opinion was unchanged. He said it as it was, even though Dodgeson might be offended.

'I trust a dog's instincts when he fails to trust a human. I have to ask myself why.' Dodgeson's puffed-up self-importance deflated instantly – like a flattened beach ball.

'His ego deserves to be punctured now and again,' Ray said to the dog once the sergeant was gone. 'Just promise me you won't do it literally,' he added.

Rudy's presence was a continuous reminder of the little girl Ray had rescued from France. He thought about the pretty French Resistance fighter surmising she'd escaped from one of the trains going east. Funny how he sometimes thought he could smell her perfume, or it could have been the scattered heads of lavender in the landing field.

Shaking his head, his thoughts went back to the little girl. An idea had taken seed in his mind. The thought of returning to that pristine house irked him. One greasy thumb print and Meg was there with a duster leaving him wondering where he could sit or what he could touch without her reacting with a duster or plumping up a cushion he'd dented. The plan he had in mind might be helpful for everyone. He certainly hoped so.

He phoned Meg and asked how she was. She went on and on about the damp dirtiness of the Anderson shelter, the queuing for rations and the lack of any decent material for curtains. He let her go on until finally she asked him how he was.

'Back safe and sound.'

'Thank goodness. I've missed you.'

She probably had. At least him being home added an extra dimension to her daily routine.

'Meg, there's something I have to tell you.' He explained about the little girl he'd brought out of France. 'She was unconscious the last time I saw her, not really with it at all. We asked her name but she doesn't seem to remember.'

'Poor thing. How old is she?'

'About ten. A nice-looking kid but very thin. Definitely in need of one of your shepherd's pies.'

He enjoyed the sound of her sudden laughter. He heard it so rarely nowadays.

'Does she have relatives here?' Meg asked.

'I don't know. Someone will try to find out. But she needs a home. A proper home. I suppose if they can't find a relative – and they won't if she's lost her memory – she'll end up in a home.'

'I hear children's homes are pretty crowded nowadays, what with the evacuees and suchlike.' There was a pause on the other end of the line. 'If they get stuck and she has nowhere to go, do you think we could...'

Ray shut his eyes. He'd purposely angled the conversation in a sympathetic direction, hoping against hope that Meg would grab the chance to have a child, even if it wasn't theirs.

'Meg. Would you?'

77

'Take her in? Of course I would.' He sensed her sudden hesitation and hoped she wasn't having second thoughts, 'Would it be allowed?'

'I don't see why not. I can make enquiries. It isn't a foregone conclusion. She may recover immediately and remember who she is and then there might be a relative to claim her. I mean, there may be. But...'

He didn't mention the dog. The dog and the girl went together like bread and cheese. He didn't think Meg could accept that. She'd refused to let him have a dog before. 'In case we do get lucky,' she'd said to him. She'd meant a child. But after four years they'd pretty much given up hoping. But if they could foster or adopt? They'd discussed it many times and would have done something positive if the war hadn't disrupted their plans.

Take it one step at a time, he told himself. In time he might be able to bring her round. For the moment the girl was the most important thing. Rudy had landed on all four paws and at least for the moment was happy enough at the airfield. The girl was still unclaimed.

After telling Meg he would do his best and saying goodbye, Ray made arrangements to visit the girl. After a good night's sleep he made the hour-long journey to see her in the hospital in Lincoln.

The hospital was a flurry of pristine whiteness, where white-hooded nurses flitted with soft footfall along narrow corridors. The girl was lying in a bed close to a window that looked out on the rustling leaves of a beech tree, through which could be glimpsed the city itself. Beyond the patchwork of rooftops rose the spire of Lincoln cathedral.

The view was handsome enough, and although it drew his attention for a little while, it was the girl he had come to see. She was lying silently, eyes closed, her face almost as white as the pillow. Ray tried to work out whether she looked worse or better than when he'd found her in that frosty field.

'Are you her father?'

Assuming visitors were being kept to a minimum, he'd barged through the ward door without reporting to anyone.

'No.'

'I'm sorry. Only relatives are allowed to visit.'

'Have you found any relatives?'

'Well, no. Not yet.'

'Then I'm about all she's got. I found her in occupied territory and brought her out. I reckon that gives me priority.'

The officious-looking nurse, her badge reading 'Ward Sister', was ready to throw the book at him – that is, until he smiled at her. She looked at him, taking in the craggy chin, the sapphire-blue eyes, the way one side of his mouth curled upwards as though he might laugh but also cry. Women were always taking a second look at Ray Malin, and this ward sister in her dark blue uniform was no exception. It didn't matter that she was in her mid-thirties and dedicated to her chosen vocation, there were times when a charming smile might persuade her to choose a man above nursing.

'So. How is she?'

She smiled in a tight, patient manner, as ward sisters and matrons are inclined to do. 'She's been through hard times but she's young. Physic-

79

ally she'll recover. Her head wound was superficial. Mentally it may be a different matter. It would help if she was placed in a proper home environment.'

She cocked her head to one side in a pertly attractive manner. Her hair was blonde and her lips very red. She was pretty, though perhaps wearing too much make-up.

'She was unconscious when you found her?'

Ray nodded. 'Yes. She was also very cold and very hungry. I don't think she'd eaten for days.'

'It does seem that way. She's very weak.'

Ray frowned while nodding that he understood. 'Has she said anything at all?'

Her crisp headdress crackled as she shook her head. 'I'm afraid not. We don't know her name. We've asked her but she just looks at us blankly before sliding back into unconsciousness.' Her voice was husky.

'Have you tried other languages?'

She eyed him as though he'd said something slightly insulting. 'We are not stupid. We've tried everything. She knows a little French, some English but mostly German. The problem isn't that she doesn't understand, it's that she can't remember who she is. Judging by how thin she is, and how poorly dressed, she's been through an awful lot. It's as though she's blocked out everything that happened before you found her. People quite often block out terrible incidents. It's all part of the survival instinct. Have you any idea what she might have gone through?'

Ray thought of the rumours coming out of Germany, some too terrible to believe. At first, they had been disregarded precisely because they were so horrible. Now they were starting to be believed.

Instead of answering the sister's question he asked, 'What will happen to her if she can't remember her name and no relatives are found?'

The sister's starched headdress crackled again as she smoothed down the sheet fold, lifting first one of the girl's hands then the other, scrutinising her work with quiet efficiency. She reminded him of Meg.

'She'll probably go to an orphanage until she recovers enough to remember who she is. Unless we can find a home environment, but in these troubled times, what with thousands of homeless and evacuees all needing accommodation...' She sighed heavily then looked down at the neat little watch pinned to the top of her crisp white apron. Ray noticed the time was detailed upside down so she could lift it up in her long white fingers and read it right away. He also read her name as Sister Rossiter.

'Sister Rossiter,' he said, bending his head so she could see he was trying to read her name.

'Edith. You can call me Edith,' she said softly.

Ray smiled. 'Edith. Can I stay with her a minute?'

She eyed him apprehensively, though her mind was already made up. 'Is it true what you said about finding her in France?' He nodded.

'Poor thing.'

'You can say that again. God knows what she went through. I found her in a field half dead with only a dog for company.'

'What happened to the dog?'

Ray grinned. 'He landed on his feet. He's living at the base with me.'

She flashed him an approving smile. 'That's very kind of you.'

His grin widened and the accompanying wink made her blush. 'I'm a very kind man.'

It was against the rules but Edith Rossiter knew she was beaten. Though she shook her head disapprovingly, her red lips smiled. 'Five minutes. That's all.' She went to fuss at another bed across the ward, closing the curtain around a groaning patient while Ray pulled up a chair.

Now how to approach this? He recalled the girl's eyes flickering and that one sweet smile when he'd promised her that the dog was going flying too. He shook his head sadly. Very lightly, he tapped her hand with his finger.

'Rudy sends his love. Hey. Do you remember him? Rudy, the dog you were with?'

Her eyes flickered open and she attempted to raise her head from the pillow.

'Now, now,' Ray soothed. 'Take it easy. Rudy is fine and living with me. You do remember me, don't you? The man who flies aeroplanes. I took both of you up into the big blue yonder. Whoosh,' he said, flying his hand through the air in imitation of an aircraft.

The girl frowned and Ray was disappointed. He'd fully expected her to respond to him mentioning the dog's name, even if she didn't know who he was. After all, she'd only met him that one night and even then, for the most part, she'd been out of it. It hooked at his heart to see her confusion. The poor kid didn't know where she was.

'The train! It's for cattle! It's for cattle!' She said it in German then repeated it in French.

It was almost the same as before in the plane: a train not going to Salzburg and meant for cattle, not humans. Whatever had happened, it all went back to the train. The Resistance fighter must have been right.

Her breath caught in her throat and her sunken eyes stared at something beyond him, something only she could see. 'Breathe!' he urged, afraid that she was choking. 'Breathe!'

He looked over to the other side of the ward. Sister Rossiter was still dealing with the patient behind the curtain.

Ray flung his cap on to the bed and leaned over the girl. 'Now listen. You're no longer on the train. You're in hospital. Think of Rudy. You and Rudy escaped. You got away. You're safe now. Completely safe.'

He almost thanked God out loud when her eyes opened.

'I'm sure Rudy remembers you even if you don't remember him. Does he know your name? Can you tell me your name so I can tell him you're safe and well?'

The interest that had brightened her, face diminished. Her jaw drooped, her eyes watered and she began to sob. 'I don't know my name.' She repeated it three times: in German, French and English.

'Are you German?'

'I don't know.'

He didn't press her that she might be French, though the spy he'd picked up in France said she had a German accent and was probably a German refugee. Whoever she was, she was well educated enough to speak three languages.

'I don't have a name,' she wailed again. 'I've lost my name.'

Ray felt cornered. He'd thought to help her remember and all he'd done was upset her. He did his best to make amends.

'No need to take on. How about we give you a name you can use just until you remember who you are? How would that be?'

To Ray's delight, it seemed the pain in her eyes retreated. She nodded hesitantly.

'Will you choose a name or would you like me to choose one for you?'

'You.'

'OK, as our American allies would say. Whatever you wish, ma' am!'

A faint smile came to her lips when he saluted.

'How about we call you Lily? Like Tiger Lily in Peter Pan, or a lily growing in the garden. You know, slim and white and smelling really sweet. Would that suit you?'

She nodded and again a faint smile appeared.

'My word! What's going on here?' Sister Rossiter looked surprised to see the child smiling. Ray suspected she'd retouched her lipstick. It looked redder than it had been.

'She's decided her name's Lily until such time she remembers where she placed her old one. She lost it somewhere. Didn't you, Lily? Just like you would a sixpenny bit, then find it in the

84

pudding at Christmas. Isn't that right, Lily?'

Lily looked puzzled.

My fault, thought Ray. The kid wouldn't know much about Christmas, especially an English Christmas – especially if she was Jewish, which seemed to be the most likely case.

'Are you Jewish?'

Lily looked at him wide-eyed and shrugged. 'I don't know. I don't know what I am.'

'Right, young lady. That's enough for now. Time for you to get some rest.'

Ray straightened and waited to be ushered out. Lily didn't take her eyes off him.

Sister Rossiter insisted on escorting him out of the ward. 'I'm not going to kidnap her, you know.'

Edith Rossiter gave him a so-so look as though she only half believed him. In fact, she was looking forward to him visiting again.

As the doors to the ward swished shut behind them, Ray lingered, a whole whirligig of questions going round in his mind. Sister Rossiter noticed. 'Is there something you want?'

'Does she have to go to an orphanage? I mean, how about if somebody offered her a home?'

A small frown puckered between her eyebrows. 'I dare say it would be considered if it was somebody suitable...'

'Right! Who do I see about it?'

The ward sister's eyebrows arched. 'Well, for a start you have to be married...'

'I am.'

'Oh.' She sounded disappointed. 'Very well. I'll give you the details.'

The woman she directed him to was in charge

85

of Children's Welfare at the local council offices, but first he had to speak to Meg. He judged there wasn't time to make the journey to London. A telephone call would have to suffice.

Meg positively bubbled on the phone. 'Ray! Well, this is a surprise. Don't tell me they've given you extra leave ... not that you don't deserve it, but ... or is it the other matter? I've been trying not to get my hopes up, honest I have...'

'Meg, listen. This little girl ... it might be a bit much for you. You see she's lost her memory, or at least some of it. She can't remember who she is so the powers that be can't trace any relatives. The chances are that unless somebody can foster her, she'll have to go into a home; you know, some kind of orphanage, unless they can find a decent foster home, though they are few and far between. People keep reminding me there's a war on – as if I didn't know. Anyway, I've asked if we might take her in, Meg. You might be getting more than a house to take care of...'

Contrary to what he'd feared, Meg was over the moon. 'Ray. Oh Ray... When?'

'Bear in mind, Meg, that things might be difficult for a while. The poor kid is half starved and can't remember her name. She's a pretty little thing but it won't be easy. You have to take that on board. It isn't going to be a sleigh ride. Could be quite a bumpy ride, in fact.'

'I don't care, Ray. Let's give her a chance. If we can.'

'I've got to go along and see the children's welfare officer at the council offices in Lincoln. They'll check our status but from what I can gather, they're pretty desperate for volunteers to take children, what with the evacuees and houses being destroyed in London.'

'When do you see these people?'

'Things will take a while, so the quicker we can get the wheels turning the better. I'm on my way there now, but thought I'd better ring you to make sure you still want to do it.'

'Of course I do! Of course we'll have her.'

'Just remember, at some point she might re-member who she really is or somebody might claim her, so I don't say it will be for ever, but at least we can give her a chance.' He paused. 'Are you sure it's all right with you?'

'Yes! Oh yes, of course it is.'

'Seeing as we don't know her real name, I've called her Lily. Your second name.'

'Ray, that is so sweet of you.'

'There is one other thing.'

'What's that?'

'There was a dog with her when I found her. I think he's the only reason she managed to sur-vive.'

Meg fell silent.

Ray closed his eyes and prayed. He'd known this would be the stumbling block but had brushed it to one side thinking that having a kid to look after would override Meg's aversion to having an animal in the house.

'Not a dog, Ray. I don't want a dog. You know I've never liked dogs. They make me nervous. I can't help it.'

Ray sighed. 'You got bitten by one a very long time ago.' He couldn't help an element of impatience entering his voice. He wanted to say, look, you're grown up now and bigger than the biggest dog.

'But they make such a mess,' she continued. 'I would be cleaning up after it all the time and anyway, it sounds as though Lily will need all my attention.'

He held back from saying that she was cleaning all the time anyway. Best to tread carefully, he decided.

'Never mind. The dog's already living with me at the base. The chaps love him. Still, it's Lily that counts. Do you think we could do it?'

'Oh yes, Ray. I'll sort out the guest bedroom right away. I'll get the decorators in and see if the bargain store has got a suitable rug in stock. The curtains might have to do, but I will wash them. I want everything perfect for her when she comes. And I love the name. Lily. My middle name. You are a sweetheart.'

'Then I'll set the wheels in motion. I'm on my way to the Children's Welfare Department as soon as I put this phone down.'

'Yes! Oh, yes. Ray. Let me know as soon as everything's been arranged. My, but I have so much to do before she comes to live with us. So much!'

Ray smiled to himself as he put down the telephone. Having a child to look after would keep his wife occupied. Perhaps she wouldn't give so much attention over to the house. He knew she did it to keep herself busy, but it still drove him to distraction. In consequence, he felt drawn to other women who gave themselves over entirely to passion for him, not for housework. Meg couldn't help what she was and neither could he.

Ray was relieved to discover that what he'd heard regarding homeless children was true. Thanks to the war, a lack of suitable housing, overcrowded orphanages and a torrent of evacuees flooding into the countryside, the people at the council offices sighed gratefully and swiftly checked the credentials of Mr and Mrs Malin. Without too much procrastination they decreed Lily Malin, as she was now recorded, would be allowed to live with them in Andover Avenue, London. It helped that Ray was an RAF flight officer and had the backing of his superior officer, a very well-known wing commander.

It took a further two weeks before the paperwork was completed, by which time Lily was ready to leave the hospital. Both Ray and Meg were there to collect her in their car and, although the little girl looked a little bewildered and didn't speak much, they assured themselves that things would improve. Extra petrol rations had been obtained in order to get Lily to her new home. Once that was done the car would be mothballed; Ray tended to use the train to get to the airfield and back.

The children's welfare officer was there to oversee the handover. 'These are her things. It's not much but they may prove useful.'

'She won't need them,' ventured Meg, feeling very pleased with herself. 'I've been given a children's clothes ration card. I've bought her some new things and now I've seen her I know what sizes to get and can buy her some more.'

Meg thought she'd done very well. Lily was to have a new beginning and new clothes were essential.

Mrs Abbott, the children's welfare officer, smiled knowingly. 'The sight of her old clothes might help with her memory. Not now, perhaps, but in time. I suggest you take them.'

Feeling slightly foolish, Meg accepted the brown paper parcel. 'We did wash them first,' Mrs Abbott added, judging by Meg's appearance that she might be fussy about such things. The clothes were beautifully laundered. There was no sign of the stitches that had once held a yellow star in place.

Meg exchanged a look of embarrassment with Ray. 'I didn't think of that. They might help. In time.'

Ray squeezed her hand. 'You can't think of everything.'

Recalling the yellow stitches, Ray wondered if he should mention taking Lily to a synagogue in London before leaving for home. He saw his wife's brightly shining eyes, her glossy hair and the look of expectation on her face. For now he would ignore Lily's religious affiliations. Best she recovered before they did anything.

'I've brought you a present,' said Meg, kneeling down so her face was level with that of the little girl. She brought out a rag doll she'd made. Its eyes were bright blue, its yellow woollen hair plaited and tied with ribbons. 'It's especially for you. I named her Loulou but you can name her what you like.'

Lily smiled shyly. 'Loulou,' she repeated and

hugged the doll close.

Lily was silent for the whole journey from Lincolnshire, where the airfields were based, to the neat suburbs of London, where pairs of semi-detached houses with bay windows stood in leafy-lined avenues.

Meg couldn't help feeling nervous. They were taking on a great responsibility and she feared not being up to it. 'Give her time,' Ray whispered in her ear. 'It's a big step.'

Meg nodded. 'I feel so privileged, but also a bit scared. I know we always said we wanted kids, but this really brings home to me what a big responsibility it is. I'm so scared of making mistakes.'

Ray grinned. 'Even the best of parents make mistakes.'

Meg laughed. 'I suppose so.' She turned to Lily, leaning beside her so that she too was looking out at the countryside.

'See how green it is, Lily. And look at the cows. Black and white mostly. Do you understand that? Black and white.'

Lily nodded. 'Black. And white.'

'Your English is very good. Did somebody teach you?'

Lily turned her head, her eyes suddenly brimming with tears. 'I don't know.'

Meg gave her a hug. 'Never mind. You'll remember in time. Oh, look! There's a tractor.'

Lily's attention went back to the passing scene.

'Perhaps her parents were teachers,' Meg whispered to Ray. He agreed it was a possibility. 'We'll find out more in time.'

When they came to London, Lily tilted her head

back, fascinated by the barrage balloons bobbing over the tall buildings of Whitehall and others in the city centre. She pointed. 'What are they?'

It was Ray who explained. 'It's to prevent enemy bombers getting too close to the buildings.'

London was crowded. Lily gazed at the red buses, the policemen directing traffic and blowing whistles. They wore white armbands so their directions could be seen at night when the blackout law meant that no lights could be visible.

Meg and Ray exchanged conspiratorial glances and held hands when traffic allowed, like they did when they were courting. This was such a big adventure for them, exciting and also a little scary.

Lily sat in the back with the rag doll Meg had made from scraps. Meg wondered if Lily might be a bit too old for the doll and chastised herself for not giving the gift greater consideration. Not that the gift had been rejected. Lily cuddled it tightly as though it were a shield against this strange world she'd entered.

The houses in Andover Avenue had been built in the interwar years, semi-detached with bay windows and neat gardens at the front, a garage and a longer garden to the rear. 'Home,' said Ray. 'At last.'

In the days that followed, Lily continued to look a little confused at times but on the whole adjusted well. It helped that Meg did her utmost to fill the little girl's life with activities and experiences. She adored taking Lily shopping for new clothes, proudly showing off the pretty little girl whose bright blue eyes regarded every unfamiliar thing with uncertainty.

Meg was becoming very fond of her, and the more fond she became the more she feared that one day Lily would remember who she was, her family would claim her, and yet again she and Ray would be childless.

'Do you think she ever will remember,' she whispered to Ray as they lay in bed at night.

He responded by kissing her naked shoulder and deeply breathing in her scent. It was her scent as well as her features that stayed with him when he was flying into enemy territory. 'Who knows? Let's just do our best for her, shall we?'

Meg sensed that Ray was aching to say something else concerning Lily but was holding it back. Lily had become as much a focus in her life as their beautiful home, which she'd always been so proud of. She gave him a playful nudge in the ribs.

'Ray. You're thinking thoughts. Care to share them with me?'

Ray rolled on to his back, one arm thrown over his face. 'I was thinking about the dog. She named him Rudy. I mentioned him to her in hospital and something seemed to click, but just as quickly seemed forgotten. It was as though she couldn't put a face to the name – unless there's more than one Rudy. I thought her seeing the dog might help her remember. It might do yet.'

Meg sat up abruptly. 'I know where this is going, Ray. You know how I feel about having a dog in the house! They're messy creatures. I've got enough to do in this house, cleaning and keeping it nice for you when you come home. If you want to keep the dog at the airfield, then that's up to you. But I don't want a dog here in this house. Ever!'

'Hey!' She shivered in response to his hand stroking her arm. 'Gently does it, old girl. You keep this place immaculate. Nothing out of place ... but it doesn't matter to me if it gets a bit messed up now and again. I really don't mind.'

Meg rounded on him. 'Is it a crime that I like things to be nice? Would you prefer me to be a slattern? Anyway, that's my final word on the matter. I'm not having a dog living here. As you said yourself, we need to give Lily time. With what's been happening in Europe, it might be best that she never remembers.'

Ray tugged her back on to the pillow.

'Darling, I know what you're thinking. I know that you're quickly becoming fond of Lily. I must admit, so am I, but we have to be realistic. In time she might remember who she really is and perhaps the name of a relative here in England. We can't ignore that. We can't pretend it won't happen.'

'But if we give her a good home with us,' Meg pleaded, 'she might never remember. She'll be with us for ever.'

Ray sighed. Meg had her shortcomings, but he still loved her. He also knew that inside that lovely exterior she had a will of iron. She didn't want the dog here, firstly because she was extraordinarily house-proud, and secondly because she had quickly made up her mind that Lily belonged to her. She'd wanted a child for so long and now she had one. If ever relatives did turn up, he could see Meg would have a problem letting her go.

He'd been given extended leave so was there

long enough to see Lily settle in and begin to speak. Just now and again a faraway look came into her eyes. At night the dream still came, in which she was on a train heading somewhere quite different to where she'd expected to be going.

Meg shuddered the first time she heard Lily screaming out, sitting up in bed, her gaze fixed on the wall opposite her. All she could do was wrap her arms around the girl while using soothing words.

'What does it mean?' she asked Ray once she'd got Lily back to sleep. 'She keeps on about a cattle wagon.'

Ray wrapped his arm around her and held her close. 'The enemy cram people into cattle wagons and send them east. A lot of them don't get there.'

Meg was horrified. 'You think she was on one of those?'

'I'm only guessing.'

'That's horrible.'

'Yes,' Ray replied grimly. 'It is.'

When the time came for him to head back for the airfield, Lily smiled up at him in such a way that it made him feel as though they had crossed the first hurdle to her recovery.

'Goodbye, Mr Malin.'

He ruffled her hair and smiled back at her, hiding the pang of regret that she didn't yet call him dad. Too soon, he thought. In time she might do. His smile was as sunny as he could make it.

'Now you two girls look after each other while I'm gone. Promise?'

Lily nodded. 'I promise.'

95

'So do I,' said a smiling Meg. 'Keep safe and get home as soon as you can. That's what we want, don't we, Lily?'

Ray's last sight of them was standing at the garden gate, Meg with her arm around Lily's shoulder, and the pair of them waving him goodbye. It hurt to leave but he kept waving until he came to a particular spot halfway down the avenue. On reaching that point, he stopped waving and never looked back.

The brick-built airfield buildings stood proud on the flat Lincolnshire countryside, grouped around the control tower standing at the centre of everything. The buildings were of simple design and practical rather than pretty. Square windows set in regimented lines sat beneath concrete roofs that would be thick with moss if they weren't scrubbed once a week. Beyond the squat buildings were the hangars and the runway. Everywhere personnel scurried around the buildings, the planes and the hangars like purposeful ants.

Ray looked around him, acknowledging with a cheery wave those who waved at him. It was good to be welcomed back but there was one greeting he craved above all others. Tilting his cap further back on his head so he could see more clearly, his narrowed eyes searched for his four-legged friend.

His gaze swept over the buildings and the neatly clipped lawns fronting the main drive. He wasn't expecting the dog to remember him, but it would certainly be a bonus if he did. His heart leapt with joy when he spotted Rudy lying down outside the door to his quarters, the dog's head resting on his front paws.

On seeing Ray the dog's head jerked upwards, his ears upright. Ray put his kitbag on the ground.

'Rudy! Come on, boy!'

The dog leapt to his feet and, barking excitedly, ran towards him. Ray was almost bowled over when the dog hit his knees. 'Steady on, old boy. You nearly knocked me over.'

Rudy's enthusiasm carried on unabated. Wagging his tail fit to fall off, the dog bounded excitedly around him.

Pleased as punch that the dog remembered him, Ray hugged and patted him. 'Hey. It's good to see you too.'

Once in quarters, Ray unpacked while Rudy lay out on Ray's bed, watching as he opened and shut doors and cupboards and put things away. 'Shame you couldn't have come with me,' he said at last. Kids and a dog. That's what makes a home. Not the latest decor, smart furnishings, everything dust-free and smelling of polish. He was beginning to hate the smell of polish. Sometimes he fancied the smell of it overwhelmed the perfume that Meg wore. He sighed.

'Never mind. We've got each other for the duration.'

Later that week Ray was stood down; no mission for a few days. He was grateful for that. There was so much thinking he needed to do. Had he been right to foster Lily? Yes. It was the least he could do, and both Meg and Lily were getting on well together. His only worry was that Meg had taken to Lily so quickly, much quicker than he'd expected. She'd be devastated if Lily did regain her memory and somebody came to claim her. To his mind he had to do something now before things went any further.

He put out the cigarette he'd been smoking and got to his feet, stretching his aching body.

His steward came in with clean laundry. 'Long journey, sir?'

'Too long. Twice as long as before the war.'

'Only twice?'

Ray laughed.

'Thought Rudy might like this, sir.' The steward brought out a bone from beneath the piled linen.

After he'd gone, Ray thought about what he must do. Meg had to be made to accept that it was only fair that Lily be given every opportunity to regain her memory and perhaps, one day, be reunited with her real family. Rudy was the key to Lily regaining her memory. At some point these two should also be reunited.

Ray was deep in thought when he sat himself down next to the dog. He ruffled his ears and spoke to him softly. 'One day you're going to come and live in my house, Rudy. What do you think of that?'

The dog raised his head majestically as though he approved and then wagged his tail.

Ray smiled. 'Yep! I think it's a good idea too.'

Meg's reaction to mention of the dog was no more or less than what Ray had expected. However, he felt it his duty to continue to persuade her that it was the right thing to do. Hopefully his persistence would start to wear down her resistance.

'This is the coward's way out,' he muttered to himself as he penned a letter outlining how the dog might help Lily regain her memory.

'The war isn't going to go on for ever and the dog will be in need of a good home. He's a splendid animal: loyal, kind and not a nasty bone in his body. I feel he should live with us...'

Meg's next letter arrived a day or two later. In it she mentioned that Lily had put on weight and was settling in nicely both at home and at school, and how easily she'd made friends.

'She's growing fast. I've had to buy material from my own coupons and make her dresses. I've also cut down some of my own including a party dress. She's been invited to a birthday party. She's so excited.'

She also described in great detail that she was making cushion covers from old curtains because rationing didn't stretch to new material, her problems with getting stains out of the hearthrug, and how difficult it was finding her favourite furniture polish. There was also a barrage balloon bobbing overhead three doors up from their house. She didn't like that either, though Lily did.

'It's so ugly and I can't help thinking that it might get punctured and lay like a blanket over the whole street, suffocating us all.'

Ray sighed. Not once had she responded to his comments about having the dog live with them. Meg was the most beautiful woman he had ever met and he'd fallen in love with her on sight, resulting in a whirlwind romance and marriage. At the beginning he'd hardly noticed her obsession with having everything spick and span. Ray's childhood home had been filled with clutter: kids,

99

two cats, a canary and a dog. There had been no chance of his mother ever having the time to present her house like something from a magazine. It was what it was and although it might not have boasted the very latest in interior design, it had been a happy house.

In the quiet of his quarters in the short time he had to himself, he shared his disappointment with the dog. Rudy sat listening, his head tilting from side to side as though he were trying hard to understand what Ray was saying.

'She's stubborn in her ways,' he said to the dog.

Letters had not worked. There was nothing for it but to try again to persuade her face-to-face when he got home.

After yet another mission over France he was now due some leave. He was looking forward to seeing Meg and Lily again, and he had a plan. Even he thought it was a bit underhanded, but perhaps if he mentioned the dog to Lily it might provoke some response. If it did, then Meg couldn't possibly refuse to have the dog home. 'Tread carefully,' he muttered to himself as he approached the garden gate.

The house was easily the best kept in the avenue. The trim flower beds were squarely fixed around an equally square lawn. Meg had refused to grow vegetables in the front garden: 'The back garden is big enough for vegetables. I have to have some beauty in my life. And anyway, what would people think?'

Tired after his journey, he pushed open the front door and breathed in the smell of lavender polish plus a faint hint of disinfectant. Not a

100

thing was out of place until he slung in his kitbag, sending it skidding across the gleaming lino. He smiled at its impact against the hallstand where everything was hung in neat rows and colour-coordinated. A blue hat wobbled and fell to the floor. He placed it on top a beige trench coat, smiling with satisfaction as he did so.

He called up the stairs to tell Meg he was home.

'Darling!' She came flying down the stairs smelling of perfume and wearing a crisp white blouse and dark blue skirt. Her hair bounced with health and he could tell her make-up was newly applied. It didn't take a genius to guess she'd been watching up at the bedroom window for him to arrive so she could make the grand welcome, almost falling down the stairs and into his arms. Just like the house, Meg liked her appearance to be perfect and adored making an entrance, like a film star at a Hollywood red-carpet event.

Ray felt his heart lurch in his chest. Meg was as beautiful as ever and he wanted her just as much as he ever had – and judging by her enthusiastic welcome, she felt the same way. They kissed and hugged until they were almost breathless.

He decided to ignore the small frown that flitted between her plucked eyebrows when she spotted his kitbag slumped against the coat stand. He guessed it was taking a lot of willpower for her not to mention it. She wouldn't. Not until her initial welcome was over.

Once he got to take a breath, he asked her about Lily. 'So my big girl looks great. How's my little girl?'

Meg looked up at him coyly, her dark-blue eyes

flashing. 'You recall I wrote to you about making her a party dress?'

'Yes.'

'She's wearing it today to a school friend's birthday party.' She lowered her eyes in a coquettish manner but spoiled the effect by glancing at her watch. He knew the signs, knew what she was going to say next. 'We've got about an hour until I collect her.'

Grasping his hand, she led him excitedly up the stairs. He too felt excited, though her glance at her wristwatch was a bit of a spoiler, making him feel obliged to keep within a time schedule. In his opinion, lovemaking should never be performed to a schedule.

The sweet smell of perfume permeated the air. The curtains were drawn therefore the bedroom was pleasantly shady. He noticed the bedclothes were pulled back to display pristine white cotton sheets and pillowcases. Everything ready. Everything perfect, like a table laid with the best linen and china ready for the main meal to be presented.

He imagined how cool they would feel against his hot flesh, and although tired from travelling all the way from Lincolnshire the prospect of lying with Meg thrilled him. It had been two months since his last leave. He wanted her but up until now he hadn't realised just how much.

In consequence, their lovemaking was urgent. He felt like a drowning man gasping for air, not able to stop until he was sighing as though he had drunk a whole ocean. All thoughts about reuniting Lily with her dog were forgotten in the intensity of the moment.

Afterwards, he couldn't believe he'd ever been tired at all. That's how it was with Meg. Even though there were things about her that irritated him, she made up for it in bed.

Meg lit him a cigarette and passed him an ashtray. He accepted gratefully and smoked slowly, knowing that the moment he finished the ashtray would be emptied and wiped out.

'So how have things been?' he asked.

Meg laid her arm across his chest and, after complaining again about the barrage balloon which he'd seen bobbing above a roof on his way along the avenue, she told him about the latest air raid.

'It wasn't anywhere near here. The East End again.'

'How did Lily respond?'

'Better than I expected, though she did cuddle up close and bury her face against me. I sang to her the whole time and told her stories. She likes stories. Luckily the explosions were a long way off. We've been quite lucky so far and it's given me time to make quite a little nest for us under the stairs.'

Ray stiffened and stared at her in disbelief. 'Under the stairs? After I put up the Anderson shelter out in the garden?'

Meg wrinkled her nose. 'I don't like going in the shelter. No matter how hard I try, it's never homely.'

'It's not supposed to be homely. It's supposed to be safe. That's why you have to go in there.'

'Oh come on, Ray. It's the East End that gets

103

bombed. It's close to the docks. I mean, whoever would want to bomb Andover Avenue? Anyway, Lily doesn't like the Anderson shelter either. It's dark and damp. She goes pale and shivers like a leaf if I try to get her out there. I don't think it's just the dark. I think she finds it claustrophobic. She gets really scared...'

Ray put out his cigarette and caught hold of her chin. 'Meg, darling, you either go to the shelter or move to the country. You and Lily cannot stay in the house when the sirens sound. I absolutely forbid you to stay. It's not safe. Things are likely to get worse. Now trust me and do as I say.'

'Ray, I think Lily was in a dark place sometime before you found her.'

'I found her in a field.'

'And before that? You don't know what she had to endure. Something bad happened that made her claustrophobic. Anyway, she's been doing so well. I wouldn't want to do anything that might reverse her healing...'

'All the same, it's better to be claustrophobic than blown to bits. I insist you go to the shelter. Any shelter!'

Ray was adamant, determined that just for once his wife would do as he said. Meg was just as adamant that she would get her own way, beguiling her husband just as she had when they first met. She swung her legs out of bed and stood there naked in the middle of the room.

'We've been quite safe under the stairs so far. It's small but not as dark and damp as the shelter. We'll be fine.'

The moment Meg tossed her beautiful head,

104

her hair falling like skeins of silk around her shoulders, Ray was helpless and knew beyond doubt that Meg would do as she pleased.

'You have to think of Lily.'

'Ray, I am thinking of Lily.' Biting the corner of her lip, she added a statement he guessed she would make. 'I know what you're saying, but I can't bear the thought of leaving my lovely home. Just look how beautiful it is.'

Meg knew how to plead with her husband – with her eyes, her smile and her whole slender, sensuous body. She spun round in the middle of the room, arms spread like a twirling ballerina and just as graceful.

Her husband sighed and glanced at his watch. 'What time do we have to collect Lily. I'm desperate to see her.'

Meg smiled. 'I thought you would be. You can collect her. I'll give you the address. I'll tidy up while you're gone.'

'Tidy up?' said Ray, not believing what he was hearing. The house was immaculate.

'Of course. I have to unpack your kitbag. It's certainly not staying where it is at the moment! Besides, I take it you've brought some washing home. And I do have to remake the bed,' she added with a beguiling smile.

There was a lot of promise in that smile. His response was exactly as she'd hoped.

'We'll only mess it up again,' he said, matching her smile with one of his own,

'Better get going then.'

With a sigh of resignation, he swung his muscular frame from the bed. He hadn't mentioned the dog. He would leave that until later.

Falling in love with Meg had seemed like a dream. Love at first sight, though back then it had been all starry-eyed and purely physical. Someone had once said to him that if you want to know how a wife will turn out, look at her mother. He had: her hair never out of place, always beautifully dressed. He hadn't thought to look beyond that, to see that the perfect house she lived in ruled her life.

A nagging thought came to him. Was he fostering Lily for purely selfish reasons, hoping her presence would occupy Meg's time so she wouldn't ask too many questions? Facing the fact that she might no longer be the love of his life was difficult. He was not an irresponsible man. It was just that at times he felt trapped and even Meg's voluptuous body was not enough to scatter his wandering thoughts.

Pushing his gloomy musings aside, he marched off to collect the little girl he hoped would save his marriage, thinking how peaceful everything seemed. Home was such a contrast to the airbase. If it wasn't for the 'blimp' bobbing around above the roofs of the houses, there would be no sign there was a war on.

CHAPTER SEVEN

The house in Forest Avenue where the children's party was being held was a mirror image of the house he shared with Meg and Lily: semi-detached with bay windows, and an arched aspect enclosing a small porch in front of a green-and-white striped door with an oval glass panel at the top of yellow and red glass depicting a sunrise. The garden was nowhere near as pristine; carrots and onions growing in disarray among the long grass. Their front garden at Andover Avenue was neat and tidy, mainly because Meg had a man in to keep it that way.

The sound of screeching, laughing, chattering children accompanied the woman who answered the door. She was about the same age as Meg, though plumper with pink cheeks. Wisps of fair hair fell untidily from beneath the turban she wore. Despite her disarray he thought she looked attractive, possibly because she oozed friendliness. He immediately warmed to her.

'You must be Lily's father,' she said brightly. 'You're the only RAF father,' she said before he could ask her how she knew.

He decided that saying he was only Lily's foster father was irrelevant.

'Jennifer Nichols. Pleased to meet you. Come in.'

The inside of the house was as untidy as it was

outside. There was muddle everywhere and he doubted it was purely down to it being presently flooded with children.

'Uncle Ray!'

He'd been away a while, but the fact that Lily still recognised him made his heart surge with happiness. And she'd called him Uncle Ray. That really surprised him.

'I've had jelly,' she said to him with great relish. 'And blancmange. I dropped some of it on the floor. Only a spoonful.'

'Sorry about that,' he said to Jennifer, who just smiled and said Lily was not the only one. 'I've got four children and they're always dropping something for me to clear up. All in a day's work with kids.' Her smile was full of happiness.

Ray thanked her for having Lily at the party.

'She's enjoyed herself and is welcome to come here any time.'

With Lily's hand in his, Ray walked back home along the leafy avenues of London's suburbia, listening to his foster daughter's chatter.

'We played musical chairs and lots of other games, but my favourite was pass the parcel. We ended up with lots and lots of paper *everywhere!* It was only newspaper but Mrs Nichols collected it all up afterwards so she could use it for lighting the fire.'

Ray smiled broadly. Hearing Lily's happy chatter warmed his heart, although when it was Lily's birthday he knew beyond doubt that the party would be strictly controlled and games would only be allowed out in the garden.

'And they've got a dog,' Lily suddenly exclaimed, then fell silent before saying. 'I think I'd like a dog.'

The words were music to Ray's ears. By the time they got home he'd told her about Rudy, the dog he'd claimed as his own without mentioning that she'd been in company with the dog when he'd found her. He was very careful about things like that just in case she got upset and was back there in whatever horror she'd gone through. The kid was confused enough and seemed to be struggling with what he was telling her.

'Is Rudy going to come home with you?' Lily asked plaintively, her blue eyes round with interest.

Ray managed a tight smile and just about restrained himself from asking her whether she remembered the dog, or the time before he'd found her. His instinct was leave her to remember in her own good time and at her own pace. However, he answered the question. 'I hope so. When this war's finally over perhaps.' It was a big perhaps. If he ever dared mention having the dog live with them, Meg cut him off sharply.

On reaching home, Lily ran bouncing into the room ahead of him, proceeding to spill out everything he'd told her about the dog that lived with him at the airfield. 'Uncle Ray found him in the war and his name's Rudy and he's coming home to live with us when the war's over, isn't he, Uncle Ray?'

Lily tilted her head back and looked up at Ray for confirmation. He was tickled pink to hear her call him Uncle Ray. Before he'd gone back to the base she'd called him Mr Malin.

'Can we, Aunt Meg?'

Meg's look locked with his. 'Let's see when we get there,' she replied.

'If possible,' he said reassuringly. The moment he saw the accusing look on Meg's face he felt less confident. His wife did not look happy. Ray instantly regretted letting Lily do the dirty work. He felt guilty.

'I know we should have talked first,' he began.

Meg looked sour. 'Yes. We should have.' She folded her arms, the stance she usually adopted – along with the accusing look she gave him when he wasn't being open about something – when she said he was being elusive.

'The war might not be over for years,' she stated in a matter-of-fact manner.

Lily had a determined jut to her chin. 'So we'll see then? Promise?'

Ray wilted under Meg's direct look before she turned away and told Lily to wash her hands. 'Tonight you can stay up late seeing as your Uncle Ray is home. Bed at eight. Dinner is nearly ready so upstairs with you to wash your hands.'

Lily bounced off happily up the stairs to the bathroom.

'About the dog,' Ray began.

Meg held up a warning hand, palm outwards. There was fire in her eyes. 'I like my house to be neat and tidy. I do not want a dog. I have to think of Lily.'

'I was thinking of Lily...'

'She's coming on fine without needing to be reunited with a mutt – a German mutt. Have you any idea how hostile people are becoming towards anything that smacks of being German?'

She was right of course. He himself couldn't understand it. A dog was a dog and even though Rudy had a military number tattooed in his ear, it seemed to him that the dog's temperament just wasn't suited to the military.

'You're right of course,' he said, resting his hands on her waist and pulling her towards him, bending his head and nuzzling her ear. 'Let's drop it for now and see what happens. Yes?'

Meg nodded but he could tell by the wary look in her eyes that she would cut him dead if he mentioned it again. Discretion being the better part of valour, he changed the subject.

'She called me Uncle Ray. And you Aunt Meg. Since when did that start?'

'A few weeks after you left.'

'You should have told me. It's a really big step.'

'I thought I'd let it be a surprise.'

'It is.'

She stepped out of his reach, bent down and opened the oven door. Her glossy hair fell forward around her face, clinging to her cheeks as she straightened and placed the pie on the table.

'You shouldn't have said anything about the dog. Nothing at all. What if it brings back painful memories?'

Ray went into the dining room, poured himself a large gin and took a slug. By the time he'd got back to the kitchen, Meg had picked up his cap nonchalantly tossed on the draining board, strode purposefully out into the hallway and hung it on the hallstand.

Ray's glass was almost empty, no more than a

thimble full swilling around the bottom. The gin had given him courage, just enough to snipe at the subject again. 'We have to face the fact that she isn't ours and her people might be looking for her. I just thought the dog might help.'

Meg looked trim and glamorous in a grey pleated dress with a white Peter Pan collar. The belt around her waist was cinched in tightly, emphasising the curves of her hips and her breasts. He'd like to make love to her right now, but knew that even if Lily hadn't been in the house, it would have to wait until bedtime. As far as Meg was concerned, there was a time and a place for everything. Bed was the place for making love. Nowhere else.

Her tone was adamant. 'Ray, I really couldn't manage a dog and I don't think it's a good idea for Lily to be reminded of whatever she went through – at least not yet. You should have spoken to me first before mentioning the dog to her.'

'I wrote to you,' snapped Ray. 'You didn't respond. You brushed it under the carpet.'

'I didn't think it relevant. I did not brush it under the carpet.'

'No! You wouldn't, would you! You don't brush *anything* under the carpet. The floor is like everything else in this bloody house, polished to perfection without a speck of dust in sight.'

Her cheeks flushed. 'And what do you mean by that?'

'Exactly what I said. Keeping a clean house means more to you than I do.'

'That's not true! Dogs are dirty! I've every right not to want extra work in my house.'

'*Our* house! It's *our* house! Correction! Our home! Or it should be!'

Realising she'd said the wrong thing, Meg did her best to back-pedal, a frown darkening her sweet face. 'I didn't mean it like it sounded. All I meant was...'

Ray glared to where his kitbag had been. Everything had been put away: dirty laundry already in the boiler, clean clothes upstairs in a bedroom drawer, shoes in the wardrobe, shaving equipment in the bathroom.

'That you like everything in its place. Including me! It obviously suits you for me to be away in the air force. I'm not here to clutter things up!'

Grabbing his cap from the hallstand, he headed for the front door. Meg ran after him.

'Ray! Where are you going?'

'I'm going for a pint.'

'Ray!'

Meg stopped halfway across the hallway, the house shaking as the front door slammed behind him.

There was no way she was going to open it and watch her husband disappear down the street. That would be too embarrassing.

Her dismay evaporated. She was right, wasn't she? Anyway, you have to make a stand, she thought. He's just not being fair.

Lily's light footfall sounded behind her. Her happy expression turned crestfallen when she saw that Ray wasn't there. 'Where's Uncle Ray gone?' she asked plaintively.

Meg uncrossed her arms and managed a reassuring smile. 'He had to go out for a moment.

113

He won't be long. Would you like to help me lay the table and get everything ready for when he gets back?'

Lily nodded. 'Yes. Can we have jelly?'

'You've already had jelly.'

'I know. But you and Uncle Ray didn't. I think he might like some. How about you?'

Meg had to smile. The fact that Lily was coming out of herself warmed her heart. She liked to think that providing her with a proper home had helped enormously. Every child should have a good home and proper routine. Ray had to understand that. A dog didn't fit into that present routine.

She dished up the evening meal – cottage pie with carrots and cabbage – with one eye on the clock. She hoped and prayed Ray would come home before Lily's bedtime.

Just as she turned off the gas tap, the sirens went off.

'Oh, not again,' she sighed. 'Always at meal-times. Lily, fetch your gas mask.' Lily did as she was told before heading for the comfortable niche Meg had created under the stairs. Meg looked frantically at the front door, back to the stairs, then outside to where the unused Anderson shelter awaited them. Why didn't Ray come? Where was he?

'Auntie Meg!'

Lily was close to panicking. 'It's all right, Lily. I'm here.'

She wound her arms around the child and hugged her close. Lily reacted almost hysterically to the sound of the sirens, fear filling her eyes, her body trembling until the sound abated, to be

114

replaced by that of explosions, though thankfully never that close. He should have understood how frightened she gets, thought Meg, her arms enfolding Lily against her bosom. If he could see how frightened she gets, he wouldn't have gone to the pub.

Lily held tight to her foster mother, her eyes tightly closed. 'Not out there,' she kept saying. 'Not out there.'

The shelter smelled of damp earth and was very dark. There was earth and sandbags all around, half of the shelter being below ground. On the first occasion she'd entered, half a dozen sandbags had become loose and fallen on top of her. She'd screamed and screamed. Meg had pulled the sandbags off her, but the experience had resurrected a similar trauma, a memory that she couldn't quite face, a memory best forgotten.

Meg eased her away, held her hand and opened the door under the stairs, all the time grumbling about Ray's absence. 'He should be here,' she muttered, feeling angrier now. 'He should be here!' Torch already lit, Meg tugged the door open, pushed Lily in first then followed on, slamming the small door behind them.

An hour or so later it was yanked open. Ray's body filled the void. He swiftly took in the sight of his wife and Lily locked in each other's arms. 'What the hell are you doing in here? Why aren't you in the Anderson shelter?'

'Lily doesn't like it out there. It's dark and damp and not good for her chest. Besides, you can see how she reacts,' she said, both hands covering Lily's head, the little girl's face buried

115

against Meg's chest.

At the sound of an explosion from far off, Ray squeezed in. 'Meg, this isn't safe. If a bomb hit the house, you wouldn't stand a chance.'

Meg's voice was firm. She had to make him understand. 'As I've just told you, Lily doesn't like it out there.'

'She'll have to get used to it. It's for her own good.'

Meg sighed. How could she make him see?

'Look, Ray. It's just the two of us here. We have to manage as best we can. I prefer it in here and so does Lily. Isn't that good enough for you?'

He caught the sharpness in her voice. 'No. It isn't good enough. I don't want you to get killed. I do have some idea about bombing, Meg. It's part of my job to know.'

Meg sighed. She didn't want to quarrel, not when they had such a short time together.

As the sound of explosions became more distant, Lily began to emerge from Meg's embrace. 'There you are, darling,' Meg said to her in a reassuring voice. 'They'll sound the all-clear soon and we can all have our supper and go to bed. All's well that ends well!'

'Hey, Lily. Not much room under here. When we next have an air raid, do you think we could all go into the shelter out in the garden? There's no room for all of us in here.'

Lily looked at him wide-eyed. 'No,' she said, her voice chilly with fear. 'No!'

A long shrill note sounded the all-clear. Meg brushed imagined dust from Lily's head and from her clothes. 'What a state,' she muttered. 'Better wash your hands again, Lily.'

Lily looked as if it was an odd idea seeing as she'd already washed them a short time ago, but she dutifully obeyed and trotted off upstairs. They waited until her footsteps sounded from along the landing before they continued their conversation.

'Meg, you'd be more comfortable out in the shelter. And you'd be safer.'

Meg stalked off to the kitchen to the half-cooked vegetables and the cottage pie she'd left on the table. Everything would need warming up, and although she was getting used to doing that, she did find it irritating.

Coping was what the home front was all about. Her husband just didn't understand how it was. As she busied herself sorting out their dinner – which was now supper – she did her best to explain how she saw things.

'Ray, it's just me and Lily here. Things are difficult enough as it is, but at least I am making sure you have a lovely home to come back to. It could be very different, you know. You do know there are looters, don't you? Imagine them breaking in here when there's a raid going on and taking all my lovely things.'

She also mentioned that Lily wasn't having so many nightmares about the train, at which Ray's face clouded. He'd been hearing more rumours from his French connections about those trains, where they were going and what happened to the people crammed into the cattle wagons.

Meg caught his expression. 'Ray. What is it?'

Ray smiled. 'I was just thinking how glad I am that Lily is improving. No kid should go through

117

what she's been through.'

He could have told her about the reports from occupied Europe, the labour camps that were really death camps, but she wouldn't believe him. Nobody would.

There were two more air raids during the time Ray was home and he insisted they go out into the shelter, though first he made sure that it was well lit inside and even took a vase of sweet-scented flowers from the living room to counteract the damp smell. Reluctant though she was, Meg accepted there just wasn't enough room in the cupboard under the stairs. Her fears about Lily getting hysterical proved unfounded thanks to Ray clowning about, making paper chains and singing at the top of his voice, though every so often the little girl's eyes would stray to the small entrance and the searchlight scouring the night sky.

'Ray, you have a loud voice though not necessarily in tune. Never mind. It's certainly enough to drown out the explosions,' Meg said to him, an amused smile brightening her features. She dreaded him leaving. Lily wasn't the only one who felt braver when he was around.

The time for him to return to the airbase came round quickly enough. He was standing in the hallway, the oval window set in the upper part of the door like a halo behind his head. His kitbag sat like a squat dwarf at his side and his uniform had only lately returned from the dry cleaners. Meg's heart raced at the sight of him, and although she loved her beautiful home, Ray was the only man in her life, the only one ever. There had been nobody before him.

As they embraced, Meg breathed in the smell of him saving it to memory: cigarettes, shaving soap, a dash of cologne and a male smell that reminded her most singly of their passion of the night before.

'Be safe,' she whispered against his ear.

Ray sighed. 'Meg, I don't want to go.'

'But you have to,' she replied, her breath sweet on his neck.

'Yes. Promise me you'll go out into the shelter if there's a raid.' He placed his hands on her shoulders and looked down into deep-blue, almost violet eyes. He brushed back a stray lock of golden hair, tucking it behind her ear.

'I promise.'

He knew her well enough to not quite believe her. 'Look. If you don't want to use the Anderson, then go to the public shelter.'

Meg wrinkled her nose. 'That's hardly a more commendable alternative. The Anderson is full of spiders and smells damp, and the public one is full of smelly people. Honestly,' she added when she saw his disapproval of her comment. 'Ray, it's not just about *being* in uncomfortable surroundings. It's what can happen when I'm not in the house. I'm telling the truth when I say that looters take advantage of empty houses during an air raid. They have no scruples, Ray.' She shook her head vehemently. 'I can't bear the thought of them ransacking my home – our home – and besides, Lily is nervous as it is when the sirens go off. You've seen it. She's only different when you're here. We're both different when you're

119

here.' Her smile was a little sad.

Ray intensified his grip, a determined look on his face. 'Meg. Promise me you'll go into the shelter – any shelter. Promise!' He shook her gently to emphasise the point.

Meg knew when it was time to give in. 'If it will put your mind at rest then yes, I promise. But really, darling, I don't think we have anything to fear. No bombs have fallen around here. We hear explosions but from miles away up near the docks. Warehouses mostly, though I understand some of the old terraced houses closest to the docks have gone and...'

Ray gripped her arms. 'Meg, semi-detached houses in suburbia can tumble down as easily as old Victorian terraces.'

Meg winced, not so much because of his tight grip but because he made her doubt the comfortable world of moquette three-piece suites, plumped-up cushions, and coordinated carpets and curtains she'd built around herself. He was saying she believed that being bombed only happened to other people, not to the likes of them living in a tree-lined avenue in a pleasant suburb of London. But why shouldn't that be so? There were no strategic targets around here. Even the barrage balloon bobbing around a few houses down seemed a waste of public money. Surely it would do better service around factories, warehouses and docks? She made a mental note to write to the authorities and tell them so.

Swiftly burying the moment of self-doubt, she surprised him with a passionate kiss on the lips and a smile. 'I'll make sure we're safe when the next air raid sounds. I promise.'

He chose to believe her, mainly because he had no choice and he appreciated a peaceful life – no questions asked about his life at the base, what he did when he wasn't on a mission, or what he planned to do for a career when the war was over.

Meg called for Lily, who was still upstairs brushing her teeth. She came dashing into the room, the legs of Loulou her rag doll dangling from beneath her arm. The doll wore a bright pink dress and had striped blue legs. Lily, who had a thing about colour, was wearing a blue striped dress and a pink bow in her hair. In a way they matched.

She flung her arms around Ray's legs and gazed up at him imploringly. Ray hoisted her up into his arms.

'Uncle Ray. Are you going now? Do you have to go?'

'I do indeed, poppet. But don't you worry. I'll be back in time for your birthday.' Basking in the adoration of the little girl, Ray's unsettled thoughts vanished and at least for the time being he appreciated what he had.

'Am I having a birthday?'

'Yes. Of course you are. Pick a date and that's when it will be. Anyway, who needs an excuse to have a party? Not us!'

'I like parties,' Lily responded, laughing. 'How about November?'

'Then I'll be back before that. Lots of times before November in fact.'

'Promise?'

'Promise.'

Meg felt her eyes growing moist as she regarded

her husband and the little girl who had come to share their home and their lives. Last night in bed, those same strong arms now holding Lily had been entwined around her. Their passion had been hot and urgent, their last act of lovemaking before Ray left to fly more dangerous missions over enemy territory, dropping supplies to Resistance units or parachuting an agent to the dark landscape below.

Meg and Lily waved him off at the garden gate, staying there until he'd reached the halfway stage where he no longer looked back but strode onwards. Meg willed him to turn back and wave. It would prove he still loved her. She didn't know when and why she had begun to think otherwise. Perhaps it was because all they did was make love; they didn't talk, not like they used to before they were married.

Before they were married.

It had never occurred to her before that a sea change had occurred once they had walked down the aisle. Before the war he'd looked after the garden, mowing it at weekends, carrying out repairs and even the odd decorating job when needed. He had grumbled about doing it, yes, but didn't all men grumble about home maintenance?

Everything would change once the war was over, just as Ray had changed once war had been declared. Eyes flashing with excitement, he'd dashed home to tell her that he'd joined up, crowing about how useful it had been to belong to the flying club at university. 'They snapped me up!'

Indeed they had, and he'd not hesitated in leaving home at the earliest opportunity. Home!

He'd left with barely a backward glance.

Once he had disappeared, her arm still around Lily's shoulder, Meg turned and looked at her beloved home. The house had been built in the early thirties and they'd scrimped and saved to put down their deposit, the builder assuring them they were making a shrewd investment. 'Bricks and mortar will never let you down,' he'd said to them. 'Not like banks. It's either a house or putting it under the mattress.' They'd had no intention of putting it under the mattress. Although Ray had been worried about maintaining a job in order to make the payments, Meg was persuasive, even petulant.

She finally won him round when a small inheritance on the death of her grandparents had meant Meg could furnish it as she pleased. Number 7, Andover Avenue was the house they wanted. It was here they would bring up a family and live until their dying day. But as much as they'd wanted a family, it just hadn't happened, so Meg threw herself into making a home.

Pale greens, soft pinks and apricots, a cool white bathroom with black and white tiles complemented with striped red and black towels; curtains made with fabrics from Liberty; furniture from a local shop that sold and made quality chairs and tables. The house was her home but no family came along. Ray had worked and she had become a doting housewife. How quickly he'd left, preferring to risk his life than stay home until he was called up.

'He's a man,' she murmured. 'Men think differently to women, do you know that, Lily?'

123

Lily beamed up at her.

Meg congratulated herself that she now had everything she wanted. Lily had filled the only empty space in her life. Her only wish at present was that the war would finish shortly and things would return to normal.

She watched Lily go running off into the garden while she contemplated what Ray had said about going to the shelter. Number 7 was the neatest, best-kept house in the street. The windows gleamed, rose bushes graced the flower beds in short, sharp battalions edged with marigolds, and the front door looked inviting. Her house looked strong and staid, as though it would always be there for her and she was sure it would.

Thinking of her promise to Ray, she sighed. It was no good. She couldn't leave all that effort empty and at the mercy of looters who, to her mind, were more of a threat than the bombs. After all, there was plenty of room beneath the stairs for her and Lily. They could cope perfectly well. Besides, she didn't want Lily's nightmares to return and, without Ray to ease the tension, there was a chance the child would suffer them once more.

Her views on looting were based on fact. A few houses in the locality had been looted while their owners were in the shelter. It was a sad scene that people could do that instead of focusing their energies on winning this war. This bloody war!

CHAPTER EIGHT

Two weeks later, in the middle of the night, the sirens rose in a frightening wail closely followed by Lily running into Meg's bedroom, her rag doll under her arm and screaming her head off. Finally uttering a single cry of fear, she flung herself on to the bed and burrowed under the bedclothes.

Jerked from slumber, Meg folded her arms around her foster daughter's slender form, hugging her close and at the same time reassuring her that she was there for her. That she would always be there for her.

Lily's body convulsed with shivers and she was holding her breath as though afraid to breathe. There had been many air raids since Lily had moved in and her reaction was always the same, despite Meg's efforts to console her and reassure her that they were quite safe. Bombs rarely fell on London suburbs. Yet again Lily would not be comforted.

'Come on. We'd better go to the shelter,' Meg whispered, remembering her promise to Ray.

Lily whimpered. 'I don't like it out there. Loulou doesn't like it either.'

Meg sighed. 'Neither do I, but we have to be brave. Uncle Ray's being brave so we have to be brave too.'

The words tumbled swiftly out of her mouth.

Once she'd made sure Lily was wrapped in her dressing gown, slippers on her feet, she flung on her own, took Lily by the hand, and grabbed her torch and bag containing a flask of tea, a packet of biscuits and some sandwiches – everything a person might need to survive a stay in the air-raid shelter.

Halfway down the stairs the torch beam went out. Meg swore under her breath. Thanks to the blackout curtains the house was pitch black. She couldn't see her hand in front of her face. She heard Lily cry out.

'Six more stairs, Lily. You can do it.'

'I don't like the dark.'

Meg didn't need to see Lily's face to know that she was terrified. In the darkness she felt a set of trembling fingers tighten over her own. Lily's fingers felt fragile, almost birdlike. And they were cold, so cold.

Anger swelled up inside her. What right did anyone have to put a child through something like this? Hadn't Lily been through enough already? Deep inside she knew it wouldn't take much to push Lily over the edge and the thought of it made her burn with rage. Hopefully the raid would once again concentrate on the East End of London. Out here would be left unscathed and her home and her world would remain intact.

On reaching the bottom of the stairs, she gave the torch a good shake. The light flickered then died again. Reluctant to steer Lily through the rest of the house and down the garden path in the dark, she felt her way to the cupboard beneath the stairs. The sirens wailed their mournful cry before

126

stopping abruptly, a sure sign that the enemy bombers were close by and that even the civil defence units were taking shelter. Feeling her way over the familiar wooden panels, her fingers finally found the door catch. One flick and it was open.

'Quickly.' She pushed Lily in first.

'It's so dark!' the girl wailed.

'Be brave, Lily. It won't be dark for long. I've got a spare torch in here somewhere.'

Lily continued to whimper.

Meg groped for the torch, her fingers finally finding the switch and turning it on. This torch was smaller than the other but its sallow beam was enough to pick out everything she needed to see. Blankets and pillows covered the blow-up bed they used to take on seaside holidays but which now served as a mattress.

Ray's words came back to her: 'Go to the shelter. Any shelter.' A clear vision of his grim expression accompanied his words. She'd promised she would do that but Ray couldn't grasp just how much she loved her home. Their home was an extension of all that she was. A man such as Ray who regarded it purely as a house couldn't possibly understand that. And anyway, there wasn't time. Lily needed reassurance right now. When circumstances allowed she would make for the shelter.

'But not tonight,' she told herself and added to Lily, 'We'll be all right in here. Shall I read you a story or are you tired?'

Lily snuggled up to her, hiding her face against her chest. 'I'm tired.'

Meg recognised that Lily might fall apart altogether. She hugged her closely. 'Then let's try to get some sleep. Then you can have an egg for breakfast when the morning comes.'

Once promised the luxury of a boiled egg, Lily snuggled down. Together they lay with their arms closely entwined, the blow-up bed barely big enough to take the pair of them. 'It'll all be over soon,' Meg murmured against Lily's silky head. 'I expect they're heading for the docks again. It's ships they bomb, not us. Andover Avenue will still be here tomorrow.'

Assuring herself that the enemy planes sounded as far away as they always did, she closed her eyes. At other times they'd been in here she'd fallen asleep immediately, the sound of enemy bombers droning in the distance on their usual path. Tonight, sleep was elusive. Something was different.

Although all was pitch black and she could see nothing, she opened her eyes. She felt Lily's body warm against her, the sweet sound of her breath and the sleepy aroma of childish hair. Something had indeed changed. The drone of the bombers seemed louder than usual. She tensed, wide awake now and listening avidly, trying to work out if they were coming their way. Surely not! It was the docks they went after, or railway marshalling yards, not the avenues of semi-detached houses erected in the interwar years.

She closed her eyes again, though not to sleep but to pray. 'Please, God. Don't let them come our way.'

God did not appear to be listening. The droning grew louder, perhaps two miles away, one mile. No, closer. The house began to shake as wave

128

after wave rumbled overhead, accompanied by the whistling of falling bombs. Lily woke up and began to scream. At the same time her arms became a stranglehold around her foster mother's neck.

Nothing had prepared Meg for the whistling scream of bombs falling close by and the ensuing explosions that made the walls tremble and the floorboards heave beneath their feet. Wave after wave of planes thundered overhead. Bombs screeched through the air before exploding. The rumble of falling debris was bad enough. Worse still was something that sounded as though hailstones were failing on the roof or pebbles were being thrown at the windows, followed immediately by the shattering of glass windowpanes.

Squeezing her eyes tightly shut, Meg buried her head against Lily's soft blonde hair, wishing she could stop her screaming, wondering what else was going on in the child's mind, what horrors had been resurrected. Stopping the explosions was the only thing that would calm the dear child, an impossible task. All she could do was whisper soothing words, stroke and hug her in the hope her reassurances would override the hellish noise and trembling house.

For the first time she truly understood how it had been for the people in the East End of London, living close to the docks. Those poor souls, their houses destroyed and their communities in ruins. She felt for them and suddenly feared for herself, for Lily and for the house she loved so much. A deafening blast sounded from overhead and the house trembled. She thought of all her lovely things covered in the same dust that was falling on her and Lily; her best china and glassware shattered, vases in pieces, glassless windows looking out at the mayhem of a world gone mad. The hellish scream of a falling bomb filled her eardrums followed by yet another explosion. The world went black with Lily still screaming.

When she came to she was choking. Covered in dust and trembling, Meg felt for the torch but it had rolled out of reach. The darkness was complete. Limpet-like, Lily had wrapped herself around Meg, all the while screaming and screaming and screaming! It was worse than the falling bomb.

Guilt surged within Meg's heart as tears streamed down her face. 'I'm sorry. I'm sorry,' she whined, only barely holding back the sobs. It was all her fault Lily was screaming. If only she'd gone to the shelter in the back garden. Spiders and dampness were more bearable than this! And what would her home be like? Everything upside down if not totally destroyed, though she'd put up with that if Lily would only stop screaming.

Making it to the shelter might help. With that in mind she pushed at the door, first with her hands, and then with her feet, knees bent so she could give it all the force she had, kicking it again and again. It wouldn't budge. Something was blocking it. With a sinking heart she realised that her home might be damaged a lot more than she could bear.

'Not too badly, God,' she murmured, her eyes closed against the darkness and the worrying thought. 'Please don't let it be too badly damaged. We'll wait until the planes have gone,' she murmured against Lily's head, kissing the top of it. Lily took no notice.

Meg became frantic. 'Lily! You have to stop screaming. You have to!' Tears filled her smarting eyes as she pleaded. The cupboard was becoming airless and she was choking on plaster dust. There was another smell she recognised. Gas. They couldn't wait for somebody to find them. They had to get out.

Lily continued to scream. Although she hated having to do it, Meg slapped her face – difficult in the darkness but she managed. Her screams reduced to a whimper before she fell into a foreboding silence.

'There, there. Close your eyes. Are you tired? Are you cold?' Lily didn't answer.

Meg felt a tugging at her heart. At least the child wasn't screaming, but the silence was almost as wearing. She'll get over it, she told herself, holding Lily close and hoping the raid would soon be over and somebody would get them out. 'Somebody will come soon,' she whispered. 'Someone will come.'

Her prayers intensified. Please God, send somebody before the gas explodes.

CHAPTER NINE

Blackness and silence. Like a tomb.

Meg was beginning to hate silence. Every so often she gave Lily a hug, afraid that the child's silence was permanent, that she'd choked on the dust and the rising thickness of gas.

'Lily? Can you hear me? We have to stay awake. Don't fall asleep. Please don't fall asleep. Would you like me to tell you a story?' Telling a story was the only thing she could think of that might rouse Lily from her silence.

The girl remained silent.

She was reassured that the child was still breathing when she heard the odd sniff or slight deviation in breathing. They didn't have much time. The smell of gas was getting stronger. But despite her resolve to stay awake, Meg began to drift into an odd sleep that seemed somewhere between dreaming and reality.

Something that sounded like a machine awakened Meg from her petrified silence. She was sweating profusely, though not from fear. The smell of gas seemed less but she couldn't be sure. Trapped in the confined space, it was noticeably warm at first, but in a short space of time the warmth increased to oppressive heat and got steadily hotter.

Fire! She could even hear the crackling of flames close by. Her heart seemed to stop beating. This could mean only one thing: her house was on fire. Fear roused her to instant action. Although her throat was clogged from dust, she began to shout at the top of her voice, banging on the door with her fists.

'Help! Help!' she shouted.

She hadn't wanted to shout for help in case Lily began screaming again but the girl didn't scream. She remained oddly silent, as though she heard nothing and had retreated into her own private world. To Meg, her silence was more frightening than her screaming.

It's my fault, she thought furiously. If only she'd gone to the shelter. If only she'd heeded Ray's warning. He'd be furious when he found out – if they ever got out. If they survived. Tears poured down her cheeks, dripping off her chin and on to Lily's head. The cupboard that should have protected them could now be their coffin and they were in danger of being burned alive.

She felt Lily move against her and felt relief. 'We'll get out soon,' she said, giving her a tight hug. Lily's soft little body stiffened like a china doll. Perhaps I'm hugging her too tightly, thought Meg. She loosened her grip but to her surprise her action had an adverse effect. Lily began to scream, this time more hysterically than she had before. 'We'll get out, darling,' said Meg, trying to sound confident. 'They're coming to get us out.'

The heat increased. Feeling as though she were melting, Meg undid her dressing gown, fumbling in the blackness to do the same for Lily. As though sensing her fear, Lily began thrashing about, her hands catching Meg's face, fighting to

133

keep her from removing the dressing gown. 'It'll be all right, Lily. It'll be all right!' Even to her own ears she was beginning to sound hysterical.

Meg clenched the hand she'd used to slap Lily, thinking it might help to do it again but she was too hot, too exhausted and too frightened to think straight. She began to cry, though softly, not wanting to frighten the dear child who so depended on her. She had to be brave and believe they would be rescued. But time was moving on and the interior of the cupboard was getting hotter and hotter – like hell must be, she thought to herself, or like the inside of an oven.

Terror and the will to survive filled her with fresh resolve. They needed to make themselves heard. Her own screaming joined that of Lily, shouting intermittently and hammering incessantly on the thin wooden door. 'We're here, damn you! We're here!' she screeched, her voice now openly hysterical.

For a while nothing changed, then suddenly there was an odd crunching and crashing sound, nothing like the sounds she had heard before. At first she thought it was the crackling of flames, timbers being devoured by fire not too far beyond the cupboard door. Wiping the wetness from her face, she listened carefully, her heart beating like a drum against her ribs, her lips cracked, her throat sore and her ears painful from Lily's continuous screaming.

Suddenly there were voices. 'Over here!' she heard somebody shout. 'There's someone alive in here.'

'Scream louder,' she urged Lily. 'Scream louder!'

She resumed banging on the door with both fists and, even though she considered her efforts feeble, she felt the blood rush to her hands and burst through the skin, damaged by the rough surface. Her shouts mixed with the screams of Lily, whose voice was breaking up into shorter staccato shrieks thanks to the dryness of her throat until she eventually went silent.

Voices from beyond the door were raised in unison, shouting for assistance, for crowbars, for strong arms to shift debris from against the door. One clear voice sounded above the others. 'Quickly now! Before that fire gets here. And mind we don't cause a draught or whoever's in there will be burnt to a crisp! And make sure that gas main's capped!'

Lots of shouting and thudding of heavy boots ensued, plus a rushing, crackling sound and crashing as though something heavy had landed on something hard.

'Wet blankets! We need wet blankets!' The same voice bellowed again, stern with intent, barking continuous orders like the rat-a-tat-tat of a machine gun.

She heard rumbling noises, booted feet, but mostly shouting against a background of jangling ambulance and fire engine bells. A few minutes passed and suddenly the cupboard door was wrenched open and a face besmirched with soot appeared against a background of flames. The fire was reaching upwards, scarring the sky with a burning glow and flying sparks.

Feeling absolutely drained, Meg bent over Lily until she heard a low rumbling sound and realised

135

it was the flames getting closer. The scene unfolding in her imagination was red and black, full of fire and hell. Her head felt as though her brain was on fire. She touched her hair and gasped. On one side of her head, hair that had once been soft was frizzled and scorched. Alarmed, she touched Lily's. Thankfully her hair was still silky.

Her rescuer's voice was reassuring. 'Come on, love. Don't be afraid.'

Wet blankets were flung over their heads to protect them from the inferno that had once been their house, the house next door and the one beyond that.

'An incendiary bomb done for all these three,' somebody shouted. Meg couldn't believe what they were saying. Three houses!

'No,' she whispered, but even as she said it she knew they were referring to her house and two of her neighbours. Number 7 Andover Avenue was gone.

Lily's frightening silence suddenly erupted into hysterical screams, her eyes widening with terror on seeing the pillars of flames, the black smoke and the equally black, sooty smelling figures moving through the darkness. Though she herself was shaking all over, Meg did her best to reassure the little girl. 'We'll be fine, Lily. We're safe now. It's all over.'

That's what she truly believed, what she wanted to believe. Everything would be all right. It was all a nightmare and very soon she would wake up and everything would be the same as it was yesterday. She shut her eyes, opened them again but everything was still the same. The shock suddenly hit her and her legs buckled.

'Steady on, love. We've got you.'

Summoning all her strength, she forced herself and those helping her to stop. 'Wait!'

Her rescuers looked at each other in mutual understanding. They'd seen so much of this already. Some people just couldn't take things in right away. They knew what she had to do.

Meg took one last look at what was left of the home she and Ray had bought together, the one she'd so lovingly cared for. There was nothing left of it now but a smouldering ruin, the top floor totally destroyed, smoke still rising in thick clouds from burning floorboards, doors and furniture. Three walls of the ground floor remained, the front door blackened and hanging lopsided on its hinges, the casement windows no more than bits of rubbish scattered over the ground.

She let out a little cry of anguish. Her whole world had revolved around that house.

'It's gone. My beautiful home is gone.'

One of her rescuers patted her shoulder. 'Now, now, love. It was only bricks and mortar. You're still alive and so is the little 'un. That's all that matters at the end of the day.'

Meg rounded on him. 'Only bricks and mortar? To me it was my home. My home!'

The man flinched at first but quickly rallied; after all, he'd seen it all before. 'Let's get you and your daughter to the hospital to get those burns looked at,' he said gently, as he made an effort to ease her towards the waiting ambulance.

Burns? Meg touched her singed hair, then her face. It stung. Suddenly she became aware that

Lily's hand was no longer in hers.

'Lily?' She was hysterical.

'She's fine. Just fine,' the man reassured her, indicating one of his colleagues.

At first Meg's stinging eyes couldn't quite make out the thing that looked like a rolled-up mat slumped over the shoulder of another rescuer. Threads of blonde hair shifted in the hot air and she recognised Lily.

'She's only sleeping,' somebody said.

The faces around her were a blur, the scene a mass of red flames and black smoke behind carcasses of brick and stone that had once been peoples' homes.

'Come on, love. There's no point you hanging around here. There's nothing left. But look on the bright side. You and your little girl are still alive. Got to be grateful for that, ain't ya?'

Meg wanted to shout at him that there was no bright side for her and that he probably still had a home to go to. Her tongue failed her. Her throat felt as though it were full of ashes. She was dazed and not quite with it, but determined they'd get through this.

Not until she and Lily were finally offloaded at the hospital did things seem clearer. She rubbed at her eyes, still stinging like hell. At first she thought the reflection in a glass door was not her but a shabby creature, face blackened by smoke, hair sticking up from her head like the wire wool she used to scrub pots and pans. Slowly, very slowly, she raised her fingertips to her hair. She was definitely seeing herself as she was now. No more glossy hair, perfectly applied make-up and smart day dress.

'I look a fright!'

The kind hand of a nurse touched her shoulder. 'Are you in pain?

Meg hugged herself. 'No. No. I don't think so.'

'We'll get you checked just in case.' Lily was placed on a trolley and covered with a blanket. 'This way.'

Her eyes fixed on where Lily was going, Meg was guided elsewhere and told to sit down. Her heart felt as though it was beating in her throat when her face was washed with antiseptic, her eyes cleaned and her throat checked.

The doctor, dark lines etched crescent-fashion beneath his eyes, was reassuring. 'You're lucky. Your lungs seem to have coped with the smoke. Breathe deeply.' She did everything asked of her and was pronounced free to go.

'What about Lily?' She looked around for her, but couldn't see her and began to panic. 'Where is she? Where's Lily?'

The doctor pressed a hand on her shoulder. 'She's behind that curtain over there.' He pointed to curtained screen that had only just been pulled into position.

She didn't wait for permission but swept across the ward, feeling sick and giddy but determined to know how the little girl was faring. Meg's breath caught in her throat. Lily was lying very still, her eyes closed. Two nurses accompanied another doctor, who was just as tired-looking. They murmured to each other as they examined her.

One of the nurses attempted to prevent her from staying. 'I'm sorry, you shouldn't be in here...'

'I was told I could see her. She's my daughter,' Meg blurted.

The doctor intervened. 'It's all right, Sister.' The nurse retreated.

'What's wrong with her?' demanded Meg. 'Is she all right?'

'I can see no physical injury, but I think she's in shock.'

She was just about to say that Lily would be better once she took her home when she remembered that she had no home. Number 7 Andover Avenue no longer existed.

The doctor took in her perplexed expression and surmised she was still in shock too. 'I think the child should stay here. Do you have relatives in London?'

Meg nodded slowly. 'Yes. My mother. She has a flat on the other side of London. My husband is in the services, the RAF, and his father lives in Wales.'

'You'd better see the almoner. I'm sure she can organise some temporary digs until you can sort something out. Something closer to the hospital.'

'My husband! I must contact my husband.'

'There's a public phone in reception.'

Still stunned by what had happened, Meg nodded and whispered thanks. She hurried to reception but had to wait in a queue. So many people were trying to phone their relatives. Eventually it was her turn.

A member of the Women's Royal Air Force answered. 'Can I help you?'

'My name's Meg Malin. I'm Ray Malin's wife. Is he there?'

There was a pause. 'I'm afraid not. He's out on

ops. Can I take a message?'

'Could you please tell him our house has been bombed – totally destroyed in fact.'

The woman promised that she would. There was something about her tone that Meg didn't like. She told herself the woman was one of those female officer hoity-toity types who looked down on civilian women as not doing their bit.

By rights she really should phone her mother and let her know what had happened. She could even ask her if she could stay with her, but she didn't want to do that. Her mother hated her routine being disturbed, even by a situation such as this. Anyway, she really didn't want to stray far from Lily's side.

'Can I stay with her for now?' she asked a nurse.

'You can, but only until we get her into a ward. Then it might be preferable if you leave her to have a night's sleep. She might be fine in the morning.'

Meg did as ordered, staying with Lily in the curtained cubicle until a bed was found for her.

The almoner, the woman who took care of patients' social care once they left the hospital, was very kind and helpful. She also looked tired out but took the time to explain the situation. 'There are so many injured tonight and just for once it wasn't the East End. We are doing what we can.'

She was also rather overweight and rushed off her feet, her face pink with effort. Members of the Women's Voluntary Services had been allotted to help her out with people who had become home-less thanks to the bombing. 'We're even putting families in surplus army barracks – not that there's many of those.'

'Good God,' murmured Meg, shaking her head and running her hand over her eyes.

The almoner assured her they could do something a bit better for her. 'So you can be close to your little girl.' True to her word, she found Meg a bed in a Methodist church hall that had been turned into a temporary dormitory. There was a notice outside: 'Please show your docket.' Meg did as ordered. Her legs were threatening to give way; the events of the day were swiftly catching up with her. She staggered a little. Somebody asked her if she was all right. She nodded.

Ahead of her was a sea of mattresses set out in rows, three or four deep to either side. Children were crying, women were speaking loudly about the dire experiences that had brought them here.

'We was lucky. My old man was on shift at the docks, the kids was round me mother's and I was doing a turn at the Duck and Feather. I used to pull pints before I was married, so don't mind keeping me hand in. Just as well I did...'

'Direct hit three houses along, but once one went, them houses either side went with it. Nothing but rubble now.'

'I left me washing on the line. New drawers and petticoat I made from some parachute silk somebody gave me. No good now, they ain't. Shame. I was really looking forward to wearing something soft next to me skin.'

They sounded so blasé about losing everything, yet Meg couldn't find it in herself to feel that way. She was angry and bitter that her house was gone.

How could they be so accepting of destroyed homes and so glibly amused by lost underwear. There was nothing amusing about any of it! Nothing at all!

One of the women caught her looking.

'There's some clothes for the taking over there, luv.' She pointed to a spot roughly halfway down the hall. 'Take what you like. It's all free. Washroom and lav is just behind it.'

'You might want to swill off the stink of smoke and get yerself tidy, luv,' said a woman with her top two front teeth missing, a cigarette hanging from the corner of her mouth and curlers sticking out from beneath the turban on her head. Four or five children were creating havoc around her. 'Not that I'm saying you stinks any different than anybody else...'

Meg headed for the very heart of the church hall. Her face was on fire. Never in all her life had she been referred to in such a way. Stink – she who was so meticulous about the cleanliness of her home and her body! The statement coming from a woman with curlers in her hair and no front teeth made it even worse.

There were four long racks of women's and children's clothes, and a shorter rack for men's clothing. Ashamed of how she looked, she rummaged furiously among the coats, dresses, blouses, skirts and hats, annoying some other women there who declared she was jumping the queue.

Meg ignored them. Her first choice was a burgundy felt hat with a large brim, big enough to hide her scorched hair. She also found a dress of similar colour scattered with tiny yellow

143

diamond shapes plus a grey checked coat. The few bits of underwear she eyed with contempt, and she took a cursory glance of the shoes before deciding that overall she had what she needed to see her through until her own clothes had been laundered.

The hand basin in the toilets was very small, but she did her best with a small bar of soap, a facecloth and a hand towel given her by a WVS woman. After that she ate some stew brought in by the ladies of the WVS, then went to bed. She'd expected to lie awake all night but instead fell into a fitful sleep. In her dreams she could hear her hair sizzling as the flames took hold. In her dreams she heard Lily screaming.

When she got to the hospital the next morning she was surprised to see that ambulances were still coming and going and stretchers were still being unloaded. Skirting the heaving melee of embattled medical staff and groaning patients, she made her way to Lily's bed. The smell of carbolic was strong and made her feel sick.

'And where do you think you're going?' The nurse had an officious twang to her voice.

'To see my daughter,' snapped Meg, her jaw hurting with the effort of keeping her temper.

'I'll see if the doctor...'

Meg swept past her. 'Throw me out if you dare!'

The nurse pursed her lips. She was used to patients and visitors respecting hospital rules and regulations. In a huff, she went off to fetch the doctor who wasn't too far along on his morning rounds.

Doctor Williams recognised Meg at once. 'Give

it time,' he told her. 'She's been traumatised. Her mind is blocking out torturous memories. I hear you were both lucky to escape,' he added gently.

Meg, the brim of her new hat pulled tightly down on one side to hide her singed hair, nodded. 'She had a traumatic time before the bombing. Not here. Lily's not her real name. We don't know what that is. She was rescued from occupied France, found wandering about the countryside with nothing but a dog for company.'

'Really?' Doctor Williams had pale skin and ginger eyebrows, which arched upwards. It worried him to learn that the child had had more than one traumatic encounter. He needed to probe further. 'Can you tell me any more about that period in her life?'

Meg tried to recall everything her husband had told her about Lily's past. 'There were some yellow stitches left in the lapel of her coat. We think she once wore a Star of David.'

'Jewish!' Doctor Williams frowned. He didn't like what he'd been told. For a child to have suffered one traumatic experience was bad enough, but for Lily to have suffered more than one, perhaps even one more significant than escaping a burning house, made matters even worse.

'Any moments of hysteria?'

Meg thought of the time they'd spent trapped in the understairs cupboard. 'Yes. We were trapped in a small space under the stairs. She didn't stop screaming. I had to hit her.' She looked guiltily down at the floor.

'Any incidences of bed wetting?'

Meg shook her head and wrinkled her nose.

145

The thought of bedwetting was almost offensive. Thankfully Lily had never done that.

'No.'

'Nightmares?'

Meg nodded. 'Yes. She wakes up screaming.'

'Has she ever told you what the dreams are about?'

'Yes. Something about being on a train going to Salzburg but it turns out not to be going there at all. Instead it goes to the butchers and everyone gets cut into pieces.'

Again the arched eyebrows. 'Butchers? The poor child. I'm not a psychiatrist, but from what I do know it sounds as though the nightmare is a reflection on some past experience.' He looked away for a moment as though unwilling for her to see his expression, reflecting on the reports he'd heard. 'Something to do with blood and death, obviously.'

'I suppose so.' Meg frowned then shook her head. 'We know nothing of what she went through before she was found. She was in a terrible condition. It got less as time went by but what with this happening...'

Suddenly realising what she'd been saying, she looked up at him sharply. 'You know now then from what I've said that she isn't really my daughter. Not my natural daughter. My husband and I took her in.' She stopped short before she could hint at the kind of job her husband did and how exactly Lily came to live with them. His were mainly secret missions and he'd warned her not to divulge too much to anyone. 'Tell them I'm with Bomber Command,' he'd said.

'I've tried to do my best for her,' she said, looking the doctor directly in the eye. 'I wish I could have spared her this.'

He patted Meg's shoulder in an act of reassurance. 'I'm sure you've done all you could. Have courage and garner hope. We will do everything we can.'

In the moments of respite from the side of Lily's bed, Meg marched up and down to the main entrance and back, willing Ray to be there, to take them both in his arms and tell her he'd found them a grand house in Pimlico, Hammersmith, Chelsea, or anywhere they could find a place to call home. He'd been summoned from the base, though it took some days for him to make his way to London. Eventually he arrived, a solid, safe figure in air force blue, his cap parked jauntily on the back of his head, like a signal that he was off duty.

There was a strained smile on his face. Like her, he hadn't slept in quite a while, though for different reasons. He couldn't bring himself to tell her that his plane had been damaged and he hadn't been able to take off from France straightaway. If it hadn't been for the Resistance... He felt mixed emotions about being trapped there. It was as though up until that moment he'd only been playing at fighting the enemy. A couple of days with that lot and he finally realised what being a patriot was all about.

Before he had a chance to kiss her, Meg flung herself into his arms and looked up at him pleadingly. 'It was a direct hit,' she said to him,

147

guilt riding in her eyes. 'Even if we'd gone to the shelter...'

He placed a finger on her lips. 'It landed at the back of the house. There's a big hole where the shelter used to be.'

Her eyes widened. 'Oh my God!'

'I went round there to take a look. You've both been very lucky,' he said. 'I don't know what I would have done if anything had happened to you.'

His arms performed a pincer-like hug that took her by surprise. She wore a headscarf instead of her broad-brimmed hat, carefully winding it around her head in order to hide her damaged hair. In her surprise the headscarf fell back on to her shoulders.

Ray's jaw dropped.

'Dear God,' he said, his eyes moist with pity as he gently fingered the scorched stubble on one side of her head.

Meg looked up at him with tear-filled eyes. 'My lovely hair.'

Ray smiled and gave her another, gentler and reassuring hug.

'Never mind. It'll grow again.'

A nurse interrupted the sweet moment to tell them they could see Lily soon. 'The doctor is with her.'

The hospital corridor was crowded with those injured and those awaiting news of injured loved ones. Ray managed to find Meg a chair. 'The last one,' he said. 'Never mind. I'm a growing lad.'

Meg had retied the headscarf so that her singed hair was hidden. She hung her head. 'Ray, I am so afraid. Sometimes I'm not sure what's real and what isn't. I can't believe that everything we worked for is gone up in smoke. As for Lily, I am really scared. She was doing so well and then this happened.' She looked up at him. He winced when he saw her pain-filled eyes.

'I know what you're saying, but try not to worry.'

'I can't help it. Lily hasn't improved. She's not uttered a single word.'

'It happens,' said Ray. Inside he felt as scared as she did. For her sake he wouldn't let it show.

Meg got out a handkerchief and blew her nose. 'I still can't help feeling that it was all my fault.'

Ray bent down so his face was level with hers. 'We have to believe what the doctors are saying is right. Give her time to get over it...'

'But Ray, she was already getting over her experiences in France and as you said yourself, we don't know half and quarter of what she went through over there. But she was improving. Until this happened!'

'They say all is fair in love and war but I don't think it is. War isn't fair to anyone. There are always innocent victims. As long as there are wars there will be victims.' His expression clouded. 'We have to help Lily get over it, Meg, however long it takes.'

Meg sniffed into her handkerchief. 'I hope she does get over it, even if it means she remembers who she is and her relatives come to claim her.'

'That's good to hear. We need to think carefully about what to do next. We need to work out what's best for everybody – whatever happens.'

149

They followed the nurse to the children's ward hand in hand, like a courting couple fearing to face what lay ahead but finding strength in each other's touch. The sight of the ward was heartbreaking. Small figures, some with bandaged limbs, others barely able to see on account of their bandaged heads, lay against white pillows. The whole ward would have been blindingly white if it wasn't for green-curtained screens and nurses in dark blue uniforms relieved only with white aprons and starched headdresses.

Lily's bed was at the far end of the ward next to a large window. The view was uninteresting, not that Lily was aware of it. Her eyes were closed, her face pale against the pillow.

Meg heard Ray's intake of breath. She understood. After all it was the first time he had seen the child in this state. It still hit her badly to see Lily lying there so still and pale. Ray had been reticent when she'd asked him to relate how it had been when he'd found her. She'd put it down to shock and also the secret nature of his work. Sometimes she sensed there was something else he wasn't telling her but didn't press him. Ray was a man in control of his thoughts and feelings. He would only share what was strictly necessary.

He smoothed Lily's hair away from her forehead. 'I'm glad I do what I do. I don't think I could drop bombs. Up there at a great height and all those people out of sight down below.'

Meg touched his arm. 'You were her knight in shining armour. You saved your loyal maiden on the first occasion. We have to fight for her again now.'

Ray said nothing but Meg sensed he was experiencing an internal battle. He loved what he did, and whatever he said about the war he loved the excitement, the living in a different world away from her and the life she'd thought they both wanted. However, she could feel his guilt. He'd been away while they'd been in danger. He hadn't been there with them and, despite all his fine words about war, it all went back to being together and looking out for each other. Nothing else mattered – or at least it never used to; now she wasn't quite so sure.

The nurse spoke gently. 'She's been asleep for quite a while. It won't hurt her if you wake her up. She has to have her supper shortly. We have a strict timetable here despite the disruptions.'

Meg wondered if the disruptions she referred to applied to them.

Ray was staring at Lily, his own face racked with anxiety, his eyes clouded as though hiding his thoughts.

'Go on, Ray. You wake her. The nurse said it would be all right.'

Ray touched Lily's cheek, leaned close and whispered her name. 'Lily? It's me, Mr Malin. Uncle Ray. Can you hear me?'

Lily's eyelids blinked open, flickering as she took in her surroundings and settled on the two faces in front of her. They were disappointed when she gave no sign of recognising them.

Meg controlled the despair she was feeling. 'She's been in here for three days – or is it four? I'm losing track. Yet she doesn't seem to know where she is. I hoped she would do by now.'

'Are you going to say hello, Lily? Lily? Can you hear me?'

Lily stared but she said nothing.

Ray sighed.

'I'm so sorry,' Meg whispered on realising that he'd firmly believed Lily would recognise him and it hurt to see she had not.

Ray straightened and turned away, his fingers twirling his cap. Blinking the tears from his eyes, he looked out of the window at the jumble of buildings that made up the hospital: the laundries, the sewing rooms and the places where things were stored. He saw a porter pushing along a trolley full of leg irons – false limbs for those who could no longer rely on their own – and felt empty, as though he hadn't eaten for days.

Her face a picture of sadness, Meg touched his shoulder. 'We have to do something, Ray. She needs a home and some normality, not a hospital bed. I need to find us somewhere to live.'

'I know.'

The fact that he cared so much for the child touched Meg's heart. He'd never had the same affinity for their lovely home as she had, but with Lily they were united. Feeling at one with his emotions, Meg raised her hand and stroked the nape of his neck.

'A new home, Ray. Somehow or another. I feel so ... so lost.'

Ray sighed and turned from the window. He'd seen enough people with missing limbs and damaged bodies. He made the effort to concentrate on what mattered at present.

'I made enquiries about a place near the airfield. There's nothing going at present. We've got foreign squadrons coming in and they've taken up all the rooms around every airfield in Lincolnshire. But you're right. She needs to be home and leading a normal life.'

'Perhaps we can find something further out of London,' ventured Meg.

Ray's loud exclamation took her by surprise. 'No! You will *not* stay in London. I absolutely forbid it.'

Meg had been taken aback by his loud voice and fully expected that Lily might have reacted in a similar manner. Despite Ray raising his voice, Lily did not react. In fact, she seemed to be far away, blinking every so often in response to the light from the window.

'London is my home.'

'Not any longer.'

'We can find something similar.'

'Meg, thousands have moved out of London and into the country. Ask yourself why. I'll tell you. It's because the countryside is safer. London has become a dangerous place.'

The two of them stood by the window. Meg kept her voice low. 'So what do we do? She isn't going to be in here for ever. Regardless of whether she responds or not, they need the beds for the injured and I can't continue to stay in the Methodist church hall. We both have to move on.'

Ray looked thoughtful. 'Leave it with me. I'll think of something. In the meantime, let's leave the doctors and nurses to do their job. Come on. I'm taking you away from all this.'

She detected a spark of the old humour about

153

him as he cupped her elbow and guided her out of the hospital.

'Where are we going?'

'A hotel. I know just the place. You and me sleeping on a camp bed in a Methodist church wouldn't be right. Much too public.'

CHAPTER TEN

The hotel was close enough to the hospital to be convenient but far enough away to attract servicemen and women on leave and in love – at least for the duration. Too expensive for commercial travellers and those needing accommodation while looking for work, in pre-war years it had accommodated middle-class people who travelled to London in cars rather than on the train. The reception area was rich in dark wood and red carpet. The brass bannister curving up with the staircase shone brightly, as did the bell they rang to attract the receptionist.

'I feel guilty,' Meg whispered. 'I mean, leaving Lily back there in a hospital bed while we book in here.'

Ray looked surprised. 'I could make you feel even more guilty and sign us in as Mr and Mrs Smith. What do you think?' Meg felt the colour coming to her face.

'Ray!' She couldn't help but smile as she tucked a piece of singed hair beneath her scarf. 'That's not what I meant.'

'No. I know what you meant,' he said softly. 'You're feeling guilty because you're not sitting beside Lily's bed. It's not going to speed things up at all. Give her time, Meg.' He paused, his look intense, his usually bright eyes almost desolate. 'And give me some time. We have precious little of it together nowadays.'

She understood. Worry was weighing them down: the war, being apart, Lily, and now not having a place to call home. This night in a hotel was supposed to be by way of respite, a time to take stock and gather every bit of courage they had. Hopefully it might recharge their batteries.

Ray winked at her as he signed them in. The manager, a weasel of a man with receding hair and a pencil-thin moustache, handed them the key. His expression betrayed no suspicion that they might not be married, though he stiffened when Ray paid him in cash, winked and said, 'Keep the change. And the secret.'

Meg blushed. 'You did it, didn't you?'

'Why not?'

'You did it. You signed us in as Mr and Mrs Smith,' she whispered.

'You cannot know for sure.'

'Yes I can. He didn't ask if we were married.'

He whispered close to her ear. 'There's a war on.'

Meg gritted her teeth. 'I'll be glad when that particular statement is dead and buried!'

Despite everything – Lily being sick, having no home and an uncertain future – she couldn't help smiling in a girlish way as though they really were two lovers away for a night of passion.

155

The room was large and full of light thanks to a bay window overlooking Hammersmith High Street. Meg walked over to it, trying her best not to let her mind wander away to Lily and what would happen to them next. The scene outside was windswept; the few people walking along were fighting with their umbrellas. Leaves roughly torn from trees skipped in waves along the wet pavements.

She felt the warmth of his body as he came up behind her. 'Cold out there. Very unseasonable.'

Meg wasn't thinking about the weather. Her whole body heaved with sobs and her tears poured on to his shoulder, releasing the tension she had felt prior to his visit.

He hesitated before enfolding her in his arms. Normally he would have stroked her hair. He'd always loved her hair.

'I look terrible. My hair...'

'Damn your bloody hair! You're alive.'

His outburst surprised her. She looked up at him through her tears. When had that strained look come to his face?

'Will you always come home, Ray?' She didn't quite know why she said it; perhaps a premonition that for some reason he would not. Her fingertips discerned the tension in his jaw. His smile was guarded. His fingers folded over hers and he kissed her palm.

'Why wouldn't I come home?' His eyes bored into hers.

As far as Meg was concerned there was only one answer to that. 'Don't get shot down, Ray. Please don't get shot down.'

'I will do my best not to.'

She buried her head against his shoulder. He kissed a patch of singed hair. She pushed him away. 'Don't do that.'

He frowned. 'Why not?'

'I look awful.'

'No, you don't. It's just hair. It'll soon grow back. You were lucky – lucky you didn't go to the shelter as it turns out.' He paused before asking the question she knew would come. 'Why didn't you?'

Meg narrowed her eyes in an effort to hold back the tears and the guilt she was feeling. 'The torch went out and I couldn't see our way to the Anderson shelter. It was so dark and the planes were so close.'

'Hey!' Ray took hold of her chin and raised her face, his eyes looking steadfastly into hers. 'No need to take on like that. You did the right thing as it turns out. My favourite girls came through it.'

'But our house...!' Tears escaped the corners of her eyes.

Ray cupped her face with his hands. 'It's no good going over and over it. Meg, surviving this war is all about getting through it whether we make the right decisions or not. I have to tell you right now that even the commanders only get it half right, but you're not to blame for what happened. Get back to your old self and take care of Lily.'

'You're right. The sooner we get back to some normality, the sooner she'll be well again.'

Ray's face clouded. 'Meg, you do realise she may never get over it. She may never remember us, let alone the life she had before.'

157

Meg shook her head. 'I refuse to accept that. She *will* get better.'

'Meg, we've already been told that there are no guarantees.'

'So we can be as patient as you like and she might still not recover?' Meg's voice rose almost hysterically.

'It's early days.'

Although her concern for Lily gnawed at her inside, it was reassuring to feel Ray's arms around her. She closed her eyes. 'I'll make sure she recovers. I promise, Ray, I *will* make sure she recovers.'

'Of course you will,' he said gently, as he stroked her hair. 'Of course you will.'

Their lovemaking that night lacked the impatient passion they usually shared when Ray was on leave. There was a nervous hesitance about it and, although Ray was as considerate as ever, the tension never fully left her body.

In the morning they had toast for breakfast with just a scraping of jam, plus a pot of tea served by a waitress who had the air of having better things to do.

'Sorry, we're out of everything else,' the waitress told them. 'First come first served at mealtimes. Eggs and bacon go first, then butter. We do have marge though.'

'Shame. I would have liked eggs and bacon,' mused Ray.

'It can't be helped. Don't you know there's a war on?'

'Really? I wondered why I was wearing this uniform.'

Miss Sniffy Waitress shoved her nose in the air and stalked off.

They both laughed. 'As if we didn't know!'

Ray began fiddling with the cutlery, a sure sign that he was on the point of stating something serious. 'Meg, I think it's going to benefit Lily to live in new surroundings. I've had a few thoughts and there's one particular idea I think would work beautifully. Away from London, of course. It won't help her recovery being among all the debris and air raids. She has to be away from all that, and on that note... Look, do you remember my Aunt Lavender? She's gone to stay with her daughter up north but I'm going to ask her if we can rent her cottage while she isn't there.'

'In the country?' The country was a foreign place to Meg. There were no buses, no taxis and Underground, just acres of fields and lots of animals. 'I don't know about that,' she murmured, hanging her head and studying her cup of tea as if it were a crystal ball capable of telling her the future. She had heard of the cottage but had never gone there. It was too far from London, and why would she want to enjoy a cottage garden when she had a perfectly lovely garden at home? Only there was no home. Not now.

Seeming not to notice her demeanour, Ray battled on with his suggestion. 'Give me a few days and I'm sure she'll agree that you and Lily can live there. It'll be good for both of you.'

Before the bombing, Meg would have procrastinated, but that was when she'd had a comfortable home. Nothing could compare to 7 Andover Avenue. The solid reality of her old home was

159

hard to shift from her mind. She had to forcibly remind herself that it no longer existed.

'So Bluebell Cottage it is,' stated Ray with an air of finality.

Deciding she had no choice, Meg nodded, without enthusiasm. 'I'll come and visit you there and I'll bring Rudy.'

'Not the dog again! I've already told you...'

'No more of that!' Ray winked. 'He's a man's best friend and although the boys at the base have adopted him as mascot – quite usual for an animal captured from the enemy – his true place is with us. Lily will love him.'

'Ray! There is no good reason for having the dog live with us. We must think of Lily.'

Ray eyed her thoughtfully. 'That's who I was thinking of. The dog might hasten her recovery.'

Meg folded her arms defensively and turned away. 'I can't see that.'

Ray felt a volcano of tension build up inside. His wife being waspish was something Ray had experienced right from the start of their marriage. At first he'd stood his ground but after a period of time he'd accepted defeat. Meg's mother had made her what she was. He should have seen that before they married. It would take a special kind of man to make his wife happy. He wasn't sure he was that man.

'I won't argue with you but would ask you to keep the dog in mind. In the meantime, I'll set the wheels in motion and arrange everything. Once Lily is better, get out of here and down to Bluebell Cottage. Promise?'

She accepted she had no option but to move to

Bluebell Cottage. 'I promise.' This time she meant it.

The only thing they both regretted was that Ray could not get extra leave in order to see them settled in. Meg and Lily would have to travel alone, just the two of them moving into the cottage.

CHAPTER ELEVEN

It was the end of June when Lily was finally discharged from hospital. She stood with Meg on the platform at Paddington Station waiting for the train to the West Country. The signs saying it was Paddington Station had been taken down – as if anybody could mistake it for what it was. Everyone knew where it was!

Keeping a tight hold on Lily's hand, Meg headed for the correct platform. In the other hand she carried a brown leather suitcase she had bought from a bombed-out shop in the West End. It was very smart, which at least in her opinion was more than could be said for its contents. The clothes packed inside it had been chosen from similar racks she'd first come across in the Methodist church hall, most second-hand but some donated by stores and shops. It irked her pride that she had nothing left of her own, though she had noted that some items were in good condition if a little dated. Other children growing out of their clothes meant that Lily did fairly well.

'We all have to make do with what we can,' the almoner at the hospital had stated. 'People have been so kind.'

Meg feigned agreement but inside promised herself that in time she would purchase new clothes for both herself and Lily. She had never had to resort to cast-offs before the war and she was adamant she would only do so now while she had no choice.

Although feeling far from amenable to this move, Meg had chatted merrily all the way to the station, trying as best she could to elicit some response from the silent girl. There was none and Meg was exasperated. Lily remained silent for the whole journey, staring out of the train window at cornfields and pastures where cows and sheep grazed. Meg conjured up a game of counting the animals. Lily did not respond. Meg did all the counting.

Lily didn't speak and rarely moved. She was like Loulou, thought Meg, the rag doll she used to love that had been left behind in the ruined house. She didn't do anything.

'Here we are,' said Meg brightly as the train pulled alongside a single platform on the up line. Tubs of colourful flowers decorated the station and more flowers trailed from baskets attached to lamp posts. It struck Meg that the countryside was far more cheerful than the city.

Her voice reflected her own uplifting of spirit. 'This will be our new home. Just smell that fresh air.'

Lily looked as if she hadn't noticed they'd arrived anywhere, as if she was seeing the same

162

surroundings she'd left behind, though the village couldn't have been more different. Upper Standwick had snuggled for centuries in Somerset's Avon Valley, the river meandering like a silver ribbon beside the straighter aspects of the eighteenth-century canal and the nineteenth-century railway line. The houses were older than either the canal or the railway and built of the same honey-coloured stone as the nearby Georgian city of Bath. Bath and its hot springs became famous in Roman times and reached its zenith during the Georgian period when men wore tight britches and women gossamer gowns.

Each village around the city huddled around its own village church, green or even duck pond. Upper Standwick was no exception. Situated on one side of the village green, Bluebell Cottage was approached over a flagstone path where tufts of speedwell and pimpernel pushed up between the cracks. A family of swallows had set up house beneath the eaves. The windows were small and square, and the trailing flowers of a climbing wisteria cascaded like amethyst teardrops over a trelliswork porch.

Meg stood dumbly at the door feeling half inclined to turn around and get the next train back to London. I don't want to be here, she said to herself, until Lily tugged at her hand. The little girl was looking up at her with soulful eyes. Even though she said nothing, Meg knew this was her signal for needing the lavatory.

'All right, Lily. Just hold on a moment and we'll get you inside.'

Her gaze alighted on a huge iron key hanging

from a nail at the side of the door. So old. So heavy. Not neat and tidy like my front door, she thought to herself before the truth hit her like a hammer, as it had so many times before. Her house was no more. Bluebell Cottage was her new home.

The key crunched in the lock and the door opened. Leaving her suitcase on the step and clutching Lily's hand, she stepped inside. 'I think it must be out the back,' she said to Lily and immediately went to the back door. The catch opened easily. The door had not been locked. *How crazy is that,* she thought to herself, *locking the front door but not the back?*

She took Lily to the outside privy where a moss-covered back door opened on to a surprisingly clean lavatory. 'Can you manage by yourself?'

Lily's response was to enter the square-built structure and firmly close the door behind her.

Meg made her way back to the house, on her way passing a zinc bath hanging from a nail. There was no bathroom. Her heart sank. How would she manage?

The day was hot but inside the cottage was cool and shady. Meg stood and took stock. There was only one large room on the ground floor that served as both kitchen and living room. She wouldn't have thought it possible that her heart could sink further, but it did. At Andover Avenue she'd had two reception rooms and a kitchen. There had also been a bathroom on the first floor.

Yes, the room was large and there was a pretty view of the garden from both the back and front windows. But further inspection revealed there was no gas cooker, no oven and only a deep butler-style sink with a single cold tap hanging over it. A cast-iron range sat in an immense inglenook fireplace, a clockwork trivet hanging just in front of it alongside a metal spike. She couldn't think what the spike was for but noted a large kettle hanging on the trivet.

Surveying her surroundings with increasing despair, the only thing she found in its favour was its cleanliness. Apart from that, it bore no relation to the house she had once lived in. Heavy beams hung low over a faded Turkish rug lying upon a flagstone floor. The windows were small and the curtains were of a dark tapestry style that only served to further obscure what little light managed to squeeze through. Overall, Bluebell Cottage could not hold a candle to her house in London.

The springs squeaked as Meg sank into one of the old-fashioned armchairs at the side of the fireplace. She wished with all her heart that she could turn the clock back but what would that achieve unless she could wish the bombers had bombed somebody else.

Lily had returned from the lavatory, standing like a statue in the middle of the room. She showed no interest in her surroundings, not looking at anything, just staring as though she'd lost her way, as she always had since the bombing.

Meg closed her eyes. It's no good, she said to herself. This is all you have. You're dependent on the generosity of other people. First clothes and now this house. Correction, cottage. Opening one eye then the other, she took in the bumpy walls, the uneven floor and shivered. Mice probably lurked in those walls. Flinging back her head, she blinked away the tears, forcefully reminding herself of the doctor's advice that Lily needed a change of scene, as far away from London as possible. It was all about Lily. She had to make the effort. Could she make the cottage look better than it was?

I suppose I can do something to improve it, she thought, while gazing critically at the dark fabric of the curtains. They would be first to go.

'Oh well,' she sighed, blinking back tears when she thought of her old home and how modern and light it had been compared to the cottage. It was dreary! It was dark and old-fashioned, but for Lily's sake, she had to put on a brave face. 'Let's take a look upstairs,' she said, sounding far brighter than she actually felt.

Lily appeared not to have heard her, standing there, staring into space, looking but not really seeing. Not until Meg took hold of her hand did she allow herself to be led to the narrow spiral staircase and up to the next floor. Two bedrooms led off the small landing at the top of the stairs. Meg pushed open the door to her right.

'This will be your bedroom. Isn't it pretty?'

The floorboards were whitewashed and creaked beneath her feet. A pink and beige rug lay between the bed and the window. A cast-iron single bed overlaid with a patchwork quilt dominated the room. A painted blue chair and chest of drawers were the only other pieces of furniture. Pink flowers dotted the wallpaper and a pair of pink and pistachio-coloured curtains hung at the window.

At least it will keep you occupied, she told herself. *You can improve on what is here.* Aunt Lavender won't mind. 'Not that I care,' she muttered to herself, her finger chasing a wandering spider along the stone windowsill.

Oh, Ray, what have we come to? She needed him and envied his being apart from all this, in comfortable quarters at the base and not relegated to living in what to her was little better than a rabbit hutch.

The view from the bedroom window was of green fields fading away to fields of corn stalks left bristling in the sun. The pastures were dotted with black-and-white cows, beyond which was a field of sheep.

For Lily's sake she made the effort to sound cheerful. 'Look at those cows, Lily. Do you see them? And sheep. And I can see people in the field helping with the haymaking. See? Just think of the fun we're going to have here. Everything is so green and fresh, and there are so many animals.'

Meg's heart ached for London, but it was imperative to get Lily to engage with their new surroundings. There was no traffic noise, just the sound of birds. 'Listen. Do you hear the birds singing?' For a moment she thought she caught a blink of acknowledgement but couldn't be sure.

Talking of animals brought Ray to mind. He'd been so intense about having the dog live with them. It wouldn't happen, though she had to admit the animal would be more at home in this countryside retreat than in a house in London.

While Meg cheerfully rattled on about how green everything was Lily stood mute, totally

167

unresponsive, not moving or saying a word.

Meg persisted. 'Look. I can see cows in the distance. And sheep. Don't you want to see them, Lily?'

Lily took one more glance then proceeded to study her immediate surroundings more closely, turning her head and staring around her as though monsters lurked in the corners. Was there nothing likely to entice the poor child from the closed world she presently occupied?

At night, Meg tossed and turned. It was hard to think of something new that might trigger a response. 'Things will improve,' the doctor had told her on the last occasion he'd examined Lily before leaving hospital. 'New surroundings would help no end. But give it time.'

'And if she doesn't recover?'

She'd seen reticence in the pale eyes viewing her through the thick glass of horn-rimmed spectacles, and knew he was weighing up whether to reassure her with half-truths or be totally honest. Swallowing her apprehension, she'd pressed on. 'I'd like to know the truth, Doctor.'

He'd nodded in a vague kind of way, pushing his spectacles upwards with one finger until they sat in the indent at the top of his nose. 'If she doesn't recover, then we may have to arrange specialised treatment in a hospital for children with psychological illnesses.'

'You mean the mad house?'

The doctor snatched his spectacles from his nose in one fell swoop – like an eagle snatching its prey. 'Mrs Malin! We do not refer to such places like that these days. Mental health is an illness

168

that can be cured like any other,' the doctor indignantly declared.

Meg refused to be intimidated. 'My child is not going into such a place whatever you might like to call it. And that is that!' She surprised herself when she referred to Lily as though they were related by blood. My child!

My child. She flinched at the thought of that conversation. Ray's warnings were ripe in her mind. At some point Lily would remember who she was or somebody might recognise her. Then she would no longer be her child. She would belong to somebody else.

Getting down on to her knees, she smiled into Lily's eyes and stroked her cheek. 'It's nine weeks or so before you begin school here, so we've got plenty of time to explore. Just the two of us. You'd like that, wouldn't you?'

Lily said nothing and did nothing.

A sharp pain stabbed at Meg's heart and for an agonising moment she felt that pain turn to anger. 'I want the real Lily back!' she wanted to shout, but she restrained herself from doing so. Shouting was likely to frighten Lily, sending her deeper into this hollow shell she now resided in.

'Let's go back downstairs,' she said, letting the curtain go and watching the spider scurrying away. Their footsteps echoed down the narrow staircase, sounding as hollow as her thoughts. She wanted Ray, she wanted her old life back, and it was only her responsibility towards Lily that kept her from catching the train back to London. She had to give the child a chance.

The hot weeks of July and August were spent

169

rambling through fields ripe with corn and filled with the laughter of land girls helping with the harvest. At least the fresh air would do both of them some good.

Most of the land girls were city girls who'd never seen a cow before, let alone learned how to milk one or drive a tractor or toss sheaves into a threshing machine. Meg much admired them. Every time they took a short cut across a field, she waved at them and they waved back.

Lily did not acknowledge them in any way. As far as she was concerned, they might as well not be there. She was totally unresponsive and Meg was at her wits' end. Only the promise of her Uncle Ray coming to visit seemed to raise any interest at all, and even then it was only a sideways look from those sea-blue eyes. It was small comfort but all she had.

Her hopes soared when a letter arrived from Ray saying he had leave coming and would be returning soon. 'He's coming home,' Meg she said to Lily, excitement spilling from her voice. 'He's coming home. Isn't that wonderful, darling?'

She vaguely recalled reading in the letter that he was bringing somebody named Rudy with him. She would prefer he didn't bring anyone. She wanted him to herself, so they could talk about Lily and how long it would be before she recovered from her ordeal on the night the bombers came. Perhaps she would have regained her memory by now if it hadn't been for that.

She went down on her knees so that she could stroke Lily's hair and smile into her uncomprehending eyes in the hope she might understand better. Yet again she fancied she saw a flicker of response, but it was so difficult to tell.

The hot day cooled into twilight. It was just after she had put Lily to bed that she remembered who Rudy was. The dog! Her mind had been so preoccupied with worrying about Lily, she'd forgotten. The last thing she wanted was a dog. This place was dreary enough without bringing a dog into it and Ray's sudden mention of bringing the dog home with him angered her, so much so that she phoned him at the base. Thank goodness Aunt Lavender had had a phone put in so she could keep in touch with her daughter in Scotland.

'I need to talk to Flight Officer Ray Malin,' she said in a clipped tone, gripping the receiver as if she were attempting to strangle it.

'I'm sorry. He's not here at the moment.'

Meg heaved a big sigh of exasperation.

'Would you like to leave a message?' asked the polite young woman on the other end of the telephone.

Meg bit her bottom lip. Her exasperation had not gone away. She was still annoyed but it wouldn't be fair to have Ray come back to a bad-tempered message. She made the effort to regulate her tone.

'Yes. Will you please tell him that I cannot possibly cope with him bringing a dog? Tell him that. Tell him not to bring the dog.'

She waited a few hours before phoning again. Ray was still not available. He never went into detail about the job he was doing. Incisive questions were met with deep silences. She only

171

knew he wasn't on ordinary bombing missions. He was involved in dangerous missions in enemy territory, but that was all he would admit to. The details were top secret.

Enemy territory! The thought of him being captured was frightening.

The only clue she had was him suggesting they might think about living in France once the war was over. The very thought of it had made her shudder, but that was when the house in Andover Avenue was still standing.

There was always fear at a time like this. She closed her eyes. 'Please come home safe,' she prayed. She derived some reassurance when Ray didn't get in touch and neither did his commanding officer. No news was good news.

She occupied herself by day with Lily and making new things for the house, keeping it clean and chasing the resident spiders from their knotty holes in the plasterwork. By night she had time to dwell on things. 'Don't let it be too long,' she whispered when the moonlight fell like a skein of silk across her bed and bats fluttered from the church tower.

The day the telegram arrived saying he was on his way home, she sprang into action cleaning, and making the place as perfect as possible almost became the obsession it had been back in London. She tried to involve Lily in tidying the cottage, weeding the garden, picking flowers to place in a vase, chivvying her along with her enthusiasm, trying to get her as excited as she was.

'What about those pink ones? You like pink, don't you?'

Lily didn't answer, only paying attention to the bright red poppies that grew in the long grass against the fence. She wasn't picking the poppies but fingering them and then peeling the red petals away so that only the coal-black stamen remained.

Fear clutched at Meg's heart. It was always red and black Lily chose, never something girly and pink. Before the bombing, Lily had been fond of colouring books and drawing, using all different combinations of colour to create a picture. Not now. She only used red and black. Red for flames. Black for the darkness of that terrible night. And the screaming. Nowadays Meg wished Lily would scream. At least it would be some kind of reaction.

Long shadows fell across the garden and Lily was still unresponsive, standing in the middle of the lawn gazing at flying insects caught in the last mellow rays before the sun went down Meg finally called it a day.

'Come on, poppet.' Taking hold of her daughter's hand, she led her indoors but left the back door open. 'There. So you can watch the sunset,' she said lightly. 'Or would you prefer to draw?'

Ignoring the view out of the open door, Lily sat down at the kitchen table and pulled her drawing book towards her, picked up a black crayon and began to plaster the lower half of the paper with blackness. Seemingly satisfied that enough of the paper was black, she reached for the red crayon and covered the top half.

Black and red. Darkness and fire.

The following morning dawned cloudy and grey, a light drizzle falling like a gauzy veil, droplets of

173

water hanging from the thirsty cabbage roses that bounced against the front wall of the cottage. The low thudding of raindrops on the zinc bath hanging on the back wall got on Meg's nerves, though it did remind her that an umbrella was needed when visiting the primitive toilet at the end of the garden.

The cottage was even darker without the benefit of sunlight. Meg tried not to think of the rain and greyness as a portent of things to come. You can't have every day being sunny, she told herself as she peered around her. She so wanted the day Ray came home to be sunny. It might help all of them be happy, including Lily.

Finally, the rain stopped. On opening the kitchen window, the smell of a wet garden came in and for a moment lifted her spirits. She placed a piece of buttered toast and a boiled egg in front of the silent waif she had brought into her life, slicing off the top and handing Lily a spoon so she could feed herself. Whatever was going on in Lily's mind, it had not affected her appetite.

Meg sipped at her tea and gazed out of the window. Birdsong and the smell of flowers wafted in, but she hardly heard one or smelled the other. In fact, she wasn't really tuned in to seeing the garden in all its summer glory. Her mind was preoccupied with all the things she needed to do before Ray came home. Even though he would bring his own ration book with him, she'd really pushed the boat out, queuing for the little luxuries that would make him feel truly at home.

Ron Place, the local farmer, had butchered a cow that was no longer giving milk and she'd been lucky enough to purchase a piece, a definite change from rabbit. Everyone in the village had access to rabbits and wood pigeons. Fresh food was more plentiful in the country and it was also much safer.

Lily had eaten her egg and toast and drank her milk. She was drawing again. Meg sighed. Red and black again. Never mind, she thought as she swilled her cup under the tap. Ray would be home in two days. He'd be disappointed in Lily's progress and perhaps decide they should move back to the city, close to the experts who might help Lily further. It cheered her to think they might *have* to move back to London, though she shook her head at the thought of the threat from overhead. London was being badly bombed.

Somebody knocking at the front door jerked her thoughts back to the here and now. 'Who can that be,' she said as she took off her apron and hung the tea towel to dry in front of the range. 'Can't go to the door unless I look my best, can I sweetheart?' she said to Lily.

Lily didn't look up.

After quickly running her fingers through her hair, Meg headed for the front door. She assumed her visitor would be another of those Women's Institute ladies pressing for her to attend one of their village meetings. 'You will be most welcome,' her neighbour Mrs Dando from across the other side of the village green had insisted, a thin-lipped smile creasing her already wrinkled face. Oh well. She would be polite and tell her plainly that she had not changed her mind.

It was not Mrs Dando.

175

A young man with a freckled complexion and ginger hair stood on the doorstep. He wore the uniform of a telegram delivery boy and the front wheel of his bicycle peered from behind the garden gate.

'Mrs Malin?'

He didn't smile. If he had smiled she might not have felt what seemed to be cold fingers gripping her heart. If he had smiled she would have thought that Ray had sent a telegram saying he would be coming home early. This afternoon's train perhaps?

He didn't smile and the colour drained from her face.

'Yes.'

'Sorry, ma'am.' He handed her a plain brown envelope, touched his cap and was gone.

She didn't know how long she stood there staring at the envelope. The postmark, War Office, didn't really register because she didn't want it to register. She didn't want to open it.

A sudden scream from the kitchen took her running to Lily's side. The girl was staring at the fire in the range. Meg had lit it in order to do some baking. Thinking to take advantage of the heat, she'd spread a few things in front of the fire to dry and there really hadn't been room for the tea towel she'd put there. The smell of scorching filled the kitchen. The tea towel had burst into flames.

The washing-up water was still in a bowl in the sink. Thinking on her feet, Meg grabbed it, throwing the water over the fire. There was a sizzling sound as steam replaced the smoke sent up by naked flames.

Lily was still screaming.

Meg wrapped her arms around her. 'It's all right, darling. It's all right.'

Lily stopped screaming, pushing herself from Meg's arms. Her face was expressionless as she made her way back to the kitchen table, her crayons and her drawing. It was as though nothing had happened. The moment was blocked out, another incident to be buried with far worse memories.

Meg squeezed her eyes tightly shut. If she didn't rein in her feelings she too would be screaming. It was bad enough coping with Lily, but now there was a message – from the War Office. Her heart was beating swiftly.

Taking a deep breath, she opened her eyes. One thing at a time. One problem addressed and another one to come. Hands shaking and heart thudding, she picked up a butter knife and slit open the envelope. The words were straight to the point.

'*We are sorry to inform you that Flight Officer Raymond David Malin failed to return from a mission and is presumed dead after his plane went down over enemy territory.*'

CHAPTER TWELVE

After receiving the news of Ray's death, Meg held herself stiffly as though she was made of cast iron. Ray wasn't coming back. He would never again complain about mowing the lawn, decorating the house or trimming the rose bushes. With hindsight she realised just how much he'd hated all those things. He'd preferred meeting friends at the pub, rambling around London streets with a drawing pad, talking to new and exciting people. The last thought hit her like a bus. She recalled how he'd seemed twice the man when meeting new and different people or socialising with friends owning as much ego as he did. Now he was gone. A light had gone out in her life.

For the rest of that day she flitted around the cottage numb from head to toe and without shedding a tear, holding everything back behind a concrete dam for Lily's sake. Long after the girl had gone to bed, she carried on polishing furniture that didn't need polishing, sweeping a floor that had already been swept three times that day, and washing items of laundry that she'd just brought in from drying on the line.

That night, once in her own bed and with the cottage creaking around her, she stared silently into the darkness awaiting tears that did not come. What was wrong with her? She felt sad so why didn't she cry? Inexplicably, her sorrow changed to anger.

'Oh, come on, Meg. This war will be one great adventure.'

No, she wanted to shout. No! It is not an adventure. It's dangerous and takes you away from your proper home.

How dare he go away! How dare he volunteer for missions over enemy territory! If he'd been more content with his home life and a more mundane wartime job, perhaps in administration

178

or training, he would still be alive.

'See,' she said, her voice shrill because she restrained from shouting, in case she woke Lily. 'If you had been content with being at home, this would never have happened. And now you're dead!'

Yes, the telegram said missing presumed dead, but she knew what they meant. Why didn't they just spell it out as it was instead of giving her false hope? She hated this war. She hated the faceless bureaucrats in Whitehall who thought they knew best how things should be worded, how best to handle a woman who had lost the man she loved. They knew nothing!

Sleep was elusive. Throwing back the bedclothes, she sat on the edge of the bed staring out of the window, unseeing as the night sky turned to grey and fingers of orange from the rising sun streaked the sky.

Memories from their first meeting, their courtship and their marriage flooded into her mind. He'd worked in the city for an insurance company and, by his own admission, was recognised as a rising star. His own enthusiasm for being well thought of did not match that of everyone else, however; especially his father.

'It was the job he wanted for me, not one of my own choosing.' His manner had been unusually bitter. 'I hate doing the job I'm doing. My heart's not in it.'

'So where is it?'

'In Montmartre,' he'd said wistfully. 'I love drawing and painting. I love France and everything French. When I was younger I had it in my

179

head to be an artist in Montmartre in Paris and follow the path of Maurice Utrillo.'

Meg had cringed at the thought of being married to a husband who didn't keep standard office hours. Luckily Ray had loved her enough to marry her and buy a house in the suburbs. He'd never get to France now, she thought glumly. Never get to choose where to live and work once the war was over.

Meg heard Lily's footsteps heading for the toilet. Lily must not see you upset, she said to herself, and made the decision not to tell Lily that Ray was dead – not yet.

The whole of the next day, the day after that and the rest of the week seemed to pass in a dream. She hoped nobody had seen the boy delivering the telegram and surmised that something was wrong. She couldn't cope with receiving their sympathy or answering their questions. Not yet. Not until she had pulled herself together and got used to the situation – if she ever did.

Keeping busy obviously helped. Even so, she found herself staring into space, though she steeled herself to make a meal for Lily. Perhaps that was why she hadn't burst into tears for a man she'd thought was the love of her life. Had something changed?

The war, the war, the war. And yet she couldn't help feeling that was only an excuse.

The sun was still shining, Lily was still ferociously painting red and black pictures, life in the village was going on regardless.

Ray's widowed father had been his usual stiff self when he'd been told the news. It was hard at times to reconcile the two men, though Ray had once told her that he took after his mother. She'd been French and he'd worshipped her.

'Her name was Françoise,' he'd told her. He'd kept a small photograph of her in his wallet. She'd looked young and pretty, more like a sister than a mother.

'I'm sorry,' she'd said when she'd first given her father-in-law the news, as though it were somehow her fault. He asked her to keep in touch, to let him know if anything materialised. 'In case he is only missing...'

Meg pressed her hand over her eyes. 'Of course,' she said, but behind the hand tears threatened. 'He's dead,' she wanted to say. 'They don't seem to know it but all they are doing is prolonging the agony.'

Her own mother fell to silence when she told her before offering to come down and stay with her for a while. 'Though I cannot possibly get there for about two weeks. I've become so involved with the WVS and the WI. It's so hectic in London at present.'

Meg had already made up her mind that a visit from her mother would not materialise. Her mother would have better things to do – better as in more supportive of the war effort. She wished to do her bit and wished her actions to be observed by her society friends. There was status in being a volunteer, working herself to a standstill without the prospect of remuneration.

During those early days she continued telephoning the few people she knew had phones, most of them in London. Everyone was sympathetic but busy, surprisingly busy, as though death and being a friend really had little to do with each other.

'There is so much going on and so much to do. Are you coming up to London? We must meet up if you are. So sorry, darling. So very sorry.'

Looking after Lily was her excuse for not visiting London, though she badly needed a shoulder to cry on. The villagers were still strangers, though they smiled and slowed as they passed as if expecting her to tell them something about her life.

Persisting in letting relatives and old friends know about Ray helped her cope. Over and over she repeated the same thing. 'A telegram came. It said he's missing, presumed dead.' Sometimes she got it in the wrong order: 'Dead, presumed missing.'

She badly needed someone to care, to act as though her loss was the only fatality in this bloody awful war. Her list was small and it was an old friend who didn't live in London who threw her a lifeline: 'Come and stay with me, darling.'

She'd met Diane in London when they were both working as secretaries at a very large law firm. Even though they were from different backgrounds, they clicked immediately. Diane was pretty and laughed a lot.

'I was supposed to "come out",' she'd told Meg. 'You know. The debutante ball and all that.'

Meg had been highly impressed. 'But you didn't go?'

'My darling Meg, do I look the sort of woman likely to fall for a chinless wonder with oodles of money but no charisma?' Meg had to admit that

182

she didn't look that sort at all. Her friend was totally bipartisan when it came to men. 'In time, I intend going back to Cornwall. My folks will be missing me.'

Though she was now married, Diane still lived in her parents' stately home in Cornwall. The War Office had requisitioned a major portion of the house. Her sympathy and generosity knew no bounds, though she did feel obliged to apologise for their straitened circumstances.

'We only have the use of the west wing for our own purposes. It's a little cramped but one has to make sacrifices in the current situation, doesn't one,' Diane had explained in her plummy accent.

From memory, Meg thought the accommodation described by Diane as being allotted to the family was far from cramped. The manor house dated back to the sixteenth century and was surrounded by a large garden with a coastal path beyond the high walls. At this time of year, a turquoise strip of sea could be viewed from most of the upstairs windows. Gulls screamed by day, freewheeling against coastal clouds and summer blue. Owls hooted at night, accompanied by the far-off sound of surf crashing against the rocky coastline.

'And where's your husband?'

She heard a sudden catch in Diane's throat. 'Ian is away at sea. He's in the Navy.'

The train journey down was long and arduous. Lily slept most of the way, her hair damp against her forehead. She stirred slightly when Meg stroked her damp locks away from her eyes, catching her breath as though something was

183

preventing her from breathing properly.

At one point she sat up, eyes staring. 'Where are we going?'

Meg was taken by surprise. Lily spoke infrequently and never seemed to know where she was.

The carriage rattled along as she explained they were off to Cornwall to stay with a friend. 'You'll like Cornwall,' Meg pronounced. Lily still had nightmares about a train journey, though not as many as she used to.

'Bodmin! Bodmin!' The stationmaster, a white-haired man with an officious air, strode up and down shouting the name of the station over and over again. There were no signs stating they were at their destination.

Meg shook Lily's shoulder. 'Come on, Lily. We're here.'

Lily started, her eyes wide with alarm, looking around her as though she didn't know where she was. Her face paled when she saw she was on a train.

Meg caressed her face. 'It's all right Lily. We're here at Bodmin. We're going to have a lovely holiday. You can paddle in the sea and...'

It broke her heart to see the look of terror on the little girl's face. Incomprehension she could cope with, but this look went far deeper. The bombing, she thought. It always went back to the bombing.

'Come on,' she said, taking hold of Lily's hand. 'Let's go and have a lovely time.'

Diane, a picture in a summery print dress and a straw hat decorated with flowers, collected them from the station. 'I'm so sorry, darling,' Diane said to her, arms around her shoulders, the long fingers of her right hand clasping a cigarette holder. 'Poor you. Poor Ray. Poor child too.'

Meg broke down sobbing on her friend's shoulder. Lily took no notice whatsoever. Even when Diane, a woman who could charm anyone, did her utmost to engage her, Lily gave no sign she'd heard her.

'Meg,' Diane said to her later that evening once Lily had been put to bed. 'Far be it from me to criticise, but don't you think that child would be better in a special hospital – or something...'

Meg responded fiercely. 'Diane, I no longer have Ray in my life. If I didn't have Lily, I think I would go mad!'

Diane nodded sagely. 'Yes. Of course you would.'

The weather was fine so the next day was spent out in the garden seated beneath a chestnut tree, dappled with sunlight and shade as leaves rustled in the warm breeze. The two women, who met in a time so different to the world as it was now, reminisced about times gone by; both watched Lily as they spoke.

Lily was standing close to the fence at the far end of the garden, her arms held straight at her side, her whole body completely still as she took in a flock of sheep grazing stoically on the salty grass that gave roast lamb from around there its unique flavour.

'Poor love,' said Diane.

'I still blame myself. We should have gone to the public shelter.'

'Hindsight is a wonderful thing.'

185

Meg nodded. 'Ray and I used to wonder what she'd gone through before he found her.'

'She doesn't remember any of it?'

Over a pot of tea, scones, jam and Cornish cream, Diane asked her about Lily's condition and the chances of a full recovery.

Meg shrugged. 'All they say is that it will take time. Nobody tells me how long that's likely to be. She rarely speaks. In fact, I wonder at times if she knows that I'm there. I'm hoping she might improve once she begins school in September.'

'Let's hope she does. Other children might very well bring her out of herself.'

Meg nodded. 'That's what I'm hoping.'

'And Ray? They have said missing in action. It doesn't necessarily mean that he's gone for ever.'

A cloud suddenly obscured the sunshine and Meg shivered. 'Missing in action, presumed dead. I'm thinking that if I believe the worst, then the best thing might happen. He might be a prisoner of war.'

Diane put out her cigarette and patted her hand. 'Chin up, dear friend.'

Diane had a way of looking at her at times as though she was cooking up something. Meg eyed her quizzically. 'I get the feeling you're planning something.'

'How about we go to the beach this afternoon?'

Meg wasn't keen but Diane had been kind. Her response was only slightly non-committal. 'Do you have one without barbed wire stretched across it?'

'Of course we do. A very small hidden cove that only the locals know about. There should be other children there. You don't have to. I just

186

thought it might help.'

They took a picnic with them and chatted excitedly, ensuring Lily was included in the conversation, talking to her as though she was as excited as they were and was answering lucidly. In fact, she made little response, but Meg was determined. She'd even made her wear her swimming costume beneath her candy-striped dress, just in case the gentle lap of waves on the shore enticed her into the water. At least it was something other than drawing those terrible memories in red and black.

They took deckchairs, bundling them into the boot of Diane's small Morris along with towels and sun hats, even though the sun wasn't too strong today and the breeze was likely to lift them skyward.

The salty smell of the sea rose up to them from the cove below, the secret place only approached by a narrow and very steep pathway of stone and clay and bits of wood forming makeshift steps. Meg gazed at the shimmering water, thinking how beautiful it was and yet how deadly. It was more than likely that Ray's plane had ditched into the sea. He might very well be buried beneath its crystal surface.

Lost in her thoughts, it was a few minutes before she realised that Diane was standing at her side.

'I know what you're thinking,' Diane murmured. 'As I have already said, they presume Ray to be dead, but it doesn't mean that he is. You have to believe that.'

Meg's response was uncharacteristically abrupt. 'I'm not a fool living on false hope, Diane. There's been no word. If he is still alive there would have been. I have to cope with the here and now. I have Lily to think of.'

Diane watched her old friend take hold of Lily's hand and begin the descent to the beach. On the surface, Meg appeared to be coping well, but they were old friends. Diane knew that inside, Meg was only barely holding on.

'You'd hardly believe there was a war on,' Meg remarked once they'd set up the deckchairs and opened the hamper.

'I know,' said Diane. 'Not a bit of barbed wire in sight, the reason being that small beaches like this are not thought a feasible option for invading armies that count their numbers in thousands. Instead we are experiencing an invasion of evacuees from London. Just look at them all.'

Meg heard the raucous voices of East End evacuees, delighted as they ran in and out of the waves or built castles close to the shoreline where the water could fill the moats they'd dug around their creations.

'I should have sent Lily to you,' she said softly. 'I was being selfish keeping her in London.'

Diane squeezed her arm. 'You couldn't see into the future. You weren't to know what would happen.'

Meg bit her bottom lip. 'I haven't told her about Ray. I don't want to upset her. Perhaps I should, you know, get it over with.'

Diane sighed. 'Leave it be for now. You'll know when the time's right.'

Their gaze was suddenly drawn to the slight figure heading for the sea. Lily did not look to left

188

or right as she walked straight through a half-built sandcastle.

The boy who had built the castle jumped to his feet, bucket in one hand, spade in the other. 'Hey! Look what you've done to my sandcastle! Are you stupid or something?'

Not content with shouting at her, he ran over and gave her a big push, sending her sprawling into the water. Lily lay there, staring up at him but not crying, not showing any sign that she'd noticed the sandcastle or heard the tousle-haired boy who'd shouted at her.

Meg had heard and got up so quickly the deckchair collapsed. 'That little girl is not well and I'll thank you not to speak to her like that!'

The boy poked his tongue out when her shadow fell over him. 'Stupid, stupid. Na-na-ne-na-nah!'

Meg slapped his face. 'Call that child stupid again and I'll pick you up and throw you into the sea! Do you hear me?'

Surprised and wailing, the boy ran to a plump lady sitting on a rock, her old-fashioned hat shading her face from the sun as she knitted plain and purl on a set of clicking needles, her stockings rolled down around her ankles. On hearing what the young lad had to say, her face crumpled like a deflated beach ball. Holding on to him for assistance, she struggled to her feet.

By now Meg had gathered the soaking-wet Lily to her breast, anger still written over her face as the big woman with the knitting came striding across, her fat arms swinging at her sides.

Diane got to her first. Meg couldn't hear what was said but could guess. Her friend was explain-

189

ing the reason for both Lily's and her own behaviour. Even at this distance, Meg could see the woman's frown and fairly cringed at the sound of a heavy hand smacking the lad's other cheek.

'I explained everything,' said Diane, striding back in her forthright manner. She glanced up at the sky. 'Now come on. We'd better get home before it rains. Have to say, though, Meg, I never knew you had it in you. Slapping that kid like that. You were always so peace-loving. You're becoming quite grouchy – understandable, of course. Still, you did surprise me.'

'There's a war on,' Meg said bitterly.

In the car on the way back, Diane dared again to broach the subject of the change she'd perceived in Meg's behaviour. 'You can't take it out on the rest of the world, my dear. They were not responsible for what happened.'

'I know that,' Meg responded sharply. 'I was responsible. I should have gone to the shelter. That's why I'm so bloody angry!'

CHAPTER THIRTEEN

Ten days later Meg and Lily left Cornwall and made their way back to Upper Standwick. The return journey was just as lengthy and tiring as the one down. First, they'd had to get to Bristol and then a branch-line train to Upper Standwick. Thankfully Lily had no nightmares but looked out of the window the whole way. The

190

only train that would call that day pulled in at Upper Standwick halt and they got off.

Meg eyed the squat-fronted cottage with some misgiving. Somewhere in the distance came the sound of a tractor and the shouts and laughter of land girls helping to bring in the harvest. When the tractor wasn't running they sang popular songs at the tops of their voices, mainly about how much they were missing their sweethearts. The words numbed her heart as the truth hit her. They might get to see their sweethearts once more, but she would not. Ray was gone.

The cottage threw its shadow over the front garden where bees buzzed among the rampant flower growth, wildflowers growing among knotted rosebushes and sweet scented stock. Despite its chocolate box exterior, Bluebell Cottage was an unknown quantity. It did not feel like coming home. Meg couldn't imagine it ever feeling like home.

The sundry brown envelopes waiting on the doormat in the hallway were pounced on, ripped open with enthusiasm and then discarded with dismay. There was no news. Thanks to Diane's positive input, Meg had entertained the hope that Ray might have been taken prisoner and a letter to that effect would be there when she got back. On the return journey to Bluebell Cottage she dared to dream that Ray would be waiting for her, alive, in the flesh, not dead at all. If he were a prisoner of war he would still be alive. Or perhaps somebody was mistaken and he was merely missing in action. Anything was better than never seeing him again.

191

There was nothing here to reassure her.

The sun outside glared with summer intensity. Lily was in bed with a slight cold and Meg had ordered her to stay there: 'Here's some warm milk. Drink it down now.' The warm milk had done the trick. Lily was sound asleep.

A cup of tea would be nice, she thought to herself, but might as well do the washing up first. As she did, a knock sounded from the front door. Wiping her hands on a tea towel, she opened it to see Mrs Dando who lived in the cottage opposite on the other side of the village green. She was holding the leash of a large Alsatian dog.

In no mood for neighbourly chats, Meg looked from one to the other and asked what it was she wanted.

Mrs Dando's crumpled face lit up. 'I brought you your dog. The RAF left it with me.'

Meg frowned. 'I don't have a dog.'

'It was your husband's dog,' Mrs Dando said brightly. 'The young RAF man who brought him said he belonged to your husband. I explained you were away and he asked if I could look after the dog until you get back as he was due to go back on ops very shortly.'

Meg was horrified – and angry. How dare the RAF dump a dog on her after they'd given her such awful news about her husband! 'I don't want a dog. I have a sick child to contend with and that, Mrs Dando, is quite enough.'

Now it was Mrs Dando who looked horrified. 'But I can't give him a home.'

'Why not? You live alone, don't you?'

'Yes ... I mean, no. I have a son. He'll be home

soon and he doesn't like dogs. I can't have him.'

'I'm sorry. I don't want him.'

'But seeing as he's your husband's dog, he's your responsibility.'

'As I have already intimated, Mrs Dando, I have quite enough responsibility at the moment. I do not want a dog!'

Mrs Dando tutted. 'Oh, dear, oh dear. What's to be done? I can't possibly keep him. Surely you could take him in seeing as he was your husband's dog, I mean, out of the goodness of your heart...'

'Who said I had a heart? At this moment in time I seem to have misplaced my heart. It's the war. The war took my husband. I have to blame the war. Everyone does, don't they!'

The woman at the door adopted a pained expression and sighed in exasperation. 'Look, Mrs Malin, it's your husband's dog after all, and you know what the alternative is.'

'Mrs Dando,' Meg responded, 'thanks to this bloody war, my Ray's gone. Shot from the sky. And anyway, I didn't know the dog was his. I understood it belonged to the airbase and is their mascot. That's where it should be. I've got problems of my own without taking on a dog!'

Mrs Dando, a pillar of the village church, pursed her lips as her face reddened with embarrassment. 'The young man who brought him said it was your husband's wish that the dog live out his days with his family. If you don't take the dog, I'll have no alternative but to arrange for him to be put down.'

Meg winced before directing a hateful glare at the Alsatian, as though it were the one who had shot her husband down. She reminded herself of the other name for an Alsatian: a German Shepherd. His origins were based in enemy territory.

The dog wagged its tail hesitantly, gazing at her with pleading in his brown limpid eyes as though he understood everything being said.

A plaintive expression on her pink face, Mrs Dando stroked the animal's head. 'He's such a lovely dog. It would be such a shame to have to put him down. Such a waste.' Her voice was sweet but it grated on Meg, who was in no mood to be placated.

'It's no good playing the sympathy card with me, Mrs Dando. If you don't want to put him down, you give him a home.'

Mrs Dando looked taken aback. For a moment she stammered to find a suitable excuse for not taking him.

'I can't. My son ... he won't ... and I ... I can't really have him because...' There followed a big pause. 'I'm thinking of moving to London to my daughter's. She only has a flat. There's no room for a dog. Anyway, he's an extra mouth to feed. I have to put my own family first.'

Meg pointed an accusing finger. 'Yes! So do I. And there you have it!'

The door slammed shut.

Left standing on the doorstep, Ivy Dando's generous breast heaved in an almighty sigh. 'Oh well,' she said, looking down into the dog's soulful eyes. 'I suppose I'd better take you back home – at least for now.' She couldn't be sure but she fancied the dog looked quite disappointed at not being able to live at Bluebell Cottage. 'I know it's

194

disappointing, but you never know, she might change her mind. Let's hope she does, shall we?'

As though in agreement, the dog gave a little whine.

Heaving another heartfelt sigh, she bustled back across the village green to her cottage, the warm little room and the kettle hanging from its trivet, waiting for her firm hand to swing it back on to the range. The dog kept pace with her, every so often glancing up as though awaiting any better idea she might have.

In Ivy Dando's opinion, taking tea was best done in company and the sight of one teacup and saucer sitting on the table never failed to sadden her. She'd done quite a lot of social tea drinking in the days when her husband was still alive, in the full knowledge that somebody was sure to come in at the exact moment she put the kettle on. She'd got out the biscuits or a home-made cake and they'd sit down with a cuppa and discuss the events of the day, and gossip about whatever was going on in the village.

Ivy sighed at the memory. Things were so different since Alf had passed over. It wasn't often now that she had somebody to talk to, and even though her current companion was only a dog, she began talking to him.

'Rudy,' she said, for that was the dog's name according to the young man who'd brought him, 'I've a confession to make. Today I told a lie. That was very bad of me. My father used to say better a thief than a liar. He was a vicar and held that telling lies was the devil's work. I never used to lie, but today I did. The fact is, Rudy, I don't have

195

a daughter.' Her expression saddened, the corners of her eyes and mouth downturned. 'I wish I did.' She almost sobbed but held back. 'Someone to care for. Someone to care for me.'

A floorboard creaked overhead. Ivy's teacup rattled in its saucer. She looked up at the ceiling, fear squeezing her chest. 'God give me strength,' she whispered in a faltering voice.

The dog sat upright, his head held high, ears erect. He was looking up at the ceiling too and growling. Ivy tried to draw his attention with a biscuit. 'Take no notice, Rudy. It's my son, Bert. He's probably wanting some food.' She frowned worriedly. 'I suppose I'd better take something up to him. We certainly don't want him coming downstairs and discovering you, do we?'

Ivy's face was tight with concern. Upstairs was trouble. Her son, Bert, had reappeared a few days ago climbing through the back window and hiding up in the attic when she was out with the dog. So far she'd kept the dog and her son apart. He'd come home so unexpectedly – in trouble again. As usual he'd bullied her into doing what he wanted.

'I'm hiding out here, right? And don't go telling anyone I'm here. Get it?'

She shivered at the thought of his bony fingers tightening on her arm as he shook her. Alf had also had bony fingers, but his had been sensitive and he'd never shook her or done her harm. Her son's fingers were cruel and she was sure he enjoyed hurting her. Bruises already dotted her upper arms and he'd only been back a few days.

Her own fault to some extent; as a child she'd

196

spoiled him. Alf had remonstrated with her that the lad would turn out bad. He had always been firm with Bert but once he was gone there was no one to curb her son's selfish violence. She'd been powerless to stop him.

Closing her eyes, she fantasised about packing her bag and not telling him where she was going, simply leaving him to find himself all alone. But there, it was only a fantasy. She was too old to run. She had to face him.

Ivy looked at the dog. She was no expert but could see he had a lovely nature. Bert wouldn't like the dog being here. What was she to do? Initially the young RAF officer had taken the dog round to Mrs Malin's cottage, but when nobody answered he happened to see her trimming her hedge and came over to introduce himself and his business. Ivy had shaken her head in bewilderment. She should have been firm and told the young man to take the dog back to wherever he'd come from, but when he'd told her that Meg's husband had been killed in action, she couldn't bring herself to do it.

Oh well, she thought. Better sort something out for his supper.

Her hands trembled. Flexing her fingers didn't help. Rudy could sense fear. She hoped he couldn't see how nervous she was, how often she glanced over her shoulder at the narrow stairs winding upwards to the first floor and the other set that led up into the loft.

Bert had always hated dogs. He'd told her to get rid of Chum, her pet terrier. He'd called it a mangy, flea-ridden mongrel. Luckily for them both, Chum had died of old age before Bert could insist she had him put down. The last thing he would want was for her to take in a dog belonging to somebody else. He won't be here for long, she told herself. Given time, Mrs Malin would reconsider and be pleased to have a memento of her missing husband.

She recalled the RAF officer standing there looking too young to even have left school, let alone fly around in aircraft. He'd seemed such a happy chap, the sort she would have welcomed as a son and totally at odds with the one she had.

Oh well. There it was. The deed was done. She'd always been a soft touch. Bert knew that, hence his sudden return home. She had no doubt he was hiding from whatever trouble he'd made for himself in London but hadn't dared asked what it was. Anyway, he'd only lie.

She thought again of the young airman and smiled. If only she'd had a son like that, so polite as he told her about Ray being killed and how the dog had come into his ownership in the first place. 'Ray found him in France,' the young man told her once he was in the house with a cup of tea and a slice of home-made cake in front of him. 'The name's Rudy.'

'Your name's Rudy?' she'd asked, her round face bright with innocence, which seemed so funny now. She'd been rewarded with a fresh-faced smile.

'No. I'm Stan Crawford. I was one of Ray's crew.' His smile had cracked suddenly. 'I wasn't with him on the last mission. Lucky for me. Bad luck for Ray.'

198

Hearing him speak of Mrs Malin's husband, Ivy had been convinced that Meg would welcome the animal and so it would be gone before her son Bert found out and went into one of his rages. He didn't often come down from the attic, but when he did there was usually hell to pay. Ivy had crumbled. *I expect the poor woman will appreciate something that used to belong to her husband,* she had told herself. Reaching for the socks she was darning, Ivy sighed. 'The trouble is, you've always been a romantic, Ivy Dando.'

At six on the dot, a thudding sounded from upstairs. Bert wanted his supper. Placing the darning to one side, Ivy went into the kitchen to prepare his meal. The contents of her larder looked in dire need of replenishing. There was cheese, some liver, two pigs' trotters and some brawn she'd pressed from a pig's head. The trotters were already cooked and mired in jelly. A few potatoes and that would serve for Bert's supper. For herself it would have to be bread and cheese. The supplies in her cupboard had to last a few more days because she didn't have Bert's ration card. Her ration card had to serve them both. On top of that she had Rudy to consider. The dog had to be fed.

Placing everything in a large pudding bowl, she placed it on a tray and took the lot upstairs, leaving it on a small table on the landing. The hatch leading into the attic opened and the ladder came down, barely missing her head. Bert's face appeared, jaw slack, his hair slick with Brylcreem and a hard, bearlike look in his small eyes. 'About bloody time!'

199

He slid down the ladder without using the rungs, bouncing on to the landing beside the table where she'd placed his supper tray. Bert's bottom lip curled with distaste as he eyed the meal she'd brought him. He poked his finger into the jelly that still clung to the heel of the pig.

'What ... the ... bloody ... hell's ... that?' Each word was accompanied by a poke at the food.

Ivy trembled. 'I can't afford much with just my rations, Bert,' she said apologetically. 'I can't very well go along with your ration card as well now, can I?'

Bert's jaw stiffened and a savage darkness came to his eyes. 'Ain't much of a meal. Not enough to feed a bleedin' sparrow. Was that the best you could do? A couple of pigs' trotters?'

'It's all I've got.'

Ivy braced herself for a pinch or a punch – it could be either.

'Never mind. If I'm still hungry I'll be down for a bit of bread and cheese. You 'ave got that, 'ave ya?'

'Yes,' she replied, reluctantly accepting that tonight she would have to go without, though she might chance a sliver of brawn. There was still the dog to consider.

'Have you emptied the jerry?'

She nodded and placed a clean chamber pot in front of him. Three times a day she had to do that.

'Can't chance going down to the lavvy can I?'

'Right. If you're all right there, I'll go and get myself a piece of toast,' she said, just about keeping the fear from her voice. She tuned as quickly

200

as her old pins would allow, leaving him sitting there on the landing gobbling down his food.

Upset by his uncaring attitude, her hunger passed so she didn't bother with toast and the bread and cheese remained in the pantry. At first she went back to darning his socks and, after that was done, stood at the kitchen door, opening it a fraction so she could hear the cutlery rattling on to his plate accompanied by a loud burp. Once she was certain he'd finished, she crept back up to fetch what he'd left – mostly bones except for a tougher bit of fat and skin.

That night, after she'd fed the dog on the bony remains of the trotters and the head from which she'd made the brawn, she spread out an old eiderdown for Rudy to sleep on, then made a cup of cocoa for herself and went thankfully to bed. Time enough to deal with the dog in the morning. Everything would look better in the morning.

The dog would have to go back to where he came from, though his prospects filled her with trepidation. She'd heard rumours that old war dogs, once they'd served their time, were put down, a terrible waste in her opinion. In this case it seemed inevitable. Despite his breeding, which at one time might have scared her, he seemed a well-behaved, intelligent animal who obeyed every command she had given him.

The only thing that unnerved her was the way he kept looking up at the ceiling. Even though Bert's tread was light without shoes on, the dog was aware that somebody was up there. She'd warned him not to make a sound. Bert mustn't know he was here. So far the dog had obeyed.

201

'Oh well,' she murmured. 'There's nothing more you can do.'

Since the dog's arrival she'd made a habit of firmly shutting the door to her living room, which she fondly called her front parlour, when she went up to bed at night. Tonight, however, because she was suffering from a pain in her chest, she didn't close it as firmly as she usually did. Without her noticing, it sprung open, leaving a gap big enough for Rudy to squeeze through.

The pain in her chest had started just after lunchtime and was still with her, though more intense. Indigestion! And nerves, of course. That's all it was; she'd always suffered from it. A good night's rest would see her all right.

Settling herself comfortably in bed and drinking her cocoa, she reached for a book with her left hand. She'd been looking forward to getting to bed and reading this book all day. Reading helped her escape the reality of her life. In a book she was a lady in distress and there was always a white knight on the horizon to rescue her. In real life there was not.

As she opened the book, a spasm of pain speared through her chest. She cried out, retracting her arm, the book falling to the floor along with the mug of cocoa, its dregs staining the bedside rug.

Even before she heard the creaking of the attic stairs, she knew her son was on his way down. He'd complained about his supper; said it wasn't enough to feed a sparrow. He'd be after his bread and cheese and she'd have to go downstairs to get it for him. He mustn't go down. He mustn't see Rudy.

Ivy sat very still, hands folded one on top of the other over her pounding heart. The doctor had told her that her heart was not as strong as it used to be. She'd always suffered palpitations. That's what she told herself this was, except she'd never experienced such pain before.

Bert ducked beneath the lintel as he pushed the door open. He had the same black hair and eyes of his father, a sallow complexion and narrow shoulders. He wore a grim expression, the corners of his mouth downturned, his bottom lip pouting in the same way it had as a boy.

'Put that bloody book down and go and get me some bread and cheese. Or is it me got to do it? Eh? Sat there reading trashy novels...'

Ivy attempted to push back the covers but couldn't, her hand grasping at her heart. He used to shout at her in the past, but now kept his voice down in case somebody might hear him. The angry shouting had scared her, but this low menacing tone was more frightening. Ivy gasped as she tried to get out of bed, the pain in her chest worsening, every breath feeling as though a knife was stabbing her heart.

'I've got a pain,' she said, laying her hand on her chest.

Bert was unmoved.

'Never mind lying there as though yer dying, go and get me more food. Get out of that bed and down into that bloody kitchen! Come on. At the double! Get me some grub.'

Seeing that she still hadn't thrown back the bedclothes, Bert did it for her, dragging them roughly away. Ivy winced and cried out. 'No,

Bert! Don't do that! I'm in pain. Terrible pain!'

A movement close to the bedroom door caught her eye. Bert turned round. The dog stood four square between the bedroom door and him. A deep growl rumbled from his throat. Its jaws stayed closed. Taken totally by surprise, Bert looked from the dog to his mother. Surprise, fear and anger took it in turns to mould his expression. Once he'd gathered his wits, he pointed a nicotine-stained finger. 'What the bloody hell is that?'

Panic surfed madly around Ivy's chest as she groped for excuses. The pain subsided long enough for her to speak, though she fought for each breath and each word pained her.

'He's not staying... He belongs to a neighbour...'

Her son's daunting presence loomed over her. 'Have you any idea what you've done, you stupid cow? He's got my scent now. He knows I'm here. Dogs don't forget and they're good at tracking people.'

'But who would...?'

'I don't care who might come after me. Could be from a number of quarters,' he said, his gaze nervously fixed on the dog. 'Get rid of him! Now!'

Ivy cringed and adopted her most pleading voice, which always came out as a pitiful whine in her son's presence. 'I can't get rid of him now. People will notice.'

'In case you ain't noticed, you silly old cow, there's a blackout. Nobody will see you.'

'I think they will, Bert. I did tell you we have an air-raid warden now... Reg Puller... You know Reg. Runs the greengrocers. He patrols the village all night long and always checks my front door in passing... I did tell you that, Bert, love... I did.'

'Another nosy old bugger!'

'I wouldn't say that, son. He just likes to make sure I'm all right.'

Bert grimaced, his eyes like coal as his glare met the more measured look of the dog. 'I don't like dogs. You know I don't like dogs.'

'I know, I know. I'll go to the police. John Carter will help find him a home.'

'Carter?' Bert's voice tightened. The very mention of the village policeman unnerved him.

'I'm sure he will.'

He grabbed her bare arm where the yellowing bruises lingered from his last onslaught. 'You'll say nothing about me being here. Got it? Nothing at all.'

Ivy winced and her eyes began to water. 'Bert, you're hurting me.'

'I'll hurt you a lot more if you don't get rid of that bloody dog! Hear me?'

'Son! Please,' she whined, her hand still flat to her chest. 'I've already got a terrible pain in my chest... Something I ate, I suppose.'

Bert grinned. 'It probably was something you ate if you had the same slop you served me.'

Ivy eased herself towards the edge of the bed, every inch causing her severe pain. 'I'll get you some bread and cheese.'

'In a minute. Now listen carefully: you do as I say. The dog goes in the morning. I don't care where, just so long as he ain't here. Right?'

The pressure of his fingers digging into her arm was unbearable. More bruises would be there in the morning. 'I'll get John Carter to collect him...'

205

'You'll do no bloody such thing! Do you want to get me arrested? I don't want any nosy parker neighbour here. You take the dog to him. You take the dog to anyone who'll have him. Got that?' His eyes bulged. He clenched his jaw, spitting the words out in rapid succession through closed teeth. 'Now get me something to eat.'

'Bert, I...'

His expression darkened. He hated it when people – even his mother – didn't obey him. Well, he would damn well make her – just as he'd done a few others in his time.

'Do ... as ... I ... say!' Cupping her face, he banged her head against the wall, not once but three times, just to ensure his message was getting through.

The dog watched. He did not understand these humans, some of whom could so easily harm the weak and helpless, while others had shown him only kindness. He recognised in this man the same cruelty he'd witnessed in the guard he'd toppled into the pit some time ago, on the night he'd befriended the little girl.

Ears laid flat on his head, he let out a warning growl.

Too absorbed inflicting pain on his own mother, Bert failed to heed the warning. Just as he was about to bang his mother's head on the wall for a fourth time, the dog's jaws clamped around his calf. Roaring with pain, he staggered backwards, tried to turn round, but the dog's jaws held him tightly.

'Look! Look, you stupid bitch! This is all your fault.'

He shook his leg in an attempt to dislodge the dog's jaws. The dog held on. Out of his mind with pain and shock, he lunged for his mother but got nowhere. The dog held on grimly. Paw by paw he was moving backwards, dragging Bert towards the door.

Bert was beside himself. 'He bit me! He won't let go! I'm bleeding!'

He put more vigour into shaking his leg, but Rudy wouldn't let go. In Bert's warped mind the blame lay with his mother. He glared at her, wanting to hurt her as much as the dog was hurting him.

'You stupid—'

Unable to reach the dog, he made a huge lunge towards her, raising his hand so he could hit her again. He'd reckoned without Rudy. The dog jerked him away, his jaws clamped firmly around his calf, its teeth slicing through skin and flesh, grating on bone.

Ivy screamed. The pain in her chest was worse now. All she could do was scream. She had no breath left for shouting.

Afraid that the air-raid warden might be passing and hear the commotion, Bert snarled at her to shut up. Having given up getting to her, he struggled his way to the door and out on to the landing, dragging the dog with him, jerking his leg, kicking out, trying everything and anything to shake the dog off.

Somehow he manoeuvred himself between the dog and the bedroom door where he put all his energy into one last effort, one almighty kick. The dog yelped and let go. Bert backed out of the room, heading for the ladder and the safety of the attic.

Although Bert was a cowardly bully, he wasn't stupid. Taking the rungs two at a time, he climbed up the ladder to the trapdoor. With luck, the dog wasn't capable of climbing a ladder. The thought cheered him until he glanced over his shoulder.

The damned creature managed the first three rungs and might have climbed higher, but Bert moved quickly. As he pulled the ladder up behind him, the dog lost its footing, tumbling backwards on to the landing. Bouncing back on to its four legs, the dog growled up at him, its open jaws and angry expression only disappearing once Bert had shut the trapdoor behind him.

Alone in his hiding place, Bert worked quickly, examining his bloodied calf, ripping up pillow-cases to bind the flesh back to the bone. The bleeding was heavy and made him feel sick. He probably needed a doctor, but there was no way he could chance doing that. Nobody must know he was here. There were people in London look-ing for him. If they found him, he'd bleed a lot more than he was at present. He'd be dead meat.

'Pull yerself together,' he muttered, wincing as the pain bit in. He wasn't the best educated of men, but he knew his main problem would be infection. He only hoped the dog wasn't suffering from rabies. People died from rabies. Or went mad. He didn't want to do either of them.

Closing his eyes, he rested his head against the wall. Sweat beaded his face and forehead, his chest rising and falling swiftly with his rasping breath. He needed a smoke. His hand shook as he reached for a cigarette. Luckily his mother had got a good stock of fags in. She'd told everyone in the village that her nerves were on edge since the beginning of the war and that was why she'd suddenly taken up smoking. Nobody would suspect that Bert Dando was back, hiding in the attic.

He thought he heard his mother cry out, but he couldn't tell exactly what she was saying – it could have been help. Now why would she cry out for help?

He grimaced into the spiral of cigarette smoke. Never mind his mother calling out for help, what about him? His leg was painful thanks to the filthy cur that had bitten him. Well, if she thought he was going back downstairs just to check on her, she was very sadly mistaken! He would stay up here and take care of himself, no harm done. It was nothing that couldn't be avenged and he would certainly do that. In fact, he'd take pleasure in it. He had the time to do it. He'd be here for a while.

Bert considered himself a clever sod in that he'd avoided being called up to serve his country. Let somebody else do it. Let the toffs do their own fighting. Bert was all for himself. He'd always looked after number one, seeking opportunities to feather his nest without too much effort on his part, such as going out and getting a job. Ducking and diving, that was the way he lived. Nick a bit, spend a bit, then nick a bit more.

At first he'd looked on the war with dismay, loathing the thought of putting on a uniform and going off to fight. It had nothing to do with him! Then the shortages began. Luckily he'd left the village some years before the outbreak of war and gone to the nearest city. Bath was an old city and, as far as he was concerned, not big enough for his grandiose ideas of getting rich with as little effort as possible. Anyway, the scale of his thieving reached the ears of the local plods. Crime was noticed in a small city and it wasn't so easy to hide. He'd realised then that he needed to be where the real action was, in a big city where criminals could melt into the background. London. That was the place where he would make his fortune – just like that bloke Dick Whittington in the pantomime he'd seen as a boy with his mother.

He couldn't believe his luck when he got to London. Riches were there for the taking and with so little effort. Avoiding local gangs, he'd set up by himself, doing the same as they did, looting houses of anything valuable while the residents of leafy suburbs, stocky terraces or handsome Chelsea flats were hiding in their cellars, shelters or Underground stations. To him, the falling bombs were a gift from heaven, not Hitler. He'd thrown back his head and laughed at them, until he'd fallen foul of a London gang, looting a house belonging to the mother of a gangland villain.

Shortly after that he'd only barely escaped the law after he'd once again avoided being called up at his London address. Loot was piled high floor to ceiling at that flat and it had grieved him to leave it all behind, but what with the London gangsters and the police, he knew it was time to lie low for a while. And where better to lie low than with his old mum in a sleepy little village where crime was centred around poaching or digging up a few spuds from a farmer's field. Also in his favour was the fact that he was only known as living at a London address. Even his call-up papers had gone there once the authorities were informed. The old lags in London knew nothing of this address. He was safe enough here, though he didn't dare show himself in the village – just in case.

He swore as he examined his leg wound. The dog's teeth had sunk deep into his flesh. There was a lot of blood. He wondered how much of a trail he'd left behind. Never mind, his dear old mum would clean it up and she'd kick the dog out. Not physically, of course. She wasn't capable of being cruel to anyone. But he was. He most certainly was. Everything would go back to normal. Nothing would have changed. He would be safe. Nobody would find him.

He didn't know anything had changed until he saw old Doctor Fudge puffing his way up the garden path accompanied by Reg Puller, the air-raid warden. He couldn't hear what was being said but assumed Reg had called to see if his mother was all right. Probably had a fall, he thought to himself, and got Reg to call the doctor. He frowned when he espied the front wheel of a bicycle sticking out from the other side of the front hedge. So PC John Carter, the village policeman, was also downstairs. Somehow he guessed it wasn't about the dog.

It didn't occur to him that something really bad had happened to his mother until the undertaker arrived from Hinton Charterhouse, a nearby

211

village, and he found himself looking down at two blokes manhandling a coffin up the garden path and in through the front door. His mother was dead?

Shocked that things had taken such a surprising turn, Bert eased himself back from the small dormer window just in case somebody might look up at the swallows' nest hanging beneath the eaves and see him. He needed to take it all in. He needed to think what he would do next.

I'll be safe, he said to himself, and he certainly wouldn't be going to his mother's funeral. *The old woman's gone and it's now my house. The village won't know where I am but will respect this place until my 'return'. It was my dad's place, after all.* He shed no tears for his mother's passing but was put out that she'd chosen such an inopportune moment. He'd needed her to feed and look after him, to get his cigarettes from the village store or on her monthly trip to the city.

He winced as he put his weight on to his leg. It would be some time before the pain was gone. That sodding dog! In his twisted mind, the dog was to blame for everything and, as he would for anyone else who upset him, he would plan to get even.

He slept for the rest of the day, but that night, disturbed by the pain in his leg, he thought through his priorities. First off, he had to plan his survival very carefully. Things might be a bit different now and, heaven forbid, he might have to do a few things for himself. Stealing cigarettes from the village store was top of his list, though eventually, once things had cooled down, he would make his way back to London.

In the meantime he would sit tight. The cottage would creak in the stillness and remain unoccupied until his mother's will was sorted out. Her memory would be respected and nobody would trespass until they had located him, Bert Dando, her one and only son. Not that they would find him, of course, though they'd be a while trying. He'd covered his tracks well and the shabby basement flat in London would be empty of stolen goods by now. It was also likely that somebody else was in residence.

Lie low and keep yer head down, he said to himself. *A walk in the park.* He took out another Woodbine and shoved it in the corner of his mouth. It wouldn't be easy, but somehow he had to manage.

CHAPTER FOURTEEN

The day before she'd died, it was Mrs Dando standing at Meg Malin's front door with the dog from the RAF base; now it was PC Carter. Some men grow up from boys into men, their faces bearing no resemblance to the happy chaps they'd once been. John Carter was an exception. He had fair hair, blue eyes and a dimple in his chin, plus a scattering of freckles over the bridge of his nose. His eyelashes were dark and totally at odds with the rest of his colouring. It was these that Meg noticed first, that and a persuasive expression halfway to a smile. She wondered why

213

he wasn't in the armed forces.

'I take it you've heard about Mrs Dando?'

Meg nodded. 'Yes. I heard.' She glanced down at the dog. 'And I know what you're going to say,' she said through gritted teeth. 'Allow me to put you straight here and now. I've got too much on my plate with my Lily to bother with a dog.'

PC Carter didn't waiver before her steadfast expression. He had a job to do, which was to attempt to persuade Mrs Malin to face up to her responsibilities. 'Mrs Dando told me the day before yesterday that the dog belonged to your husband and was apparently brought here by a young RAF chap. I understand you were away at the time.'

'Yes. I was in Cornwall when he called.'

PC Carter adopted a pained expression. 'I understand you not wanting the dog, but I doubt anyone else round here would want him either – things being the way they are, and seeing as he belonged to your husband, it seems to me–'

'I thought he belonged to the RAF. Surely he'd be of more use to them than to me? I understand the military are asking for dogs that can be of service in England's hour of need.' The statement was delivered in a bitter tone. The nation had taken her husband and now they wanted to land her with a dog she didn't want.

PC Carter shook his head. 'I wouldn't know, Mrs Malin. I only know what I was told by Mrs Dando, God bless her soul. It was a heart attack, you know.'

'So I hear.'

The village policeman paused. She knew he was

giving her time to reconsider, but she wasn't going to. Her mind was made up. She felt exasperated. Why was it this dog kept ending up on her doorstep when it was clear she did not want him?

Meg shook her head vehemently. 'I don't want him! I can't! I've a very sick little girl to deal with. I do not have room or the patience for a dog.'

PC Carter poked at the peak of his helmet and shook his head disconsolately. 'Well, let's give it a bit of time, shall we? Let's see what can be done. I'll take care of him until you've had time to make up your mind or another offer turns up. Shall we do that? At least until after the funeral?'

Meg bit her lip. Constable John Carter had such an open, trusting face and happy disposition, and wanted everyone else to be as happy as he was – as though a whole village could be completely happy all the time. A little unrealistic in her opinion but it wouldn't hurt to agree.

'If you don't mind.'

'Of course I don't mind. How are you settling in?'

She shrugged. 'Well enough. It's very different from London.'

'I should hope so. Some of your neighbours' families have lived here for centuries and are not always welcoming to outsiders. The war has changed all that – especially the evacuees,' he added with a laugh. 'Little scamps, some of them.' There was kindness in his eyes when he smiled.

'I imagine so. It's very kind of people to take them in.'

'I take it you'll be going to Mrs Dando's funeral.'

215

'I didn't know her very well.'

The policeman looked taken aback. 'That don't matter. You live in the village and it's traditional that everyone goes to a neighbour's funeral. It's always been that way.'

'Then I suppose I'll be there,' said Meg.

In London you only went to the funerals of people you knew very well, mostly relatives. Still, she couldn't be mean and the policeman was still beaming at her while telling her there would be beer and sandwiches at the pub afterwards. 'The money for it was set aside in her will though even if it hadn't been, the village would have clubbed together.'

'When is Mrs Dando's daughter coming down?'

PC Carter looked surprised. 'Daughter? Mrs Dando didn't have a daughter. Only a son – a right wastrel if I recall. We're trying to find him to tell him his mother's passed over. He was last heard of living in London. Nobody's seen him since. Got a bit of a criminal record around here and up there. Certainly never deserved a mother like Ivy. And now he inherits the cottage. Don't seem fair somehow.'

'Oh. I must have been mistaken. I was sure she told me she had a daughter.'

'No. Definitely not.'

'I'm sorry for lumbering you with the dog, but I just can't...'

PC Carter waved his hand dismissively. He wouldn't tell her that one look at her and her wish was his command, but that was how he felt. 'Look. I can't promise and it might be that I can only keep him at the station house for a few days.

216

After that … well... I'll have to make other arrangements.'

Meg cringed at the thought of what 'other arrangements' might be but she'd made a decision and at least for now she was sticking to it. She didn't want a dog. She wanted Ray.

'I would appreciate that.'

He lingered, eyeing her with a mix of personal interest and sympathetic concern. 'I'm sorry about your husband, Mrs Malin. It's a shame after losing your house in London. I can only offer my sympathy and hope you do decide to settle here permanently once the war is over. It's not a bad place. Cosy and friendly. P'raps in time you'll grow to love it.'

She knew he was only trying to be friendly and it wasn't in her nature to be so testy. Losing Ray had changed a number of things in her life, the most surprising of which was her reluctance to be too friendly with anyone. It would be some time before she allowed anyone to break through the barrier she'd erected around herself since arriving in the village.

'You'll find it a lovely village,' he said to her before swinging his leg over his bicycle saddle and bidding her goodbye.

'I can see it is,' she responded, though without any genuine enthusiasm.

Upper Standwick was a village where little had changed in centuries. Thatched cottages huddled around a Saxon church that was said to have been built by Edgar the Peaceful, the grandfather of Edward the Confessor. The village store sold everything from buckets to beans. A red pillar box

217

stood sentry on the pavement alongside a red telephone box. Locally grown vegetables and fruit were displayed in wooden packing cases outside. So were cabbage and carrot seedlings in case you preferred to grow your own. But although the village was idyllic and peaceful, except for the drone of aircraft from the American airbase close by, Lily did not respond as Meg had hoped she would.

Once the policeman had gone, Meg stood in the middle of her living room shaking her head frenziedly and hugging herself. Her gaze stayed fixed on a fuzzy photograph of her husband proudly wearing his Royal Air Force uniform. Raymond had been the only man she'd loved. They'd met when he was eighteen and she was sixteen, and had been inseparable ever since. She'd never foreseen losing him like this. Like having her house bombed, such things only happened to other people. She'd never expected him to be shot down and still couldn't believe he was dead. Other people got killed, not the people she loved. Tears spilled from the corners of her eyes.

'I want you back, Raymond, not your bloody dog!' Her voice was a mixture of despair and anger. He had mentioned the dog in his letters. With what was almost fatherly pride, he had also told her the dog warned them of enemy bombers heading for the airbase even before the sirens wailed.

Every night once Lily was in bed, she reread Ray's last letter. The village policeman had unsettled her, reopening the hurt she felt at losing her husband. She needed to hear his voice and the only way she could do that was by reading his words. As Lily scribbled away with her crayons, Meg took the letter from the old oak bureau sitting just in front of the window and read it again and again. He mentioned the dog's name was Rudy. She'd never really taken it in before.

Controlling her sobs she swiped at her tears, pasting on a smile that hinted at a happiness she did not feel. 'Would you like some lunch now, Lily?'

The little girl gave no sign that she'd heard her. Lily continued to live in her own private world. Of late she'd begun whispering to herself. Sometimes Meg fancied she was talking to somebody she could not see, an imagined friend with whom the child could confide. *Not me,* thought Meg, and it cut her deeply.

Meg forced a smile as she leaned over Lily's shoulder. As usual, she was drawing pictures with red and black crayons. The subject of the pictures was always the same: red flames sprouting skyward from blackened buildings.

'You're going to wear those two colours out. How about using pink and green for a change? You could draw some flowers like the pinks and carnations out in the garden?'

The little girl gave no response but carried on scribbling with the red and black crayons, which she dug fiercely into the paper until there was no blank whiteness; nothing except the redness of flames and the darkness of destruction.

Meg sucked in her bottom lip in an effort to hold back a threatening sob. Although she still held on to the hope that Lily would recover, it seemed a

219

long time coming. She was unchanged to how she had been in London, rarely speaking or playing with toys, never reading a book as she'd used to do. All she did was draw scenes of that night, the scenario playing out in her brain, again and again and again.

Meg told Lily to put her things away. 'It's lunchtime.'

Lily never made a sound. Never made a move but sat there like stone.

Meg sighed. 'I'll help you put your things away...'

Her hands paused. The pictures were different. Still red and black but not a fire. Not a building. Rather, a pyramid of bodies, black as night, each one outlined in red. Another depicted a train, the carriages completely lacking windows. A third caused a cold shiver to shoot down her spine: an adult figure, legs akimbo, and a blob of red that looked like a baby.

CHAPTER FIFTEEN

Meg was one of the few people in the village not to dwell on the death of Mrs Dando, though it did strike her as strange that the old lady should lie about having a daughter in London. Was it just so Meg would take the dog? Probably. What other reason could there be?

It was Lily's first day at school. Concerned about how she'd react, Meg explained everything about the village school to her; the fact that there were only forty pupils and that she could take her time settling in. As usual, she got no response. If Lily was worried at all, it didn't show. Meg carried the worry for both of them. She couldn't help it.

'They said it was a heart attack,' said Alice Wickes, one of the young mothers Meg had seen around during the last couple of months since they'd moved into the village. They'd kept bumping into each other at the village store, which doubled as a post office. Meg wasn't interested in starting up a friendship but Alice was the sort who wasn't easily rebuffed. It was as though Meg was a challenge to be overcome. Meg was also from London and in Alice's eyes that somehow made her exotic.

'I'm sorry to hear that. I didn't know her very well, but she seemed a kind woman.'

'She was.'

Meg went on to tell her about the day she'd come to the door with the dog. 'She told me she had a daughter in London and was going to live with her. She said there wasn't enough room for the dog.'

Alice frowned. 'Ivy didn't have a daughter.' She giggled. 'Not unless there was a guilty secret from her youth, but I doubt it. She never left the village. There was only her son Bert and the further he stays away from here the better!'

Meg noted her attitude echoed that of PC John Carter. She couldn't be sure but she also thought Alice looked very uncomfortable at the mention of Bert Dando's name.

'I expect she said it purely to get me to take the dog.'

'Will you take him?'

Meg shook her head vehemently. 'Certainly not. I've got enough to cope with.'

'Of course you do.' Alice nodded in understanding. 'How's Lily?' she whispered, cupping her hand over her mouth and glancing at the silent little girl.

'About the same,' Meg pronounced through gritted teeth. She didn't like people continually asking after Lily's condition. Everyone in the village did it. Nosiness, she decided. They didn't really care. They were just nosy. She could imagine how the matter was discussed behind her back.

Poor little mite. Should have been evacuated. Now look at her. Lost her wits. Best for her to be in a place where they take care of kids like her...

It wasn't apparent that Alice noticed her discomfiture. 'Perhaps being at school will help,' she suggested. 'You know. All the other kids around her.'

Meg nodded stiffly. The suggestion had been made before. 'Perhaps.'

In her heart of hearts, she really hoped it would, but how was Lily going to learn anything if she refused to speak and only scribbled in black and red?

'Still, there's such a lot they can do nowadays...'

Meg didn't respond but squeezed the little girl's hand in an effort to reassure both of them. 'Your first day at a new school,' she directed at Lily. 'It looks very nice, don't you think?'

'How about we meet up soon with the kids?' suggested Alice. 'Your little girl needs to make friends around here and not just in school. What do you think?'

Meg had to admit it was a good idea and found herself gradually warming to Alice's open attitude. 'I think it would do her good.'

Alice nudged her with her elbow. 'I think it will do you good too.'

Meg felt the barrier she'd built round herself gradually falling down. She needed a friend and so did Lily. They had to get on with things and live again.

Lily continued to silently ogle the old village school with eyes as big as saucers. Beyond its iron gate a set of steep steps led upwards. To the left the arched windows of the main schoolroom looked out on to School Lane and the golden fields, shorn of their harvest, sloping down to the valley floor.

As this was her first day, Meg was allowed to take Lily to her classroom. She also had a chance to speak to the teacher and briefly outline the reason for Lily's odd behaviour.

'I'm hoping that making new friends at a new school will bring her out of herself.'

Miss Pringle, a colourless person as grey in face and hair as the clothes she wore, eyed Meg over the top of a pair of wire-framed spectacles. She appeared to listen but it was hard to tell whether she was sympathetic. Her long thin face showed no sign of emotion.

'We'll see about that,' she finally stated. 'I've been a teacher at this school for over thirty years. I do *know* quite a lot about difficult children.'

Her manner made Meg feel as though she were

a child. She felt herself colouring up.

Miss Pringle ordered one of the older girls to take Lily's hand and sit next to her. 'Cecily! You will be her monitor.'

It was a terrible wrench on Meg's part to leave Lily there. Once or twice she looked round, fancying she heard the little girl running after her, not wanting to be left in the care of strangers. Each time it was another little girl or boy, never Lily.

Feeling unsettled and unhappy, Meg made her way through the throng of chattering children. Bluebell Cottage was going to feel very empty without Lily being there during the day. *But I'll have time to clean the place from top to bottom*, she reminded herself. *Just as I did at Andover Avenue before Lily arrived.* At one time she would have looked forward to making her home sparkle, but that was then and this was now.

Once outside, Meg met up with Alice again. 'Will you be going to the funeral?' Alice asked.

'Mrs Dando's?'

'Who else?'

Meg thought of the woman who had come to her door and the dog reputed to have belonged to her husband, and she suddenly felt regret at the way she'd spoken to her. 'I hardly knew her. But I suppose I should.'

'She was kindly but a bit of a busybody. Still, nobody's perfect. The whole village will be there. That's how it is here. Christenings, weddings and funerals. The whole village turns out.'

And I'm certainly not perfect, Meg thought to herself. She began to wonder if leaving the poor old dear to look after her husband's dog might have contributed to Mrs Dando's demise.

Alice suddenly doubled over with laughter. 'Forgot to tell you. The dog escaped. That daft John Carter took him for a walk – the dog doing the walking and him riding his bicycle. The lead got tangled in the front wheel, John fell off and the dog ran away. Isn't that funny?'

Meg had to admit that it was. 'So where is it now?'

'It's hanging around the village. He said he'll capture it when he can, but seeing as it's got four legs, it runs faster than he does and the front wheel of his bicycle is bent. It seems a nice animal. Somebody should give it a home. Will you reconsider?'

Meg shook her head. 'I've Lily to think about.'

'He's not really daft,' Alice ventured suddenly. 'In fact, he's quite good-looking in a country boy kind of way.'

Meg knew she was talking about the village policeman and her stomach tightened. She knew very well where this was going. 'So why isn't he married?'

'Hasn't found the right girl. He's in his late thirties, you know.'

'I didn't know.' She felt Alice's eyes regarding her sidelong. 'Don't even think about it,' she snapped. 'I'm going to remain a widow for a very long time. Perhaps for life!'

'Sorry, I'm sure.' Alice took on a hurt look that wasn't repeated in her tone of voice. Although they barely knew each other, Meg had sensed from the first that she wasn't the type to be out of sorts for long.

'It sounds as though your husband was the love of your life,' Alice went on. 'Lucky you.'

'Yes,' said Meg. 'Lucky me.'

Yet she didn't feel lucky. She felt deflated and confused. There was no doubt in her mind that she and Ray had been physically compatible. Lovemaking was the one time when they'd been completely at one. But what about those other times when she was throwing all her energy into their home, doing all she could to encourage him to be just as enthusiastic? How close to that imagined idyll had their love truly been?

Overhead, a cloud blotted out the sun.

CHAPTER SIXTEEN

In his youth, before London and the prospect of greater fortune had called him away, Bert Dando had prowled the countryside at night, poaching from the river and the woods, and stealing the odd lamb for selling on to a crooked butcher in town. He was good at skulking in the darkness, a skill that would come in very handy in the days ahead. For a start he had to figure out a way to get more food now his mother was dead and the supplies in the larder were running out, and all the cigarettes nearly smoked. That would come later. Top of his list was avenging his mother's death – and his leg injury – on that bloody dog! Once he'd located it, that is.

The spectacle of PC Carter getting the dog's lead tangled around his front wheel had sent him into fits of laughter. It had been even funnier to see the village bobby running after it, finally panting to a standstill, hands resting on bent knees as the dog sped away.

The dog had not left the village. He'd seen it lurking around, people giving it scraps to eat. Stupid sods, the lot of them. Soft in the heart and soft in the head. The dog was a vagrant, not a pet. Couldn't be a pet seeing as it depended on peoples' kind hearts to keep it alive.

Bert Dando had never been famous for having a kind heart. Quite the opposite, in fact. The sooner that dog was disposed of, the better. Revenge simmered in him like a firework – light the blue touchpaper and stand well back. In time he would explode. In the meantime he studied the dog's habits, peering down at it from his attic room.

The dog slept under the bench next to the duck pond. Perhaps it hunted the paddling ducks. He couldn't tell. He didn't care. In time he might be hunting them himself if he didn't soon find some money and head for London. He'd searched every drawer and every china teapot for money. His mother had hidden it everywhere, some for food kept in the teapot, some for coal in a tin decorated with the heads of King George V and his wife, Queen Mary. It was something, though hardly enough. If all else failed, he'd have to hitch-hike his way to London – there were plenty of army trucks going that way. Hopefully his misdemeanour was forgotten, or those who would have his

227

guts were dead. He hoped for the latter.

Yep! His mind was made up.

'I'll get the better of that mangy hound yet,' he vowed, as he puffed on one of the few cigarettes he had left. The dog might be clever, but so was he. All he had to do was wait until the small hours when the village was asleep, and even the air-raid warden was tucked up snugly in his sandbagged bunker next to the village hall.

Supper was bread and cheese accompanied by a mug of cider drawn from the barrel kept in the scullery. There was always a barrel of cider in the scullery and another in the outhouse. His father had drunk cider and so did he. 'Cider gives you courage,' his old man had said. Not that his father had seemed to have much of that. He'd been a soft touch, even though he'd tried to keep Bert in line when his mother couldn't. *Women! They're the ones who need to be kept in line – by any means necessary,* Bert thought.

After that was consumed, he had a little nod. 'Got to rest before you do the job,' he muttered to himself as he settled down on the narrow bed his mother had helped him drag up into the attic.

It was dark when he awoke and there was no moon and no lights in cottage windows. The village was in blackout. He heard the church clock strike midnight. The time was ripe. Dressed from head to toe in dark colours, he took the stairs two at a time, uncaring that they squeaked under his weight. Nobody was around to hear. He'd spotted a tin of corned beef in the larder. He hated opening the thing with its stupid little key, but needs must. Once he'd done it, he cut it in half.

One piece was enticement for the dog. The other would serve as his supper the following night. Rather than chance the front door – just in case some old biddy couldn't sleep and was peering out from behind her curtains – he went out the back door and closed it behind him.

Sniffing the night air gave him great satisfaction after being stuck in the attic. He'd always loved the night: the darkness, the excitement of being out on the prowl and up to no good. He'd poached rabbits and skinned them where he found them. He'd done the same with stolen spring lambs. His prey tonight was a bit different but he'd do the same, imagining the faces of those who fed the dog seeing its naked flesh without that thick fur coat. Smiling into the night, he padded away from the cottage on tiptoe towards the village green, the bench and the duck pond.

In his right hand he held a long piece of wire that would serve as a leash. Once it was round the dog's neck, he would pull it tight, drag the creature off and keep tightening it until the last breath had left its body and the wire was cutting into its flesh. But first, he had to capture it. Having seen and felt the damage those fangs could do, he would be extremely careful. The corned beef was the lure. Despite the scraps he was being fed, it couldn't possibly be enough for such a large dog. The corned beef would be irresistible. Once the dog took the bait, he would quickly tie another piece of wire he had with him around its back legs, then pass a loop from the long piece over its head. The dog, preoccupied with trying to free its back legs, would be taken by surprise.

As expected, the dog was lying beneath the bench, the pond in front of it and a low wall and bushes to its back. It should be an easy task to sneak up along the front of the bench and slip the wire around its back legs. Yes, dogs heard sounds humans couldn't hear, but Bert was an experienced hunter. He was good at treading softly. Only his scent might give him away. He was banking on the dog thinking it was somebody from the village wanting to feed it.

Thanks to the government-enforced blackout, the night was incredibly dark. Bert grinned to himself. He could cope with black nights. One of his old poaching mates had reckoned he had owl eyes. Perhaps he did. He was good at seeing in the dark.

The dog heard him coming, raised its head and growled.

'Here,' he said softly, extending his hand and the piece of corned beef. 'Look what I've got for you.'

The dog's nose twitched and it freely took the offering. Before it knew what was happening, the wire was being wound around its legs, though not quickly enough. The dog leapt to his feet, head low as it bounded out from beneath the questionable security of its bench. Bert only managed to get the wire around one back paw. The dog yelped, more surprised than hurt. Then it growled and hurtled towards him.

A trifle deterred, Bert stepped backwards, determined to stay away from the dog's sharp teeth. The length of wire he'd chosen was very long. It trailed along the ground behind the dog, enough for Bert to step on. The dog yelped as it came to an abrupt halt, the wire tightening around its paw.

Grabbing the wire with both hands, Bert gave it a good pull. The dog spun round, its snapping jaws only inches from the front of Bert's already injured leg. Swearing under his breath, his temper more foul than usual, he tried to drag the dog backwards.

'I'll teach you a lesson you'll never forget,' he muttered under his breath, spittle spotting the corners of his mouth, his eyes slits of anger. He tried to throw the other loop of wire over the dog's head but kept missing, the dog lowering its head so that the wire slid harmlessly along its back and on to the ground. Bert wrapped the wire tightly around his hand in an effort to strengthen his grip, determined the dog would not get away. It had to pay. Anyone who upset his plans had to pay a price. For the dog, it was death.

Rudy was forced to leap on three legs, his trapped paw wrenched out behind him. He heard a noise he did not like. A stick, as thin as a whip, swished through the air, landing on his back just once before he turned in a tight circle, his jaws open, growling as he attempted to bite the front of his assailant's leg.

Recalling another black night, another cruel man raising a stick to him, sent Rudy into a frenzy. He remembered what had happened, the little girl he'd tried to protect, the dark nights when he'd had to hunt for food, the times he'd dug up potatoes for the little girl, on one occasion stealing a farm labourer's lunch from an empty barn.

231

The man who had trapped his paw did not know his history and so did not realise he had awoken a deep-seated anger. This man was ignorant, a bully who enjoyed picking on the weak, those who could not fight back.

Gleefully triumphant, Bert dragged the dog backwards, meaning to take it back to the cottage, down to the garden shed where all manner of tools were stored. His cruel imagination visualised the lower branches of the apple tree, strong enough to accommodate the hanging of a dog while he skinned it. After that he would take what remained and dump it on the village green. The villagers would not know who was to blame. He chuckled at the prospect of watching them run round like headless chickens from his attic window.

His grip tightened, the wire now around his wrist as he dragged the dog backwards, slipping on the wet grass, the reeds of the pond close behind him. Two paths crossing the green merged at this point, a favoured vantage point for people walking across the green to stop and feed the ducks en route. Constant footsteps had worn the path into a muddy stew. The dog struggled but kept on his feet.

He brought the stick down again, connecting with the dog's back. It yelped, spinning round on its back legs. Then it was Bert who yelped as the wire tightened around his wrist, trapping his skin, digging in until the wire drew blood.

Bursting with fury, he raised the stick again. 'I'll teach you...'

The dog tugged backwards, tightening the wire

around Bert's hand. He gritted his teeth to stifle his cry of pain. He dropped the birch switch, gripping his wrist, keeping his voice low as he swore even worse punishments for the dog as he sought to free his trapped flesh. Concentrating on his grip rather than his feet, he loosened the wire. As he did so, the dog leapt to one side, yanking the end from his hand, then leapt backwards.

Behind him was the duck pond. There was a splashing sound as his back legs hit the water. Fuelled by temper and his determination to catch and punish the dog, Bert spun too quickly on the wet, muddy ground. 'I'll get you, you mangy cur,' he muttered, biting his bottom lip so that he didn't shout. In doing so he tasted blood. Another reason for lunging towards the animal he blamed for his pain.

Reeds from beside the pond whipped at his legs. He was close to the water, closer than he'd judged himself to be. Unbalanced and hurting, he began to topple over the stones enclosing the pond water, reaching out for something to steady his balance but clutching only at reeds. His temper up, his ego deflated, his legs went this way and that, his feet slipping on the slimy mud beneath the surface.

The last sound Rudy heard as he limped away on three legs, his fourth paw dragging behind him, was a loud splash. He kept going until he'd made the edge of the village and a thick copse fringing the brook that fed the duck pond.

Hidden from view, he collapsed onto a cushion of tough grass where he began to lick the blood

233

from his injured paw. He was panting and thirsty and would shortly drink and sleep, though not until he was sure he was safe.

Muttering all manner of retribution, back at the duck pond Bert clambered through the reeds, roosting ducks scattering and quacking as he made his sodden way to the bank. A torch flickered over the ground some way off and a voice shouted, 'Anyone there?' Bert kept his head down.

PC John Carter flashed the torch around the perimeter of the pond before assuming a fox was responsible for the disturbance. The beam from his torch flickered like a firefly then was gone.

Carefully, Bert pried the reeds apart. The torchlight was moving off. He waited until it was out of sight before he eased himself out of the smelly goo and on to the bank, keeping low to the ground all the way back to his mother's cottage, though not before strangling the nearest duck to hand. Roast duck for supper, to be cooked in the wee hours while everyone was sleeping. Nobody would smell it and he would eat well. At least he had something for his trouble.

CHAPTER SEVENTEEN

Mrs Trinder, who owned the post office, tackled Meg about the dog three days after its escape from PC Carter's clutches. 'I hear it was your husband's dog. Is that right?'

Mrs Trinder had a habit of holding on to whatever a customer wanted until they had answered her question, while her eyes fixed them with a hard stare over the top of her wire-rimmed spectacles.

Meg felt her cheeks grow warm. 'As far as I know, the dog belonged to the RAF. I dare say they'll come back and collect him.'

'So they should, poor creature! He appears to have a wire around his back paw. He must be in great pain dragging it along behind him like that.'

Meg got her stamps but if she thought that would be the last mention of the matter, she was very much mistaken.

Waiting for her outside the school gates after dropping off her daughter, Alice brimmed with curiosity. 'Have you seen your husband's dog? In a right bad way, he is. Looks as though he's got an injured paw. Probably got caught in a poacher's snare. PC Carter has been trying to catch him again but he doesn't seem to want to be caught.'

'And when he does catch him?'

Alice sighed. 'He'll probably be put down.'

Meg hardened her emotions. She had to concentrate on Lily. The state had taken her husband; it was their responsibility to deal with the dog. 'It's probably for the best.'

'Do you think so?'

Alice sounded surprised. Meg fixed her gaze on the school entrance, determined not to meet the look on Alice's face.

'I've been working on doing so much to make the cottage more comfortable. I've made new cushion covers, counterpanes and curtains. A dog would only mess things up.' She threw Alice

235

a reassuring smile. 'I don't think Aunt Lavender will recognise Bluebell Cottage by the time I've finished with it.'

'I doubt she would notice.'

'You don't think so?'

'She likes dogs.' The small statement seemed to linger in the air between them.

Meg fought down the feeling that she was being selfish. Ray would have tried to persuade her, but Ray wasn't here. And if he was? Doubt nagged at her for the rest of that morning and was still there when she was outside the school gates again later waiting to collect Lily. Before the children came out en masse, she saw that Miss Pringle was waving to her from the main entrance. Recognising that she wanted a word, Meg walked over.

Miss Pringle peered at her through the pair of spectacles perched halfway down her nose. Her voice dropped to little more than a whisper. 'I have no wish to cause you any undue concern, Mrs Malin, but I fear we are not getting very far with Lily. I think it's time to consider other options.'

'Options?' Meg felt her heart beating faster. The school term had only just begun and Lily was already an object of concern. She knew very well what Miss Pringle was about to say. Doctors had trod the same path.

'Perhaps it's time you looked into sending her to a special school where her medical condition could be treated at the same time as she is educated.'

'No!' Meg's snapped response hung like a knife in the air between them. 'I will not allow that. If

236

you are unable to do anything with her, then I shall teach her at home...'

'The authorities may not allow that.'

Miss Pringle's tone was even and amenable enough, but Meg was still outraged. 'I don't care what they will allow. The child deserves better. My goodness, she was airlifted from France by my husband. We cannot imagine what awful things she went through there. We have to try.'

Miss Pringle held her head to one side, her sharp eyes regarding Meg with a mixture of pity and resolve. '*You* have to try, Mrs Malin. I have the other pupils in her class to consider. Please give it some thought. I really do think it might be for the best.'

Over my dead body, thought Meg. Once Lily's hand was in hers, she stalked off quickly. Only when she'd calmed down and they were passing the village green did she feel Lily's weight dragging on her hand.

'Come on, Lily. Don't dawdle. Let's get home...'

Lily seemed oblivious to the tug Meg gave her. Her gaze seemed fixed on something or someone over her shoulder. Meg had been mulling over what Miss Pringle had said but buried her irritation and switched her attention to Lily. 'What is it, Lily? Do you want to see the ducks? I haven't got any bread with me, but we could bring some later if you like.'

Lily blinked and slowly, very slowly pointed a finger. 'Rudy!'

Meg swallowed. A word. A simple word but every word counted. Much more than that, she'd said the dog's name. She remembered the dog's name! Trembling, she got down so her face was level with that of the little girl. Suddenly the day seemed brighter. She took in Lily's expression and was sure something had changed.

'Rudy? How did you know his name is Rudy?'

Lily did not answer, but Meg was now certain that she did look brighter. Or was it coincidence? She racked her brain. Was this the first time Lily had seen the dog? She hadn't seen it when Mrs Dando had brought it over or recently when the dog had escaped PC Carter's clutches and hid out in the village. At least, she didn't think she had. Yet she'd recognised him. She must have done to have said his name.

Meg turned and looked at the dog. He was drinking pond water, the ducks keeping a respectable distance. He was standing on three legs, his fourth paw lifted and a length of wire hanging from it.

'Rudy,' Lily repeated.

Meg swallowed. Dare she believe that Lily was beginning to remember? She licked the dryness from her lips and thought carefully about how to handle this.

'Do you recognise him, sweetheart?' she asked, the words hesitant and trembling.

Lily appeared not to hear, her gaze still on the dog.

Prejudices against the animal, which were mainly about hairs on cushions and doggy smells, fell into insignificance. Lily had said something. It was quite amazing. Meg made a snap decision. She stepped on to the wet grass of the village green and stretched out her hand.

238

'Here,' she called. 'Come on, Rudy. Come here, there's a good dog.'

Lily seemed to be eyeing the dog as though she were concentrating very hard.

'Hold out your hand,' Meg said to her, hardly believing she was encouraging the dog to come to them, she who had wanted nothing to do with him.

Lily stood stock-still.

Meg took hold of Lily's hand, unfolding her fingers from her palm. 'Ask him to come,' she said, barely able to control the excitement in her voice. 'Go on, Lily. Click your fingers. Like this,' she said, clicking her own. 'Call him over.'

To Meg's great delight, Lily responded, clicking her fingers as best she could. Her fingers were just too soft.

'Call him,' Meg urged. 'Go on, Lily. Call him.'

Lily opened her mouth. 'Rudy,' she said, her voice barely audible.

The dog's ears were already perked with interest and he was gazing in their direction. At the sound of Lily's voice, his tail began to scythe through the wet grass. He gave a loud bark.

'Say hello,' Meg further urged, expecting nothing but hoping for everything.

'Hello,' said Lily.

Meg was astounded.

At the sound of her voice, the dog ambled closer, sniffed at her outstretched hand, looked up at her and wagged his tail more vigorously, whining and brushing his head against Lily's arm as though delighted to see her. Meg lay her hand on the dog's head and heard Ray's voice, saw the

239

words in his letter: 'if, after the war, we could give Rudy a home...'

Despite his injured paw, the dog seemed healthy enough, his eyes bright, his nose wet. She'd read somewhere that a healthy dog always had a wet nose. She wasn't sure how true it was, but on this dog it glistened.

Lily was stroking Rudy's head while the dog looked up at her adoringly. 'Look, Lily. He's a nice dog,' said Meg. She couldn't believe what was happening, couldn't believe what she was contemplating. Ray had claimed the dog but she recalled its history. Ray had brought the dog and the child to safety. Dog and child had escaped from a war zone.

The little girl, traumatised by both her experiences before coming to England and the bombing raid, was finally beginning to communicate and all because of a dog. Such a small step but such a large one too. Meg pushed on, wanting Lily to speak again, to say more, to remember all of her past, even if some of it pained her.

'And his name's Rudy,' said Meg, wanting to be sure she hadn't imagined Lily speaking, desperate to hear her speak again. 'Rudy. Say it Lily. Say his name.'

Lily pursed her lips. 'Rudy.'

Closing her eyes, Meg threw her head back. Miracles did happen. The key to unlocking Lily's mind had been here all along. Why hadn't she seen that before? Ray had understood all about dogs. He'd grown up with them, had even tried telling her how they could help people get better. She'd found that difficult to believe. Yes, there were dogs

240

for the blind. She could understand that. But other illnesses too? She didn't know and didn't care. All that mattered was helping Lily. She owed it to Ray. Her mind was made up. If there was any chance, any at all, she was going to take it.

'I think Rudy should come home with us,' Meg whispered to Lily, her heart hammering against her ribs. 'What do you think?'

'Yes,' Lily whispered. Meg almost leapt into the air. She found herself wishing she'd brought a piece of rope to tie around his neck, perhaps borrowing the washing line if she couldn't find anything else.

'Come on, Rudy. Come with us.'

Her worries about not having brought a lead vanished. The dog trotted along beside them, his head pressed loyally to Lily's side. Lily placed her hand on the dog's head, patting him as they walked along and every so often the dog gazed lovingly up at her.

Meg was ecstatic, though one old niggle remained. She could hear her mother's words tolling in her ears. 'What about the dog hairs? I do think a child like Lily should live in a pristine environment. And the smell! That doggy smell!' It struck Meg then that she'd inherited her fastidiousness from her mother. Her mother, too, had been house-proud and it had rubbed off.

So far her mother hadn't visited Bluebell Cottage, but Meg was in no mind she'd find it lacking, especially when compared to her own house or even Andover Avenue. So far her superintending the WVS and other war work had kept her away. Let it stay that way.

241

Meg also recalled that she'd never been too keen on her and Ray fostering a child. 'It's up to you, but really, someone else's child... And a foreigner at that.'

So far Meg was very pleased with the improvements she'd made to Bluebell Cottage. She'd made new curtains and her mother had sent her a rug from London. She'd also painted the walls white and festooned the place with flower displays. A church jumble sale had proved a worthy source of discarded ornaments, cast-off clothes and bits of material suitable for changing into useful and pretty things. Bluebell Cottage would never be Andover Avenue, but at least she could make it bearable for however long she had to live in it, possibly until the end of the war. Then she would return to London, or that's what she'd always thought, but now she wasn't so sure.

The dog was still with them, limping along at Lily's side. Hopefully he would follow them all the way to Bluebell Cottage, then she could attend to that sore leg. The piece of wire trailed behind him and she could see it had dug in deep, the fur above his paw coated in blood.

'Come on, Rudy. Come on,' she said, feeling sorry for what he'd been through, partly as a result of her refusal to give him a home. 'I'll make it up to you,' she whispered.

As they walked along the verge of the village green, a self-satisfied thought came to her mind and a smile to her face. The dog had chosen to be with them. Other people in the village, including PC Carter, had tried to seduce the animal with food and kind words. Nobody had succeeded

242

enticing him home. It struck her then how little encouragement she had given the animal. It was with a sense of pride that the dog that had escaped the village policeman wanted to be with them.

Feeling more hopeful than she'd been for a long time, she sneaked glances at the two close companions – child and dog. They were all three of them in a row. Just like a family.

At the place where a trio of weeping willow trees trailed feathery fronds into the duck pond, the dog fell back and Lily stopped too. Alarmed, she turned round to see where he was. Surely he hadn't deserted them now?

He had not. Rudy was standing rigidly, his head raised and staring into the distance. Meg's hope that he was the answer to her prayers was instantly dented. She had to get him home. Lily, too, looked alarmed, her little jaw dropped, her eyes full of concern.

'Rudy?' Her voice failed to carry.

Meg wished again that she had something to tie around his neck. She would drag him home if it meant Lily would be on the road to recovery.

'Rudy. Come on, boy. Come on! Heel!'

Heel. She didn't really know what it meant but had heard people out walking their dogs use the word. The dog glanced at her before turning his eyes skyward, gazing into the far distance as though seeing something nobody else could see. Or perhaps he can hear something, thought Meg.

I need to get a lead, she decided, thinking she could hurry home and find something. She tugged at Lily's hand. 'Come on, Lily. Let's keep

243

walking, then the lovely doggy will follow us home. Shall we do that? And then I can run back with something to put around his neck.'

Lily was standing absolutely still, fascinated by the dog's sudden behaviour. Disappointed, Meg decided there was nothing to be done for now but was determined to have another go. She turned to Lily and, in a disconsolate voice, urged Lily to march on with her. 'Come on, Lily. Supper and then bed.'

The little girl stubbornly refused to move.

Meg sucked in her breath and rubbed at her temple. Somehow she felt cheated. Everything had been going so well. 'Do you remember who he is?' Meg asked tentatively.

'Rudy.'

'Yes. Rudy. But he doesn't want to come home with us today. We'll come back for him tomorrow.'

Lily turned her gaze from the dog and looked up at the sky, her eyes suddenly as big as saucers and her bottom lip trembling.

Telling herself she had already done her best, Meg lost patience. 'Oh, come on, Lily. Come on!' She gave Lily's hand a tug.

'No!' cried the little girl, her attention firmly fixed on the sky. 'No!'

Meg shivered. She could see nothing up there herself, so what was Lily seeing? Her thoughts went back to what Miss Pringle had said. *'If she doesn't improve by next spring, then you will have to make other arrangements.'*

Meg had pleaded for more time. Next spring wasn't that far away. Miss Pringle had relented. *'All right. This time next year.'*

244

Meg stared at Rudy and told herself she had not imagined Lily's response to him. She had visibly improved before her very eyes. A part of Meg resented that. It was only right that a mother should be the centre of a child's universe. Not a dog. Surely not a dog!

But I'm not her mother. Not really.

'That dog's going to get shot if he's not careful. Or he might die anyway if somebody don't take a look at that bad paw.'

Not realising anyone else was close at hand, Meg started. The speaker was Cliff Stenner, who kept the village inn, the Bear and Ragged Staff, an old thatched place with low ceilings and small windows that smelled of sawdust and hops. He was standing with his hands tucked into the pockets of his baggy trousers, studying the dog with a deep frown and narrowed eyes.

'Why is he likely to get shot?'

Cliff Stenner dug his hands deeper into his pockets as though that was where the answer lay. 'Farmers don't like stray dogs around. They kill sheep or harry them when they're lambing.'

'That's not fair. He's got an injured paw.'

'I know. I've been trying to catch him and take him home with us. He'd be a good dog to have in a pub. Alsatians are excellent guard dogs.'

'I won't let that happen. He was my husband's dog,' Meg declared, surprising herself that she was fighting the dog's corner.

Cliff raised his eyebrows. 'Sure of that now, are you?'

Meg stated that she was. 'Do you have any idea how he injured his paw?'

245

'Looks to me as though he somehow got it caught in a wire snare.'

'Do many dogs get caught in traps?'

'Enough. It's not unusual for dogs to get trapped in snares put down by poachers to trap rabbits or even foxes. Some animals chew their paw off rather than stay trapped. But that's a big dog. A strong dog. He managed to get away and pull the wire with him. Poor devil. It's still around his leg but he won't let anyone close to him.'

'I managed to get quite close. For a moment he seemed to be following us home. Now he's just sitting there staring into the distance and nothing I say will move him.'

There was a rasping sound as Cliff rubbed his chin. He frowned as he looked at the dog, then looked in the same direction as the dog. 'Odd behaviour. A thunderstorm, perhaps? Or...' His voice melted away and his expression clouded. Born in the country, Cliff respected the instincts of animals. He was no military genius, but he had a suspicion that Upper Standwick was about to get dragged into the twentieth century.

'How is he surviving?' Meg asked him, though she sensed his thoughts were drifting.

'People are feeding him.'

'I've decided it would be best if he moved in with us.'

Cliff shrugged. 'Up to you, love. It's your business. I would have given him a billet if he'd let me near him. A few others tried too. Thought we'd get him to the vet and then think about what to do next, but the blighter just eats the food then runs away regardless of his injured leg. And this is where he mostly ends up. He was sleeping under that bench old Percy Smart had put up by the terms of his will. It was his favourite place in the village. Sat there day after day feeding the ducks. Not sure where he sleeps now.'

'I take it you mean the dog.'

Cliff laughed. 'The dog. Yes. Old Percy sleeps over in the churchyard. Been there five years or so.'

Rudy turned his attention from whatever he'd been looking at in the distance, his attention suddenly switching to Lily. Meg heard him whine plaintively.

Lily's eyes flickered for a moment. 'Rudy?'

To Meg's ears, Lily sounded as though she were questioning whether that was indeed the dog's name. There was a swishing sound as the dog's tail thrashed through the grass.

'He seems fascinated by Lily.'

Cliff shrugged his bulky shoulders again. 'He must like kids.'

Lily reached out her hand. The dog came to her, but turned quickly away as though something more important had caught his attention. Suddenly the dog was barking excitedly, his front legs leaving the ground with the effort.

'Hello. That's different.' Cliff looked impressed. 'I wonder what he's hearing that we can't. Marvellous hearing, dogs. Better nose than us too.'

Meg's heart began to race. 'Is it an air raid?' The memory of the London bombing turned her legs to jelly. She narrowed her eyes. What did the dog see? What did he hear? She herself saw nothing.

Cliff did the same. His eyes weren't as good as

they used to be but his instinct wasn't so bad. He felt a bad thing was coming. The dog, however, knew it was. 'Barking at nothing,' he muttered, not wishing to frighten Widow Malin.

Despite his injured paw and the length of thin wire trailing behind him, the dog began running in circles like dogs do when they're chasing their tails, stopping every so often to look back at the two humans and small child as though surprised they couldn't hear what he was hearing.

Cliff's brow furrowed into ridges. 'We've never had an air raid here.'

Meg felt suddenly cold. 'Please tell me nothing's changed. I had enough of that in London.'

Cliff shook his head vehemently. 'There's nothing here to bomb...' He paused as a thought struck him. 'Or there wasn't. Not before the air-base was built, anyway...'

Only seconds after his words faded away, the wail of an air-raid siren filled the air.

'God's teeth!' Eyes wide with alarm, Cliff scanned the church tower. A black-robed figure was just about discernible. The air-raid siren was situated on the roof of the tower and the church-warden was turning the handle.

'So they know about the airfield,' exclaimed Cliff. 'Well that's our peaceful existence interrupted, though hopefully they won't come this way, but in case they do, there goes the church-warden doing his job. Better get to safety.'

Meg felt as though her blood had turned to ice. She had come here to Upper Standwick to escape the bombing and it scared her to think it had followed her here.

'But there are no shelters here, are there?' For Lily's sake, she attempted to control the trembling in her voice. Lily squirmed when she grabbed hold of her hand.

'Just a few Andersons. But never you mind. Come with me. The Bear and Ragged Staff's got deep cellars. We'll be safe there.'

Trying not to let Lily see her panic, Meg walked hurriedly along at Cliff's side, dragging Lily with her. She was aware that the dog was following close behind them, limping along at a pretty fast pace. Yet Cliff had said he didn't go with anyone and he was following her now just as she'd wanted him to.

At the very instant a plume of smoke appeared in the direction of the airbase, Cliff's wife, Gladys, appeared at the pub doorway, waving frantically.

'She's seen something from the upstairs window,' said Cliff, huffing and puffing as they increased their speed, his face turning as puce as a beetroot. 'We've got a good view of the airfield from there.'

Other villagers were also moving swiftly in the direction of the village inn, everyone well aware that the old thatched pub had deep cellars and at least they'd have company.

Just as they reached the pub door, an old chap called Tom Morris, wearing moleskin trousers tied at the knees with string, doffed his cap and stepped aside so Meg and Lily could go in first. 'Get the youngsters in. I'm an old codger and I've lived my life,' he exclaimed through the few teeth that remained in his head.

'There'll be no room in the cellar at this rate,'

249

Gladys Stenner remarked, her face as red as her husband's with the effort of dashing for keys, then down the stairs and opening the cellar door, then back up again. 'Right! How many wants to go into the cellar?' she shouted.

'Well, you can count me out,' said Old Tom. 'In case Jerry bombs me, I'm having a last pint at the bar. Set 'em up, Gladys.'

'You'll have to wait. You're always first in the bar.'

'And I intend being the last!'

'There's beer in the cellar,' somebody said.

'Yes, but it ain't tapped and ready to draw,' chuckled the old man.

'He certainly knows how things are done,' said Gladys as she helped those who wanted to shelter down the cellar steps.

'No dogs,' she said, when Rudy appeared to follow.

Cliff put her in the picture. 'He's injured, Glad. It's the one I've been trying to get hold of.'

Gladys loved her husband but when it came to on-the-spot planning and knowing the rules, she was the one who took charge. 'You know how it is, Cliff. Rules is rules. No dogs allowed. Especially strays.'

'Just because he's a stray?' said Old Tom from his spot at the bar. 'Somebody must own him.'

'He belonged to my husband,' Meg blurted, feeling instantly guilty that it hadn't been so long ago she'd wanted nothing to do with the animal. 'He used to live at my husband's airfield. At Waddington. He was a mascot.'

She couldn't remember whether that was really

the case, but in Lily's interest she felt obliged to stand up for him.

'Then he's a war dog,' said Old Tom. 'Dogs that live with servicemen usually are. Even get pay, they do. Usually got some skill that's appreciated by the military.'

'I reckon you're right, Tom,' said Cliff, nodding as he supped back half a pint of bitter and passed another over the bar to the old man. 'In fact, I'm sure that dog heard them bombers coming before we did. Now that's what I call useful. In fact, he heard them bombers even before the church-warden turned the handle on the air-raid siren.'

'Then he deserves to be saved,' declared the old man. 'Anyway, he can have my place in the cellar. I like dogs. Dogs have got more sense than a lot of humans I know.'

The dog followed Meg and her daughter down into the cellar, finding a place next to them and settling down. Meg hugged Lily to her side. The dog sat snugly against Lily, glancing at her with a protective look in his eyes. Lily returned the dog's glances. Sometimes their looks seemed to lock together as though they were exchanging thoughts. It made Meg wonder what horrors the pair of them had been through.

Laughter at Old Tom's words followed them down into the cellar until the door was firmly closed. Cliff had stayed up there too.

'Leave Old Tom in there and the barrels could be supped dry,' said Gladys. 'Nobody can drink like Old Tom.'

'I prefer to be down here,' said Meg and truly meant it. Although she'd heard the public air-raid

251

shelters in London were quite jolly, she couldn't believe they compared well to the pub cellar. People talked to her, asked how she was, how Lily was and did she need anything in particular?

'Always willing to help out.'

The same words were used over and over again. That was the way it was in the community that was Upper Standwick.

A sudden thud brought dust floating down from the ceiling. Everyone gasped and Meg drew Lily closer. The sound of explosions seemed far away. Some people screwed their eyes shut and stuffed their fingers in their ears. One or two elderly women sat knitting, comparing patterns and wool as though nothing else was going on.

Gladys did her best to reassure everyone. 'You can bet your life no bombs will fall here. They'll save them for the airbase. Upper Standwick is God's little acre. Nothing will ever fall on this village, you mark my words.'

Meg was inclined to ask why she thought that, but something else had caught her attention. Lily's head rested against that of the dog and both arms were wrapped around him. The dog's jaw hung open and just for a moment Meg could believe that he was smiling. But dogs didn't smile. Did they?

'Poor love,' said Gladys, looking down at the dog's damaged paw. 'I wonder if he'll let me take that wire off him?'

She made a move towards Rudy, her fingers barely brushing the harsh wire. The dog growled.

'Ooh,' she said, quickly withdrawing her fingers. 'Sorry, I'm sure. Still,' she said, leaning to-

252

wards him. 'It'll go septic if it don't come off.'

Meg conceded that she was right. 'Do you think you can do it?'

Gladys nodded. 'I think so, though somebody will have to hold him. I've seen his teeth.'

Meg knew little about dogs but she badly wanted this one to survive. Taking a deep breath, she decided to make an effort. 'I'll do it.'

She placed her arm around his neck. 'It'll be fine, Rudy,' she said, speaking the dog's name as she stroked his head. 'We're just trying to help you. Ray would want you to be good. So just keep still. There's a good dog. How about you stroking him, Lily? How about you telling him to be a good boy?'

Lily spoke to him in German. Meg was astounded. The dog was putty beneath the child's hands.

Gladys heard what Lily had said. She exchanged a swift look with Meg before doing her bit to gain his trust. Meg offered him her hand. He sniffed it thoroughly before his nose ran up her sleeve. He did the same to Lily, though lingered longer, sniffing up and down the arm of the blue cardigan she was wearing.

Meg wondered why that was before remembering she had made the cardigan from wool unravelled from one of Ray's old jumpers. The dog sniffed up and down Lily's arm one more time before lying calmly down, his head on his front paws.

The dog's interest in the knitted wool that had once been worn by her husband gave Meg an idea. Taking hold of Lily's hand, she burrowed

253

her daughter's fingers into the thick fur encouraging her to soothe him again. 'The poor dog's been hurt,' she explained to Lily. 'If we stroke him and talk to him, he might let us take that nasty wire off his paw.'

Lily's fingers curled into the thick fur and for a moment Meg thought she would retract her hand, but she didn't.

Gladys looked relieved. 'Well, that seems to have worked. Now to cut that wire. Cliff keeps his tools down here. There's bound to be something we can use.'

After clattering around in a wooden toolbox, she came up with a pair of wire cutters. 'Keep talking to him,' she whispered to Meg. 'And you keep smoothing his fur, young lady,' she said to Lily.

Gladys shifted to put herself in line with the dog's back leg. The bombing was momentarily forgotten as anxious eyes focused on the dog and the pub landlady. One woman whispered to her neighbour, 'If she's not careful, he'll bite her.'

'He wouldn't dare,' her neighbour whispered back. Those who heard smiled and nodded agreement. They all knew, some from experience, that Gladys Stenner, with her big arms and sharp tongue, was not a woman to cross.

Soothed by the petting hands and softly spoken words, the dog seemed almost as though he were anaesthetised, his eyes half closed. Gently and very slowly, Gladys cut the wire, then laying the cutters to one side, prised it from where it had bitten into the dog's flesh. Meg bit her bottom lip when she saw blood trickling into the dog's fur. If only she'd taken him in, this might not have happened. Poor dog.

'There, there,' murmured Gladys once the wire had been removed and she was bathing the raw wound with a pad of wet cloth. A gasp of relief flowed like warm air in the stark confines of the cell. The dog heard it and opened his eyes. He wagged his tail, obviously glad it was all over.

Gladys's knees cracked as she got to her feet and flung the wire cutters back into the toolbox. 'There. That's him settled, though I don't mind saying I'd like to get my hands on the poacher who laid the trap. Cruel bugger!'

'Well done, Gladys.' Everyone clapped and smiled.

The dog heaved a big sigh then lifted his head, rubbing it against Lily's sleeve and gazing up at her, gratitude shining in his eyes. Lily smiled and buried her face in the dog's fur. Meg felt a great urge to pinch herself. In just a few hours, Lily had made more progress than she had in months and all thanks to the dog. They seemed so close, so fond of each other. It gave rise to a question.

'Have you had Rudy all your life?' Meg asked.

Lily seemed to think about it before shaking her head. Her smile disappeared. The corners of her mouth were downturned and a look Meg could only describe as deep blackness came to her eyes.

'So when did you meet him?'

Lily looked confused. It was as though she was trying to remember, but something was stopping her.

Gladys came back from putting the toolbox away, swiping at her forehead and shaking her

255

head as the sounds of bombing continued. 'Will it never end?'

'At least it's a fair way off.'

'Definitely the airfield, not the village.'

'Thank God!'

Just as Cliff had surmised, the enemy was concentrating on the airfield. The next two hours in the cellar flew by. Meg was surprised just how jovial such a gathering could be. Women knitted while others talked, laughed and sang songs. Alice was taking it in turns with other mothers to read stories to the children. The atmosphere was a world away from the isolation under the stairs where she'd thought she'd be safe. In fact, it was almost possible to forget that an air raid was going on.

The thin wail of the all-clear went unnoticed. It wasn't appreciated that it was all over until the cellar door opened and Cliff, who'd stayed behind in the pub bar, appeared, his face wreathed in smiles. 'The churchwarden's sounded the all-clear. Sod the opening hours. The bar is still open for all them who need a drink to steady their nerves.'

There wasn't exactly a rush to the bar, though enough to make it worthwhile for the Stenners to serve them.

Meg declined. 'Thanks all the same, but I'll be getting on home, Mrs Stenner.'

Darling Gladys, her hair crimped in the grasp of steel curlers, gave her a cheery wave. 'That's all right, me dear. You get on with that little 'un of yours. Looks as though she might have found a new friend. Your husband would have liked that, wouldn't he?'

'Yes,' said Meg, feeling a lump rise in her throat. 'He would.'

As they squeezed out through the doorway, Meg saw that Lily's free hand was still buried in the thick ruff of fur around the dog's neck. Once outside, she paused and took a deep breath.

'Mrs Malin.' Constable John Carter looked hot and harried beneath his policeman's helmet. 'Took shelter in the pub, did you?'

'Yes, I did.'

PC Carter's gaze fell to the dog and back to her. 'You look pleased with yourself. And you've got the dog. Well if that don't take the biscuit.'

A few hours ago, Meg had been adamant she would not give the dog a home. Now here she was with him in tow on her way back to Bluebell Cottage. A little embarrassed, she nervously tucked a swathe of thick blonde hair behind one ear. 'I believe Rudy is my responsibility and he seems to have taken to Lily. Anyway, I owe it to Ray.'

PC Carter nodded quietly and the warmth in his eyes lit up his face. 'I'm pleased to hear it. If you ever get stuck... Come to me.'

Meg nodded. 'I will, and thank you for all you've done.'

'I didn't do anything much – just fell off my bike and the dog took off, but honestly, if you do encounter any problems coping with him...'

'Food could be a problem, but I think we can manage.'

PC Carter tapped the side of his nose. 'There's plenty of rabbits around here. Two or three a week should do the job, don't you think?'

Rudy didn't flinch when the policeman patted his head. 'Handsome fellah. Do you have a collar and lead for him?'

'No, I don't.'

'Think I might have a collar and lead somewhere. If I find them, I'll bring them round.'

Meg thanked him for his generosity before hurrying on, Lily and Rudy keeping pace. It was a great relief to Meg that Lily had barely noticed they'd experienced a bombing raid. After London, she would have expected her to panic, but she appeared quite calm. Her feeling of relief was further encouraged when Lily began to skip.

'Lily! You're skipping.'

Lily looked up at her and laughed. 'Rudy's come home.'

The dog lolloped at a brisker pace. Meg began to skip too. So there they were, all three of them trotting and skipping happily along the road. She began to laugh, the first time she had laughed since losing Ray. Or perhaps even before that.

Her mood was euphoric and in consequence her mind seemed to wake up to the possibilities, things to do that would elevate both her spirits and contribute more to Lily's healing. 'Tomorrow we'll make carrot cake.'

Lily laughed. 'With carrots?'

'With carrots,' echoed Meg, hardly daring to hope that this breakthrough would continue. She wasn't sure she had all the ingredients for a carrot cake, but the promise and the events of the day made her buoyant. They'd survived the raid intact and in good company, the villagers carrying on with their lives as though knitting and singing could win the war. Better still, Lily had not reverted back to the haunted child she'd been before Rudy had attached himself.

They were closing on the cottage gate, half hidden beneath a trellised arch of worn wood and an overgrown climbing rose; its scent distinguishable even before the mass of blooms was sighted. Meg placed her hand on the gate, paused and looked at the dog. Rudy looked up at her and wagged his tail, almost as though waiting patiently to be invited inside.

As though he perceived Bluebell Cottage as his home.

Lily reached out her hand. The dog took a step forward, sniffed and licked her palm. Lily giggled.

What a wonderful day, thought Meg. It was as though something had cracked and splintered inside the little girl – like winter ice on a frozen pond. 'Rudy is very glad to be home and he's never going away again.' She said it boldly, hurriedly yet gently. Her heart seemed to stick in her throat as she watched Lily's face. The dog entered the cottage, sniffing around a bit before collapsing with a sigh as his body met the coolness of the old flagstones.

Meg's thoughts were in turmoil, as she looked at all the improvements she had made. The cottage was more cheerful than it had been, the floor cleaner and the colours of the faded Turkish rug were brighter thanks to her hanging it out on the clothes line and giving it a good beating. After dislodging the dust, she'd laid it down on the floor and given it a vigorous scrub. The result was pleasing. The room looked and smelled clean. Everything was in its place and she wanted it to

259

stay that way. She'd never liked dogs very much and might take some time adjusting, but for Lily's sake she would do that.

Telling Lily to go and wash her hands, she stood alone with the dog and her thoughts. Ray had told her how he'd found her and the dog, but had known very little about what went before.

'Rudy. What did the two of you go through?' she said softly.

The dog opened one eye, its tail sweeping the flagstone and disturbing the fringe of the Turkish rug. Somebody knocked on the door, causing the dog to raise his head. PC Carter was standing there, a leather lead and collar hanging from his right hand.

'I thought you might be able to make use of these. I don't know who they used to belong to, but they've been in the station for ever. I thought you could do with them.'

Meg thanked him. The policeman lingered. She had a few scoops of tea left in the caddy so invited him in. Lily came back from washing her hands, then promptly lay down beside the dog. Both of them closed their eyes.

'Great pals,' remarked PC Carter.

'It would seem that way.' He didn't pry as to her reasons for refusing the dog a home in the first place and for that she was grateful.

He'd also brought her along two rabbits and some offal that he explained was horsemeat. 'The horse died of old age. The rabbits were trapped. Everyone will be fed well on this lot. I've even got carrots, onions and potatoes if you've not got any yourself.'

She thanked him and, feeling happier than she'd been for a long time, decided it was only polite to invite him for dinner the following evening. 'I'm also going to make carrot cake. So if you'd like to come...?'

CHAPTER EIGHTEEN

Constable John Carter was just an ordinary village policeman and regarded by all as a confirmed bachelor. He'd had girlfriends but none he felt serious about. At thirty-seven years of age he was still single. He hadn't met or pursued anyone who tickled his heartstrings so presumed he'd remain a bachelor all his life – that was until Meg Malin had come along.

Due to the tragic circumstances of her husband's death, he had respected her widowed status. He'd made no advances, but he could at least be friendly, though even there he judged it best to tread carefully. The business with the dog had finally given him the opportunity he'd been waiting for. The fine collar and leather lead had been there in the outhouse at the back of the police station when he'd first taken up residence. Nobody had laid claim to it and he didn't have a police dog. Meg Malin needed it.

He congratulated himself on the brilliant idea of offering her rabbits for the dog and was pleased as punch when she'd invited him for dinner the following night. It was the first date he'd had in years. Not really a date though. He reminded himself that the little girl would be there and smiled at the image of them together. *Almost like a ready-made family,* he thought to himself, barely curbing an embarrassed smile. *All supposition. Pie in the sky.* Still, a man could dream.

He arrived with a bouquet of flowers, the remains of summer blooms interspersed with fronds of cow parsley and thick red leaves from some shrub in the garden that he didn't know the name of. Meg opened the door wearing a blue dress, her hair caught back in a fine silvery snood. He couldn't be sure, but he also thought she might be wearing lipstick. Though he was no expert on the world of cosmetics, he didn't think he'd seen her wearing lipstick before. Lily was sitting at the table, the dog at her side and the smell of rabbit stew was enticing. He fancied also that some baking had been done, as promised.

Rudy got to his feet and wagged his tail. John offered him the back of his hand when he sauntered over. He gave it a quick nuzzle before going back beside Lily. 'He let me in then,' said John, as Meg took his coat and the bottle of Cyprus ruby wine he'd brought with him. The wine had been bought for Christmas three years ago but had remained hidden at the back of the sideboard ever since. 'I hope that doesn't mean he'd let anyone in.'

'I don't think so.'

'It was left over from last Christmas,' he said as he handed over the bottle, but didn't say which Christmas. 'I think it's still drinkable.'

'That's very kind of you. Rudy seems to recognise who is a friend and who is an enemy,' said Meg, feeling profoundly protective of the animal.

'Something in his background,' said John. 'If you train them in your ways from a puppy, that's the dog you'll get. Quite an intelligent one by the looks of it. And he's known kindness. You can kind of tell.'

'I think so,' Meg said quietly, and realised she meant it. They spoke of generally pleasant things over dinner and he helped her with the dishes once Lily was put to bed.

'It's a little weak,' she said to him as she poured two cups of tea.

'Getting used to it,' he said, and Meg laughed. 'Everyone is.'

The dog was stretched out. Every so often his tail would brush the flagged floor as though he approved of certain aspects of their conversation. He was also replete following a tasty meal of rabbit bones, stew and soaked bread.

'I take it your husband didn't own the dog when he was a puppy, so where did he get him from?'

Meg carefully put her cup down in the saucer, her eyes downcast. At the mention of Ray she couldn't help but turn into herself. Things were bound to get easier.

'I'm sorry,' said John on seeing her hesitation. 'You don't have to tell me...'

Meg held up a hand to stop him going on. 'It's all right. I try to avoid speaking his name. Silly, I know. They do say time is a great healer, but let's face it, all the grieving in the world isn't going to bring him back.' She paused and waited for his reaction. 'You probably think I'm hard-hearted,' she said when he continued to stand there without saying a word. Finally, he shook his head. His smile was slightly lopsided.

'No. Not really. Life goes on.'

'Unless he is only missing in action... Action was what it was all about for Ray. He loved the war.' She frowned. 'Funny, I'd never really accepted that before, but it's true. If he'd been given a choice between staying at home or going off to war, he would still have chosen war – even if he could have stayed home.'

John poured the dessert wine, noticing its colour and thinking that its thick consistency was very close to blood. He wanted to hear her voice again but not hindsight comments relating to her husband, which stirred him to false hope at a time when he felt the niceties of grieving were not yet over.

'To peace,' he said, raising his glass in a toast.

'To peace.'

'So where did the dog originally come from? I'm intrigued.'

'I'm still not sure. I can tell you as much as I know, but it isn't much. Very little, in fact. Ray was always very secretive about his missions in France. I'm not sure I should even be mentioning them to you. But that was how he found them, you see, while he was over there.' She frowned as an odd thought surfaced. 'At times I think he used to prefer being over there to being with me in London. More exciting, I suppose...'

She rubbed at the sudden chill at the nape of her neck. Up until this moment it had never occurred to her that this might indeed be the case.

John interrupted. 'Dangerous, though.'

His comment brought her back from her thoughts. 'Lily and Rudy were found together. Lily was in a dreadful state, very thin and unconscious. She regained consciousness long enough to insist that she wasn't going anywhere without her dog. Where she came from and where the dog came from is unknown.'

'You don't think they lived together?'

Meg eyed him warily. 'Ray thought at some point Lily had a Star of David sewn to her coat.'

'Jewish.'

'Yes.'

John tried to work out why she was eyeing him so warily. 'What is it?'

'Rudy has a number tattooed inside his ear. A military number. Ray thought he might have been a dog used by the German army to guard prisoners.'

John raised his eyebrows. 'Jews?'

She nodded. 'Possibly. It's the most likely explanation.'

John slumped back in his chair. 'I'm amazed. You wouldn't want anyone to know that – public feeling being what it is.'

Meg shook her head and, sighing, reached to pour more wine. 'Apparently Rudy was something of a trophy to Ray's RAF colleagues. Dogs, once employed by the enemy, instantly become mascots. Ray loved him.' She looked up suddenly. 'I would prefer nobody knows about the number and where the dog might have come from. Nobody would know unless you peered into his ear.'

'Your secret's safe with me.'

265

'Thank you.'

John winced when she raised her eyes. Talking about Ray and things past had darkened her eyes. They were now much brighter and full of hope. She went on to tell him about her day.

'Yesterday I think a miracle began to happen. My little girl – she's only my foster child but to me she is indeed my little girl – responded to that dog. Suddenly she was speaking again. It's early days, John, but I truly believe her healing has begun.'

'You mean she might also remember her past?'

Meg nodded.

'Doesn't that worry you?'

Meg nodded again. 'Of course it does. She used to have nightmares. I'm hoping she won't have any more. On the plus side, she might remember her real name and that of her parents. She'll want to go with them. I do realise that.'

'If they're still alive,' John murmured.

Meg silently acknowledged what he was saying.

'I have both you and Mrs Dando to thank for keeping Rudy here. Without you two there might never have been a chance of this happening. I'm grateful, I really am.'

John smiled. 'Glad I could be of some service. Shame about Mrs Dando though.' He frowned. 'Odd, too. She definitely died of a heart attack but there was some blood on the landing. We couldn't find any bleeding on her and there's no sign of forced entry. All we can think is that the dog caught a rat or something and ate it. Dogs sometimes do.'

'It's possible. He liked Mrs Dando. He still stops at her garden gate and looks in as though expecting to see her.'

John was intrigued. 'Does he now?'

It was gone ten when John shrugged himself into his coat and Meg shepherded him to the front door. He paused before leaving. There was so much he'd like to say but he settled for, 'Thank you for a lovely dinner.'

'Thank *you* for a lovely dinner. I don't know where you got those rabbits, but they were first class.'

There was a sudden narrowing of space between them, a pregnant pause in conversation as both weighed up the possibility of a goodnight kiss. But the awkward moment was swiftly shattered as the dog dashed between them, bounding to the leafy convenience of a laurel hedge where he paused to relieve himself.

John wished her goodnight. Meg waited for the dog to finish before going back inside.

PC Carter walked away from Bluebell Cottage deep in thought. He was thinking about Meg, the little girl and the dog. He'd been touched by the story of Meg's husband finding Lily and Rudy together in occupied France, the pair of them bound by some inner understanding. That was the thing with animals, they still had instinct, able to size people up with a look or a sniff. A good dog that, he thought to himself.

Thinking of the dog took him back to thinking about Ivy Dando. He could do with making more enquiries, and if you wanted to know anything in this village you went to the pub. Upper Standwick was hardly a hotbed of crime, most of it confined to poaching or warning the local pub landlord not to serve drinks after hours. So even though he was off duty tonight, it was in that capacity that he called in at around quarter to eleven that night and pointed out the time.

'P'raps it's a bit fast,' he said, frowning as he pulled back his coat sleeve and peered at his wristwatch. 'Mine's just before ten twenty-five.'

'Best have a half while I check it,' offered Cliff.

This scenario was acted out quite frequently. PC Carter didn't need any newfangled detecting methods to find out what was going on in the village. All he had to do was call in at the pub and, after a half of bitter, he knew everything. Old Tom went on about the air raid and Gladys told him about the dog and how she'd removed the wire from around his back leg.

Carter swiped at the froth from the beer that clung to his ginger moustache. 'Poor thing must have been in some pain.' He frowned suddenly. 'Funnily enough, there were bloodstains up on Mrs Dando's landing. But I swear the dog wasn't injured then. I would have noticed it.'

Cliff frowned. 'I didn't know that. So he couldn't have got it trapped in a snare when he was with her.'

The policeman shook his head. 'No. His leg was injured after that.'

'After he toppled you from your bike,' Cliff said with a smirk. There were chuckles all round.

Carter ploughed on regardless. 'It still doesn't explain the blood on the landing and the spots of it on her bedroom carpet.'

'He didn't bite her by any chance?'

Carter shook his head. 'No. Ivy Dando died of a

heart attack. There wasn't a mark of anything else on her.' He frowned as a sudden thought hit him. 'Though the doctor said she had a few bruises he couldn't explain. But definitely no bite marks. Yes, definitely a heart attack. And she'd spilt her cocoa and her book was on the floor. Still, the blood must have come from somewhere.'

'Are you having it tested? I'm group O by the way. The doc told me so.'

'No point. The doctor confirmed how she died so that's that. He said bruises at her age aren't that uncommon. Old folk are prone to falling down and bruising themselves.'

'I do that meself,' said Old Tom and everyone laughed.

'Yeah, but that's from the drink!' More laughter.

Carter remarked on Gladys removing the wire from around the dog's back leg. Cliff replied, 'That dog must have been in pain for days. No wonder the poor thing wasn't keen to have anyone take it off. It's a miracle he let anyone at all. He let my Gladys do it. Didn't make a peep when she did.'

'I wouldn't stand any nonsense if he did,' Gladys interjected.

Cliff's belly wobbled as he laughed. 'And don't we just know it, my sweet!'

Even after Carter's watch had been adjusted and despite being officially off duty, he left to do his last round. Cliff was unsure that he'd got it right about the dog but was in agreement with the policeman that it had been hale and hearty, using all four legs right up until Ivy Dando's funeral.

Gladys told him not to dwell on it. 'P'raps Ivy

didn't notice it was injured. She did wear glasses.'

'Leave it out, love. Carter confirmed he wasn't injured right up until he toppled from his bike. The dog caught it in a trap at some point. Still, don't it make you wonder? I mean to say, if it weren't the dog's blood on the floor, whose was it?'

Gladys gave it some serious thought. 'Liver,' she finally exclaimed. 'I expect Ivy had a bit of liver for her supper and spilt some of the gravy on the floor. John said himself it was only a few spots.'

Cliff frowned as he nodded, but although his wife had a point, he wasn't entirely convinced. He'd have another word with PC Carter at some point just to make sure he'd heard right and the blood spots had been found on the floor upstairs not down. Drinking cocoa in bed was one thing. Eating liver was another.

CHAPTER NINETEEN

After the soaking he got the night the dog had got the better of him, Bert Dando hung his wet clothes over the beam running through the attic room. He was so livid that he chose to ignore the air-raid sirens. Neither had he cared about the sound of bombs dropping in the distance. Not one bomb had fallen on him in London and he wasn't expecting one to get him here in Upper Standwick.

So instead of worrying about bombs, he put his

mind to ferreting out some of his old clothes from the chest where his mother had stored them. The clothes were old but not what he would call worn out. As he got out what he needed, he threw aside the mothballs his mother had put in with them, not quite realising what they were or how strongly they smelled. He'd never had a nose for smells.

He had bathed his cut wrist in the sink downstairs, being careful to throw the water outside on the garden and leave everything as clean as possible. That damned dog! First, it had bit his calf and now it had injured his hand. It was neither here nor there that it was his own fault due to snaring the animal with the deeply cutting wire. Bert didn't think that way. Everything should have gone according to plan but the dog had turned the tables and injured him again. *Never mind, Bert,* he said to himself, *you'll get even, my old son.*

On his way back from falling into the pond, he'd stolen a truckle of cheese from the storeroom in the dairy along the road. There were at least twenty-four truckles drying out and it wasn't likely one would be missed, especially as he'd taken one from the very back. The truckles were used in sequence, drying out sometimes for a year before they were used. There would also be no sign of forced entry. This was Upper Standwick. Doors were left open, neighbours entered freely.

Cigarettes were more of a problem than food. The village store sold cigarettes but the only way of getting his hands on any was to break in and steal them. He couldn't do that just yet, not until he was really desperate and close to leaving. Breaking in might give him away and he didn't want to be discovered, at least not until he'd taken his revenge on that bloody dog!

In the meantime he would survive, though he wasn't too sure he liked the silence of the house. Much as he hated to admit it, he was missing his mother. It came as quite a surprise to find that he'd got used to the sound of her bustling about downstairs. The old woman had looked after him, cooking reasonable meals and doing his laundry. His culinary skills only stretched to fried bacon, egg and a bit of fried bread, not that he had such luxuries. For the moment he would use up everything that was in the kitchen larder, preferably eating it cold during the day. Tinned stuff was best. Beans, corned beef, tinned pineapple rings and peaches. Night-time would be the best time to cook anything up, but even then he would have to be careful. Not having a good sense of smell made him vulnerable, in which case he would have to curtail cooking to the dead hours of night. As for laundry, well, as long as his thick jumper and tweed trousers were comfortable and kept him warm, that was enough for him.

Thanks to the home-made cider from the scullery, he slept well that night. In the morning he was hungry and, although he preferred to go downstairs only at night, his need was greater than his fear of being discovered. He took the tin of treacle from the back of the larder, carrying it upstairs with him, spooning it into his mouth until half the tin was gone. He didn't bother making tea, washing down his odd repast with more cider.

272

Between eating and drinking he propped himself up to look down at the outside world, village life going on all around him. This was the one thing he did like about his lone existence: peering unseen from the attic window, watching the ebb and flow of people passing by, knowing he could watch their daily lives unfolding without them knowing he was there. He grinned when he saw the vicar, nodding his small head on his giraffe-like neck and smiling at Mrs Crow, a woman of rotund proportions and a sharp tongue, chairwoman of the flower-arranging committee and well known for being the font of all gossip. When he was a boy – well known as the biggest scamp in the village – he'd climbed over her garden fence to steal cherries. Nobody in the village had a cherry tree except her.

One day she'd caught him, grabbed him with her staunch hand, pulled down his trousers and plastered his bottom with brown paper spread with honey. His dad had been alive then, seen the state he was in, found out the truth and given him what for. He'd never touched honey since then, though Bert hadn't let things rest there.

Continuing to harbour a grudge, he'd gone back in the middle of the night three years after his father had died and trod all her dahlias into the earth. Every year it was an accepted fact that she would win the dahlia contest at the village horticultural show. She didn't that year and there was nobody around to point the finger at him. Nobody to chastise him either. His father would have suspected his involvement and tanned his backside, but his father was dead and gone by then, and if his mother had known she'd never dare mention it. He'd had her under his thumb and, truth to tell, he missed having somebody to bully. Still, it wouldn't be too long before things in London would have cooled down and he could go back to live life high on the hog. But not until he wanted to. He still had that dog to deal with.

The village kids were in his front garden playing hide and seek, carefully keeping to the lawn without trampling the flowers. Very considerate of them. His eyes narrowed. The grass was growing. He suspected somebody in the village would be along to cut it. No doubt that meddling air-raid warden, Reg Puller. A wicked grin came to his face along with a wicked thought. He'd love to rush out there and clip them all around their ears, or kick their errant little backsides and shout, 'Get out of my fucking garden!'

When PC Carter cycled past, he ducked down out of sight. Even a simple village policeman like John Carter made him nervous. He did the same when the air-raid warden strolled past early in the evening. Must be the uniforms, he decided.

The pair of them had a habit of inspecting the cottage, making sure nothing had been disturbed since his mother's death, walking up the garden path and ducking under the rose arch at the side of the house and into the back garden. They even chased out the kids playing there. He kept dead quiet when he knew they were around.

His favourite subjects were the young women who he leered at in private while appraising each one in turn. Some of them he remembered from school. Some of them he'd bullied. He grinned at the thought of it. There were many pigtails he'd pulled, many sweets he'd stolen from hands weaker than his. He espied Alice Grey, who he recalled had married Peter Wickes, so she was Alice Wickes now. He grinned at the thought of how he'd targeted her when she was younger. They'd been strolling across a summer meadow when he'd thrown her to the ground, tearing at her underclothes as she screamed and cried. Nobody had come to her rescue.

'And don't you go saying anything or that's your reputation gone. Nobody will want to marry you if they knew you were a tart.'

She'd protested that she wasn't a tart. That he'd been too strong for her. He'd liked the thought of that, him being strong enough to do as he liked with her. The downside was that she'd never gone out with him again. Never allowed herself to be alone with him at all, hurrying away at the sight of him. He wondered if she still remembered what had happened?

For a while after that he'd been sweet on Pammy Fielding, a girl of buxom proportions, a ruddy complexion and well known for being easy to entice into a hayrick for a bit of rough and tumble. Since living in London his tastes had changed. Plump, rosy-faced girls, no matter how willing, just didn't appeal. He'd tasted city girls and developed definite tastes. Village girls were no longer for him.

One or two of the girls he recognised pushed kids along in prams and pushchairs. The looks of some of them had improved since their schooldays, though none of them roused any desire.

Bert preferred the London girls with their loud laughter and their scarlet lipstick. The village girls were like dormice compared to their town cousins. There wasn't a woman in the village he'd go out of his way to seduce.

He maintained that view until he saw her, the young woman who walked her blonde-haired daughter to school. The woman's hair was so golden it glowed when hit by sunlight. She moved gracefully, like the racehorses he'd seen in the paddock at Kempton Park. He'd been a bookie's runner then, loved the money and loved to watch the horses, their muscles rippling beneath their lean forms. Graceful, they were. And so was she.

He'd watched her every day, making a point of getting up earlier on schooldays than at weekends so he could enjoy the sight of her walking by. Looking at her was a pleasure he relived in his mind all day. He'd never seen her with a man so presumed she didn't have one. He could tell from the way she dressed that she wasn't local, and smiled appreciatively. He knew a London girl when he saw one. 'Just my type,' he muttered to himself and licked his lips.

This morning she was accompanied by a dog, an Alsatian with sharply pointed ears and a way of lunging into his collar as he walked along. Bert's jaw clamped hard; he recognised immediately the dog his mother had taken in, the one who'd wrapped its teeth around his calf.

As his eyes hardened and he ground his teeth, he rubbed at the wound in his leg. It was slowly healing thanks to the contents of his mother's medicine chest but it would leave a scar. He'd failed to catch and deal with the creature the night he'd fallen into the village pond, but he wouldn't give up now. The dog would get what was coming to it.

True to character as the bully he was, Bert never forgave any perceived slight or wound received from others, but seeing the dog with the woman he considered just his type riled him and, oddly enough, even made him feel jealous. What right did the vicious creature have to be walking with such an elegant woman? If he had his way, he would be the one walking with her.

He saw Mrs Crow plough along the road, stopping to speak to the London woman, her round face as wizened as a raisin, her small mouth pecking at her words like a bird dissecting a pike of ripe millet. The woman with the dog looked taken aback. It occurred to him that Mrs Crow might be picking on her. For what reason he didn't have a clue, but he didn't like it. In one fleeting moment, he'd claimed the elegant woman with the dog and the little girl as his personal property. Not that she'd know about it, but then, she didn't need to.

Bert frowned. He couldn't hear what was being said, but didn't like the look on Mrs Crow's face. She had her angry look, one he knew well. Head in the air, Mrs Crow stalked off, leaving the woman with the golden hair looking upset. Well that was typical, but he was having none of it! He wouldn't have let the old bitch get away with upsetting her if he'd been there. He'd have dealt with it. He stretched his neck as far as he could until the woman he'd become infatuated with was out of sight. Mrs Crow had been her usual nasty self to the good-looking woman. He was convinced of it.

Suddenly he espied PC Carter chasing after his London beauty on his bicycle and heard him call out her name.

'Meg!'

The name drifted softly upwards. Meg. So that was her name. He vaguely recalled his mother telling him about some woman and her daughter who'd come to the village from London following a heavy air raid, and that her husband had been in the air force but got killed. This had to be the one. But where the hell did the dog fit in?

Both the dog and the woman had entered his life without him inviting them. He was becoming obsessed with both but for different reasons. The dog would be disposed of. The woman – Meg – was his for the taking. That was the great thing about these dark nights. At some point he would creep up on her and get what he wanted – just as he'd done with the woman who was now Mrs Alice Wickes.

All that morning he spent planning what he would do about Mrs Crow in retribution for her treatment of the lovely Meg. The contradiction between his intention to rape the lovely lady and to defend her against Mrs Crow's sharp tongue was wasted on him. What Bert wanted, Bert got.

After setting the matter straight in his mind, his thoughts turned to what he would do in London when he went back there. The old lady didn't leave much money in the house when she died. He needed to make some more, but in the meantime this village was set for a wakening.

At lunchtime he sneaked down into the kitchen and made himself a corned beef sandwich. There were about five tins of corned beef in the larder, plus a loaf of bread he'd stolen from the back room of the bakery when nobody was looking. It would do him for a week or so, toasted once it turned stale.

As he munched on his sandwich and drank tea flavoured with condensed milk, he mused over Mrs Crow and the dismayed look on Meg's face. He grinned salaciously, thinking himself quite the man, the hero of the hour who would avenge any slight from Mrs Crow. If he had happened to look in the mirror, he would have seen that his reflection was hardly the stuff dreamboats are made of. But it wasn't what she wanted that concerned him, it was what he wanted, and what he wanted he always set out to get.

'Meg, my girl. I'm here for you.'

As for Mrs Crow, she ought to be taught a lesson. *And you, my son, are the one to teach her,* he thought as he chewed. He considered how best to upset the old bitch. What was her passion, the thing she loved above all others?

Dahlias! *There you are,* he thought to himself. *You do the same as you did in the past, me old china!* It was a pound to a penny that she probably still did grow dahlias, as keen to win the cup she'd won every year since time immemorial. He'd trample them into the ground just as he had before. Imagine her face! He chuckled at the thought of it.

He spent the afternoon sleeping and stealthily walking from one room to another, down the stairs, up the stairs, a cigarette hanging from his mouth. Each cigarette stub was saved and broken apart to remake a fresh one. It wasn't ideal but it was all he had until he got back to London.

As darkness fell, he took the remains of the corned beef, some more bread and a cup upstairs. The one thing he was careful about was hiding his tracks, just in case some nosy bugger peered through the window. Nothing had changed since his mother's death, everything was in its proper place.

Slowly the darkness invaded every corner of the attic room until the moon came out from behind a bank of clouds and silvered the blackout with its chill white light. Good enough for me, Bert thought to himself. His plans were made.

It was close to midnight when he made his way down the stairs into the kitchen. Standing by the back door, he breathed heavily like a greyhound at the White City, panting to be chasing the hare. He waited until the time was right. The clock in the church tower struck at the same time as the moon retreated behind a cloud. Keeping close to walls, bushes and trees, he moved swiftly out through the back gate, along the little-used path that ran between Malago Brook and the rear walls of a whole terrace of cottage gardens.

Mrs Crow's cottage was detached and stood in its own generous gardens. It was said in the village that you could smell her garden before setting eyes on it. She grew all kinds of flowers, most of them heavily scented, the dahlias being an exception, though like everyone else in the village, nowadays she grew more vegetables than flowers. But she still grew flowers. He was sure of it.

A shaft of moonlight struck the back wall of the garden he sought. He recalled there being a trellis-work arch over the back gate thickly covered with some kind of climbing plant. Keeping low behind a ramshackle shed with hoes and garden rakes hanging from its sides, he narrowed his eyes. The moon served him well. The trelliswork arch was right in front of him, picked out by moonlight and throwing a shadow on the back wall.

Darkness fell like a blanket as he inched forward, carefully holding the hinges of the gate to stop them from squeaking. If he remembered rightly, Mrs Crow's beloved flowers were on the right-hand side of the uneven garden path. This was it, he thought joyfully as his feet sank into the earth. This is where she grows her pride and joy. Silently and quickly he began to trample the unseen plants into the earth, kicking and jumping on each and every leaf that brushed his legs. Given the chance, he might willingly have gone all over the garden until every single plant was laid low. As it was he had no wish to be discovered. Mrs Crow wouldn't know who'd destroyed her plants and in consequence, she would be beside herself and the village would be up in arms.

Back home he took off his boots at the back gate and scraped the mud off into the water butt, the mud falling beneath the fly-speckled water. Nobody would be any the wiser as to who had paid a nocturnal visit to Mrs Crow's garden. He had covered his tracks well. Up in the attic he lit a cigarette, smiling at the thought of what he had done and imagining how that old cow would react. The village too. Smug vicar. Officious policeman.

Pompous Mr Puller, the air-raid warden. He bore grudges towards all of them and taking revenge brought delicious thoughts to mind. They all deserved some of the same treatment, acts of revenge by person or persons unseen. In the absence of anyone else, they'd turn upon each other.

Bert swelled with pride. Yes. That's what he would do. It was the best ruse he'd ever had and what's more, he would enjoy doing it. Just for a few weeks until he judged it safe to return to London. But first, he wanted a close encounter with the lovely Meg, though to do that he had to get rid of the dog. He had to get her alone.

CHAPTER TWENTY

Meg sniffed the air and closed her eyes. The smell of the two plum cakes she'd just taken from the oven was quite delicious. Normally she would only make one for consumption by herself and Lily. Today she had baked two and for very good reason. Although identical, Meg knew there were more plums in one than the other. The one with the most plums in was for Mrs Crow by way of a peace offering.

'I'm sorry,' she'd said to her when they'd met head on in the street yesterday. 'I really hadn't noticed that Lily picked your flowers. And anyway, they were growing on the verge outside your garden wall. I didn't know they were yours...'

The way Mrs Crow pursed her lips was akin to

sucking on a lemon. Her words were sharp as needles. 'That's the trouble with people like you from the city. You know nothing about folk like us and the way things are done round 'ere.'

'I really am sorry, Mrs Crow. I didn't notice her picking them. She always used to like making daisy chains in our garden in London.'

'They are marguerites, not daisies. And they weren't growing in your garden in London. They were growing in mine.' Mrs Crow jerked her chin disapprovingly at the chain of flowers Meg had thought were wild moon daisies hanging around Rudy's neck.

'I didn't realise the flowers growing outside your garden wall were yours. I'm sorry,' Meg repeated. 'I promise she won't do it again.'

Lily had looked from her mother to the po-faced woman berating her about the lovely necklace she'd made for her dog.

Mrs Crow heaved her awesome breast, her nostrils flaring like a mettlesome horse. 'Most people in the village have dug up their flowers, gone over to growing vegetables to eke out their rations. I am one of the few people in the village still growing enough flowers for the bereaved to place on the graves of their loved ones and to decorate the church to the glory of God. I'm sure you can see my point given your own recent tragedy.'

Meg had felt her face burning. She really hadn't noticed what Lily was doing, absorbed as she often was nowadays with wondering if Ray really was dead and, if so, was he at the bottom of the sea or blown to bits? 'I'm sorry,' she'd said again.

A curt nod and the confrontation was over. Mrs

283

Crow moved on.

She couldn't help wondering about her husband, just in case he was found alive and well. It was a forlorn hope, but all she had. Every day she watched the postman making his way around the postboxes of the cottages bordering the village green, hoping and praying that he would stop at Bluebell Cottage and hand her a letter saying that a mistake had been made; that Ray was alive and a prisoner of war. Waiting for years for him to come home would be preferable to the prospect of living a life without him by her side.

'You must not pick Mrs Crow's flowers again,' Meg said to Lily. 'Do you understand?'

The girl nodded solemnly.

'Promise?'

'I promise,' she said.

Meg was thankful that she'd replied in English. While Lily doted on the dog and rarely drew houses with flames coming out of their roofs – a fact Meg was extremely grateful for as she began to emerge from her shell, she sometimes reverted to German, as though her English had got a little lost along the way. Deep down, Meg feared her speaking in German. She worried that if she remembered more German, she might also remember something of her family. If she did so, then they could be traced and Lily would be lost to her. It was a selfish notion but she couldn't help it.

Following the altercation, Meg had felt obliged to make amends for Lily picking her flowers. She felt guilty, given Mrs Crow's reason for still growing them when everyone else had turned their

284

gardens over to the growing of vegetables.

As it was Saturday, there was no school. 'Come on,' she said to Lily. 'Let's take this lovely cake to Mrs Crow, shall we?' After wrapping the cake in a clean tea towel, she placed it in a basket. 'Rudy can stay here,' she said, as Lily picked up his leash.

Two sets of soulful eyes looked up at her accusingly, one pair brown, the other blue. Meg sighed. 'We're taking a cake to an old lady. It would be better if we leave Rudy here.'

Lily's bottom lip quivered; Rudy whimpered. The two pairs of eyes continued to gaze at her imploringly.

Meg knew when she was beaten. She sighed but said firmly. 'All right. You win. But no picking flowers. Understood? As for you,' she said, turning to Rudy. 'You will stay at the garden gate until I've done what I have to do. Is that clear?'

Rudy wagged his tail. Lily smiled.

It wasn't unusual to see PC Carter's bicycle outside Mrs Crow's cottage, so Meg thought nothing of it but sauntered up to the door, the basket containing the plum cake banging against her hip. People dropped in on each other all the time. Lily and Rudy followed behind her, the dog's leash wound tightly around Lily's fragile hand.

Meg turned at the front door and pointed at the dog. 'Sit!' Rudy sat down, his ears up, eyes alert. 'Lily. Put the lead down and come with me.'

Lily glanced over her shoulder.

Meg noticed her pensive look. 'Rudy will still be there when we get back. Now come on,' she insisted.

Lily patted the dog on the head and gave him a

hug. 'We'll be back soon. Be a good boy.'

Meg felt something shift inside. More words, though she had to admit that Lily spoke more to the dog than she did to humans. But that didn't matter. Lily was coming out of herself and the world felt a more beautiful place. Rudy wagged his tail.

The front door to Japonica Cottage was open. Not quite used yet to the ways of the village, Meg paused at the door, reluctant to enter until properly invited. 'Hello? Is anyone there?' She pushed the door open gently. The smell of bees-wax and the sweetness of late-flowering roses wafted outwards from the interior.

'Come in, whoever you are!' The voice was brusque. Definitely Mrs Crow.

A wave of warmth came from the cast-iron range sitting in the old inglenook fireplace. A series of sepia-tinted photographs sat above it on the solid oak mantelpiece. Meg presumed them to be family photographs: young men in uniform, women in leg-of-mutton sleeves and high tight collars. Two cats lay on separate cushions on a window seat, their tails lashing, their eyes staring at the strangers as though hostile at having their privacy invaded.

Mrs Crow was slumped in a chair, her hand over her eyes. She was sobbing silently. PC Carter was standing over her, a reassuring hand on her shoulder. 'There, there,' he soothed.

Mrs Crow's head jerked upwards, her face creased with dismay. 'Never mind "there, there". All my plants ruined. And done deliberately!' A finger as gnarled as an old twig pointed towards the open back door. 'Trampled. The whole lot's been trampled.'

'We don't know that for sure... It might have been cows or sheep.'

'It weren't no cows or sheep!' Mrs Crow cried. 'Did you see any hoofmarks? No, you did not!'

Mrs Crow's splinter-bright eyes spotted Meg standing at the door and one side of Lily peering out behind from behind her hip. 'If you've come to sympathise, don't bother, and if you want flowers there aren't any. Not many vegetables either.' Her tone was less than welcoming.

Meg was taken aback. 'Has something happened?' She looked at the policeman for explanation.

Carter took off his helmet and wiped his brow. 'Mrs Crow's prize dahlias have been trampled into the ground.'

'Not just my dahlias. Everything! Delphiniums, lupins... Everything, even my vegetables.'

'That's terrible,' said Meg. 'Who would do such a thing?'

'Who indeed!' Mrs Crow's eyes blazed with indignation, so much so that for a moment Meg felt that she was suspected of the dastardly crime.

Swiftly realising that wasn't the case, she gathered her thoughts in order to say the right thing. 'It seems very odd that someone would trample the vegetables. A thief would have taken vegetables, surely, unless he wasn't hungry or had no one he could sell them to.'

Carter frowned as he nodded. 'My thinking exactly.'

'Jealousy,' snarled Mrs Crow, her eyes glittering. 'That's what it is. Do you know how many years Fred Grimes has been pushed into second place with his dahlias? Twenty years. Twenty years! He couldn't beat me so he's finally lost his mind and decided to destroy me!'

'Now, now,' said PC Carter, his tone as long suffering as his expression. 'You can't say that for sure, Mrs Crow. There's no evidence. Besides, old Fred's pins are a bit dodgy. I can't see him doing anything like that.'

Mrs Crow was like a dog with a bone. 'It was him. It has to be him!' She'd decided Fred Grimes was the culprit, and until somebody proved otherwise, that was the way it would stay.

PC Carter sighed. He had been village policeman long enough to know that the peaceful idyll was not always what it should be. There were rivalries over matters city folk would consider too trivial to pursue. Winning prizes at the annual horticultural show was small fry to them but red meat to the likes of Mrs Crow and Fred Grimes.

He was determined to wrap this up as quickly as possible. His feet ached in the new boots he was presently breaking in, and he was desperate for a cup of tea and a visit to the bathroom. With that at the top of his agenda, he straightened his helmet and got ready to leave. Normally he'd get a cup of tea for his trouble, but Mrs Crow was in no mood for making anyone tea. He wasn't likely to get another cup at Japonica Cottage until the whole case of the downtrodden dahlias was put to bed.

His attention shifted to Meg, who was nice to look at and more amenable to deal with. He would have liked to thank her again for the rabbit stew the other night, but didn't dare do that in front of Mrs Crow or the news would fly around the village. 'Was it me you came to see, Mrs Malin?' He eyed her hopefully.

Meg shook her head. 'No. I came to see Mrs Crow.' She attempted a smile as she raised her basket. 'I've brought a peace offering,' she said to the old lady.

Mrs Crow eyed her quizzically, a deep frown wrinkling her tanned forehead. PC Carter lingered, keen to know what this was all about. Mrs Crow noticed and instantly gave him a piercing look. 'I expect you've got things to do.'

Carter recognised he was being dismissed, and Mrs Crow wasn't the sort you got into arguments with. Clearing his throat, he got to his feet, his knees cricking as he did so. 'I'll be off then.'

'Yes,' snapped Mrs Crow. 'You be off then. We've already agreed on that.'

The policeman eased himself past Meg and her daughter, smiling at Meg and patting Lily on the head. 'No doubt I'll be seeing you around, Mrs Malin. Anything you want, I'm always around.'

'Thank you.' Meg returned the smile, noting that he'd called her Mrs Malin in Mrs Crow's presence whereas over dinner she'd been Meg.

Whistling nonchalantly, he strode off down the garden path and into the high street. After a few yards he remembered he'd left his bicycle, came back and collected it.

Meg summoned up all her courage and turned round to face Mrs Crow. 'I've brought you a plum cake. It's freshly baked.' She tried not to sound nervous.

289

A pair of deep-set eyes narrowed to glass chips and looked at her sharply. 'Why?'

'Because of Lily picking the flowers... To say we're sorry...'

The moment the words were out of her mouth, Meg realised they could be easily misunderstood and instantly regretted them. 'I mean, the other day. Not this. Certainly not this. It wasn't her that trampled your flowers. I mean, she only picked the ones outside on the verge. She wouldn't go into your garden without being invited and certainly not overnight. Honestly she wouldn't.'

Mrs Crow made a huffing noise that sounded as though it could be disbelief, then shook her head. 'I am not stupid, Mrs Malin. Somebody wearing big boots destroyed my flowers, not some dainty little thing like her.' She waved her hand dismissively at Lily, then suddenly jerked her head forward and addressed the little girl directly. 'You like flowers, child. You wouldn't step on them, would you.' It was a statement, not a question.

Lily's eyes widened as she shook her head.

'No, she wouldn't,' Meg added emphatically. 'But she did pick your flowers without asking permission. That's why I baked you this cake.' She placed her basket on the kitchen table, pulled back the tea towel and took out the plum cake.

Mrs Crow sat back in her chair, produced a lace-edged handkerchief from her pocket and blew her nose. 'Push the kettle back on to the hob. I could do with a cup of tea and a piece of cake. The cups and saucers are over there on the dresser. Let's see how good a cake maker you are.'

Meg crossed the flagstoned floor to where an

290

oak dresser took up almost the whole wall. A range of mismatched china of every description hung from hooks or stood upright, propped against the wooden slats at the back. The teapot was hidden beneath a knitted cosy. The cups were blue-striped Cornish, thick and serviceable.

Meg made the tea and placed the pot, a cup and saucer, sugar and milk on to a tray along with a slice of cake on a matching plate. She wouldn't dare pour a cup for herself or slice a piece of the cake, and anyway she didn't particularly want to. She'd made amends and that would do.

Feeling just a little contrite, she paused by the door. 'Are you going to be all right?'

Mrs Crow helped herself to a bite of cake and grunted. 'I'm going to have to be, aren't I?'

'Then I'll be going. Let me know if there's anything you want.'

Mrs Crow grunted again before taking another bite of cake. 'You make a good plum cake,' she shouted after Meg as she made her way out of the door.

Meg threw her a thankful smile.

'And shut the door behind you. I've had enough visitors for one day. I don't want any more!'

'I will indeed,' Meg murmured beneath her breath.

Lily ran on ahead, straight to the place where they'd left Rudy tied to the gate post of the field next door. He wasn't there. Lily whirled around on her heels looking for him and calling out. 'Rudy! Rudy! Where are you?'

Meg felt leaden. Frantically she looked and shouted just as Lily had done. Suddenly she saw

291

him. 'There he is!'

He was on the other side of the village green, ranging up and down the hedge surrounding Mrs Dando's cottage, pausing each time he got to the closed gate. The gate had remained closed ever since Mrs Dando's death.

'Rudy!'

Lily dashed across the village green. Meg followed behind her, wishing she were wearing more sensible shoes as she sprinted over the green grass. Lily shouted Rudy's name again. The two collided and Lily threw her arms around his neck. The dog licked her face in greeting before his intelligent eyes returned to fix on the front door of Mrs Dando's cottage. He seemed very agitated, pawing at the garden gate, whimpering as though in sorrow for the lady who had been kind to him.

Meg was still dwelling on Mrs Crow and the flowers. She had no patience this morning for a stubborn dog. 'Now what's this all about, Rudy? It's no good looking for Mrs Dando. She doesn't live there any more.'

The dog whimpered.

Meg looked up at the cottage windows, small squares beneath overhanging eaves of red pan tiles. Above them was a dormer window set into the main structure of the roof, its panes of glass as small as those on the first floor. The windows stared vacantly back, like dead eyes reflecting the clouds and scene around them.

She shook her head. The dog's behaviour was a mystery unless he was remembering Mrs Dando and how kind she'd been. Meg ruffled his ears. 'Mrs Dando is gone, Rudy. You live with us now.'

292

The dog whined one more time but seemed to understand.

'Come on, Rudy. We have to go home,' said Lily, tugging him gently until he finally wagged his tail and did as he was told. 'Why did he run away?' asked Lily as they made their way back to Bluebell Cottage, her big eyes full of concern.

Meg shook her head. 'I don't know. Perhaps it was because he suddenly remembered Mrs Dando. She was very kind to him when he first came to the village.'

Neither Meg nor Lily noticed the twitching of a curtain high up in the attic window. Neither did they see Bert Dando's nervous look. He'd covered his tracks regarding the damage he'd done to Mrs Crow's garden. Nobody could have traced him – except for the dog. Everyone knew dogs had a keener sense of smell than humans. Still, as long as he lay low for the next couple of days, he should be all right. Two days was enough time to sort out old grievances and destroy that bloody dog!

Now for my next trick, he thought to himself, gloating at the prospect of what he intended to do next. Fred Grimes had once scolded him for throwing stones at his garden shed. He guessed Mrs Crow would accuse the old man of trampling her garden seeing as the pair of them had been feuding for years. Well, how about adding a bit of ammunition to the warring pair? Give them something to fight about?

Bert chuckled, got out the last cigarette in the packet and began to make plans.

293

CHAPTER TWENTY-ONE

Fred Grimes lived in a cottage that didn't have plumbed-in water, which meant that each morning he had to fill his kettle from the old pump outside the back door. Come winter, summer, spring or autumn, he was a man who rose early, revelling in the freshness of morning when it seemed the world was empty of people, most of whom were still in bed. Dew-spotted cobwebs strung between golden rod and wild poppies, glistening like jewels in the morning light. Fred relished this time of year, loving the freshness of it after the over-exuberance of summer; the crispness of a new September day.

On this particular morning, he took only one deep breath before he saw the desecration of his garden and his jaw dropped. Stiff-kneed or not, he tottered back inside as quickly as he could, slammed the kettle down on the kitchen table, grabbed his overcoat and dashed out. It pained him to run, but he went as fast as he could down the garden path and out of the gate, heading for PC Carter's house.

Carter glanced at his watch when he heard the frantic knocking on his door. 'Now what?'

Fred was red in the face, his hand was on his chest and he was breathing heavily. PC Carter opened the door wider. 'You'd better come in. Take a seat and tell me all about it.'

Fred almost fell on to the proffered Windsor chair – Carter's favourite. For the moment he would stand. 'Don't hurry. Get your breath first, Fred.'

Fred took great gulps of air. 'It was her! I knows it was her,' he cried excitedly. 'It's revenge for what she thinks I did to her garden. But I didn't do nothing. Nothing at all! The old witch! And now she does this!'

Carter, his own kettle just boiled and the teapot ready for the first brew of the day, rubbed at the bridge of his nose and the corners of his eyes with finger and thumb. 'Your garden's been trampled?'

Fred nodded. 'Yes. It bloody well 'as.'

The village policeman sighed. 'Look. I'm just about to pour myself a cup of tea. We can talk about it while we have a cuppa. How will that be?'

Fred was in no mood for polite conversation, until he perceived the whiff of bread fried in bacon fat. 'I can spare you a piece of fried bread too if you like,' said Carter, observant even at this time of the morning.

Fred slid his backside further back into the chair. 'Don't mind if I do.'

The news of yet more vandalism spread through the village like wildfire. Nobody could believe that Fred had trampled Mrs Crow's garden and vice versa. After all, Fred's knees had been shot for years. Getting as far as the post office was an ordeal and everyone knew he might take all day to plant a row of potatoes or a line of runner beans. Lurking around at night just didn't sit well with a man with dodgy legs and breathing issues.

In the absence of clues or local suspects, other

possibilities were suggested. *'Somebody from the base. They're Yanks. Big and brash. Saw them in the pub the other night. Loud lot and full of themselves.'* But nobody could quite see why a bunch of American air-force personnel would want to trample the plants in peoples' gardens. *'A prank. They'd do it as a prank after too many drinks at the Bear and Ragged Staff.'*

Kids from the village were also put forward as possible suspects, though every parent in the village insisted their children were tucked up in bed all night. It was also pointed out that the air-raid siren had sounded, which meant that the children were accounted for, as was everyone else for that matter. Everyone had taken refuge in whatever they used as an air-raid shelter, be it Anderson shelters or a cellar if they had one, or the cellar of the village inn if they didn't.

PC Carter scratched at his head. 'There has to be an explanation,' he said to Fred, having called in on him following his initial investigations.

'Somebody with a grudge against me,' Fred replied.

'And somebody with a grudge against Mrs Crow.'

'Well, that shouldn't be too difficult,' Fred grumbled. 'There's more than one in this village who'd like to trample her into the ground, let alone her plants!'

Unwilling to get further involved in a feud he knew for certain had lasted at least thirty years, he ambled off back to the station, popping into the Bear and Ragged Staff on the way. Over half a mild, he confided to Cliff that, although it looked as though the old folk were spatting at each other, he couldn't actually see them as out-and-out vandals.

'It certainly isn't Mrs Crow carrying out a reciprocal action. She's just not up to the job. She said herself her legs aren't what they were and everyone knows Fred suffers from arthritis, so although they might be competitors in the horticultural stakes, neither of them are physically fit.'

'Then it has to be a stranger,' said Cliff, his brawny arms resting on the bar top.

Carter took a good draught of his beer, thinking it might help fill the gap where his second slice of fried bread should have been, the other having been offered to Fred. 'A stranger would have to be hiding out somewhere. Nobody's seen anyone lurking around, not even the gypsies. Nobody's seen them around since harvest time.' The village was used to the gypsies appearing at harvest time, as casual labour to help with the harvest, though there were less of them now since the arrival of the land girls.

Cliff suggested, 'Blokes wanting to avoid being called up?'

Carter agreed that it was a possibility.

After he'd gone, Cliff couldn't help thinking that this kind of thing had happened before, but his memory wasn't quite what it was so the details were vague. That's the problem with memories, he thought to himself. Memories of things that happened so long ago tend to fly away like dandelion clocks.

CHAPTER TWENTY-TWO

Bert Dando lingered in bed the morning after he'd trampled Fred's garden. He finally awoke to the sound of heavy rain and wind, so heavy it rattled the glass in the windows. Rotten weather, he thought to himself, turning over and trying to get back to sleep. Sleep didn't happen. He was feeling too pleased with himself. He'd set the two old people against each other, but he wasn't done with this village yet. *Next stop,* he thought, rolling over on to his back.

It had been a long time since he'd been enjoyed the company of a woman and he was beginning to feel it. He could wait until he got back to London of course, but he just couldn't get Meg Malin out of his mind. He wanted to be in her company, just for an hour or so. But how to swing it?

Somehow he had to get her alone and persuade her to do what he wanted. Night-time was the best time but so far he didn't think she ventured out much at night. After all, there wasn't much in the village to venture out for unless it was for a drink at the pub and she didn't look the type. Did she take the dog for a walk at night? Somehow he didn't think so. It was aggravating but he was a patient man. He'd get what he wanted in the end. It was just a case of waiting for the right moment.

Getting Meg alone also meant arranging for the kid and dog to be absent. How exactly was he going to do that? Tall order, the lot of it. *Be patient, my boy, just like you used to when you were out poaching.*

Something unplanned and surprising happened a few days later. Even from his lofty eyrie he could read every word of the poster pasted on the trunk of the old beech tree standing between his cottage and the other side of the village green: DANCE. VILLAGE HALL. He could see it all: the date, time and everything. A smile spread across his face. The opportunity had come and he would grab it with both hands. It was just a case of careful planning.

He watched as people, mainly women, gathered around the poster chattering excitedly. He saw Alice there and Meg too. He saw Alice say something to the woman he fancied, saw Meg shake her head. Alice was wearing a persuasive look.

'Well, I'll be blowed! You're a lucky man, Bert, me old son!' They'd be going to the dance. Both of them.

This would be his chance to get Meg to himself. The blackout would be in force. The village hall would get warm inside because of the blackout curtains and so many people milling around. Inevitably people would come out to take the air. All he had to do was wait for Meg to do just that. It wasn't a definite that she would, but he was optimistic. As a widow, he didn't expect there to be a man with her and anyway, there weren't enough men in the village to go round. Yes, the night of the dance would be the best time to carry out his plan and he looked forward to it. He looked forward to it very much.

Bert was correct in that Meg and Alice were discussing the village dance. Alice was being persuasive but Meg was reluctant.

'Alice, I don't know if I really want to go. Not yet. Not until...'

'Meg,' Alice said gently. 'It's tragic that Ray is gone, love, but you have to go on living. Haven't you heard of that old saying? All work and no play makes Jack a dull boy. Grieving for ever shortens your life and you'll end up with wrinkles. Wouldn't want to be old and wrinkled before your time, would you? Come to that, I bet Ray wouldn't want that either. Live again, Meg, or you'll turn into a moaning Minnie and everyone will keep away from you.'

Meg laughed. Although Alice was married with three kids, her husband away at sea, she refused to be downhearted and thought she deserved a good time. 'My Stan wouldn't want me to be miserable. I've got to keep me spirits up for when he gets back. Anyway, I don't suppose he's leading the life of a monk. Well?'

Meg smiled and shook her head. 'I don't know what I'd do without your cheerfulness.'

Alice's round cheeks glistened like dewy apples. 'That's what I'm here for.'

'What about Lily? I can hardly take her to a grown-up dance.'

'Of course not! Our Annie's in the family way and won't be going. She's promised to look after my three. One more ain't going to make much difference.'

Annie was Alice's sister. It had come as some-

300

thing of a surprise when Meg found out that both Annie and Alice were married to their cousins. It seemed to happen in the village quite a lot and nobody seemed to take much notice of it. The village resembled a close-knit family and any excuse for a party was leapt on. But with all that had happened, Meg couldn't help feeling that she shouldn't be socialising until she knew for sure that Ray wasn't ever coming back, though Alice was very persuasive.

'I'm not sure... There's the dog to think of.'

When she'd first taken the dog in she tolerated him in the house, busily running the carpet sweeper over the worn rug once he was out of the way. At night she'd insisted he slept outside – until Lily reverted to one of her tantrums. Now he lay on the end of Lily's bed, his head on the cardigan she'd made for Lily from one of Ray's cast-offs.

Alice wasn't giving up easily. 'Meg, I have to point out to you that dogs are supposed to be left to guard your house. You don't have to guard them.'

Meg nodded. 'I'm just worried. You know how Lily used to be before he came along. I don't want her backsliding.'

'For one night?' Alice looked incredulous. 'It finishes round about ten so you can fetch her then. Lily and the dog will still spend the night together.'

'I suppose you're right.'

'Of course I am! Anyway,' she added with a sly wink, 'the Americans are coming. Have you seen them? I think of Clark Gable every time I see one.'

'You mean they all look like Hollywood film stars?'

301

'You bet they do! They can get a bit fresh if you're not careful, but I think we're adult enough to cope with that, don't you?'

Meg relaxed a little. 'I suppose so. I expect there'll be a few young girls there anyway.'

Alice pulled a face. 'You can say that again! No doubt a whole cartload of those trollops from Trowbridge will be there. Anything in trousers and there they are.'

Old Fred, who was now in the habit of coming round to tidy the garden at Bluebell Cottage and look after the vegetables, laughed when Meg asked him if the girls from Trowbridge were really as fast as Alice made them out to be. 'What you don't know, you're suspicious of – and jealous,' he added, tapping the side of his nose. Meg wondered if Alice regretted marrying her cousin. She certainly must have been very young at the time. She now had three children and couldn't be much more than twenty years of age.

Autumn days of red and gold persisted long into October. The harvest was in and the wheat and cornfields were sharp with stubble, like golden spears sticking up from the earth. A white mist shrouded the morning sun but had lifted by the time Meg fetched Lily from school.

Meg waved to Fred as she left the cottage. He was planting spring runner beans. Rudy was trotting along obediently at her side. Alice was at the school gates when she got there with her youngest, Reginald, in the pushchair. Little Reggie was about two years old. 'My parting gift from Stan,' Alice had told her happily when Meg had asked her how old he was. 'Can wait for another one,'

302

she'd added.

'Any news?' Meg asked.

'Funny you should ask. I had a letter this morning. Three weeks, he reckons.' Alice hunched her shoulders in excitement. 'Can't wait. But I'm still going to the dance. He won't be home until after that.'

Meg swallowed the pang of jealousy that sat like a stone in her chest. 'That's lovely for you.'

'Managing to feed that dog all right then?'

Meg said that she was. 'Cliff from the pub brings me bits of offal and the odd rabbit and pigeon when he's been out shooting. PC Carter brings me rabbits. I cooked one for dinner and he brought round a bottle of wine...'

'Did he now!' Alice said teasingly.

Meg felt her face getting hot. 'He's just being kind.'

'He's almost as good-looking as the Yanks, and don't say you haven't noticed.'

'He's just a friend!'

'Of course he is. He'd say the same to you about the dog. Nobody's going to break into your place, not if Rudy's got anything to do with it!'

Meg ruffled the soft fur between the dog's ears. In response, Rudy half closed his eyes.

'Seems as though he's been with you for ever. Mark my words, he's the loyal type. Knows who he likes and that's it.'

What Alice knew about dogs could possibly be written on a postage stamp but Meg accepted her comment graciously. Rudy was a lovely dog and liked who he liked. She shuddered at the thought of what his behaviour might be towards some-

303

body he despised.

'And Stan won't mind you going to the dance?'

Alice seemed a little ruffled. 'No. Of course not.'

Meg sensed there was something Alice was holding on to, a little secret from her past that occasionally brought a blush to her face. She knew from village gossip that she'd had to marry Stan, but that it wasn't that unusual. Most girls in the village had been in the family way when they'd walked up the aisle. Still, she decided she had a point.

'I think you could be right about the dog. He's very intelligent.'

'Go on,' said Alice. 'Tell me more.'

Meg told her about Rudy focusing on Mrs Dando's garden gate as though he was looking at her. Alice drew in her breath. 'Oh my! Perhaps he can see her ghost. I've heard animals see and hear things that we don't see.'

'He heard the bombers before we did. I'll give him that.'

'Well, there you are.'

Meg couldn't quite see the point of this exclamation. Alice was one of those people whose 'informed' opinion on most things was not necessarily correct.

There were only about forty children in the village school, aged from five to fourteen, the older ones sometimes supervising the small fry. A teacher came out of the double doors first, holding a brass bell with both hands. On the dot of four she rang it, the noisy clanging sending the birds flying from the lower branches of a copper-leaved tree. Before the last note had fallen away, a wave of children flooded through the opening, satchels slung over their shoulders, hair awry and all chattering twenty to the dozen. Thanks to the crisp October air, the children were all rosy-cheeked. Lily looked brighter than she had for a long time thanks to her association with Rudy the dog.

Meg said goodbye to Alice just after they passed the post office. She smiled down at Lily, pleased at the change in her. 'I think we'll have cheese on toast for supper. How will that be?'

Lily nodded. 'Yes. What's Rudy having?'

Giblets, thought Meg, but knowing Lily would probe as to exactly what they were, instead said, 'Some things Mr Puller brought round.'

Meg had been surprised at how many people had rallied round with food for the handsome Alsatian. Reg Puller kept a large flock of chickens in the orchard behind his house and, following the killing off of some old broilers, had brought round a bag full of innards.

'He'll like that. Won't you, Rudy?'

Rudy, liking the sound of Lily's voice, wagged his tail. Yet again he had the love and attention of a little girl, just like the one he'd been brought up with. She'd had fair hair too.

A figure stood just in front of the garden gate. Meg gave a start. For a moment she thought it was Ray, though he was wearing a trench coat over a suit, not a uniform. When he removed his trilby, she could see the man's hair was fair. Suddenly a great surge of hope speeded her footsteps as a thought occurred to her. Was it about Ray?

305

Had they found him?

'Are you looking for me? I'm Meg Malin. Is it about my husband?'

The man ran his fingers around the rim of his hat. He hadn't expected to see such an attractive woman before him and for a moment he forgot what he'd come here to say.

'Mrs Malin? Pleased to meet you. My name is James Amble.'

She shook the hand that was offered.

The man glanced from her to Lily and lingered on Rudy. Something in the dog's expression changed. He didn't wag at the stranger as he did at most people. He wasn't showing any aggression but he did appear wary. Not that Meg was paying that much attention. If the man had news of her husband, she wanted to hear it right away.

'Have you found Ray? Is he alive?'

For a moment he looked taken aback before he shook his head sadly. 'I'm sorry. No. That's not why I'm here. It's about the dog.'

'The dog?'

'Yes. I understand your husband took the dog under his wing on his return from France.'

Meg frowned. 'Yes. That's what I understand. His colleagues adopted Rudy as a mascot.'

'And he was brought to you following the loss of your husband for which of course you have my deepest sympathy.'

Confused as to why he was here at all, Meg shook her head. 'I'm sorry. I don't understand. What's the dog got to do with this? What is it you want?'

He took a deep breath as though what he had

306

to say next was unpalatable. He could see that it would be. The arms of the little girl with the pale hair were wrapped around the dog's neck. Even a fool could see she was fond of it.

'I'm here to take the dog. There's been a counterclaim of ownership. Your husband signed the dog over to the RAF and the dog lived with him there. A sergeant there confirms the fact. He'd advised that the dog should be kennelled with the rest of the military dogs, but your husband insisted it slept in his quarters.'

'But my husband brought him out of France. It was his dog!' Meg couldn't help raising her voice.

'And then he brought the dog to the base where it lived with him. In order to obtain permission, he signed the animal over for military uses.'

'No!' Meg shook her head vehemently. 'No! You can't take Rudy.'

Mr Amble's expression was a mixture of smugness and sympathy, but more the former than the latter. 'I'm afraid I can. You can look at the form your husband signed if you wish.'

'Yes! I do wish.'

Meg was aware of her hands trembling as she perused the form. There at the bottom was her husband's signature. 'I'm sorry,' she said, shaking her head, 'Rudy was my husband's dog. He brought him out of France with this little girl...'

'Mrs Malin...'

Lily was squatting next to Rudy, her arm around his neck looking panic-stricken. 'What is it, Auntie Meg? He's not going to take Rudy away, is he?'

'No,' snapped Meg, slamming the form back

into Mr Amble's outstretched hand. 'No, he is not.'

Mr Amble sighed. 'You may be aware that a great many breeders of guard dogs have cut their kennels to a minimum, plus many people have had their pets put down. Even kennels of hunting dogs – bassets, otter hounds and fox hounds – have been reduced until we have peace. The trouble is that nobody realised it would leave us without any suitable animals for war work: guard duty, message running, sniffing out bombs and rescue situations. Dogs like this are in great demand, doubly so seeing as he was captured from the other side. He has a military identification number tattooed in his ear. He's been trained and is used to receiving military orders. Mrs Malin, both the Royal Air Force and the Army are in dire need of intelligent dogs for various duties. Your animal here fits the bill. I can ask you politely to let me take him now, or I can leave you and your little girl to get used to the idea before he joins the fighting forces. I can give you time. Let's say three days.'

Meg's jaw dropped. A few weeks ago she would have welcomed somebody taking the dog off her hands – but that was then. Things had changed.

She felt Lily tugging at her sleeve. 'What's he saying, Auntie Meg? He doesn't mean Rudy, does he? He can't take Rudy!' The shrillness of her voice increased with each short sentence.

Meg gripped Lily's hand and tried to reassure her. 'Leave it to me, darling.' She turned back to the man. 'I really don't understand. My husband said the dog was his and it was brought to me after he went missing presumed dead. Rudy means a lot to me and to Lily here. Surely you can reconsider?'

The man shook his head. 'I'm sorry. If you refuse to hand him over, then we will have no recourse but to refer the matter to military law.'

'Over a dog?'

Sensing that despite her mother's reassurances, this was to do with her beloved Rudy, Lily began to cry.

Their visitor gave the child a brief glance but held his ground. 'If need be.'

'Look, Mr Amble. You don't understand the situation. My foster daughter was traumatised after we were bombed in London. It was the dog who helped her recover. I can't let him go. I just can't!'

Mr Amble shrugged, pressed a fold into his hat and put it back on his head. 'I'm sorry. I have been instructed.'

'Are you a policeman?'

Mr Amble looked perturbed. 'No. As I have already told you, I am acting on behalf of the War Office, specifically for the Royal Air Force, and as such...'

Lily burst into tears. 'Don't let him take Rudy! Don't let him take Rudy!'

Meg wrapped her arms around the girl. 'I have no intention of doing any such thing, darling! Rudy is our dog,' she said, glaring at their un-welcome visitor. 'His home is with us.'

'Mrs Malin...'

'That's my final word on the subject!'

Mr Amble tipped his hat. 'I will be in touch again. Probably with the police.'

Lily and Rudy clamped to her side, Meg pushed roughly past him, stalked up her garden path and went into the cottage.

Lily was still crying. 'Auntie Meg...'

Meg bent down to her, cupped her sweet face with both hands and looked into her eyes. 'Now listen to me, Lily. Rudy is our dog. Nobody is going to take him from us.'

That night, once Lily and Rudy had eaten and were settled down for the night, Meg stared out of her bedroom window. The moon was the only light outlining the scene beyond her window. The whole village seemed to be sleeping, though for an instant she did think she detected a figure melting into the bushes between her and the village green. She tensed, hoping against hope that the figure was Ray and that he'd finally come home. The bushes moved again. And just for a moment...

No. Just the wind. Only the wind and hot tears blurring her sight.

Lily would be devastated if the dog was taken away from her. She'd made such progress since he'd arrived, and although Meg still hated dog hairs over the furniture, she would put up with that if it meant Lily recovered and could lead a happy, full life. The sky was full of stars. Wish on a star, she thought, but her eyes were drawn to the more intense light of the moon, so she wished on that.

'Let Ray come home,' she whispered. 'Let him come home.'

CHAPTER TWENTY-THREE

Meg felt herself a bit of a fraud, bending this way and that over a dog, but she had every intention of fighting tooth and nail to keep him. She recalled vividly what the officious Mr Amble had said. 'If you don't hand him over now, then I'll be back with the police.'

Lily had looked up at Meg wide-eyed as she tucked her into bed. 'I won't let them take Rudy,' she declared defiantly. 'He's my very best friend. I won't let them. I'll run away if I have to and take Rudy with me. Like before...!'

'Before?'

Lily's eyes adopted a faraway expression. 'We ran away from bad people.'

'Do you remember who they were?'

A faint frown creased Lily's smooth brow. 'Bad men. They shouted. They wore uniforms. They had dogs. One of them was going to kill Rudy.'

Meg's heart was in her throat. She wasn't sure she wanted to hear everything, but had to steel herself to do so. 'But Rudy escaped?'

Lily nodded. 'Yes,' she said softly.

'There, there,' Meg said soothingly, smoothing Lily's hair back from her face. 'Rudy lives with us and will always live with us.'

Lily turned, regarded her over her shoulder. 'Rudy won't bite good people. He only bites bad ones.'

311

Although she wasn't at all sure what Lily meant, Meg agreed with her that Rudy only bit people he didn't like.

Now in bed, Meg tossed and turned for a while and finally slept a deep sleep only after she had reached a decision about what to do. She wouldn't mention it to Alice, but she would mention it to PC John Carter. If Mr Amble came back with a policeman, that policeman would be John. Could she persuade John not to carry out his duty? She didn't know for sure but she had to try.

The following day after walking Lily to school, Meg headed for the police house. PC Carter beamed when he saw who was on his doorstep.

'Come on in,' he said, holding the door wide open. 'Take a seat. Fancy a cup of tea? A decent cup,' he added with a smile. 'I've just collected my ration.'

Meg responded to the invitation, sitting herself down in the same Windsor chair that old Fred had favoured when he'd come to report the desecration of his garden. As John brewed up, she took the opportunity to look around. There was nothing official-looking about the police house where he lived. The living room had been converted into an office. The kitchen where they were at present was the room John mainly used. Plump cushions sat in the window seats and there was a thick rug in front of the kitchen range.

Taking hold of a cloth pot holder, John scooped the kettle from the hob and made the tea. 'I don't suppose you've come with any information regarding the big-booted garden trampler, have you?' he asked, his voice laced with humour.

312

Thrown off balance for the moment, Meg frowned. 'Was the person who trampled Fred's garden big-booted?'

John grinned and raised his eyebrows. 'Size tens. I found a few clear footprints. Checked it against the happening at Mrs Crow's. Definitely a pair of size tens. So I know it wasn't you.'

'Or any of the village kids.'

'No,' he said, passing her a cup of tea. 'Definitely an adult. Nobody's owning up to Upper Standwick's biggest crime for years. Nobody has a clue and that includes me.' He sat down opposite her, his cup and saucer close at hand. She felt his eyes on her and when she smiled, he smiled too.

The pensive manner turned forthright. 'I'm hoping you're going to say that you're here to ask me to dinner again. Or the village dance. I don't mind which.'

Meg shook her head. 'That isn't why I'm here... Though I dare say we can arrange something,' she added, on seeing disappointment register in his eyes.

His happy countenance reappeared. 'Glad to hear it.' He held his head to one side like an inquisitive boy, though unlike a boy, the look in his eyes was deep and penetrating. 'So how can I help you?'

Meg toyed with the teaspoon sitting in her saucer, a frown puckering her brow. She told him about Mr Amble and his intention to use the law to take the dog away.

'I dare say he'd make a good services dog.'

'But he's Lily's dog! John, Lily was badly trau-

313

matised even before the bombing raid. She's German. As I've already told you, my husband found her and the dog in a field, huddled together against the cold. She was barely alive...'

John stared at her. He would have liked to take her in his arms, but that was the stuff of novels. He knew he wouldn't be allowed to do that until this business with the dog was sorted. 'So this bloke reckons your husband signed the dog over to the RAF.'

She nodded. 'You have to understand how important it is that Rudy stays with Lily. The child doesn't even have a name, not her real one anyway. We don't know what that is. It was only the warmth of the dog that had kept her alive. That's what Ray said. He brought both of them back in his aeroplane along with... Well...' She paused, then looked at him directly. 'Somebody else he'd been sent over to collect.'

She looked down at her hands, principally at her wedding ring. It seemed a little tight nowadays. So did the waistband of her skirt. Country living, she supposed. There was more food in the country than in the city.

'I appreciate you confiding in me,' John said softly. 'That poor little kid. I understand what you're saying, though I'm not sure what I can do to help.'

'John, if this Mr Amble does ask you to assist in taking Rudy, will you help him or will you help me?'

He looked at her wide-eyed, aware of the challenge in her voice and wincing at the sight of her expressive eyes, the long lashes, the arched brows.

314

He'd often dreamed of her eyes, her hair, and kissing that generous mouth. Faced with her and her question, he didn't know quite what to say.

'You're putting me on the spot.'

She was indeed. On the one hand he would move heaven and earth to please her. On the other hand he was a policeman and had a duty to perform – if he got asked to do it, that is. He expressed this to her in as gentle a way as possible.

'Perhaps I should go,' she said, the legs of the chair scraping the floor as she got to her feet.

John also got to his feet. 'There's no need to take off. I didn't say I couldn't help, just that I have to do my duty – or at least appear to do my duty.'

They stood either side of the kitchen table. If it hadn't been between them, perhaps they would have thrown their arms around each other. As it was, their countenance was restrained despite the emotions raging beneath the surface.

Meg thought about what he'd just said. 'Are you saying you won't help him take Rudy?'

John shook his head and smiled a thought-provoking smile. 'I'm suggesting that if I don't know where he is, I can't possibly help this man from the War Office take him.'

The look she gave him was uncomprehending but at the same time relieved. 'You're saying I should hide him?'

He shrugged his shoulders. As yet he hadn't put on his tunic so was still in his shirtsleeves. John was a broad-shouldered man and the sleeves were tight around his biceps and across his chest. 'How about another cup of tea,' he said as she

315

slumped back down into the chair.

It seemed so simple. The dog had wandered the village in those days following Mrs Dando's death. A few people had tried to catch him including Cliff Stenner at the Bear and Ragged Staff, all to no avail. It would come as no surprise to anyone that he'd run away again.

'I can't just turn him loose,' she said after considering the options.

'No. There's always the chance he might be caught, but he can't be in your house, that's for sure.'

John poured more tea and Meg shook her head. No, he could not be in her house but he had to be in a house where he felt at home.

'And don't tell me where you plan to hide him,' said John, just as she opened her mouth to speak. 'Tell me no secrets and I won't tell any lies. Right?'

'Right.' Even to her own ears, her voice seemed far away. She walked away from the police house with a warm glow inside. Not only had John given her a way out of her problem, he was a genuinely caring man and a good friend.

On reaching the gate to Mrs Dando's cottage, she paused and looked up at the windows. They still seemed vacant, reflecting nothing today except the emptiness inside. It was obvious that Rudy had been happy in the short time he'd spent with Mrs Dando. For that reason she didn't think it at all odd that he loitered outside her gate, gazing at the house as though fully expecting the old dear to come out of her front door.

Meg recalled Alice's comments about Ivy's ghost still living there and, although she hadn't taken her comment seriously at the time, Meg did wonder if there was any truth in it. Rudy wouldn't be frightened of the old lady's ghost so for that reason alone it was the ideal hiding place.

The most difficult bit would be ensuring Lily kept the secret to herself. It did cross her mind not to tell her, merely to say that he was in a safe place, but she'd seen how frantic Lily had become when she thought he was being taken from her. Meg sighed as she entered Bluebell Cottage. There was so very much to consider but she would face the challenge. Mr Amble must not take Rudy, so if she had to hide the dog and lie that he'd run away, then so be it.

Rudy was lying on the floor. He raised his head and wagged his tail in welcome. Meg bent down, stroking between the dog's ears as she spoke to him softly. 'Rudy, you're going to a new home for a while, but only for a little while. You'll be a good boy, won't you?'

The tail wagged again. His head went back to the floor and he closed his eyes.

Back at the police house, PC Carter was placing the dishes in the washing-up bowl. There was just about enough water in the kettle to wash the breakfast things and his dinner plate from the night before.

For a moment he looked at that single dinner plate thinking how lonely it looked. One dinner plate. Bachelor meal for one. Up until now he'd never bothered too much about wanting company. He'd had lady friends but none had stirred his feelings to the point of wanting to settle

317

down. Then Meg Malin, had come along.

What a kind lady, he thought, *taking in a little girl whose background was completely unknown to her.* But it was more than that, of course. He wanted them to be more than friends but knew he had to give her time. She hadn't long lost her husband and he didn't think her the sort to rush into things. *Give her time,* he told himself. *Be her friend and see where that goes.*

Leaving the dishes to drain, he wiped his hands on the tea towel and prepared to fasten his shirtsleeve cuffs. As he did so he thought about what Meg had said about Lily. Nobody could possibly guess what the little girl had gone through. It was even more intriguing to hear that she and the dog had been found together; a little Jewish girl and a dog with a military number tattooed in his ear.

Like Meg, he couldn't fathom how they'd come together. But whatever had happened had left the little girl without her memory. If only the dog could talk. It couldn't, of course, but its presence had helped Lily's progress. In time, as long as the animal was giving her comfort, she might remember even more. The girl and the dog were inseparable and that was a fact.

'It's her dog,' Carter said thoughtfully. 'Not Ray's dog. It wasn't his to sign over.' The truth of his statement was like being pricked with a sharp pin. He looked out of the window, across the village green to the cottages on the far side and the top of the church tower showing above the trees. It was like a revelation. 'It's her dog!'

Feeling akin to St Paul on the road to Damas-

318

cus, he dashed out of the station house, looking to see if Meg was still in sight. He could just see her about to cross the village green and heading to Mrs Dando's cottage. He was about to run after her but was accosted by a red-faced Cliff Stenner, who puffed a bit before settling back from a trot into a more refined pace better suiting a man of his age and rotund physique.

'John. I've had a break-in.'

As if that wasn't enough, the Reverend Gerald James also stalked over, his cassock floating like a pair of black wings behind him. 'The collection box has been stolen, plus some items from the Harvest Festival Display.'

'What sort of items?'

'An apple pie, two loaves of bread and some fruit.'

PC Carter turned to Cliff. 'And you?'

'Food and cigarettes. Plus a pair of clean long johns from off the washing line. I did say to Gladys they might just have blown away. I mean, who the bloody hell pinches a pair of long johns? But she won't have it.'

'The church was open so there is no sign of forced entry,' stated the vicar, who, being a great Agatha Christie fan, thought he knew a thing or two about crime in general and murder in particular.

Cliff added details of his own break-in. 'Whoever it was got in through the cellar window. It's only a slit, but anyone skinny enough could slide through all right.'

Carter sighed. His revelation about the dog and the little girl had to be put on hold. 'Right,' he

319

said. 'Let's get on with it.'

The moment Meg pushed open the gate of Homeside Cottage, Rudy sprinted to the front door. Once there he sat down, head back and his attention fixed on the door as though fully expecting someone to open it. Even though she thought it a useless exercise, Meg tried heaving the big catch upwards. Just as she'd suspected, it wouldn't budge and there was no big key hanging from a nail at the side of the door.

Most of the old cottages in the village had these old panelled doors that had an iron latch and a huge keyhole for the key, which most people kept hanging from a nail outside. Neighbours went in and out other peoples' houses at will. Everyone was honest and crime was just something they read about in the newspapers; something that happened in places like Bristol or Bath, anywhere but a village of small population where everyone knew everyone else.

Even though Mrs Dando was dead and gone, Meg had still expected to see an old iron key hanging from a nail. She decided that either PC Carter or Reg Puller might have it, just so they could check on things now and again. Her intention had been to see what it was like inside and perhaps get Rudy used to being there alone, at least in the daytime while Lily was at school. But she certainly wasn't going to gain entry through the front door.

Seemingly understanding what the problem was, Rudy dashed along the path that led around the side of the house and through an archway of tangled climbing roses into the back garden. Meg followed and found him sitting at the back door waiting for her to catch up. The back door of Mrs Dando's cottage was protected from the elements by a ramshackle, door-less lean-to of glass and mismatched pieces of wood.

A smell of fermenting apples came from a barrel stowed on a ledge in front of her. Droplets of liquid squeezed out from the barrel tap formed a small puddle on the floor. Meg touched her finger to the oozing tap and tasted it. So, sweet old Mrs Dando had kept a barrel of scrumpy cider out back. Well, good for her!

Rudy was sitting as still as a stone statue, his eyes fixed on the back door. Meg wondered at the training he'd once been given. He was such a gentle dog yet so instinctive and obedient. She also wondered what he was hearing and smelling seeing that she couldn't.

Meg tried the back door by giving it a gentle push, but it didn't open either. Shielding her eyes with her hand, she peered in the kitchen window. The curtains were drawn just as they were at every other window. Meg eyed the lean-to, which vaguely resembled a greenhouse. Even though it had no door, it could provide sufficient shelter for a few nights. Being an obedient dog, Rudy would stay here if told to.

'Just for a few nights,' she muttered.

Rudy turned his head. His eyes were unblinking. Nothing else about him moved, not even his tail.

Meg frowned. She couldn't help get the impression that the dog was trying to tell her something.

321

'If only you could speak,' she said, sorrowfully shaking her head. 'What is it, boy? What's wrong?'

Meg looked at the back door. Its dark green paint was peeling away from the wood like strips of skin. Sighing, she got to her feet. 'We can't get into the house, so we'll have to hide you here. Now, shall we do a dummy run, as my Ray used to say when he was in training? You stay here. Stay! Do you understand me, Rudy? Stay!'

She walked backwards at first, fixing him eye to eye as she repeated the order to stay over and over again. Once she was sure he would obey, she walked swiftly to the corner of the house. Once there she turned and looked at him, pleased to see he hadn't moved. His gaze was fixed on her as though he understood her command but not the reason why. This will be a trial run, she told herself as she strode back to the garden gate and out into the street. Half an hour should do it.

CHAPTER TWENTY-FOUR

Bert Dando had been eating a slice of apple pie when he'd heard the garden gate bang open and seen the lovely Mrs Malin heading for his front door. He'd also seen the dog, that bane of his life. At the sight of it he'd clenched his teeth so hard he'd nearly choked on a piece of pastry. What the devil was she doing here?

At first she was out of sight to him, though he knew she had to be standing by the front door.

Beside him on the floor lay the house keys, the big old iron one for the front and another for the back. On hearing the heels of her shoes clip-clopping along the side path round to the back of the house, he did the same. There was no attic window at the back of the house so if he wanted a clear view he would have to go down to the first floor.

Shoeless, he tiptoed from the attic, down the stairs and along the landing to the back bedroom. Peering through the gap in the blackout curtains, he found himself looking down on the top of her head. She wasn't wearing a hat, which gave him the pleasure of admiring her glossy hair, as golden as autumn sunlight. He heard her talking to the dog but couldn't work out what was being said.

He was totally surprised when she left without the dog, telling him to sit and stay and not to move. What was that all about, he wondered? Was the dog there to guard the house? Did she suspect there was someone here and the dog would prevent his escape?

'Just yer imagination, me old mate,' he said to himself as he took one of the cigarettes from the packet he'd nicked from the pub and lit it up. Leaning back against the wall dressed in the clean underwear he'd stolen from a washing line, he blew smoke circles up into the room, watching them disintegrate in the cold draught from the window. Good job he'd taken the long johns. He'd been in two minds, but finally took them anyway.

As he smoked he imagined yet again what it would be like to get Mrs Malin alone. Not long now until the village dance. Who was going to notice another bloke hanging around there? Not in the blackout, they weren't. In the meantime he would cut himself another slice of apple pie and a bit of tinned ham – he'd had enough of corned beef. Shouldn't feed it to a dog, he reckoned.

That dog. His thoughts went back to it and wondered at Mrs Malin's reason for leaving it outside his back door. He looked again out of the back window – the dog was still there. Thank goodness he'd brought his haul of food and such-like up here.

Thinking of the food gave him an idea. A cube of corned beef remained in its tin. He retrieved it from the attic, noticing how dry and even more unpalatable it was than usual, though a dog might eat it. He returned to the back window.

Carefully, very carefully, he opened the window just a crack, wide enough to throw out the piece of dried corned beef. The meat landed just outside the entrance of the lean-to. He saw the dog come out to investigate and was sure the corned beef was eaten.

Bert smiled to himself. He'd been considering various ways of getting the dog out of the way so he could have his wicked way with Mrs Malin. Ultimately he'd prefer the dog to be dead. All he had to do was slice up a bit of corned beef or Spam and sprinkle it with some of the rat poison kept in a bottle under the sink. Yes, he thought to himself. Give meself a minute to finish this fag and that's what I'll do.

Unfortunately for Bert Dando, Meg collected Rudy half an hour later before heading off to

324

collect Lily from school, though the child was old enough and more settled now to come home alone. It was just that she wanted to see Lily's face light up when she saw Rudy.

The outhouse smelled of mouldy rags, turpentine and something else. She wrinkled her nose. Was that mothballs she could smell? The old rags probably. She didn't usually bother putting Rudy on the lead. He usually followed wherever she led and obeyed immediately. On this occasion he began to whine and paw at the back door, looking up at her expectantly as though waiting for her to open it.

'We can't get in, Rudy. There's no one at home.'

The dog wasn't easily persuaded. Meg eyed the door wondering if she should try it again. She turned the handle and gave the door a hard shove. The door opened a fraction before it scraped stiffly at the floor. It would take more effort and be noisy if she pushed it. The smell of old food and, again, mothballs came out through the crack.

Rudy thrust his twitching nose into the gap. 'No, Rudy. We'd better go. Come on. We have to meet Lily from school.'

As expected, Lily was over the moon to see Meg and Rudy. Once they were back in the cosy kitchen sitting in front of the glowing range, Meg made herself a cup of tea and flopped in a chair. She felt so tired.

'What have you been doing?' she murmured after gratefully sipping some tea. Closing her eyes, she lay her head back and almost dropped off to sleep. 'Oh, come on,' she muttered, as she opened her eyes. As she placed her cup and saucer on the

325

table, a button popped off the side fastening of her dress. 'Blow it! Not another one!'

Her gaze drifted to the photograph on the mantelpiece of Ray in his air-force uniform. Four months he'd been gone. Four months since they'd last gone to bed together and made love... And then it dawned on her. Four months! Why hadn't she noticed?

The answer came swiftly. Because you've been too absorbed in getting Lily sorted out to notice that something isn't quite right with you. It had been more than four years since she and Ray had got married and decided to start a family immediately – only a baby hadn't arrived. And now, with Ray gone and having fostered a child, here she was. After all this time, she was pregnant!

CHAPTER TWENTY-FIVE

PC John Carter solemnly inspected both burglary scenes, not that there was much evidence to go on. Anyone could walk into the church and take whatever they wanted, and Cliff Stenner freely admitted that he never actually locked the back window, his reason being that it was very small and therefore only a very small person could squeeze through.

Carter shook his head. 'I'm not so sure. Somebody with slim hips could slide through. An adolescent perhaps?'

Cliff had to agree. 'Nobody my size,' he added,

rubbing his stomach to emphasise the fact he was a bit on the large side.

Carter suggested to the vicar that he might like to lock the church door. The vicar was horrified. 'I cannot withhold help to anyone who needs it. The church door has to remain open to any troubled soul who wishes entry.'

While he was with the vicar, the policeman sniffed the air. 'If you don't mind me saying so, I smell mothballs,' he remarked.

The vicar pulled in his chin as though the policeman had landed a punch on it. 'Well, it certainly isn't me! My wife will not allow such things into the house – or our wardrobes! No. It certainly isn't me.'

It wasn't that strong a smell, but taking a deep breath, he had noticed the same smell at the pub. 'Ever use mothballs?'

Cliff shook his head. 'Camphor! Can't stand the stuff.'

Both men insisted their clothes were scrupulously laundered. Cliff was even more resolute than the vicar. 'Only my funeral suit is kept in mothballs, and even then it's taken to the dry cleaners in Bath when I'm in need of it, and it's kept upstairs in the spare-room wardrobe.'

The fact that only money and food had been stolen – plus some cigarettes from the Bear and Ragged Staff – brought PC Carter to the conclusion that the theft had been carried out by a vagabond, a tramp hiding out in the countryside, and whoever it was smelled strongly of mothballs. He voiced his conclusion to both Cliff and the vicar. Both men agreed with him.

'There are so many homeless people nowadays, what with the bombing,' stated the vicar. 'There are kind people about who give them cast-off clothes – hence your smell of mothballs, Constable.'

'And quite a few deserters unwilling to die for their country,' added Cliff with resolute scepticism. 'Heard of one over Dursley way, living rough in a disused cow byre.

Carter nodded thoughtfully. 'I think you're right. Food is more valuable than anything nowadays, though the perpetrator did nick the money in the collection box. That couldn't have been very much – could it?'

'No. I'm afraid not,' replied the vicar.

'Just in case it was kids, I'm going along to the school this afternoon to give the youngsters a good talking to – just in case.'

PC Carter didn't dwell too long on the string of crime in his beloved village, except to wonder about the smell of mothballs. He would indeed be calling in at the school and asking Miss Pringle's permission to give the kids a talk on the sin of stealing and not owning up to a misdemeanour – more of a deterrent to future petty crime than presently applicable. On his way there he would drop in on Meg Malin and tell her what had popped into his mind regarding their dealing with Mr Amble.

The balmy autumn days were behind them now, the air today crisper with a foretaste of winter. Gold, bronze, red and yellow leaves still clung to the branches of trees. The leaves looked like blobs of paint against an azure sky. Here goes, he thought as he pushed open the garden gate of Bluebell Cottage, where a few remaining bees collected nectar from late-flowering blooms and spiderwebs hung in gauzy splendour from withering leaves.

Truth to tell, he had butterflies in his stomach. Nobody else in the village had that effect on him, only Meg. My goodness, he felt like an adolescent youth all over again when she was around. She always looked so fresh, peachy skinned, glossy haired and neatly dressed. He thought about the night he'd had dinner with her. They'd promised each other they would do it again and he was sure they would.

He smoothed his hair before rapping the wrought-iron knocker. Footsteps tapped across the flagstone floor and the door was opened. It wasn't so much that she looked surprised to see him as a little taken aback, agitated even.

'Oh! John. It's you.'

He saw her frown. 'Have I come at an awkward time?'

'No. Of course not.'

Her hair swung around her head as she shook it and he wondered at the colour: not just plain gold but light gold with darker streaks. How he longed to run his fingers through that hair and bury his nose in its smell. Perhaps one day he would.

After taking off his helmet in order to duck more easily under the low door lintel, he followed her into the cottage noting how much work she'd done on the old place and remembering how impressed he'd been when he'd first seen it. The walls had been painted and new curtains hung at the window. He was no expert but guessed other things had been renewed and replaced. It certainly looked far cosier than when Miss Lavender had lived here. A cake sat cooling on top of the kitchen range. It smelled good. His stomach rumbled.

Rudy got up from his favourite spot, stretched and greeted John with a cheerful wag of his tail and a quick sniff of his proffered hand.

'Nice to see you too, old chap,' John said to him and patted his head. 'But it's your mistress I've come to see.'

Tea plates clattered lightly and a stiff drawer groaned as she opened it, extracted two knives and closed it again. She turned to face him, her lips smiling and knife held in her right hand.

'I take it you'd like a piece?'

'I would indeed.'

She cut a sizeable piece, placed it on a plate and slid it to his side of the table. A little steam still rose from it and made his mouth water. 'That looks good.' He bit into the cake and found it moist in texture. 'Delicious.'

'You didn't know I was baking a cake, did you?'

Mouth full of cake, he shook his head.

'So to what do I owe the pleasure?'

'It's about the dog.'

Her smile diminished, though the welcome remained in her eyes.

'This business with your husband signing over the dog to the air force...' He looked down at the interior of his helmet. He'd had the words well rehearsed but now, standing here face-to-face, he felt suddenly awkward. She'd fed him cake but was standing at a greater distance than on his last visit. He read it as some kind of portent, a sign of some change in her emotions. He launched into what he'd come to say, the words falling together in logical sequence.

'I've got some great news. As I see it, your husband had no business signing the dog over because it wasn't his to donate to war service. The dog belonged to Lily. He brought both of them into this country.'

'So should I still hide him?'

'I think so. We have to get this man Amble's agreement that Lily is his rightful owner. He might huff and puff a bit. Eventually he's got to concede defeat. In the meantime it might be safer if the dog was hidden until it's all settled.'

'Thank you. It was very kind of you to look into the matter.'

John felt as though his face had been slapped with a wet kipper. Somehow he'd hoped for Meg to throw her arms around him in gratitude and offer to cook him another dinner to thank him. But she didn't. Her distracted air was unexpected but he steeled himself to go on.

'Well. Thought I'd come and tell you my conclusion right away,' he said fiddling with the chinstrap of his helmet. Better be going now. I'll see myself out, shall I?'

She nodded. 'Thank you for coming to tell me,' she said again.

He turned round to face her and smiled. 'It was no trouble. I was only doing my duty.'

But I wasn't just doing my duty, he told himself as he left the cottage behind. *I was hoping for you to throw your arms around my neck and tell me how wonderful I am.*

Heavy-hearted, he plodded through the village to the school, wondering what had caused the change in Meg's attitude. He stopped and eyed yet another poster for the village dance. He'd been hoping that they might be a couple by the time this came round. Still, it wouldn't hurt to ask her if she was still willing to have him accompany her. Hopefully she'd say yes, but meeting up with her today made him doubt himself. She'd seemed just a little off-handed, as though she had something on her mind. Shame, he thought, sighing heavily. He'd thought they were getting along so well.

Meg ran her hand over her forehead and closed her aching eyes. She still found it hard to believe that after four years of marriage and becoming a widow, she was finally expecting a baby. The saddest thing was that the child would never know its father. Ray was gone.

The next saddest thing was that although it was still early days, John Carter had looked a likely candidate to fill the gap left by her husband. He was different to Ray, though in some ways very alike. John had remained a policeman despite the call to arms. He loved the life he lived and, unlike Ray, was not lured by the promise of danger and adventure. Home was most definitely where his heart was.

Would he still want her once she told him her news? Her slim figure was about to expand, and their burgeoning friendship was likely to suffer or at least be put on hold. At some point she would have to tell him, though first on the agenda was a visit to the doctor.

The doctor congratulated her and confirmed that she was indeed about four months pregnant. She left the surgery in a dream, almost colliding with Alice Wickes who was on her way to collect her children from school.

'You look as though you've seen a ghost,' said Alice. 'Are you feeling all right?'

Meg looked at her as though she was a stranger. Eventually she said, 'I'm feeling ... I'm feeling...' Her voice trailed away. Goodness, but her throat was so dry.

'You can tell me how you're feeling on the way to school. Come on or we'll be late. Might earn ourselves a black mark from Miss Pringle if we do that!' She laughed.

'Oh my goodness. Yes. School. Though Lily insists she can go and come back by herself. She changes her tune if I've got Rudy with me.'

Side by side they headed towards the village school. Although she could feel Alice's eyes on her, Meg couldn't immediately voice her amazing news. She was still having trouble digesting it herself, chewing it over before sharing it with somebody else. But Alice was nothing if not persistent.

'So come on. What is it you're feeling that's made you look as though you've found a five-pound note you didn't know you had?'

'What?' Stirred back to the fact that this was an ordinary weekday afternoon and that she wasn't dreaming, Meg burst out laughing. 'I'm sorry, Alice. I don't quite know who to tell first, though it might just as well be you.'

'That sounds as though I'm the last resort,' said Alice, feigning hurt feelings. 'Thanks very much. By the way...'

'What?'

'Your cheeks have gone pink.'

Meg's cheeks reddened even further as she stated the best news she'd had in months. 'I'm pregnant. Four months, the doctor says.'

'Oh, Meg! You are lucky.'

Meg smiled sadly and her eyes moistened. 'I wish Ray was here. He'd be over the moon. Four years and nothing. Four months he's been gone and I find out I'm expecting.' She shook her head. 'I'm still finding it hard to take in.'

They came to a stop at the school gates where Alice patted her hand. 'Meg, I am so pleased for you. Fancy that. Your Ray leaving you a goodbye present.'

'He couldn't have chosen better,' said Meg. 'Except I wish he could be here. He would have been so excited.' She could imagine his joy, his infectious laughter and the way he would have told everyone he knew that he was going to be a father. At long last he was going to be a father.

'When are you going to tell Lily?'

Meg's fantasy faded away. Ray wasn't here. He'd never be here again. 'After I've told my mother,' she replied. 'I'll write to her tonight. Then I'll tell Lily.'

'Isn't she on the phone?'

'Yes, but mine isn't working properly at the moment. You know how it is. With the war on private phones go down all the time, usually when you need one.'

Alice's eyes sparkled and her smile was more than cheeky. 'John Carter's got a phone. Ask him if you can phone her from there.'

Meg chewed her lip nervously. 'I'm not sure I should. It is rather private.'

'And he's sweet on you,' Alice added suddenly.

'Nonsense!'

Alice tore some of the crust from the bread she'd just bought and gave it to her youngest to chew while grinning up at Meg. 'You're blushing. Did you think I didn't notice?'

'We're just friends. And anyway, he'll keep away now I'm expecting.'

'Why should he? You're still a widow, Meg.'

'Don't say that!'

'Sorry, I'm sure. But it's the truth. And you're attractive. Wish I had your hair. Wish I had your legs too. Look at mine! I've got stumpy legs. Ma said I inherited them from her. Comes from the women of our family working in the fields.'

The pall of silence that fell on the pair of them didn't last for too long. Alice gave her a nudge with her elbow. 'Go along and ask to use his phone.'

'I'm not sure. Anyway, I haven't quite got used to it yet. One moment everything is as it was, then suddenly this happens.'

'Good job you're not too far gone or you wouldn't fit into your new dress, the one you were making for the village dance.'

Meg was shocked. 'Alice, I can't possibly go dancing, not when I'm like this.'

Alice looked at her uncomprehending. 'Why ever not? You're not too bumpy yet.'

'Well...'

At that moment the children flooded out of the school, hair awry and clothes dishevelled, their single thought to get away from school and back home as quickly as possible.

'How come they go to school neat and tidy and come home looking as though they've been dragged through a hedge backwards?' Alice asked.

Meg was inclined to agree with her. Shiny-eyed Lily came rushing out, one ribbon trailing from her hair, the other one just about hanging on. 'Come on, Lily,' said Meg, offering her hand. 'I've some news for you.'

Lily's smile vanished. 'Where's Rudy? The man hasn't come for him, has he?'

'No,' said Meg, shaking her head vehemently. 'No. It's something marvellous that I've got to tell you and nothing to do with Rudy. But first we have to call in at the police house on the way home. I need to use the telephone.'

Her eyes met those of Alice Wickes over Lily's head. 'He won't refuse you,' Alice called out. 'I guarantee it.'

Meg was thankful for the cool breeze fanning her cheeks as she walked hand in hand with Lily to the police house. The last thing she wanted was John noticing her pink cheeks and thinking perhaps that it might have something to do with him.

'Why did Rudy stay at home today?' Lily asked her.

'Because I had to go to the doctor.'

To her surprise, Lily failed to ask why she'd had to go to the doctor. Of late, Lily had been full of childish curiosity about everything. She glanced at the little girl's face and saw she was frowning down at her shoes as if she didn't like the look of them.

'My daddy used to be a doctor – I think – a professor. It might have been a professor,' she said softly.

Meg was stunned. Had she heard correctly? She counted to ten and cleared her throat. 'Are you sure of that?'

She nodded.

'Can you remember his name?'

Lily looked up at her and Meg was taken aback by the terror-filled look in the little girl's eyes. 'Rudy,' she said, her voice barely above a whisper. 'Rudy.'

'And your name? What was your name?'

Lily frowned as though she were thinking very hard. Her eyes filled with tears as she shook her head. 'No. No, I don't remember.'

By the time Meg got to the station house, she was visibly shaking. PC Carter had been looking out of the station window, a cup of tea in hand. Even from this distance he perceived her pale face and alarmed expression. Setting down his cup and saucer, he swiftly opened the door.

'Meg! Here. Let me help you.' Cupping her elbow with his hand, he guided her into the police house, aware of the lightness of her arm on his as he swiftly got her to a chair. 'Has something happened? Can I get you a cup of tea?'

'Yes,' Meg replied. She wasn't one for believing a cup of sweet tea cured everything, but in this instance anything that might help would be gratefully received. Somehow she had to find the right words to explain why the two of them couldn't risk becoming any closer. Why they had to remain just friends.

John feared the look on her face. He'd never seen such a look in her eyes before. Initially he'd felt a leap of joy when he'd seen her approaching. Now, as he noticed her shaking hand, he felt a bolt of concern shoot through him. He'd do anything for Meg Malin. Absolutely anything, and that included taking on any worry she might have and getting it sorted. He noticed her hand was shaking and instinctively reached for her fingers, holding them in his palm as though they were violets and in danger of being crushed.

'Is everything all right?'

'There's something I have to tell you.'

'Is it about Rudy? Or Lily?'

Meg lowered her eyes and shook her head. 'No. Something else.'

'Can I go out into the garden?' Lily piped up, seemingly unperturbed now she knew this visit had nothing to do with her or the dog. Only mildly interested in grown-up conversations, she adored the long grass and fruit trees crowded in the police house garden. John said she could, which gave Meg the opportunity to speak to him alone.

'Nice of you to call on me,' he said, flashing her a white-toothed smile.

'I need to speak to my mother in London. I've got some very important news I need to tell her. Is it possible I could borrow your telephone?'

John was slightly disappointed that she didn't entertain a desire to visit him on his own account, but readily agreed that she could use his phone. 'I'll pop out and give Lily a hand climbing up the apple tree. I'm pretty certain she's out there to gather a few windfalls. Be my guest,' he added, nodding to the phone on his desk.

'John!' She touched his arm and he turned immediately. 'There's something I must say.'

'Right.'

'It's Lily. Just now she told me that her father was a professor and that his name was Rudy.'

John's eyebrows arched in surprise. 'Did she now? What do you think brought that on?'

'I had to go to the doctor's this afternoon so I didn't have the dog with me. She asked me where I'd been and I told her. Somehow it triggered a memory. I thought I should tell you before you go out there.'

He nodded. 'Leave it with me.'

A gentleman through and through, he didn't ask her reason for visiting the doctor and, at this moment in time, she didn't seem quite ready to tell him. Fallen leaves rustled and crackled beneath his boots in the garden, and the air was as spicy as cider. Meg had been to the doctors and he couldn't help being concerned. He hoped it was something trivial.

Meg's mother sounded breathless. 'Is something wrong?' asked Meg.

'Dust,' she said. 'There's dust everywhere and Mrs Bush, ungrateful woman as she is, has given her notice. She's off to work in an armaments factory. I have to do everything myself.'

Meg's mother had always had a daily in three days a week to clean her house and had tried persuading Meg to do the same. Meg had insisted that she could manage. Actually she was in two minds: yes, a daily would have helped alleviate her housework load, but Ray wouldn't agree, citing that as she didn't have children she had the time to do it herself. Pointing out the truth had hurt, but she had conceded that he was right. After that she'd thrown herself into housework, keeping herself busy and her home clean and ordered.

'Mother, I've got something important to tell you.'

'You're moving back to London! There! I knew it. I knew you wouldn't want to bury yourself in that place. You're a town girl, not a country mouse...'

'Mother! I'm not coming back to London. Well, not in the foreseeable future anyway. That's not why I'm phoning you. I'm pregnant...'

'Not coming back to London! Expecting? Did I hear you say that you're in the family way? But how could that possibly be? Ray's been dead for ... what is it? Six months?'

Meg gripped the phone. 'Four months! It's four months, mother, since Ray was posted missing, and I'm four months gone. Four months *pregnant!*'

'There's no need to shout and no need to use *that* word. It's unladylike.'

Meg barely controlled her anger, gripping the telephone receiver as though she might hit someone with it – more specifically her mother! 'Well,' she said determinedly, 'aren't you pleased you're going to be a grandmother?'

'Of course I am, darling.' There followed a significant pause. 'However will you find a nanny out there in the country?'

Meg sucked in her breath. A nanny! 'So many nannies and other servants have joined up, I doubt I would get one. Still, if I move back to London I won't need a nanny. Wouldn't you just love looking after your very first grandchild?'

She could easily imagine the look of horror on her mother's face as she envisaged sticky finger-marks over her polished mahogany dining table and dirty footprints over her pale green carpet.

The pregnant pause was monumental.

'Did you hear that Buckingham Palace was bombed again? I mean, how dreadful that even the king and queen's home should be bombed. London isn't even safe for them. I don't blame anyone evacuating their children and moving to somewhere safer.'

Meg took it that her mother's urging for her to return to London was at an end thanks to the prospect of looking after a baby.

'So what will you do with the changeling?'

'You mean Lily?'

'Yes. I really do understand why you took her in, but surely you'll need to make room now you're expecting your own child. I suppose you can re-turn her to the authorities? Unless a relative turns up out of the blue.'

Meg turned cold. 'Mother, I have to go now.'

'Thank you for sharing your good news. And think carefully about the German child. Children get very jealous about new arrivals.'

Once she'd severed the connection, Meg went to the back door. The autumn afternoon was drifting into twilight. Orange tones were being replaced by grey and green tints, and the breeze had turned slightly colder. John was helping Lily collect autumn windfalls from beneath the bare-branched apple tree. Wormy ones and those wasps had eaten into were tossed on to the compost heap for digging into the vegetables. Those destined for a pie or crumble were being pushed into the gaping mouth of a hessian sack laid purposefully in the damp green grass.

'You two look busy,' said Meg after swiftly pasting on a smile.

The grown man got to his feet. Lily looked up only after she'd thoroughly examined what looked from a distance like an unblemished apple before throwing it on to the compost heap.

'So how's your mother?' asked John, at the same time passing another apple to his young accomplice.

'Same as always.'

Deciding he wasn't going to hear anything more about her conversation, he asked if she was still going to the village dance.

'I'd like to escort you there if you're willing. If you want me to, that is.'

She fancied he was on a knife-edge and couldn't refuse him, but first she thought it only fair that he should know her condition. 'I am still going and would love it if you went with me.'

John beamed from ear to ear and she fancied his ears turned pink with pleasure.

'There's just one thing I think you should know. You too, Lily. I'm expecting a baby.'

John's jaw dropped and Lily dropped an apple.

'I won't mind if you want to change your mind about taking me to the dance.' Her thoughts

342

turned to what her mother had insinuated. She had to get that straight with him. 'It is Ray's baby,' she proclaimed with a toss of her head, her blue eyes sparkling with intensity. 'I know that for sure.'

Lost for words, John's arms dropped to his side. Both the look in his eyes and the tone of his words were infinitely tender. 'I wish he were still here for you, Meg. I'm sure he'd be very pleased.'

Without any warning, Lily flung her arms around Meg's waist.

'Whoa there.' Meg gathered Lily in, stroking her foster daughter's silky hair. Over Lily's head she exchanged a look of understanding with John. He shook his head. No. Lily had not said anything else about her father or the life she'd endured before Ray had found her in a French field.

'Come on, Lily,' Meg said gently. 'Time to go home. Now who's going to tell Rudy about the baby? You or me?'

Lily tilted her head back and looked up at her with big frightened eyes. 'Will you still want me when the baby comes? Will I still be your little girl?'

Meg felt a tightening in her throat. She held back a sob. 'I'll always want you, darling, and you'll always be my little girl. For ever and always.'

'Meg, I'm happy for you,' said John.

'Thank you.'

'Now how about the dog? Didn't you say Mr Amble is due back tomorrow?'

'Yes, I did, and I've found somewhere to hide him. We'll take him there for an hour tonight, just so he can get used to it. Lily will help me hide him from the nasty man, won't you, Lily?'

CHAPTER TWENTY-SIX

Bert Dando had not been sure whether Meg Malin and the dog would pay another visit or not. Something was happening and he'd heard her telling the dog to be a good boy because he had to be hidden but only for a very short time. Hopefully she would be back, though he couldn't be 100 per cent sure.

It was getting dark when he heard the squeaking of the front gate and footsteps hurrying around the side of the cottage. He'd prepared the meat early, soaking it in the rat poison his mother had kept under the sink. 'Enough to down an army,' he gloated as he placed the meat on a tin dish.

After washing his hands, he'd crept quietly downstairs, through the kitchen and into the back porch. Luckily no neighbours overlooked the back garden. There was nobody to notice that someone was residing in the late Mrs Dando's cottage. Heaps of fallen leaves had blown into the back porch. He had been wondering how to screen the dish of poisoned meat from Meg. Slipping the dish into the leaves would do just that. The dog would sniff it out anyway.

Creeping into the back bedroom, he squinted out from the side of the blackout curtain and made out three shapes: an adult, a child and a dog. He heard the little girl tell the dog to be a good boy. They'd be around to see him tomorrow once the nasty man had gone. Nasty man? He smiled to himself. Not as nasty as me.

Unaware they were being watched, Lily gave Rudy a big hug before she followed Meg back along the side of the cottage and out of the gate, though only after they'd filled his water dish from the rain butt and lay his rug out on top of a pile of leaves. They also left him a large marrowbone given to Meg by the butcher.

Rudy sniffed the air. He couldn't understand why he was being left here but his new people were good people and he loved them. He'd whined and looked up at them meaningfully before they'd left but couldn't make them understand that this place was a bad place inhabited by a bad man. All he could do was prevent the bad man from getting out of the house. Perhaps that was why he had been left here. He was on guard duty all over again, though this time he was not being ordered to guard or attack the weak. The man in this house was just the same as the guards who'd goaded their dogs to attack men, women and children. He was cruel and a bully. Rudy, his heart full of love for his new family, would do his duty.

Ignoring the delicious bone, he laid his head on his paws, heaved a big sigh and nosed the piles of leaves. The leaves fell away, exposing the piece of corned beef. Rudy sniffed at it. The smell was enticing and it would take no effort to eat, unlike the marrowbone which had little meat left on it. He sniffed it cautiously, detecting something in the smell that was different to the piece he'd eaten the day before.

Just as he was about to shove his nose into it

more closely, the broad wings of a barn owl swooped low over the garden. Rudy lifted his head, his ears tuning in to the sounds of the night: the crying of foxes, the hooting of the owl perched close by, the barking of badgers ambling from their sett. He again turned to devour the piece of corned beef, but the scream of a rabbit caught his attention.

Despite being told to stay put, his natural instincts made him restless. Like his cousins, the wolf and the fox, he had a taste for fresh meat and the sounds of the night – wild sounds – sent his blood racing. The corned beef couldn't possibly be enough. The call of the wild things, the smell of peaty earth and the lure of dark shadows were just too strong.

Lily woke up in the middle of the night. In her dreams she'd heard a baby crying, but when she awoke all she could hear was the friendly hooting of a barn owl. Everything was darkness and, as she lay there, fragments of the dream came back. People crowded around her, though a mound of them lay on the floor. A woman lay on top of the mound, her neck stretching as she screamed. An older woman and a man tried their best to console her. Eventually the screaming stopped but the hushed silence that followed was far worse. The silence was all-encompassing.

On waking she felt all over the bed for Rudy. It was Rudy who had broken that terrible silence, the one when she was surrounded by red and black, blood and the stench of death. Rudy! Mr Amble wanted to take him away. She wouldn't let him do that.

Her thoughts were jumbled. She vaguely recalled Aunt Meg telling her that nobody would
guess he was hidden in Homeside Cottage. They
could search here both inside and out but they
wouldn't find him. The bed usually sagged
beneath his weight, but tonight it was completely
level, the spot he usually occupied coldly empty.
What if he was frightened being hidden away? It
just wouldn't be fair. There and then, she made
up her mind to go to him. He had been there for
her, now she had to be there for him.

Quietly, so as not to disturb Aunt Meg, she got
out of bed, dressed and went downstairs, being
careful to step over the stair halfway down that
had a determined squeak. Her boots were on the
floor and her coat was hanging on a peg above
them. Once she was ready, she let herself out of
the front door, closing it softly behind her.

A full moon silvered the frosty night and her
breath misted like silver silk in the chill air as she
rushed along to Mrs Dando's cottage. At one
point she saw Mr Puller coming along, shining his
torch at windows in case somebody had left a
light on. Nobody had of course. They wouldn't
dare, besides which, at this time of night everybody was in bed and there hadn't been an air raid
on the nearby base for some time. Lily hid behind
a hedge until he was gone. Once he'd passed by,
she carried on with her mission, keeping low and
running silently just as she had in France where
she and Rudy had first teamed up.

France! It had popped into her head so easily.
She remembered being with him, scavenging as

they'd headed west. West! Her father had told her to keep heading west! Remembering her father brought her to a sharp standstill. Her father, Professor Rudolph Westerman. And her name was Leah Westerman!

Memories flooded into her mind and she experienced a tightness in her chest. Her legs felt like jelly, as though the memories that now filled her were too heavy to carry.

'Rudy!'

There was no time to confront the painful memories. Her parents were far away and it had been quite a few months since they'd stressed the need for her to escape. The only link between them was the dog that had saved her. And now she must save him. She had to get to Rudy.

When she got to the cottage gate, she was careful not to let it squeak, just in case Reg Puller was coming back her way and heard it. Slipping through, she headed around the back to the porch, her path lit by moonlight.

'Rudy,' she whispered as she turned into the back garden of the cottage. The moon had lit up the front of the cottage, picking out its lumpy outline and making its small windows glitter. But the back of the house threw a heavy shadow over the garden. Lily called Rudy's name again. There was no response. He didn't run to meet her as she'd expected. All was silent.

Her heart began to beat faster. Where was he? Something seemed to stir above her. For a moment she thought she heard a window creak open. Betty Wickes, who was in her class at school, had said the old place was haunted. Lily

348

shivered and her misty breath trembled with her as her teeth began to chatter.

'Rudy?' Her voice quivered. She couldn't see him. It was so black here.

Bert Dando was dead to the world having finished off half a gallon of scrumpy so he failed to hear what was happening outside. In his dreams he was standing with skinning knife in hand, the dog lying dead at his feet. In his dream he saw the villagers screaming in horror at what he'd done. The best part of his dream was seeing a submissive Meg Malin, too afraid to run from him, willing to do anything he asked of her.

PC John Carter couldn't sleep, tossing and turning, thinking about the various events that had happened in the village; first the trampling of the flowers, then the burglaries. Was he right in thinking that it was down to more than one person or were the events connected? The burglaries certainly were. The perpetrator had left behind the unmistakeable smell of mothballs.

There had been no hint of the smell in the trampled gardens, but these had not been confined spaces so it would not have been noticeable. Although it wasn't his habit to patrol the village at night unless there was some poaching or sheep-rustling going on, tonight he felt he needed to. Kicking back the bedclothes, he hesitated between wearing a civilian sweater and dark trousers or his uniform. Deciding it best to patrol in his official capacity, he opted for his uniform but in the dark he failed to notice he'd done the buttons up wrong.

The night was crisp and had a shiny cleanliness about it thanks to the full moon. Settling his chinstrap into a comfortable position, he stalked off listening to the night sounds, his hands clasped behind his back. A duck quacked in the village pond, an owl hooted in the distance and a bat barely skimmed his head on its way to the church tower. The scream of a small creature, possibly a rabbit, was followed by the cry of a vixen calling to her mate. Of late there were a lot of foxes in the woods and copses bordering the village. Little was seen of them during the day, their preference being to come out late at night to hunt rabbits and small animals, raid hen coops and scavenge for any bits of food left out.

It was purely on a whim that he pushed open the gate of Homeside Cottage. He checked it twice a week, though purely during daylight hours. To-night he'd make an exception. Moonlight played on the windows, which looked out on the village like empty eyes. He gave the door a push. It remained steadfastly locked. The windows were unbroken and tightly shut. Wouldn't hurt to take a look around the back, he decided. The back of the house was in darkness so he didn't see anyone hurtling towards him until they collided.

'Hey! Steady on.' He found himself holding a small arm, a child's arm. He turned on his torch and saw it was Lily Malin. 'Lily! What are you doing out at this time of night?'

He shone his torch into the child's pale face. Her stunningly blue eyes were bright with tears.

'I can't find Rudy. We hid him here and now he's not here.' She sounded close to hysterics.

Carter couldn't believe what he was hearing. Her mother had hidden the dog here. He'd thought she would have hidden him in the garden shed or somewhere more adjacent. It seemed an odd choice until he recalled the dog had spent some time here with Mrs Dando, and that he still showed an interest in the old place each time he passed it.

'Can you help me find him? Please?'

Bending his knees until he was level with her face, he smiled. 'First we'll get you home to bed. I'm a policeman. It's my job to find missing dogs.'

'I want to stay and find him.'

Carter sighed. 'Have you considered how worried your Aunt Meg is going to be when she wakes up and finds you gone? Have you thought about that?'

Lily shook her head.

'Right. Then let's get you home and leave the dog finding to me. Come on.'

Carter paused before taking hold of Lily's hand. The night air was fresh enough but he detected something other than damp grass and cow dung from the next field. Just to confirm his suspicion, he breathed in a good lungful of night air. Outside the lean-to the air was crisp and fresh. Inside he smelled the unmistakeable stink of mothballs.

He flashed the torch beam over the back door. It looked as though it were tightly closed. Laying his palm on the scratched paintwork, he gave it a push. It was barely discernible but he sensed a narrow gap appeared between the plank door and the jamb. He put his nose to the gap and smelled food. Something or somebody was in there and

351

he thought he knew who it might be.

It was hard not to stare when Meg answered the door to his urgent knocking wearing a blue dressing gown, her hair smothered in moonlight and trailing round her shoulders. At first there was warmth and then outright surprise on seeing Lily rubbing her eyes and yawning.

'Lily! What's going on?'

'I found her round at Mrs Dando's old cottage in a bit of a state because Rudy wasn't there.'

Meg caught hold of Lily's shoulders and brought her face down to her level. 'Whatever were you doing round there?'

'I thought he'd be lonely all by himself. But when I got there, he wasn't there. Where is he, Aunt Meg? Where's he gone?'

Meg shook her head, which sent her hair falling forward around her face. 'I don't know, darling. But one thing I do know is that you are not going out looking for him. Off to bed with you. It's a school day tomorrow.'

'Now don't you worry about that dog,' said John, addressing the little girl directly. 'I think I know where he might be. I'll get him settled and be round in the morning to tell you so. Will that be all right?'

Meg pointed towards the staircase. 'Bed for you, young lady.' The little girl stopped in her tracks and, although her eyes were red-rimmed, gave Meg an odd look as though she were seeing a stranger before her, not the woman who had looked after her for some months.

Rain that was not much more than mist had

begun to fall, making John reluctant to leave the cosy interior of the cottage and the lovely woman who lived there. 'Are you well?'

'Yes.' As she nodded, she pulled on the tied belt around her waist as though it would somehow form a barrier between her, the expectant mother, and him, the man who couldn't get her out of his mind.

'Suppose I'd better get on,' he murmured, trying his best to maintain an air of friendly aloofness.

'Not like that,' Meg said, suddenly reaching for the buttons of his tunic. Momentarily startled, John didn't at first grasp what she was doing. 'You must have been in a rush,' she said, smiling as she adjusted his tunic buttons.

'Right,' he said, a pale pink flush colouring his cheeks. 'A chap has to be well turned out.'

'Yes. You're an important man in the village. It's only right you make a good impression.'

'Yes. I suppose you're right.'

Meg smiled and thanked him before saying goodnight.

Once the door was closed he heaved a big sigh. Learning of Meg's pregnancy had come as something of a shock. He supposed a woman expecting her dead husband's baby wouldn't be interested in a new man entering her life. She certainly seemed a bit cooler than she had been.

'Oh well,' he muttered, disappointed because he'd dared to dream. 'No point crying over spilt milk.'

The cottage was in pretty much the same state as he'd left it except that water dripped from the overhanging eaves. Some of it found its way into

353

the collar of his tunic. Just to make sure all was safe and sound, he shone his torch over the windows but there was nothing to see. Seeing as batteries were becoming scarce, he turned it off again even though it meant finding his way around the back of the cottage in darkness.

Once he entered the blackest shadow he turned the torch back on again. In its yellowish light he picked out the lean-to porch, a poor affair of bits of odd wood and glass panes. He saw the shelves first, the barrels of scrumpy cider and odd bottles of weed killer and methylated spirits. Sniffing the air persuaded him he had not been mistaken: mothballs, just the same as at the two burglaries.

Directing the beam down to the ground picked out Rudy's blanket bed, a dish of water, a half-gnawed bone and a tin plate with something resting on it, something that looked like a snout and a black nose. Please God, don't let it be the dog. He couldn't bear telling Lily the bad news.

The beam from his torch picked out a canine muzzle resting on the dish, saliva frothing around a rictus grimace. Carter felt the grip of tension between his shoulder blades. Fearing what else he would see, he held the torch more tightly. First the beam picked out a glassy eye, then a pair of pointed ears and a tawny red coat. There was no sign of life.

A sound somewhere further down the garden caught his attention. He shone the torch in that direction and detected movement. A long lean form picked out by moonlight strode purposefully towards him. Carter pushed his helmet back on his head. 'Well, I'll be blowed...'

He couldn't believe what he was seeing. There was Rudy charging down the garden path with a rabbit hanging from his jaws. Relieved, he burst out laughing. He recalled the night noises he'd heard earlier. Perhaps the dead fox lying in the porch had been called by its mate. The vixen had received no answer. Perhaps she'd dropped the rabbit she'd caught or perhaps Rudy, not satisfied with just a bone and water, had gone hunting for food. Like Lily, the dog had learned to look after himself.

Panting and looking mighty pleased with himself, Rudy dropped the rabbit on to the policeman's highly polished boots. He picked it up. 'Come on, old chap. Let's get you settled for the night and that rabbit skinned for tomorrow.'

He picked up the water dish, blanket and bone. The dog took a quick sniff at the fox before nudging it with his nose. 'Poor thing,' said Carter, frowning. He'd come back tomorrow to deal with the dead fox. Might even be able to tell how it had died. It wasn't unusual for people to keep rat poison in their garden sheds and outhouses. The plate was a bit suspicious. He'd ask Meg if she put it there. If she didn't, then who did?

Before leaving he looked up at the back of the house. It looked secure enough and he knew that Reg Puller made a point of checking for any sign of forced entry. So far he'd reported that nothing was disturbed. The house was unchanged since Ivy Dando's death.

Still, it wouldn't hurt to check it out. A second job for tomorrow.

After tucking Lily in bed, Meg hadn't felt like sleeping. Instead she went downstairs and made herself a cup of tea. As she sipped at the sugarless brew, she looked around the cosy kitchen-cum-living room. Her eyes settled on the oak bureau where she kept all her paperwork. Ray's letters were bound together with a purple ribbon. She had a sudden yearning to read them all again. Once the ribbon was untied, they slid apart like a pack of cards.

Meg took the last letter from its envelope and read it through again and again. When she'd first read it, her tears had spotted the paper so that the ink began to run. It surprised her that she could no longer cry and it wasn't just because she'd evaluated their marriage and decided it was not perfect. From what she could see, there was no such thing as a perfect marriage.

On reflection, she decided that it wasn't only that. She was expecting a baby and not only was it a part of Ray, it was a new dimension to her life, as though she were an explorer and had found a new and enchanting island that held a wealth of new experiences.

Having a nice home hadn't mattered that much to him; she knew that now. But he'd had a strong sense of what was right and what was wrong. It also went without saying that he would have loved their unborn child, perhaps to the extent that he might have been less adventurous, more content to stay home. To Meg this meant more than anything. Being home together was between them. Other people had shared his other life. Nobody else had shared his home life but her. At

356

least she had that, even though deep down she knew he hadn't been a settled man, certainly not the sort to contentedly mow the lawn on a weekend or plant runner beans, or shop with her for curtain fabrics. However, he would have made a wonderful father. Of that she was sure.

'You have to go on living,' Alice had said to her. 'Especially now.'

Meg spread her hand protectively over her stomach and smiled. Well she certainly had good reason to go on living. There was far more to live for now.

Up in her bedroom, Lily lay awake thinking about what had happened in her life. Faces she'd forgotten came and went, but she knew her name and those of her parents. She could even recall fragments of her life in France. What she couldn't seem to get into focus was the period following her time living in France. She knew that in France it had only been two rooms and that food was scarce and life was dangerous. But after that she remembered nothing, so what was the point of telling Meg that her real name was Leah?

The faces faded away. She wanted to call for them to come back and help her relive her time with them. Without anyone needing to tell her, she knew for sure she would never see them again. They were dead. The smell of the cattle wagon, the bodies she'd been buried under, were like messages in solid form. Like Uncle Ray, that was the way they had gone. That was the way many more would go.

Meg had become her lifebelt in a tumultuous

sea. She was all she had to cling to. Her foster mother had the kindest eyes in the world, a fresh complexion, and although she often smelled of baking nowadays, she brought bunches of sweet-smelling violets to mind – just like the ones growing in the woods. Thinking of Meg helped her fall asleep.

After hiding Rudy in the back room, Constable John Carter shook Mr Amble's hand but had already decided to dislike him.

'I've a warrant,' said the other man loftily.

Carter unfolded the document and began to read. Mr Amble fidgeted and frowned. Carter was giving it a thorough perusal.

'You don't need to go through it with a fine-toothed comb. It says there that the dog was legitimately signed over to the Royal Air Force by Flight Officer Malin.'

'Hmm,' said Carter, holding the document in both hands, one at the top of the paper, one at the bottom. 'It would indeed be a legitimate document if Flight Officer Malin had been the legitimate owner. The fact is that Mr Malin did not own the dog so it wasn't his to sign over.'

Mr Amble's fleshy face turned the colour of cooked crab. 'Please explain yourself.'

Carter nodded. 'Certainly. Flight Officer Malin rescued a little girl and a dog from France. The dog belonged to the little girl. Ray Malin was only looking after it until the little girl was better again. Unfortunately she lost her memory so he had to look after the dog longer than expected, which meant he had to take him on to the base.

The dog cannot belong to the Royal Air Force because it didn't belong to Flight Officer Malin, and so he couldn't sign it over. The dog belongs to the little girl.'

Amble stiffened. 'Can you prove it?'

'The little girl has lost her memory, but we can approach the cloak-and-dagger brigade in London and get it confirmed, or Flight Officer Malin's commanding officer. A report was made at the time of the mission. It shouldn't be too much bother. I'm surprised you didn't look at the history of this case before coming down here.'

Looking totally demoralised, Amble took back the warrant. 'This is most unconventional,' he said through gritted teeth.

'But very legal,' Carter countered.

'Perhaps I should go and speak to this little girl – in the presence of her parent or guardian, of course.'

'Her foster mother. We think her parents are dead.'

'Then if I could talk to her perhaps, let her know she would be doing the country a service if she handed the animal over...'

'Mr Amble,' the policeman stated in his most official voice while barely controlling the urge to aim a left hook at the smug man's jaw. 'Mrs Malin has lately lost her husband; missing in action, presumed dead. Can you not be a little bit more considerate of her and the child's situation?'

'There is a war on, Constable Carter.'

'Yes,' Carter snapped. 'And Mrs Malin has already paid the price. She's sacrificed her husband. What more would you take from her, eh? How about we just let sleeping dogs lie, as they say. Give this one a wide berth and leave a family to heal.'

Amble blustered about coming here in his official capacity, but Carter knew he had him beat. Pompous to a fault, he thought.

Amble shook his head. 'Well, I don't quite know how to handle this...'

'Tell them back at your office that a mistake was made. The dog is no longer available.'

'Very well. But I must advise you the animal may still be requisitioned.'

'Well. Better get on with sorting it out, old chap, while there's still a war to fight.'

PC Carter watched from the window as Amble slid into the back seat of his government car. Fancy that – a car, and a state car at that, just to collect a dog. But that was government for you. He gave it five minutes after the car drove off before opening the interconnecting door between the room used as his police office and his private living accommodation. This was where he had hidden the dog. He smiled as he imagined Amble's surprise had he known.

Rudy was very alert, almost as though he wanted to hear the outcome of the meeting between the government official and his good friend John. 'Well,' said Carter, getting down on one knee so he could more easily ruffle the dog's thick fur collar. 'That's him done, at least for now. How about we go home and make a full report to them that count?'

Meg opened the door, invited him in, and made a big fuss of the dog before asking if John would like a cup of tea. 'Only if it's no bother,' he said

360

to her.

'Take a seat. I wouldn't have asked if it were any bother. Besides, I'm grateful for what you've done. A cup of tea is the least I can do.'

He told Meg all about his exchange with Mr Amble. Meg laughed when he told her Rudy had been on the other side of the door.

'Hidden just a few feet away.'

'What would you have told him if he'd insisted on going through that door?'

'That Rudy was Ted, a police dog, and should not be approached. One word from me and he'd chew his leg off.' Meg's peal of laughter was a joy to John's ears.

While her back was turned making the tea, he spotted Rudy looking at him enquiringly, then looking at Meg, then back at John. He almost felt like blushing. Was the dog reading his mind? Perhaps. John winked. The dog's jaw dropped, his tongue lolling out. In a human, it would be a wide grin.

'Dogs are clever fellahs, don't you think?'

Meg threw an amused look over her shoulder. 'I think they are. In fact, I'm sure they are.'

Once the kettle had boiled and the tea was poured, she sat opposite him and smiled. 'Enjoy your tea. It's only the second time these leaves have been used.'

'Refreshing enough for me,' said John. He eyed her speculatively. 'You look really happy today.'

It was true. There was a bloom on her face that had been sadly absent since coming to the village. She was also a little plumper than she used to be, but not overly so. To him she was quite stunning.

361

Would she still fancy coming to the village dance? He told himself probably not; after all, she was expecting a baby. With that in mind, what she said next surprised him.

'I was wondering if you're still on to take me to the village dance?'

'Yes. Undoubtedly. As long as you can cope with dancing, that is.'

Meg threw back her head and laughed. 'I'm not ill, John. I'm only in the family way and I'm not so big yet that I can't enjoy myself at a dance.' Her expression turned serious. 'But I will understand if you don't want to escort a pregnant widow when there are lots of single young females in the village who'd jump at the chance of going with you.'

'Not at all!' John exclaimed, determined not to miss his chance. 'I couldn't think of anyone I'd rather take than you. I mean that, sincerely I do.'

Meg's smile was sweet and her eyes glistened. Her expression changed when she added, 'You do realise it might set tongues wagging?'

There was rich amusement in John's eyes as he thought what fun that would be, but he had more respect for Meg than to say it. 'Please be assured, Meg, I wouldn't do anything that might sully your reputation. You mean too much to me...'

He saw her gaze drop down to his hand. Unwittingly he'd covered hers with his. He swiftly snatched it back.

'I'm sorry. I shouldn't have done that.'

To his surprise, she reached out for him, cupping his jaw in her hand, her face alight with emotion. 'Yes, you should have, John,' she said softly. 'Despite my condition, I need affection. I appreciate your friendship, but I also appreciate your affection. And your respect.'

CHAPTER TWENTY-SEVEN

It was the night of the village dance and Constable John Carter was thinking what a lucky man he was to be having a date with Meg Malin when the unforeseen happened. He was just about to button up the trousers of his best suit when a call came through from Rethman's Farm that a sheep had been found with its throat torn out.

The farmer concerned had made up his own mind about the likely culprit. 'Damned dogs! People dumping them out here in the country rather than doing what's right and proper!' Carter knew Farmer Rethman was referring to people abandoning dogs to find their own way in the world rather than facing up to rationing restrictions or having them put down.

The farmer was one of the few in the area with a phone so there was no excuse not to traipse out there and investigate. If it had been over ten miles away he would have left the call until the morning, but this particular farm was only five miles distant. He could get there on his bicycle in roughly half an hour.

'It would be tonight,' he muttered to himself as he stepped out of his suit trousers and into his uniform.

Before heading for the farm, he got the young lad from next door to take a message to Meg. 'Tell her I've been called out on a case so I'll see her there. Have you got that?' Young Tommy Potter wiped his nose on his sleeve, said he fully understood and accepted a penny for his trouble.

Alice was there when the message was received, having called round to tell Meg that Lily had settled in perfectly with her kids under her sister's care. 'She's reading in bed. Right little brainbox, isn't she!'

Meg smiled in agreement. She had to admit that Lily did love reading almost as much as she loved drawing. At least I get other colours nowadays, she thought.

'How do I look?' Meg was wearing a blue-and-white-flowered dress beneath her coat.

'Like a film star.'

Meg gave her a telling look. 'Does my bump show?'

Alice, who was wearing a red dress that would look better on somebody slimmer, shook her head. 'You're lucky. By the time I was four months, I looked as though I'd swallowed a beach ball!'

Satisfied that she didn't look too pregnant, Meg reapplied a smidgen of lipstick, pressed her lips together, studied her reflection and decided it would have to do.

Bert dined on some of the mutton he'd stolen from Rethman's farm. At the same time he congratulated himself for selling some of it on the black market in Bath, cutting the sheep apart in the field, leaving the fleece and taking only the meat. He congratulated himself still further on slitting the throat of one of the sheep, ripping it out with the teeth of a fox trap. Clever old Bert Dando! The police wouldn't be looking for him. They'd be looking for an animal with jaws big enough and strong enough to rip out the throat of a sheep. There was only one dog in the vicinity that fitted that picture and, with a bit of luck, the finger of accusation might point in the devilish creature's direction.

He grinned at the thought of what he'd done. The poison hadn't worked but smearing the animal's reputation would do the job. The farmer would be beside himself, demanding the animal be put down. Only he, Bert Dando, would know the truth.

From the attic window he heard and saw the shadowy figures of Alice and Meg, their progress lit only by torchlight. The two women were going out on the razzle. Lucky them. Lucky him too. He guessed the little girl was being taken care of somewhere else. Only the dog remained in the cottage. The sound of the women's shoes and their excited chatter soon melted away, and the night was once more silent and dark.

Bert crept out from the bushes in the lane at the side of Bluebell Cottage. His first choice would have been to enter via the garden gate, but he'd heard it squeak loudly when the women had left earlier. Best if he climbed the back wall and swung down from the lower branches of the apple tree he recalled growing there from way back. As a child he'd free-ranged through every garden in the village, taking anything he wanted, including apples.

He made a crouched landing from the tree on to something that felt remarkably like a cushion. Lucky me, he thought to himself. Keeping low, he made his way to the back door. Like most back doors in the village it was of a simple plank design. If it was locked, the planks would be easy to pull off, but he guessed it wouldn't be locked. That was the kind of village it was.

Hammer in hand, he kept to the path, his feet never straying on to the turned earth of the garden so no footprints would be left. Thieving in London had taught him a lot and so too had some of the criminals he'd encountered. A wooden lean-to shielded the shambolic back door from the worst of the weather. The back of the house was pitch-black making the lean-to hard to distinguish, but from memory he knew where it was and its approximate size.

Inside the construction was somehow even darker than outside. Bert clutched his hammer, relishing the thought of what he was about to do. Reaching into the darkness, his fingers met the iron latch that was keeping the door closed. It was stiff but lifted when he gave it a tug. Suddenly, just when he was about to push it inwards, a light came on. Surprised, he jumped back and collided with the zinc bath hanging on the wall. The bath jangled against the uneven wall like a church bell on Sunday. The dog began to bark.

Before anyone could challenge him, he was off, stumbling through the dark garden, branches scratching his face as he climbed the apple tree. The sharp stones set into the top of the wall to hinder intruders cut into his palms. He swore when he dropped the hammer on the garden side. His fingerprints would be on the handle but there was nothing he could do about it. Resigned to whatever happened, he let himself go, landing on the gravelly surface of the lane.

Inside Bluebell Cottage, his hearing attuned to the smallest sounds, Rudy heard the footfall of feet on loose stone. He barked wildly when the back door rattled as somebody on the outside tried to force it.

PC Carter, having just returned from Rethman's Farm, decided to do a quick walk around the village before making his way to the dance. All seemed peaceful until he closed on Bluebell Cottage. Rudy was barking, his tone sharp with warning. As he neared the cottage he saw the light in the downstairs window. Meg wasn't usually so careless, but perhaps in her present state she wasn't thinking straight. He'd heard women acted differently at certain times of their lives. Pregnancy was one of those times. Forgetting the blackout, she might even have considered leaving the light on as a deterrent to burglars, especially after hearing about the recent thefts in the village. Whatever the reason, he couldn't leave the dog barking like that. Best, he decided, to let Meg know and have her deal with it.

Heads turned when he entered the village hall, carefully closing the blackout behind him. He saw Meg talking with an American airman and immediately felt a pang of jealousy. He waved to get her attention and beckoned her over. She saw from his expression that something was wrong.

The smile dropped from her face.

'What's happened? Is it Lily? Is she all right?'

His greatest wish had been to dance with her tonight. It peeved him that he had to drag her away instead. 'Nothing to do with Lily. Sorry to interrupt your evening, Meg, but your dog's been barking fit to burst. I thought you might like to know. Not that there have been any complaints,' he added briskly. 'You don't have to come. I can see you're enjoying yourself.'

Meg immediately thought of Mr Amble who had come to take Rudy away. It occurred to her he might be trying to take him from behind her back. She couldn't allow that. 'I have to go,' she said, sliding her arms into the coat John presented to her – a blue one he recognised among all the others hanging from coat pegs behind the double doors. She called to Alice. 'I have to go.'

'Do you need company going through the dark?' asked the American she'd been talking to.

'No need,' said Carter in an authoritative manner, slightly miffed that somebody had filled his absence. 'I'll escort Mrs Malin all the way. It's my job.'

Meg allowed herself to be escorted from the room. 'I shouldn't have come,' she said to John as he held the door open for her. She was worried. If only she hadn't been persuaded to come to the dance. She'd really thought they were safe – that Rudy was safe. She couldn't let him be taken now. 'Do you think it's Mr Amble?'

'I wouldn't have thought so. Anyway, do you know you left a light on?'

She paused in the act of fastening her coat as

368

she walked from the hall. 'No, I did not!'

'Hang about while I get out my torch.'

'Hurry.' Meg didn't hang about for very long. She was off, John following behind, the light from his torch throwing a spotlight on the ground for her to follow. They ran most of the way, Meg desperate to find out what was wrong. To John it might appear that she was unnecessarily concerned, that Rudy was merely barking because he'd been left alone. She tried to persuade herself that Rudy had only heard foxes out in the garden.

Bluebell Cottage sat innocently in the darkness – except there was a light showing and Reg Puller was bent double at the front door looking into the letter box. Rudy was still barking. The light from the downstairs window went off. Reg was full of pompous authoritarianism, straightening up the moment he saw them. 'You're showing a light,' he stated gruffly.

'I didn't leave a light on,' Meg snapped indignantly. 'Anyway, it's gone off now.'

'Well somebody did! Don't tell me the dog did it.'

'I left the curtains open so Rudy could see things by moonlight.'

Reg sighed. 'An enemy plane can see a light at ten thousand feet! Do you not realise that?'

Meg felt cornered. 'I apologise but I really didn't expect Rudy to turn the light on.'

'The dog turned the light on?' Puller sounded disbelieving. 'Thought you'd have known better...'

PC Carter interceded. 'Let's go inside, shall we?' The light that had shone from the window came on, then went off again. Then on, and off again. Carter sucked in his breath. 'Is somebody mucking about?'

'Perhaps the electricity's tripped,' suggested Reg.

The door creaked on its hinges as Meg pushed it open. Carter gently nudged her aside. 'Let me...'

He didn't get to say another word. The light went on. Rudy dropped his paw from the switch and rushed excitedly to greet everyone. Meg burst out laughing. 'I don't believe it!'

PC Carter, smoothing the front of his jacket, chuckled and shook his head. Only Reg, full of bumptious self-importance, pulled a face and took out his notebook. 'That light was turned on in direct contravention of the blackout rules...'

Meg eyed him with amazement. 'Do you mean you're going to fine my dog?'

'I'm not a fool, Mrs Malin. The dog belongs to you...'

'And there's not an air raid in sight,' interrupted Carter, who couldn't help grinning like the Cheshire cat. Reg had started acting like Field Marshal Kitchener the moment he put on an air-raid warden's uniform.

'All the same...' began Reg, his snowy-white moustache quivering like a bunch of thistledown.

'Let it be, Reg. We came as quickly as we could. Can't you see the dog is agitated?'

Carter was quite right. The dog was running backwards and forwards between where they were stood and the back door. Carter headed for the back door.

'There has to be a reason.' His fingers on the latch, he turned round to face the air-raid warden with a more serious expression on his face. 'We've had two burglaries recently. In my estimation, the dog and you, Reg, might have prevented another one. Did you see anyone at all?'

The hands holding the notepad and pencil went limp and his air of self-importance intensified. 'I might have heard something, but I was only out front. I never went round the back.'

'Time we did then, Reg. Better let the dog go first.'

Rudy was lost in the dense darkness of the back garden. Reg followed PC Carter's example and got out his torch. Meg stood by the back door, watching the beams from the flashlights flutter over the frosty ground, and the bare stalks of gooseberry, blackcurrant and raspberry bushes. She wrapped her arms around herself, her breath rising in a silvery mist. In an effort to keep the cold out, she half closed the back door, hooking her foot over it so it would not swing back open. As she stood there, she thought of John Carter and smiled. How clever he'd been to include Reg in the hunt for an intruder who might or might not exist.

For a moment all was silent, men and dog out of earshot, tramping through the top end of the garden where Fred Grimes had planted seedlings for spring harvesting. The air was fresh and clear. Meg took a deep breath, its freshness reminding her of chilled water. Another sniff and she discerned something else in the air. She'd always had a good nose for smells and this included the perfume she and Lily made from rose petals; such a fragile smell but to her pungent and sweet. This other smell was far from being sweet or fragile, but it was certainly pungent.

371

Many years ago, her mother had taken her to visit an aged aunt. The aunt had worn the most antique clothes, mostly serge or bombazine and always black. Her mother had held a handkerchief to her nose, informing the old woman that she had a cold and didn't want her to catch it. The old woman had kept those clothes for years in an upstairs wardrobe. Meg had noticed the smell, and after the visit was over and they were on the train back to London, asked her mother what it was.

'Camphor,' her mother had replied. 'Aunt Frederica uses mothballs, which are made from camphor.'

Beams of light swept from side to side down the garden path. Preceded by torchlight, PC Carter and Reg appeared out of the darkness, the dog loping along behind them. 'Nobody out there,' said Carter. 'Though we did find this.' He held up a piece of brown cloth. 'We found it on one of the lower branches of the apple tree.'

'Can I see it?'

Even before she put her nose to it, Meg suspected she knew what she would smell. 'It's mothballs. I smelled it here too.'

'It is,' said Carter in a matter-of-fact manner. 'The same smell I detected at the two recent burglaries. The same as in the outhouse at Homeside Cottage too.'

Reg was shining his torch on to his watch face and mumbling something about getting back to his round.

'Reg. You reckon you've checked Homeside Cottage regularly since old Ivy died?'

'I have.'

'And you've never found anything disturbed?'

'Never!' Reg barked, absolutely beyond challenge.

But Meg did challenge him. 'When I tried the back door the other night, it wasn't locked. The door was stiff and only opened a fraction, but it did open.'

Reg almost exploded. 'That's impossible! I checked everything. Nobody's broken in there. I would have noticed.'

'Reg, I'm thinking I might take a look around the old place. Strike while the iron's hot, if you like. It's police business but I'm asking if you'd mind going with me. I do realise you have pressing duties of your own, so you can say no if you want to. I should also add that there might be a dangerous criminal inside. With that in mind, I think we should requisition the dog to go with us – that's with your permission of course, Mrs Malin?'

'Of course. I'm sure he'll be of use to you both.'

'I'm sure he will. I can't get the fact out of my mind that if he didn't turn the light on, then who did? And if he is indeed clever enough to do that, he did it to draw your attention, Reg. The dog's familiar with your routine.'

'Bloody hell! Apologies, Mrs Malin. Didn't mean to swear.'

'So what do you say, Reg?'

'Let's get the blighter!'

Meg marvelled at the way John had swung the air-raid warden on to his side. By now, Alice had brought Lily round so Meg couldn't go with them.

'Did you have a good time,' she asked Lily as she escorted her up to bed.

373

'It was fine.'

Tucking Lily in and wishing her goodnight had become something of a ritual so it came as a surprise when Lily stood in the doorway, effectively barring her entry. 'I'm old enough to get into bed by myself.'

Meg smiled in understanding without betraying what she really felt. 'Of course you can.' For a moment she just stood there as though waiting for Lily to change her mind.

'You can go now. I'm not a child,' Lily said again.

Meg took a deep breath, weighing up her hurt with a need to understand. 'Of course you're not.'

Once the door was closed, she stood out on the landing for a while, trying to work out what had happened to cause her foster daughter to behave like that. Harbouring a deep sense of foreboding, she descended the stairs, rubbing the cold from her arms as she entered the warmth of the kitchen. The grandfather clock in the living room struck eleven o'clock. Normally she would have taken herself off to bed, snuggling down beneath the green satin eiderdown she had bought from Mrs Crow, who had wanted money to buy replacement seeds for her flower garden. 'It used to be on my mother's bed before she died,' Mrs Crow had told her. Before moving to the village, Meg would have shunned purchasing anything second-hand, let alone the unwanted coverlet of a dead woman. The war had most certainly changed all that.

Tonight she would await Rudy's return and the thought of it brought a smile to her face. Her own parents, her father more so than her mother, used to wait up for her to come home from a dance or the cinema. Now here she was waiting up for a dog! After making a cup of tea and busying herself for a bit, Meg pulled up the sleeve of her cardigan and checked the time. Half past eleven.

Lily awoke from a frightening dream in which she was surrounded by barking dogs, their fangs bared and bloodlust in their eyes. She tried to sit up and would have screamed but she couldn't breathe and a terrible weight pressed down on her. Again and again she tried to catch her breath and sit up but each time she couldn't. Besides the weight there was a nasty cloying smell that made her want to vomit. But she mustn't vomit. She must stay very still and very silent.

Some inner voice told her to be calm, that she was only dreaming and what she was seeing had come and gone. Returning to that place would only ever happen in her worst nightmares. The time and the situation were long gone. Feeling suddenly relieved of the oppressive weight and the sickening horror, she kicked off the bedclothes and sat up. The room was dark around her. She was alone in the bed. Something, someone, was missing.

Rudy!

She'd got used to the weight of his body denting her gaily patterned bedspread, and when the dreams came she automatically stretched out her hand to touch him. The feel of his coat was reassuring, and when she touched him he acknowledged the gesture with a contented murmur.

Dealing with the blackout night after night had honed her sense of direction. Using both hands to feel the doorjamb, she stepped out on to the landing.

'Rudy! Rudy? Where are you?'

A rectangular glow came from downstairs before Meg stepped between the stairs and the room behind her. 'Lily, go back to bed.'

'Where's Rudy?'

'He's gone to help PC Carter apprehend a dangerous criminal.'

She didn't know for sure whether anyone at all was in Mrs Dando's old place, but if there was he was there without permission and therefore might very well be dangerous.

'Really?' Lily sounded quite surprised, but more than that, she sounded proud. Rudy was her dog and as far as she was concerned, there was nothing he wasn't capable of.

'Now go back to bed. I'll send him up as soon as he's back.'

Lily went back to bed and Meg went back to her chair and a pile of sewing. Lily was growing and she was making things that would fit her better. The light was dim and the sewing was monotonous. She rubbed at her eyes, willing herself to stay awake. Was it her imagination or was the grandfather clock slowing down? Her impatience getting the better of her, she opened the cavity at the front of the clock, took out the bold brass key, opened the glass cabinet covering the clock face, and wound it up. A quick glance at her wristwatch, a present from Ray on her twenty-first birthday, proved the old clock wasn't that far out.

For a moment she was tempted to turn off the light and open the curtains. At least she would see John return, probably with Reg though she hoped not. It was late and although it might send tongues wagging, she didn't care. She'd make tea and they'd toast bread in front of the range. She could only spare a scraping of butter, but it wasn't really eating or drinking that mattered. They would be sitting close to each other and could share their feelings until dawn.

Eventually she heard the latch lift and the door slide slowly open. Rudy came in first with his tongue hanging out. After lapping the contents of his water dish, he darted up the stairs. She heard the thud of his paws above her before he flung himself on to Lily's bed.

John came in with a trickle of blood running down his cheek. 'It's not serious,' he said, when she got to her feet and ran her fingers over it. He grinned. 'I gave him a bigger clump than he gave me.'

'Sit down!'

'Yes, ma'am.'

Meg fetched a bowl of water and a clean flannel. He winced when she touched his face, but told her to carry on. 'So what happened? Who was it?'

'Bert Dando! I should have known. I reckon he was there when his mother was alive. He tried to kick Rudy and shouted something about keeping his fangs away from him. Now I know where the blood on the landing came from. Rudy took a bite out of him. Must say, it couldn't happen to a better bloke! I'd bite him myself if I could! Anyway, the police came out from Bath in a car and took him with them. Apparently they've had

377

police in London asking after him, so I dare say we won't be seeing him for a while.'

Meg poured the water down the sink and refreshed the teapot with boiling water from the kettle. She finished filling their teacups just as the grandfather clock struck two o'clock.

'This is nice,' she said after the first sip.

'Nothing like a good cup of tea after arresting a no-good like Dando.'

'That isn't what I meant.'

'No. I suppose not.'

Perhaps it was the late hour, the fact that they were unlikely to be interrupted, but John found himself stating exactly what was in his heart. 'Meg, I know it's early days since you lost your husband, and you're about to give birth to his child, but I have to tell you that you're rarely far from my thoughts.'

'I know.'

'You do?' John's eyebrows arched in surprise.

Meg sat thoughtfully, a small frown creasing her brow. 'It's funny. In the past I would never have been so honest about my feelings. But that was when I was living in a London suburb where the men were out at work all day and the women were too busy housekeeping and child-rearing to have time for friendships. Not for real friendships anyway. I've only lived in Upper Standwick for a few months, yet I've had some very in-depth conversations with other women here. I think the fresh air must have something to do with it. Yes, people can be nosy, but they're not really prying into your private business, they're just interested. I never knew it before, but a village is like one big family.'

John wrapped both hands around his cup and thought about the sleepless nights when after seeing Meg during the day he couldn't get her out of his mind. What if she turned him down flat? What if there was somebody else or, the worst scenario of all, what if Ray wasn't dead? What if he came back? *Then all your dreams would be over, mate, and that's it and all about it!*

He started when her fingers suddenly brushed his hand.

'John, I appreciate you caring. I really do.'

'More than caring.'

'Yes. More than caring; but let's get things in perspective. I would need more than one parachute to make a wedding dress if we tied the knot before the baby is born! Just look at me!'

They both laughed, but once the laughter had finished, John took both of her hands in his and they sat there for a moment, both deep in thought as they looked into each other's eyes. The grandfather clock ticked in time with their hearts until, chiming the half past, they were reminded of how late it was.

Meg let the blackout curtain fall behind them both. A surge of night-time air made their faces tingle. Meg stood aside so John could get by.

'Goodnight,' he said softly and kissed her cheek.

She reached up with both hands, cupped his face and brought his lips down to hers. Her kiss was firm and eager. John responded, his arms around her. He buried his face in her hair.

'You smell as fresh as a daisy,' he said softly.

'And you feel as strong as an oak.'

He left her there while the going was good. It

just wasn't form to ask a pregnant woman if he could go to bed with her. Let the baby be born first, let a little time elapse while they got used to the idea, and then they would marry. After that there was nothing to stop them.

CHAPTER TWENTY-EIGHT

It was an early spring evening and Meg perceived a fluttering deep inside that she put down to how fresh the air felt and that milder weather was on its way. Buds were sprouting in the apple orchards, the mallards on the village pond were building nests among the reeds and spring lambs had appeared like fallen clouds in the lime-green fields.

Alice Wickes and her sister had invited Lily to go with them to the pictures in Bath and then stay for a sleepover afterwards. Meg decided it was only polite that she and John should escort her foster daughter to the bus stop and wait there with everyone else for the bus to Bath. After that, they intended walking to the station house where John had promised her a hearty meal was waiting.

'I've even got a bottle of wine, though I think Mrs Matthews at the village store has had it in stock since the last war. Still, it might have improved with age.'

Their route from the bus stop took them past Bluebell Cottage. Everything should have been quiet, but wasn't. They heard Rudy barking excitedly, a quick outburst like a blast of gunfire.

'He's missing you. That's all it is.'

'Rudy never barks for no reason.'

'I would think his missing you is reason enough.' He hesitated before adding; 'I'd miss you if you weren't around.'

'Are you sure Bert Dando is safely locked up?'

'Absolutely.'

'Tell you what, John. You go on. I'll check and then catch up with you. How would that be?'

He touched her shoulder briefly and kissed her cheek. 'Don't keep me waiting.'

A slight breeze brushed at her hair and pinked her cheeks as she hurried up to Bluebell Cottage. The fact that the garden gate was open came as something of a surprise; she was sure she'd shut it. Almost on tiptoe, she hurried up the garden path and pushed open the front door.

The room was filled with a warm amber light, yet she turned cold. The light was already on, but she was sure she had turned it off before going out. Her gaze alighted on the table lamp on top of the bureau shedding a brave light in a confined pool. Another table lamp sat on the small occasional table to the side of an overstuffed Victorian armchair. Her favourite chair, re-covered in pink rosy chintz that she thought brought the outside garden into the room.

For a moment she couldn't move. Someone was sitting in the armchair and at the sight of him all her lovely thoughts about John Carter turned to guilt. The dog, Rudy, lay across his feet but perked up on seeing her. Ray!

Even sat down, his presence dominated the room. 'Meg.'

Meg was transfixed. He wasn't holding out his arms, yet surely he should have been? Surely he was incredibly happy because he was home. Her feet had felt immersed in clay, but with a great effort she now managed to step forward. 'Ray?'

He was wearing his uniform and twirling his cap with both hands, just as he used to do. He looked tired, pouches of skin beneath his eyes. His skin seemed stretched too tightly over his cheekbones. It struck Meg as odd that neither of them was rushing to embrace the other. At one time they would have collided into a traffic jam of limbs, kisses and avid caresses. Not stay still like this.

'Where's Lily?'

'With a friend. I was going out tonight but then I heard the dog barking and came back. We have had problems in the village, you see.'

He nodded. 'Sorry about that. It was my fault. A bit foolish thinking he'd recognise me straight-away. Glad you took him in though. He's a good dog.'

Rudy raised himself into sitting position, looking up at Ray in adoration. In response, Ray leaned down and patted him on the head.

'Yes. He is.'

She saw Ray's steely gaze take in the changes in a cottage he'd known since boyhood. 'You've certainly got Bluebell Cottage looking trim. Better than trim. Homely, in fact. And you've kept the dog. I thought you said you'd never have him in the house. Have you got over your problem with dog hairs?'

'This is the country. Things are different here.'

'I suppose they are. Not like Andover Avenue

though, is it? You loved that place.'

'That was then. This is now.'

Meg frowned. Something was very wrong here. They were speaking in stilted sentences to each other and there'd been no hugs and kisses, nothing like a homecoming was supposed to be. Something had changed and there was one obvious thing above all others.

'Ray. Are you injured? Can you walk? Sorry,' she blurted. 'That came out so crass...'

'No. Not at all.' Ray took a deep breath. 'The fact is, Meg, I'm not coming home. Not even after the war is over.'

Meg told herself that this wasn't happening, that she'd expected an entirely different homecoming – when she'd expected one at all. 'I thought you were dead.'

'I was badly injured. The plane was hit when I was over there to fly somebody out. My French friends rescued me. Nicole looked after me. For a very long time, in fact. I'm sorry, Meg, but I have to be honest. Nicole is carrying my child. I cannot abandon her. Once the war is over, I'm going back. I have to stand by her. You understand that, don't you?'

The look in his eyes appealed for forgiveness. Meg sank on to a nearby chair. Never had her knees felt so weak. She clasped her hands so tightly her knuckles turned white. Her look was intense.

'I used to dream about you coming home. I mean, they told me you were missing presumed dead, but I said to myself, well, that means he might be alive. Sometimes I accepted that you

383

were dead. The rest of the time – less and less as time went on – I hoped and I waited...'

Him falling in love with somebody else aroused mixed feelings. There was a kind of anger – but not hot and furious. The anger derived from those moments when she'd imagined how his home-coming might be – if he was still alive. In her imagination his strong arms swept her off her feet, such was his delight in finding out they were about to have a child. In the dim light of Bluebell Cottage they sat separately, each in their own space. He didn't know she was expecting a child. His right to know seemed irrelevant. He wouldn't be here to see the child grow up because he was opting to stand by another woman and another child.

With indifferent determination, she plucked at the buttons of her coat. Bought before the war began, its voluminous layers hid her rounded belly. Once all the buttons were undone, it fell away.

'Your French woman isn't the only one expecting a baby.'

The grandfather clock beat the seconds that silence reigned. Deep-set eyes stared above gaunt cheekbones as Ray got to his feet, unable to drag his gaze away from what she was showing him.

'Is it mine?' His voice was small, incredulous.

The man he had been, and still probably was, would not forsake his own child. She knew that for sure, but did it really matter? He had committed himself elsewhere. Some people, especially her mother, might think she was mad and should determine to continue with her marriage no matter what. She could hear her voice now. *The child is his. He has to stand by you and fulfil his*

384

responsibilities.' Meg thought carefully and very quickly about what both of them truly wanted.

'Did you know this woman, Nicole, from other missions?'

He nodded. 'We weren't lovers before, but when I was injured... We'd always been drawn to each other. I'm sorry, Meg. I did love you, but the war...'

'Of course,' she interjected fiercely. 'It's always the war. It bears the blame for a lot of things.'

'The man who brought you home...' Only half a sentence but she heard the assumption.

'John Carter. His name's John Carter. He's a policeman.'

She sensed where this conversation was going. Ray was asking her if John Carter was the father of the child. The old Meg Malin would have put him straight there and then. The new Meg Malin was less inclined to give him the satisfaction of knowing one way or another. Her new life had taken hold far more quickly than she could ever have imagined. Up until Ray's reappearance she had coped with this war alone, her only company a refugee child and a dog. She'd got used to living in Upper Standwick, used to the villagers' kindness and their independent attitude.

John Carter's name hung in the air between them until finally Ray's broad shoulders heaved as though a ton weight had been lifted from each one. 'Seems I shouldn't have worried about leaving you alone.'

Meg managed a weak smile and a non-committal answer. 'No.'

Her husband was not a fool; indeed, no man

385

was incapable of working out how many months it had been since they'd gone to bed together, but it all depended what he *wished* to believe. Ray had made his choice. He wanted Nicole and the baby she was carrying. Meg couldn't believe how easy she was finding it not to try to persuade him otherwise. Somehow the air was cleared, each laying out a path for the future.

'I won't let you down,' he said to her. 'Everything will be done fairly. I don't wish for any acrimony. Anyway, it seems as if you, too, have found happiness with someone else, though I know it's because you believed I was dead. You've also got Lily to think about and living in this village.'

She didn't ask him what he meant about living in the village, but guessed he thought they were all busybodies who couldn't mind their own business; she had no wish to disillusion him. Living in a village was as though everyone was related; everyone was family.

They talked further about the arrangements after they were divorced.

'The rules are that I pay you alimony until such time as you remarry. I can manage that,' he explained. She knew he could. His father was a director of an insurance company. 'I presume you'll stay in the village and not move back to London. You know you can stay here in the cottage if you please. Aunt Lavender has decided to stay up north, but no doubt she'll be glad of the rent. I'll pay that too, until such time as you remarry.' He paused. 'I presume you will.'

Meg had a great urge to bang her hands against her ears so she couldn't hear him racing ahead with all these arrangements. It struck her he wanted to end their marriage as quickly as possible and have all the details tied up with string. Well, she might as well let him get on with it. He wanted to be with his French lover. She wanted ... this life ... the village ... a warm community she'd grown used to and loved, including John.

'Yes. That's quite acceptable. In fact, I've become very fond of Bluebell Cottage, but there is also a police house, which John lives in.' She instantly wondered what John would think when she told him about this. John being a father to someone else's child who they now knew was still alive.

'Good,' said Ray, nodding approvingly. 'So when's the baby due?'

Meg placed a hand on her belly. She felt a pain and also a heaving as the baby prepared to enter the world. She grimaced, her lips stretched taut, showing all her teeth. 'Right about now.'

Ray looked as though she'd slapped both sides of his face. His high colour disappeared and his speed crossing the room to the telephone would have put a greyhound to shame. 'I'll phone the doctor.'

Meg pushed a cushion behind her back and leaned more comfortably against it. She would not panic. Ray seemed to be doing quite nicely on his own.

'Yes, Ray. Do that. But once he's on his way, I want you to leave.'

One hand on the receiver, he looked back at her; his mouth open and an incomprehensible look in his eyes. To his mind she might very well be expecting another man's child, but he'd never

387

seen such a glow on her face, such a look in her eyes. 'You look lovely,' he said. 'You really do.'

After speaking to the doctor, he went back to where he'd been sitting, picked up his overcoat and took out an envelope. 'This is a letter from the man Lily was supposed to go to. His name's Daniel Loper. He lives in Cambridge. He's willing to give Lily – or rather Leah – a home as her father would have wished.'

Meg turned abruptly, which sent the pain jarring down her spine. She winced but pressed on with what she wanted to ask. 'But she doesn't have to live with him?'

He shrugged. 'I suppose not. Not if she doesn't want to.'

Meg winced as another pain shot through her.

'Look. Can't this wait until later? One thing at a time, eh?' His expression was that of a man unwilling to get too embroiled in women's problems, especially childbirth.

The look made Meg angry. She clenched her teeth as the pain rolled over her. 'Don't you want to stay and see it born? You know, as a prelude to the birth of your French child?'

His face turned pale. 'War is more like my bag. Not this. Sorry, but it scares me to hell. I'd better get going.'

If it wasn't for the pain she would have laughed loud and long. Her big brave husband was scared by the prospect of being involved with childbirth. But there was one other thing she wanted to know. 'Wait! One moment. What about her parents? Are they still alive?'

Ray shook his head.

'Do you know for sure?'

'We now know for sure that the so-called labour camps are death camps.' He paused and his eyes became hooded. 'I can't tell you the details.'

'Oh. I suppose it's more top-secret information.'

Still wearing the hooded look, he shook his head. 'No. It's just too horrible.'

Once the cottage door was closed behind him he took a great gulp of fresh air. The night smelled acrid, spicy with mud from turned fields and buds bursting from willow and shrub. Soon everything would be bright green with new leaves and the air would be filled with birdsong as they mated and laid their eggs. Everything was being reborn – including his life. That's how it had felt when he'd closed the door behind him. The old life was gone and as much as a part of him wanted to believe the child was his, he chose not to. He had a new life to go to once the war was over. Nothing, he realised, would ever be the same again.

CHAPTER TWENTY-NINE

Ray Malin was carrying far more guilt than he'd admit to. Nicole, with her peachy complexion and glossy dark hair, haunted both his day and night-time hours. Her dark eyes reflected the colour of the elfin fringe curling around her face. There was something almost childlike about her looks that was not reflected in her character. She was the toughest, most independent woman he had ever met. Not for her the domestic scene or traditional behaviour of a woman waiting for marriage. It hadn't even mattered to her that he was already married. She had decided she wanted him and told him so. He'd never known a woman to be so outspoken and her breathless non-conformity had tipped the balance. He had ended up wanting her as much as she wanted him.

Even though it appeared Meg had been unfaithful to him, some small vestige of responsibility remained. Nicole was the love of his life, a passion he could not resist. However, he'd once loved Meg and couldn't abandon her without making sure she'd be all right. Feeling suddenly colder, he turned up his coat collar, got into his car and drove to the police house.

He drew the car to a stop outside the station house, took a deep breath and stepped out to confront whatever awaited him. For a moment he paused, one half of him suggesting that it wasn't his place to vet the man who had slept with his wife. The fact was that he couldn't help himself. If he didn't do this, a small amount of guilt would walk with him all the days of his life. It had to be done now.

Constable John Carter was taken aback. Seeing a stranger in uniform standing on his doorstep threw him for a moment, until Ray introduced himself.

'Ray Malin. Come back from the dead, so to speak.'

PC Carter took the extended hand and shook it while doing his best to hide his dismay. Not the best way to end the day, he thought. Up until now, he'd been pretty cheerful. At lunchtime he'd gone round to Meg's for lunch. He'd helped her hang the new curtains she'd made and even lent a hand getting the cot together – an awkward job if ever there was one. He couldn't have felt more involved if the child was his; in fact, it felt as though it was his. More than that, he was already thinking ahead, planning when he would ask Meg to marry him.

The man standing at the door of the station house changed all that.

Twilight was turning into an inky dark night. 'Pleased to meet you, Mr Malin. Better come inside. I've just drawn the blackout curtains.'

Ray followed the man he assumed to have lain with his wife into an office area complete with reception desk and cupboards set into recesses either side of the chimney breast. A gas fire bubbled and spat in the grate. John jerked his chin at the old fire and apologised for its sputtering. 'It's not working properly.' He bent down and turned it off, at the same time hiding his despairing expression.

As he stood up again, his smile was warm enough, but he felt far from happy. 'Good timing, you coming back right now; just in time to see your offspring coming into the world.'

Carter's expression was totally open. If it hadn't been, then Ray might have accused him of being a liar and a knave. The expression was that of a man who always told the truth when it really mattered.

The words Ray had planned to say, about the policeman standing by the woman he'd got pregnant, stuck in his throat. Instead he said, 'Ah! Yes.

Very opportune indeed.'

'Got plenty of leave, have you?'

'No. I'm leaving almost immediately.'

'Oh.' John's enforced cheerfulness disappeared.

Ray twirled his cap in his hands, his expression hooded and inward-looking. 'I'm going away. Things have happened. I wanted to ask you a favour before I leave.'

Carter waited. He didn't know what to say, and whatever he said might be the wrong thing. Best to say nothing.

'Meg and I have been apart for a while. She thought I was dead and I...Well, being apart gave me time to think. We're separating. Eventually we'll get divorced. I won't be back, but I would like to think that somebody is looking after her and the baby. Will you do that?'

Carter frowned. Desiring Meg was one thing. Her husband asking him to look after her was quite another. Ray didn't seem to know he was doing something that the policeman found unpalatable. 'Mr Malin, I'm here for her if she wants me now she knows you're still alive, but that's her decision. Not mine and not yours. She values her independence.'

Ray set his cap back on his head and slapped it flat with his hand. 'Yes,' he said thoughtfully. 'I can see that.'

Driving back to base, he almost laughed at the fact that Meg had *let* him believe that the baby she was carrying was not his. It was pure coincidence that PC Carter had told him the truth. He could doubt him but the man's open look didn't allow him to do that. Carter had been telling the truth.

However, it did sadden him. They hadn't been apart for that long, yet this cruel war had torn them apart – or had it in fact forced them to see each other as they really were? He'd found Nicole. Meg, whether she saw it or not, had stepped back from her old self and found someone new.

The doctor's wife phoned through news to her husband that Mrs Malin had started her contractions. He was already out on a call to a farm four miles south of the village. Tired but dedicated, he wiped his sweating brow with his handkerchief, his answer determined by how long it would take for him to get back. 'I'll be there as soon as I can. She should be all right for a while, but just in case, get a message to Alice Wickes. Ring the pub. They'll get a message through.'

Alice was cutting up an old blanket to make a winter coat for her eldest when Gladys Stenner came round, opening the door without knocking to tell her the news. 'It's coming, Alice! It's coming!'

Everyone took notice when Gladys Stenner shouted. Alice leapt to her feet, then looked round at her kids. Gladys noticed. 'I'll stay and look after the youngsters if you like. Cliff can manage on his own.'

Lily had been conscientiously making a teddy bear for the baby from old blanket cut-offs. Now she was on her feet running for the door, scattering the materials for her sewing project behind her.

Alice shouted after her. 'Lily! Come back here this minute.' Lily disappeared, leaving Alice eyeing the fragments of material, cotton, pins and needles that now lay scattered on the floor. 'Dear, Lord,' she sighed to herself, palm on her forehead. 'Gladys, could I ask you to pick all this up while I put on my coat and go and see what I can do?'

'Say no more. You get out there.'

No doubt woken by his mother's shouting, a demanding wail sounded from upstairs. 'Oh no. He'll wake everybody if I don't see to him.'

Gladys was picking up the scattered bits and pieces, squinting in order to see the pins and needles better. 'The doctor said there was no need to panic. He seemed to think nothing would happen for a few hours yet.'

Alice tucked her chin in tight to her neck and gave Gladys a withering look. 'Yeah! And he said all my labours would be over within twenty-four hours. Wishful thinking. Forty-eight and counting! I'll just go up and see to the little 'uns before I head over to Meg's.'

Afterwards, Alice got her coat and managed to hook out her old shoes that she'd squashed into the coal scuttle for burning. They looked worn out but retrieving them from the scuttle was like rescuing old friends. Comfort before pride, she said to herself. 'The kettle's on the hob and there's a stewed batch in the teapot,' she shouted over her shoulder.

As each pain rolled over her, Meg took deep breaths and then the door slammed open. 'Lily! I thought you were the doctor.'

Lily threw off her coat and patted Rudy on the head. Then all the bravado, the courage to face

394

her foster mother giving birth, suddenly drained out of her. Meg frowned. 'You look worried. What's the matter?'

'I'm frightened. You're not going to die, are you?'

'I'm not ill. I'm having a baby.'

Lily felt tongue-tied. She was remembering another time, another place and another woman giving birth. Where was that? She couldn't quite remember but knew it had happened. The memory took root like a weed just beneath the surface of a pond.

'Lily, go back and stay with Alice.'

Lily shook her head. 'No. I can't. I have to stay. I have to...' She didn't know what she had to do, only that it was encapsulated in her memory. 'You should be in bed. I'll help you up.'

Another pain speared through Meg's body. 'I can wait for the doctor, thank you.'

'No, you can't. You have to lie down. Babies are born when you're lying down.'

Another pain. 'Less of your cheek, young lady.'

'It's not cheek. I've seen it before. You have to lie down.'

Meg had always thought that Lily's startlingly blue eyes and fair hair made her look younger than she actually was. Tonight she seemed more than her age, not because of any change in the colour of her eyes or her hair but because of her serious expression.

The pains came sharp and fast now, disrupting her resolve and her train of thought. 'I suppose I should be...' she conceded.

'I'll help you up there.'

'I think I can manage...'

It wasn't just another pain that made Meg hesitate, but the fact that Lily was filling the kettle, lighting the gas, then fetching and folding clean towels from the clothes dolly that hung before the range. Her self-assurance was quite amazing, and in consequence her expression had acquired a maturity Meg had not noticed before.

With firm resolve, Lily helped Meg from the chair. 'Come on. The baby will be coming soon.'

Meg chortled. 'Oh yes. And how would you know that?' She didn't see Lily's expression, the sudden flash of recognition in her eyes. Déjà vu. Something happening that she'd seen happen once before.

'I told you. I've seen it before. You have to lie down. I have to help you.'

'Where?'

'I don't know!'

'Lily, we have to wait...'

'*No! No!* I don't want you die. I don't want you to die!' She threw herself into Meg's arms. Meg grimaced while caressing the blonde hair she loved so much. Meg gave herself up to the pain, which was swiftly taking over. She would accept whatever Lily said.

Lily, determined to help her foster mother up the stairs, forced herself to concentrate on the here and now and not on the sudden memories threatening to engulf her and turn her to jelly. The train, the pile of bodies, the woman who had died in labour along with her newborn child, threatened to swamp her mind – it all came flooding back. If she were to think clearly, they had to be kept at bay. Doing that meant accept-

396

ing what had happened without breaking down. She had to think clearly.

Rudy padded across the flagstone floor to the bottom of the stairs, his melting brown eyes full of sympathetic interest. One paw was already on the bottom tread when Lily turned round and told him to sit and stay. Meg glanced over her shoulder. If it hadn't been for the pain, she might have made a quip about him looking like a nervous father. But she didn't. The pain was enough to bear, though when she thought about the child's father it wasn't Ray who came to mind. It was John's worried frown.

The bed linen had been changed that morning and Meg couldn't help but feel relieved at the prospect of sliding between those crisp, cool sheets. She pulled back the covers.

'Wait there.' Lily dashed off downstairs, returning with two clean towels and some sheets of yesterday's newspaper. By the time she had returned Meg had got herself ready, removing her outer clothes, then her underclothes and putting on a clean nightdress. For a moment she stood there, her hands holding her stomach as another contraction ripped through her and something that felt as heavy as an anvil pushed downwards between her legs.

'You need to lie on the bed,' Lily said to her.

'That's what I want to do.'

As she lay back on the heap of pillows she was racked by another contraction. When she attempted to reach for the bedcovers, her whole stomach seemed to heave sideways then downwards. She'd never had a baby before but knew

397

that it was coming. Fast! Very fast.

What happened next should have been in a blur of pain and discomfort, embarrassment even, that a young girl was lifting her nightdress, then feeling her naked belly. Lily gasped and her eyes opened wide as she peered between Meg's parted thighs. 'Don't worry,' she said, suddenly glancing up. 'I know what to do.'

Meg felt herself opening up. Somehow it seemed part of her, yet not part of her, almost as though she were watching the event rather than being the chief participant. The look in her foster daughter's eyes was hypnotic and held her attention.

'It's coming,' Lily whispered, her face bright with amazement. 'I can see its head.'

Meg got herself up on to her elbows, trying her best to peer between her knees and see what Lily was seeing. 'Lily, you must run and get somebody...'

'It's all right. The woman on the train was a midwife. She told the lady having the baby what had to be done. I remember what she said. You have to turn the head so that the shoulders come through sideways.'

Meg paused. This was such a lot for a young girl to do.

'I've already done it. I know what to do. I've seen it done before.'

Meg thought she'd heard wrongly. Lily was just a child...

It was as though her whole womb, stomach and intestines had flushed out of her body and on to the crumpled newspaper. There was also a feeling of relief followed by a piercing cry. Keen to see her newborn and to know whether it was a boy or a girl, Meg pushed herself up back on to her elbows. 'What is it? What is it?'

Before Lily could answer, the bedroom door burst open. 'Oh my God!' Alice's expression was one of amazement.

'Boy or girl?' asked Meg, her face glowing with delight even though the aftermath of the birth pains were still sending spasms of movement over her stomach. Alice placed the child in a towel and raised her up so Meg could see. 'A little girl!' Meg almost choked on a mixture of laughter and tears.

Alice turned to Lily. 'Did you do this?'

Lily nodded. 'Somebody had to.'

'You?' Alice was incredulous.

Lily spoke slowly as though she were explaining the details of a film recently seen at the cinema. 'I saw it done once before. It was on a train. I saw it all.' She didn't add that both mother and baby had died in a pool of blood.

Alice took over and was closely followed by Doctor Fudge.

'You go on outside and play. Or take that dog for a walk,' Alice ordered her. It was obvious Alice had overlooked the fact that it was dark outside and all the other kids would be in bed. Even Samuel Golding, a boy who had saved her from the loneliness her nationality and her dreams had bequeathed her.

Rudy followed her out into the twilight of a March evening. Raindrops from earlier dripped like pearls from the eaves and the air was fresh with damp grass and newly formed buds. The familiar figure of PC John Carter set his bicycle against the hedge and pushed open the garden gate. He took off his helmet as he approached her, undid his top button as though he were sweating streams and eyed her nervously.

Instead of jumping around John's knees and wagging his tail furiously, Rudy circled him as though wanting to reassure and escorted John to the front step where Lily was sitting. John got the message and sat on the end of the step, with Lily at the other end, chin supported on knuckles, and the dog between them.

'It's a girl.'

John wondered at Lily's perception before it came to him that asking the gender of the newborn was only to be expected. 'Auntie Meg is fine. They're both fine.'

'I'm glad to hear it.'

'Are you going to marry Auntie Meg now the baby's been born?'

In all other awkward circumstances, licking his lips would help grease his response. In this particular instance and asked this particular question, John was lost for words and no amount of licking made his lips any moister.

'Do you think I should?'

Lily fixed him with a piercing stare that made him wince. He'd seen magistrates look at poachers in the same way before passing sentence, as though they knew that they were going to lie even before they opened their mouths. The stare turned solemn.

'You'd make a good father.'

He smiled. 'That's the best compliment I've ever had.'

He thought of Ray Malin, the baby's real father. His visit and its purpose had knocked him sideways. Something had broken between Mr and Mrs Malin, something that could not be mended. Ray hadn't said as much, but the message was there. He was going away. Look after my wife, though to John's ears the message was that the coast was clear. He'd been right to reprimand her husband that it wasn't up to him whether she was inclined towards him or not. Not that he doubted she was. Something warm had grown between them. Just friendship at first and so far their affection had been restrained to reassuring hugs and occasional stolen kisses.

John, Lily and Rudy the dog sat silently watching the bats weaving around any obstacle in their way before circling back to the church tower. Once the bats were gone they continued to sit, listening to the night sounds and watching a waning moon flit in and out of lacy clouds.

The beam from a flashlight suddenly swept over them. 'What's this then? The three wise monkeys?'

'We're waiting to see the baby,' returned John.

'I've made it a teddy bear – well almost,' added Lily.

Rudy gave a single woof.

Reg Puller grunted something about expectant fathers and stalked off. As though he thinks I'm the father, thought John, feeling immensely proud that he might. He sat, lost in thought, waiting for Lily to say something rather than having to speak himself. However, he did wonder how she was feeling about the baby, whether she might be jealous.

'I'm looking forward to seeing this baby. I expect you are too.'

'I've already seen it. I brought it into the world.'

John fell to silence. There was something deadpan about her voice, as though bringing a baby into the world wasn't all that difficult. 'You sound very knowledgeable.'

'I saw a baby being born once before. I was on a train. It was packed with people. The woman was lying down near to where I was stood. I saw everything.'

John felt as though his tongue had cleaved to his mouth. For a moment he just did not know what to say. All he could do was express genuine surprise. 'Lily. I had no idea...'

'I lost my memory, you know. It started coming back some time ago. Now, watching the baby arrive, I know everything. My name came back some time ago but didn't really mean anything and I didn't want to tell Auntie Meg. I didn't want to upset her.'

John's speechlessness continued for a moment. He felt wonder but also surprise – and pity. The poor child. But he must not expound pity, that could only upset her. 'I like the name Lily. Will I like your new name?'

'Leah. My name's Leah. Leah Westerman. My parents are ... were ... Rudolph – Rudy – and Rachel Westerman. I don't think they're alive. I would feel their presence if they were alive, wouldn't I?'

John's jaw dropped. His face paled. 'I don't know. Some people can, but I don't know.'

Lily cleared her throat and began to recite the

bits of her life she now recalled. 'I think we were Jewish. Not that we practised it very much, but in Austria that didn't matter. We were what we were, and we were quite rich. We moved to France. Then everything was taken from us and we were put on that train. My father feared I would die at the labour camp. That's why he took me off the train and placed me on the pile of dead people. He told me to pretend that I was dead.'

The bright shining moon was hidden by cloud so he couldn't see her face when she fell to silence, as though shrouded in thought. He didn't need to see to know that tears were brimming in her eyes.

'You can't know for sure that your parents are dead...'

'I feel it!' Her interruption was forceful and un-questionable. 'I remember how it was back in Austria when I was younger. All the nastiness happened bit by bit. My father lost his job. I wasn't allowed to attend my school. I loved my school. Such a shame,' she added, almost as though she was talking about a favourite hat. 'Then we lost our house and ran away to France. My father said it was a very liberated country and that we'd be safe there. Then the Germans came and we were loaded on to a train. People said we were being sent east to a labour camp. The train didn't have seats. It smelled of cows and there were too many people packed in it and they began to die. That's where I saw the woman giving birth and other women helping her. That's how I knew what to do.'

John sat stunned, his hands clasped in front of him, his mind racing. This child wasn't yet old enough to leave school and get a job, but she was speaking as though she'd already lived half a lifetime. He didn't want her to tell him any more. He wasn't sure he could stand it, even though it was her who had experienced these things. He wanted to make her whole again and make everything normal. Normal things. That's what she needed.

'I suppose we might venture inside now, make a cup of tea or something?' he said nonchalantly.

She got up without speaking. Night had descended long ago but nobody had thought to draw the blackout curtains downstairs. The light from the range and the table lamps helped alleviate the gloom.

The grandfather clock struck two o'clock. John stood and glanced up the stairs while Lily filled the kettle and hung it from the trivet before the range. John placed his helmet on the table. Muffled conversation came from upstairs, plus the odd creaking of a floorboard. He didn't want Lily to return to the memories of her past. He tried to sound bright when he said, 'I wonder what she'll name her.'

'I think she wanted Ellen for a girl. Edward for a boy.'

Not Raymond for a boy. John's spirits were lifted. 'A nice name.'

He eyed the girl as she fetched crockery and a blue and white tea caddy from the dresser. She had an unreadable look on her face, yet she seemed full of confidence as she went about the task of making tea, pouring milk, spooning the very smallest amount of sugar into each cup.

What was going on in her mind, he wondered. Her memories had resurfaced. He only hoped she could cope with them.

'What about your name? How do you want to be called? Lily or Leah?'

The teaspoons tinkled in the saucers. She set each cup carefully in its saucer as though being accurate about such things was terribly important.

'I've thought about it. It's early days but even once I've got used to my memories I think I would still want to be called Lily. Ray saved me. Meg gave me a home and, if I want to follow the Jewish religion, I can. That's what's so important in this country and in this world. You can be whoever you want to be. That's what freedom means. I think my parents would have wanted that. It's all that's left of them. At least, I think it is.'

CHAPTER THIRTY

Nothing had prepared Meg for her feelings towards Ellen Mary Malin. She spent hours staring at the round little face, the way it puckered just before crying for her feed, the way her eyeballs moved beneath gossamer eyelids.

The doctor advised she stayed in bed for at least a week, and Alice Wickes and Gladys Stenner, both of whom popped in every day, advised she make the most of it and stay there for a fortnight. Meg was adamant she would do no such thing. 'I've had a baby. I'm not an invalid.'

405

'Stay,' ordered Gladys, pressing a meaty hand on her shoulder when she dared to push back the bedclothes and swing one foot out of bed.

Reluctantly, Meg obeyed, but only until Gladys had left the cottage. With Ellen in her arms, she went downstairs and, when the phone rang, held the baby in the crook of her arm while she answered it.

Her mother was congratulatory. 'I would come down, but there's such a lot going on here. Is the child doing well?'

'Very well and the birth wasn't so bad.'

'Ugh! Lucky for you. I myself had a terrible time when I had you... It was touch and go, you know.'

'Yes. I do know.' Meg rolled her eyes. She'd heard what a difficult time her mother had had giving birth to her a hundred times before. Nobody had suffered quite as badly as her mother had – and that was with the best of medical care!

'What a shame Raymond isn't here to see his offspring. I suppose at some stage we will hear where he's buried?'

'I'm getting divorced.'

She heard her mother's intake of breath and could easily imagine the shocked expression on her face. 'What are you saying? Surely it cannot be...?'

'We're getting a divorce. There's no acrimony. We both agree it's the best thing to do. He'll be happier with his French mistress and I'll be happy with... Whoever, somebody else.'

'Meg! You cannot possibly mean that. A French mistress? What a terrible scandal! And divorce.

Now listen carefully, my dear...'

Meg knew by her mother's tone of voice that although deeply shocked by what she'd told her, she was going to do her best to bring her daughter back from the brink. But the brink of what? Happiness?

'Getting divorced will attract the utmost scandal. You'll never be able to hold your head up again. People will not wish to include you in social activities...'

'Mother, I have no wish to be involved in the kind of social activities you think are so important. I'm going to stay here in Bluebell Cottage. Ray has arranged everything.'

'You'll be all alone! Just you and the baby!'

There was no doubt in Meg's mind that her mother was more concerned for her own reputation and how she would explain things to her close-knit and narrow-minded social group. Ellen, snuggled in the crook of her arm, began to make snuffling noises. It was getting close to feeding time again. Meg jiggled her up and down.

The dog raised his head at the sound, pricked his ears, then lay back down again and closed his eyes.

'It won't be just me and the baby. Lily and the dog are here too. She has remembered that her real name is Leah Westerman, though she has decided to remain as Lily.'

'Oh. And what about her family? Surely if you now know who she is, they can be found and will no doubt want her back.'

'We don't think so. We think she's an orphan and that her parents are dead. We're her family now and I have to say, I think we are a proper little family. I've also made many friends in the village.'

'Does that include a man friend?'

Her mother sounded scandalised, the words hissed rather than spoken. Meg imagined the clenched teeth, the fiddling of bejewelled fingers at the familiar pearl necklace. It would have been easy to deny there was no 'man friend', but Meg was averse to lying about where she expected her life to go.

'Yes. If you must know, it does.'

The following silence simmered with shock. The last few words they spoke to each other were delivered as though both of them had distanced themselves from the very heart of the conversation. At no point did her mother offer to come down and run the house while Meg recovered from the birth. Not that she wanted her to come down and upset everyone with her own dogged view of how a household should be run – how a village should be run, by the time she'd finished.

Her last comment was regarding Lily. 'What will you do with the child now that you have a baby of your own?'

'I dare say I'll appreciate her very much.'

As Meg fed the baby, one leg curled beneath her in the expansive softness of the old armchair, she thought about her mother. Lavinia Moorehead set great store by marrying the right man, living in the right place and always being well presented – which included the house she lived in. Nothing was ever out of place. As a child, Meg had never been allowed to actually touch the beautiful furnishings and, when she got out her toys to play

408

with, she was expected to put them away in exactly the same place as she'd got them from.

With hindsight, she now realised she'd married Ray because her mother had thought him exactly the right sort for her. Perhaps she'd also married him in order to escape her mother's influence, her first attempt at flying to freedom. She realised now that she had always done her best to please her mother, hoping perhaps for some affection in return.

Ray had been a lovely man, but they'd been suited to doing different things with their lives. Being house-proud had filled a void in her life, the void she didn't recognise as lack of affection. She didn't love her husband as she once had and somehow, deep down, he knew it. In exchange, he didn't love her anymore either. They would always be friends; she knew that, but both of them appreciated that their lives were their own.

Alice and Gladys were the next to be told that Ray wasn't dead. 'He was wounded. The Resistance took care of him and helped him escape.'

The two women remarked that this was a miracle and went on and on about the possibilities for the future. 'He's not dead? Well, that is wonderful news. Will you both return to London or remain buried in the country?'

'No is the answer to your first question, and likewise to the second. I will be staying here at Bluebell Cottage with my daughters. This is where I want to be. Ray wishes to be in France. He's in love with somebody else.'

There! She'd said it. The two women stared at her, then glanced at each other, unsure what to say next. So they said nothing. Silence reigned.

After they'd left, she turned her head so she could see out into the garden. She pondered on continuing to let Ray believe that Ellen was not his daughter. Was she being unfair? He'd gone from Bluebell Cottage to the station house. She wondered what conversation, if any, had passed between Ray and John. She might ask him or she might not. Perhaps in time he would tell her anyway. He'd promised to visit her soon – once she was feeling up to it.

Lily came in from school, her face flushed and her eyes shining.

'You look hot.'

'I ran all the way.' She came over and gently placed her hand on the baby's head. 'You shouldn't be out of bed yet.'

'Who told you that?'

'The doctor.'

'Well just because he's a doctor, doesn't mean to say he knows everything. I'm feeling very well. Very well indeed.'

'I'm feeling very well too. There's a letter on the table addressed to you.'

'What?'

'A letter,' repeated Lily. 'Shall I get it for you?'

'If you would.'

'I'll make you a cup of tea while you read your letter?'

Meg brushed at her eyes, then began to read the letter.

My dear Mrs Malin,
   It has been brought to my attention that a certain

410

Leah Westerman has been fostered into your care. Her father, Professor Rudolph Westerman, was an old friend of mine and, back before the war began, I promised that if anything should happen to him and his wife I would offer the child a home.

This is what I am offering now, though it should be pointed out that with my bachelor status in mind, my offer would have to go through official channels.

I am not of the Jewish faith, but all my old friend cared about was that his daughter be brought up surrounded by kindness. Please let me know your thoughts on the matter

Yours sincerely,

Professor Daniel Christian Loper

There followed the address of his lodgings within a campus of Cambridge University. Once the tea was set down on the table, Meg hesitantly passed the letter to Lily. She feared losing her foster daughter, who she had come to love immensely. John had helped her make the decision when she relayed to him what Ray had told her before. *'She has the right to know. She has the right to choose.'*

Hands clenched in front of her, she explained the contents. 'It's all about you from a Professor Loper, who was a friend of your father.'

A pair of bright blue eyes quickly scrutinised the letter that could greatly change her life. After carefully folding it up, she placed it next to the cup and saucer. 'I'm not going. You need me here.' Her eyes looked at Meg in pleading. 'Do I have to go and live with him?'

Meg shook her head. 'No. You don't have to go.'

'Good. Because I'm not going.' Her tone was

411

resolute. Meg thought she looked unshakeable.

'I dare say you have a choice.'

'My home is here. With you and Ellen, Rudy and Uncle John.'

Meg blinked, surprised that even a child had sensed there was something between her and John Carter. 'John doesn't live here.'

'But he will do when you finally get married.'

Tears in her eyes, Meg looked down at her sleeping child. Full of her mother's milk, Ellen had fallen asleep.

'Can I stay? Will we be a family?'

Meg smiled. 'Of course we will. Sit down and I'll let you hold her.'

Eyes shining with delight, Lily sat obediently in the old armchair that Meg had covered with a patchwork of multicoloured squares. The chair was quite wide and when she'd first arrived at Bluebell Cottage, wide-eyed and silent, she'd looked quite lost in it. Not so now. In a matter of months she had grown into both the chair and her new environment.

After letting Rudy out of the back door, Meg stood with her back facing the girl and baby, sipping at her tea and looking out at the garden. Spring bulbs were daring to poke their heads through the soil. The weather had turned mild. A warm spring was expected.

She heard a bark, then the howl of a dog from somewhere in the village. Rudy heard it too, lifted his head and howled in response. She guessed it was the Alsatian bitch Cliff Stenner had acquired from the US base.

'They said she was too soft,' he'd told her.

Too soft. 'Just like Rudy. A well-matched pair then.'

Cliff had grinned from ear to ear. 'Funny you should say that...'

Meg heard him going on about breeding puppies, but in her head she was applying the saying 'a well-matched pair' to her and John. She decided it was very apt.

The knock at the door was expected. Even before she looked round, Meg knew who it was. Not that she could see his face as he entered, as it was hidden by a massive bunch of flowers – winter greenery mixed with dahlias and chrysanthemums that could only have come from the hothouse up at the old manor house. Growing prize-winning specimens had been the colonel's joy in pre-war days. He didn't grow so many now, though it seemed to her as if almost every single one was in the bouquet Constable John Carter had brought for her.

'Oh, John. How kind.'

She lowered her face into the multicoloured bouquet, not smelling much from the hothouse flowers, but the wild greenery was as spicy as newly cut grass.

'You look quite the little mother,' he said to Lily.

Lily smiled. 'No. I'm her big sister.'

The look in John's eyes was unfathomable. Meg watched him: his mannerisms, his setting his policeman's helmet on the kitchen table, carefully as though he were placing it so that the measurements from all angles were identical.

He pushed his hands in his pockets, took in Meg's glow of health and felt a great surge of

413

satisfaction. 'I wanted to come round sooner ... but I wasn't sure of the formalities.'

Beneath the bare branches of the apple trees, Rudy recognised John's voice. He came bounding down the garden path, the back door swinging wide open as he crashed through it.

'Hey there, boy. Go a bit steady. We've got a baby in the house now, you know. Though I have to say I appreciate the welcome. I would appreciate a welcome like that every time I went home to the police house.'

Meg pushed the tea cup across the table. 'That's not a home, John. This is a home. It's also a ready-made family. If you want it.'

A rush of cold air came in through the back door as the girl and dog rushed out into the garden, heading for the tree at the end of the path. Feeling his face colouring up, John looked out of the kitchen window. 'Can't answer right away,' he said slowly, his comment bringing a frown to Meg's face. 'I need a second opinion. Maybe even a third.'

His blood raced as he headed over to the dog and the girl. The apple trees were coming into flower and the breeze was sending a shower of petals on to them both. They were stood very still, their eyes glowing with wonder.

'I was wondering how you might feel about me joining the family. What do you think?'

Lily gave him a very grown-up look. 'You're going to marry Auntie Meg.' Her tone lacked surprise.

Both dog and girl continued to gaze up at the pale pink flowers, some of which floated down

414

and tickled their cheeks. John looked to where they were looking. 'It's very pretty.'

'I think so.'

'And Rudy?'

Lily nodded. 'It's where we come to remember. I think I will always come here to remember.'

'Your parents?'

She nodded.

'And Rudy. Does he come here to remember somebody close to him?'

She nodded. 'Yes. I don't know what her name was but I think she was a lot like me. That's why we became best friends.'

When he went back into the house, John told Meg what Lily had said. Meg reached for his hand. He jumped. Her touch was so unexpected, but he loved the look in her eyes.

'We all need a friend whether times are good or bad. I'm glad they have each other. I'm glad we do too.'

EPILOGUE

Meg Malin wore a blue suit to her wedding, which she'd saved for from her clothes ration for months. Lily had persuaded her that not only did she need to buy new clothes for herself, but that Lily, too, would need a new dress if she was going to be a bridesmaid. 'And Ellen needs shoes. Her first pair. It's important she has shoes.'

'But it's a registry office wedding!'

415

Meg found herself outnumbered. Even John, bless his heart, was adamant she needed something new to wear.

'New bride, new husband, new outfit. It stands to reason.'

Thanks to the war and the fact that couples were not only severed by military considerations but also because they'd found they'd grown out of each other, divorces were on the increase. In fact, the divorce courts had begun sitting during the night in order to cope with the demand.

Meg's mother declined to attend the wedding ceremony.

Within a year of getting married, Meg was carrying John's child. By the end of the war their second baby had arrived.

It was hard to believe that the war had finally ended, but everyone in the village talked of nothing but the surrender of Germany. Already plans were being made for a party to celebrate the event, and the church bells that had been silent since the beginning of the war rang lustily.

On their wedding anniversary, Lily babysat while John took Meg to the cinema, which he promised would be followed by a fish and chip supper. The main feature was *Brief Encounter*, but a newsreel came on before that. Normally the chatting and canoodling would have continued unabated, but on this occasion a deathly silence descended.

'This is Richard Dimbleby reporting...'

Both Meg and John stood stiff as stones as the horrors of the death camps unfolded in black and white on screen. When it finally ended, Meg whispered in John's ear. 'We mustn't let Lily go the cinema until they're no longer reporting this.'

John gave her a silent nod and squeezed her hand. There was no need for words. They both knew now for sure that Lily was never going to see her parents again. It was their responsibility to see her grow up and help her become the young woman they all could be proud of.

The publishers hope that this book has given you enjoyable reading. Large Print Books are especially designed to be as easy to see and hold as possible. If you wish a complete list of our books please ask at your local library or write directly to:

Magna Large Print Books
Magna House, Long Preston,
Skipton, North Yorkshire.
BD23 4ND

This Large Print Book for the partially sighted, who cannot read normal print, is published under the auspices of

THE ULVERSCROFT FOUNDATION

THE ULVERSCROFT FOUNDATION

... we hope that you have enjoyed this Large Print Book. Please think for a moment about those people who have worse eyesight problems than you ... and are unable to even read or enjoy Large Print, without great difficulty.

You can help them by sending a donation, large or small to:

**The Ulverscroft Foundation,
1, The Green, Bradgate Road,
Anstey, Leicestershire, LE7 7FU,
England.**
or request a copy of our brochure for more details.

The Foundation will use all your help to assist those people who are handicapped by various sight problems and need special attention.

Thank you very much for your help.